THE PRESIDENT'S MISTRESS

"A Mount Everest among cliff-hangers."
—*Washington Post*

"The ultimate insider's book . . .
so damned close to the truth that I kept looking over my shoulder as I read it."
—Joe Goulden, author of *The Superlawyers*

"Much more than just an exciting evening's entertainment.
Pat Anderson knows the Washington scene from Camelot to the latest primary polka. His new thriller is not only a 'good read' but a thought-provoking, informed commentary on the people we occasionally choose to run our lives from that citadel at 1600 Pennsylvania Avenue."

—*Chicago Daily News*

"Superbly exciting thriller."
—*Cleveland Press*

The President's Mistress

by Patrick Anderson

PUBLISHED BY POCKET BOOKS NEW YORK

THE PRESIDENT'S MISTRESS

Simon and Schuster edition published 1976

POCKET BOOK edition published November, 1976

This POCKET BOOK edition includes every word contained in
the original, higher-priced edition. It is printed from brand-
new plates made from completely reset, clear, easy-to-read type.
POCKET BOOK editions are published by
POCKET BOOKS,
a division of Simon & Schuster, Inc.,
A GULF+WESTERN COMPANY
630 Fifth Avenue,
New York, N.Y. 10020.
Trademarks registered in the United States
and other countries.

ISBN: 0-671-80762-5.
Library of Congress Catalog Card Number: 75-37533.
This POCKET BOOK edition is published by arrangement
with Simon & Schuster, Inc. Copyright, ©, 1976 by Patrick
Anderson. All rights reserved. This book, or portions thereof,
may not be reproduced by any means without permission of
the original publisher: Simon & Schuster, Inc., 630 Fifth
Avenue, New York, N.Y. 10020.
Cover photograph by Terry McKee.

Printed in the U.S.A.

For Michael Korda
My partner in crime

1

"JOBS NOW! Jobs *now!* Jobs *now!*"

The chant rose from the throats of the thousand men and women who filled Lafayette Square and echoed across Pennsylvania Avenue to the window on the upper floor of the White House, where the President of the United States stood alone, watching and listening.

Now, Charles Whitmore mused. Whatever it is, they always want it *now.* Jobs *now.* Peace *now.* Freedom *now.* He'd heard all the chants over the years. What they never understood was that the U.S. Government can do almost anything, given enough time, but it was equipped to do almost nothing *now.*

I can't even walk across that street *now,* Charles Whitmore thought bitterly.

He sighed and put on his glasses, the glasses the public never saw because he was vain about his rugged good looks, and strained to make out individual faces in the crowd, wanting to read its mood, wanting to think he'd made the right decision in letting these people demonstrate in Lafayette Square. The Secret Service had wanted him to keep them blocks away, over on the Mall somewhere, but Whitmore had obeyed his own political instincts and opened the square to them and issued friendly statements, hoping thereby to defuse what could be an ugly and embarrassing situation. But of course you never knew about a crowd. Whitmore had ignited

1

a few crowds in his day, and he knew their passions were uncertain, explosive, like a woman's.

Like a woman's. He repeated the phrase to himself and laughed mirthlessly at a private joke. Two problems confronted him on this fine April afternoon, and the people chanting for jobs in Lafayette Square were the lesser of the two. They would go home by nightfall, perhaps peaceably, perhaps not, but in either case they'd be gone soon. But his other problem was a woman, and that problem, Whitmore feared, was not going away so easily. Charles Whitmore sighed again, slipped off his glasses, and turned away from the window.

* * *

A buzzer went off on Ed Murphy's desk as the President passed by his office. Murphy broke off his telephone conversation, raced out the door, and fell in beside the President just as he reached the Oval Office.

"Come on in, Ed," he said.

The two men settled in their accustomed spots, Whitmore behind the big preposterously ornate desk that Queen Victoria had given to Rutherford B. Hayes, and Ed Murphy in a plain black wooden chair drawn up close beside it.

The Oval Office had rarely looked more grand. Soon after Whitmore had entered office, his wife, a woman of uncommon good taste, had taken its redecoration in hand. Now, brilliant indirect lighting flowed down from the pure white ceiling onto a pale yellow rug and bright furnishings in shades of gold, green, and salmon. The Peale portrait of Washington still hung above the mantel, but Claire Whitmore had replaced the vulgar gold curtains behind the previous occupant's desk with elegant green ones. She had also added a Massachusetts Hepplewhite-style chest of drawers, a Federal card table made in Salem, Massachusetts, around 1810, and an elegant grandfather clock of similar vintage, among other items. Mrs. Whitmore's restoration efforts had won the acclaim of the nation's historical societies, but less interest from the actual occupant of the office. Urged to add his own personal touches, he had asked that the busts of Franklin Roosevelt, Harry Truman, and John Kennedy be installed in the office. But the truth was that Charles Whitmore would have been just as content to do his job in the White House attic. He didn't see furniture. He saw only people and problems.

"How was it over there?" he asked Ed Murphy.

"It could have been worse," Murphy said. By his standards it was a cheerful report. "The speeches weren't bad. They gave you credit for the jobs bill."

"What kind of people?"

"A mixed bag. Mostly blue collar. Maybe twenty percent black. Some couples who brought their kids and a picnic lunch. Plus the usual fringe of do-gooders and weirdos."

"Will it blow?"

"It could. There's an undercurrent. Rumors. Grumbling. People saying you're gonna send in the troops later on."

Whitmore winced. "Jesus, Ed, I've done everything but invite them to dinner. What do they expect?" He sat up straight in his chair and pounded his fist on his desk. "Damn it, I want to go *over* there. I want to *talk* to them."

"Forget it," Murphy said. "There's too many nuts over there and all it takes is one."

Whitmore beat his fist into his open hand in frustration. They'd been through this debate a hundred times and it always came out the same. There were too many madmen in America for any President to go anywhere he wanted to.

The two men sat in silence for a moment. A knack for silence was one key to Ed Murphy's success. Everyone else in the world was trying to sell Charles Whitmore something. Ed Murphy was an instrument waiting to be used.

"You know, I've got this other problem tonight too," Whitmore said finally.

Murphy frowned slightly. "Donna?"

"Yeah."

"It's still on?"

"She thinks it is."

"What do you think?"

"I think it's gonna be damn tough. I've got this mess out front and now Claire says she's canceling her trip."

"See Donna tomorrow or the next day."

"She says she won't wait." Whitmore got up and began to prowl about his office like a newly caged tiger, lithe and furious. "You know what I am?" he demanded. "I'm a prisoner in this blasted place."

"You asked for it."

"The hell I did. I'm still human, aren't I? I have *some* rights, don't I?"

Ed Murphy did not reply. They both knew the answer. Whitmore was *not* human any more. He was a god, and was so regarded by friend and foe alike. He could destroy the earth or send men to explore the planets. What he apparently could not do—unlike the gods of ancient mythology, who were allowed more freedom in such matters—was to keep an appointment that night with a young woman who was not his wife.

Whitmore stopped pacing and leaned against his desk. "I've thought about marrying her. Did I ever tell you that?"

Ed Murphy stared at his boss without replying.

"Sometimes I think, Screw it! This job isn't everything. Four years is probably a better deal than eight. Quit when you're ahead. If I got out after one term, I'd only be fifty-six. I'd get me a farm somewhere. Donna and I could have a kid. I'd have a hell of a time."

"You'd be miserable," Ed Murphy said. "You'd be slogging around your farm and some idiot would be here in this office and you'd be a basket case in a month."

"Okay, okay, I'd be miserable," Whitmore conceded. "But there's another way. I might could marry her and make it next time too."

"And cows might fly," Ed Murphy said.

"It's *possible*," Whitmore insisted.

"No way," Murphy shot back stubbornly. "You can have Donna or you can have this job, but you can't have them both."

Whitmore glared at his assistant. "Damn you, do you always have to be right?"

"I try," Murphy said, never smiling, and then he stood up. "I better check our friends across the street," he said.

"Okay, Ed, fine. Thanks."

Whitmore watched the short pudgy Irishman shuffle out of his office. Ed Murphy had been a down-on-his-luck newspaperman when he'd joined Whitmore's staff a dozen years earlier, and the strangest part was how little Whitmore had learned about him in all that time. He didn't know what Murphy's motivations were, what his dreams were, or even what his politics were, if he had any. All he knew was that Ed Murphy was the only man in the world he trusted absolutely.

Whitmore's secretary buzzed and he picked up the telephone. "Sir, Mrs. Whitmore wants to see you."

He groaned. It was a bad day and Claire wasn't likely to make it any better. "Wait five minutes, then ask her to come down."

The President got up, gazed out into the Rose Garden for a moment, then went back upstairs to the window that overlooked Lafayette Square. The people were still chanting there, many of them pressed against the police barricades that kept them from crossing Pennsylvania Avenue to demonstrate on the sidewalk in front of the White House. There was, Whitmore thought, no logical reason for those people to push against the police barricades, except that the national mythology had led them to believe that the rainbow ended at 1600 Pennsylvania Avenue, that somehow the solutions to all their problems were to be found inside that big white mansion. Charles Whitmore understood; he had believed that for a long time himself. Now he was there and he knew better.

You poor bastards, he thought. You can't get in and I can't get out.

*　*　*

A dozen blocks from the White House, in his small row house in Georgetown, Ben Norton was just getting up. He fixed himself coffee and a bowl of cereal, treated himself to his longest, hottest shower in nearly a year, dressed in slacks and a sport coat, and in the late afternoon strolled down to M Street. He stood on the corner for a few minutes, with Georgetown stretched out before him like a carnival midway, suddenly intoxicated by the sheer joy of being home again. He smiled at a pretty girl who was smiling at him, then started up M, past bars and boutiques, past students and blacks and freaks and gays and bureaucrats and tourists and dowagers and diplomats and secretaries and journalists and hustlers of every variety, until finally he pushed his way through the swinging doors at Nathan's.

"Hey, Mr. Norton, welcome back," Pete called from behind the bar. Pete was a burly red-bearded fellow who for some years had been working his way through law school by a combination of bartending and dope dealing. "When'd you get back, man?"

"Early this morning," Norton said. "I slept all day, started to go by my office, thought better of it, and here I am. How about a draft?"

Pete grinned and drew him a beer. "Man, it's been a while. Where was it you went? London?"

"Paris."

"How was it?"

Norton was a big man with a judicious look about him. He pondered the question for a moment.

"How was Paris?" he said. "Pete, for food and wine, it's number one. *Numero uno.* For women, it's maybe number three, depending on your tastes. For plumbing and heating, it's not even ranked. Not a bad city, actually, but I'll take Washington."

"Hey, you used to work for Whitmore, didn't you? You gonna go be a big enchilada in the White House now?"

"Not me, pal. I'm in private practice now, and I like it that way."

"Yeah?" Pete replied skeptically. "Some guy was in here the other day asking about you. Who your friends were and all. I figured he was an FBI type checking you out for some big job."

"What'd he look like?"

"Kind of strange. Dressed sharp and all, but up close there was something crazy about the way he looked at you. When he left, I thought, This guy is too weird to be FBI."

"They grow 'em pretty weird," Norton said. "What'd you tell him?"

"Oh, that you were a big cocaine dealer, and into white slaving, stuff like that."

"Good boy," Norton said. "With that endorsement, they'll make me Secretary of State."

Pete gave his lopsided doper's grin and wandered off to serve some other customers. Norton wondered if the White House might be running a check on him as a first step toward offering him a job. It was possible. He shrugged and picked up a Washington *Star* that someone had left on the bar. There was a small article on the front page headed "Jobs Rally Held," and a bigger story headed "Whitmore's Hundred Days," which concluded that the new President, in his first three months in office, had come on like gangbusters. That did not surprise Ben Norton. He had worked for Whitmore for three years in the Senate, and politically he had unqualified respect for his ex-boss. Of course, he hated the son of a bitch too, but that, as Jay Gatsby said in another context, was only personal.

When Norton put the paper down, he felt the excitement of his homecoming slipping away. There was no one in the bar he knew, he didn't feel like bar hopping, and it looked like a lonely evening ahead. He thought of some girls he might call, then realized he didn't want to call them. He sipped his beer and soon he was doing the thing he had promised himself not to do, thinking about the past, thinking about Donna.

* * *

When Claire Whitmore entered her husband's office he did not stand up and she did not sit down. They had been through that bit of protocol before. They had been through everything before. Whitmore sometimes wondered how he had managed to marry the only woman in the world who was absolutely immune to his celebrated charm.

"Isn't it time for you to go?" Whitmore asked.

"I'm not going, Charles."

"For God's sake, Claire," he said wearily. "We're trying to downplay this demonstration. Business as usual. If you cancel your speech, it looks like we're overreacting."

A tall woman, she had the angular features that are sometimes called aristocratic, sometimes called horsy. Society writers usually described her as "handsome" or "stately." Her husband thought of her as a grim, unyielding woman, and it rarely occurred to him that he had given her much to be grim about.

"Charles, I simply cannot *leave* with a thousand people encamped on my doorstep. It would look as if I were running away."

It suddenly occurred to Whitmore that Claire was the only person left in the world who called him Charles. Donna called him Chuck. Everyone else called him Mr. President, at least to his face. He decided to make one final stab. "Claire," he began gently, "I'm asking you, please, make the speech. It'll help. The publicity will take the edge off this thing over in the park. And we could put something in your speech about how concerned you are about the people who're out of work. It'd be good for you."

She felt herself weakening, as dazzled by him as she'd been thirty years earlier when he'd been the president of the student body and she'd been the richest girl on campus. He could sound so *reasonable* —even when, as now, she didn't believe a word of what he was saying. He didn't need *her* to make news for him, and in the past he'd never worried about her image as a humanitarian. She smiled a bit as she studied his proud, shrewd, inscrutable face. She thought he was the most interesting man she'd ever met. She thought him capable of anything, literally *anything*.

"My plans for the evening are firm, Charles," she said. "Perhaps we should talk about *your* plans for the evening."

"*My* plans?" he replied. "My plans are to sweat out this demonstration and then maybe to meet with some economists later on. Does that meet with your approval?"

But his heart wasn't in it. Claire didn't bluff. Claire waited until she had you cold, then she let you have it, right between the eyes.

"Charles," she said grimly, "I have information that a certain young woman is in Washington—"

"Damn it, Claire!"

"—who supposedly had left Washington for good—"

"Do you really think—"

"—and if you *see* her, if you *speak* to her, if you so much as utter her *name* in my presence . . ."

He slumped down in his chair and lit a cigar. The masculinity of the gesture seemed to salvage some dignity from his defeat.

". . . I will pack my bags and leave!"

Whitmore leaned back in his chair, studied the ceiling, then sent three smoke rings sailing toward it. For a moment he thought he heard the silence broken by the "Jobs *now!*" chant, but he guessed it was only his imagination, for this office was soundproof. But not wifeproof.

"Don't threaten me, Claire," he said smoothly, once again the riverboat gambler of his self-image.

"It's not a threat, it's a fact."

"You'd be insane to leave. You went through a lot to get here."

"Perhaps that was the insanity, Charles. The fact is that if I left, my life would improve in every way that matters, whereas your life, insofar as politics is your life, which it is and always will be, would become rather difficult. Think about that, Charles, and perhaps you'll make your plans for this evening rather carefully."

She smiled and left the office. Whitmore sat at his desk chewing on his cigar and pondering his next move. She had him by the balls—he knew it and she knew it too. She could destroy him, just by walking out and filing for divorce, and he wouldn't put it past her, not for a minute. Yet he found himself smiling, savoring the challenge. Somehow, he thought, he could control the situation, could get what he wanted, as he always had. The immediate problem, he decided, was not Claire, who had said her piece, but Donna, who was waiting to say hers. You always let people talk. Friend or foe, you gave them their say. Whitmore blew a final perfect smoke ring, grinned at the madness of it all, and reached for the phone.

* * *

"Ben, you old rascal, when'd you get back?"

Norton looked around and found himself face to face with Phil Ross, a newspaper columnist who'd been his neighbor in Georgetown for several years.

"Just today," he answered. "How about a drink?"

"Okay, a quick one," the columnist said and called for a vodka martini. Phil Ross was a nervous pinched-looking man in his forties. When Norton had first known him, he'd been a happy-go-lucky reporter, but since he'd won a syndicated column he'd grown increasingly somber.

"You went with Whit Stone's law firm, didn't you, Ben?" Ross asked. "Went over to Paris on some conglomerate deal?"

"That's right," Norton said. "It was a hell of a deal. Five governments involved, seven oil companies, and the construction of supertankers and deep-water ports. And you would not *believe* the intrigue, Phil, with those damn Arabs involved."

The columnist nodded automatically, but Norton saw his eyes starting to glaze over. He reminded himself that he was back in Washington, where no one gave a damn what happened in Paris, what happened anywhere except the White House, the Capitol, the CIA, and the Departments of State and Defense. Norton decided to change the subject.

"Tell me about Whitmore, Phil," he said. "It's strange to come back after almost a year. When I left he was still a dark horse for the nomination. Now he's President. How's he doing?"

The columnist stared into his glass of vodka as if it were a crystal ball with the secrets of the universe swirling in its depths. "It's a strange situation, Ben," he said finally. "Whitmore could be one of the greats, no doubt about that. The country needs leadership and he's got the potential, no question. And he's off to a decent start."

"So what's the rub?"

"The human element," Ross said with a little smile. "Pride. Isolation. Hubris. I keep hearing stories about erratic behavior. He blew his stack at the Majority Leader the other day for no good reason. And there are stories about his drinking and mistreating his staff."

Oddly, Norton's instinct was to defend his ex-boss.

"He drives himself so hard, Phil. The temper is an escape valve."

"Hitting people?"

"Who did he hit?"

"Forget I said it. It's all off the record. But I'm disturbed, Ben. I helped elect the man and now I'm worried. Sometimes I think he's drunk with power."

Norton nodded distractedly. Ten minutes of political gossip and he wanted back in the game. It was in his blood. He felt like a kid with his nose pressed against the candy-store window.

"I've got to go," the columnist said. "Let's have lunch. Call me." He started for the door, then turned back. "Oh, I meant to tell you, I saw one of your old girl friends the other day."

"Which one?" He tried to sound casual.

"The one who worked in Whitmore's press office on the Hill. That tiny girl with the wonderful brown eyes. What was her name?"

"Donna? Donna Hendricks?"

"Yes, of course. I thought she'd left Washington."

"So did I," Norton admitted. "Where'd you see her?"

"Just a few blocks from here. I was crossing Wisconsin, up by the French Market, and a limousine almost ran me down. I looked in the back window and there she was, curled up on the seat like a little doll. And who do you think was with her?"

Norton looked blank.

"Your old friend Ed Murphy."

Norton's hands tightened around his beer mug. "Are you sure?"

The columnist smiled. "Well, neither one of them is someone you'd mistake for anyone else, are they?"

"That's true," Norton muttered as the columnist waved and walked away. Then he sat staring into the empty mug. He felt sick.

* * *

She answered the phone on the first ring.

"It's me," he said. "I'm sorry I kept you waiting. It's been a bad day."

He smiled as he spoke. How long had it been since he'd said those words? Being President was never having to say you're sorry.

"How bad?" she asked.

"Bad, badder, baddest," he said. "Bad as hell. On top of everything else, Claire canceled her trip. I just don't see how I can get away tonight. It's damn near impossible."

"That *is* bad," she said gently.

He wished she would scream or curse, do anything but sound so calm. He could feel her slipping away from him. He was uneasy about the telephone too, that on top of everything else. If he could trust the Secret Service, it was the most secure telephone in the world—debugged every day, its lines changed each week. But could he trust them? Could he trust anyone? Even Donna?

"If you'd just wait a day or two."

"No, Chuck, I won't wait. You asked me to come and I came, but I won't wait. I don't like being alone in this house. I fly back tomorrow. It's tonight or not at all."

The finality of her words frightened him.

"There may still be a way," he told her. "I'll try to work it out."

Donna felt herself close to tears. "Chuck, Chuck, Chuck, can't we please stop this fantasy? It's over and dead and we're just going to keep bleeding and suffering until we admit it. Look at us—we're a mile apart and there's no way you can come here or I can go there. It's ridiculous and it's driving me crazy and I just can't go *on* like this any longer."

He felt her pain and for a moment he hated himself for what he was doing to her. "Donna, I want to see you and touch you and talk to you, just like it was last time. I want that more than anything on earth. I'll work it out somehow. I know this is hell for you, but just hang on a little longer and I'll work it out and we'll be together and then it'll all be all right. Please."

As he spoke, she shut her eyes and tried to hold back the tears. He had such a beautiful voice. He could speak to ten thousand people in an auditorium and make each one feel as if he or she was the only other person there. And when he spoke to a woman, one woman alone, it was almost too much to bear; it was like soaring in space, it was as if the two of you ruled the universe. She remembered a night when they had lain in bed till dawn, with him talking about his youth, about a summer he'd spent working in the oilfields and hitchhiking around the West, and the fights and the women and the crazy characters, and when he finally stopped talking she was crying. "Your voice," she'd said. "You should have been an actor." "I am," he'd said and laughed richly at the admission.

But that was gone now and she had made up her mind what she must do.

"I'll call you back, as soon as I can," he promised.

"I'm tired of sitting here waiting for the phone to ring, Chuck," she said. "I may go out for a while. I think I'll take a walk."

"A walk? Where to?"

"Just a *walk*. You know, like normal people do on pretty afternoons? I'm a normal person now, Chuck. That's what I've been working on all these months."

"You always were," he said. "That's why I loved you."

His choice of tense stunned them both.

"Maybe I'll go down to Lafayette Square and demonstrate against you," she said. "I could carry a big sign, like the people who think the end of the world is coming. 'Whitmore Unfair to Working Girl. He Done Me Wrong. Seduced and Abandoned.'"

"That's not funny, Donna."

"I didn't mean for it to be."

Another silence. He felt himself losing control,

and that frightened him more than anything in the world.

"Donna, did you bring your—your manuscript?" he asked finally. "Your book? Whatever you call it?"

"Yes, yes, I brought it. God, you make such a big deal out of it, I'm sorry I mentioned it."

Now he was patient, paternal, the man of the world. "Donna, you just can't go putting anything down on paper. You've got to be careful."

She wanted to scream. She knew too well how he manipulated people, flattered them, jollied them, bullied them, did whatever he had to do to get his way. "Chuck, I am living a quiet life in a little town in California and sometimes I scribble down a few thoughts and persuade myself I am writing a novel. It's my sole remaining fantasy and I wish you'd leave it alone."

He was unpersuaded. The idea of her writing a book, any book, made him uneasy. What could she write about except him? Every son of a bitch was writing a book these days—Presidents' assistants, Presidents' secretaries, Presidents' barbers, Presidents' butlers—and he wasn't about to be the first one to have his mistress write one.

"Donna, you've got to be careful what you put on paper."

"All I'm putting on paper is my *life*. My own little insane snafu of a life."

"Yes, but I'm part of that life. Those letters I wrote you—"

"Forget the letters!" she cried. "Forget everything. I don't want to talk any more. It isn't doing any good."

"I'll call later," he said. "Will you be there at eight?"

"I'll try to be," she said. She would not be pinned down. She could have that small victory.

He said goodbye and she put the receiver down, very gently, as if it were a bomb that might explode. She sat staring out the window for a minute. The dogwoods were in bloom. She cursed Charles Whitmore bitterly. Then she started on her walk.

* * *

Whitmore cursed too as he put down the phone, and because he could think of nothing better to do he buzzed for Ed Murphy. Murphy entered the office moments later, followed by Nick Galiano. Galiano was a short muscular man in his late forties who had small bright eyes, a broken nose, and one of America's last surviving crewcuts. He was wearing a rumpled wash-and-wear suit and a plaid sport shirt, open at the neck. He was grinning when he entered, but as soon as he saw the President's face his grin vanished. Cut Whitmore, they said, and Galiano bleeds.

"Bad day, Boss?" he asked.

"A killer, Nick. Sit down and fix yourself a drink."

Whitmore's mood lightened just a bit as Galiano winked and duck-walked across to the bar. John Kennedy once said that the White House was a bad place to make new friends, so he would stick with his old friends; Whitmore felt the same, and Nick Galiano was an old, old friend.

"One for you, Boss?"

Whitmore debated the issue briefly. "Yeah, just a light one." He turned to Ed Murphy, who had taken his usual chair beside the desk. "What's happening across the street?"

"I just got back," Murphy said. "I don't like the feel of it. It may blow."

"Then what happens?"

"Our people are there. They'll grab the troublemakers the minute they make a move. They'd like to grab 'em *before* they make a move."

Whitmore shook his head. "Wait it out."

Nick Galiano handed Whitmore a rather pale Scotch and water. "How's that for a light one, Boss?"

"Thanks, Nick."

Galiano walked over and sat down on one of the sofas across from the fireplace, where he sipped his drink and stared gloomily at the wall.

"Ed, I talked to Donna," Whitmore said.

Ed Murphy said nothing.

"She says it's tonight or never. It may be never the way things look."

Whitmore got up and began to pace again. Ed Murphy waited. Over on the sofa Nick Galiano was slumped down as if he were about to fall asleep.

"I asked her about that damned *manuscript* of hers," Whitmore said. "She said she had it with her and it was hers and I could go take a flying leap. Damn it, Ed, I don't know what she's up to. Maybe she wants to write a best seller about me. You never know what women will do. They'll do *anything.* They'll fuck you coming and they'll fuck you going and they'll fuck you standing still. Jesus Christ, what am I supposed to do? I've got a mob on my front porch and an economy about to collapse and sixteen wars about to break out and that damn Hoover file still floating around somewhere and now I've got *Donna* writing a *book!* It's just too goddamn much!" He stopped pacing long enough to kill his drink. Nick Galiano jumped up from the sofa, grabbed the empty glass, and poured another one.

"I trusted her and now she's out to screw me and we've got to do something about it," Whitmore continued. "I don't know what, but *something!* The crazy broad could ruin me!"

Ed Murphy's face was grim. Nick Galiano handed the President a second Scotch and water, several shades darker than the first one, and Whitmore sat down again. His hands were shaking. After a minute Ed Murphy got up and left the office.

*   *   *

Donna set out on her walk with no destination in mind, just enjoying the sun and the flowers and her

memories of Georgetown. Only when she passed the
Biograph Theater did she realize she was headed for
Lafayette Square. Once, back when she had worked
for the Peace Corps, it had been *her* park. Her office
had overlooked it, and on all but the coldest days she'd
go down to have lunch on *her* bench and feed *her*
squirrels and watch *her* old men play checkers. But
that was far in the past, and it was not her park today.
The people massed there were chanting "Jobs now!"
just as she and her friends once had chanted "Peace
now!" but there was something different in the air, an
ugliness that frightened her, and after only a few minutes she hurried away. It was late afternoon, there was
a chill in the air, and the walk back to Georgetown
seemed longer.

Near the corner of Thirty-first and M she stepped
into a liquor store. On a dusty shelf at the back of the
store she found what she wanted, a bottle of Mirabelle
plum brandy. Chuck loved the stuff, and it would be
a special gift for him if he came to see her that night.
Her anger with him had cooled now. Seeing the demonstrators in the park had made her feel sorry for him
—he had so many problems, and she was only adding
to them.

The clerk in the liquor store was a gangling youth
with pimples and haunted eyes who blushed and stammered as he counted out her change.

"You've given me too much money," Donna told
him.

"Huh?" The boy's face turned pale and his hands
shook, as if she'd accused him of some terrible crime.
"Okay, lady, I'll count it again. I didn't mean no
harm."

"You mustn't be so generous," she said, and, to try
to quiet the panic in his eyes, she touched his hand
and gave him her fullest smile.

"You're nice," the boy said. "You're beautiful."

Donna smiled again, a little sadly, and gathered up
her change and hurried from the store. Somehow the
exchange had pained her. She was tired of men falling

in love with her, tired of giving and giving and giving and getting so little in return. She thought you had to be selfish, tough as nails, to survive in this world. And yet she just went on giving.

She had walked only a dozen steps when she glanced across M and saw the last person in the world she wanted to see.

Ben Norton was emerging from Nathan's. He looked just as she remembered him, a big bulky man with straw-colored hair that tumbled every which way, shambling along with his hands in his pockets and a quizzical smile on his face. You saw it all at the first glance, she thought, his gentleness, his humor, his decency—everything but his brains and his toughness, which took longer to understand. She thought he looked lonely and she wished he had a girl with him, some little bird, as he called them, but the birds rarely appreciated Ben. Of course, she hadn't appreciated him either, Donna thought bitterly. She wished she could dash across the street and throw her arms around him and take them back to where they'd been two years earlier, before all the incredible complications had entered her life. But you could never go back. They'd been through the anger and the tears and the apologies and they could only go forward now. She and Ben had been so close, as close as two people can be, but now she could not cross the street to speak to him. It was too late for that. She watched with tears in her eyes until he was out of sight, then she hurried on toward the house on Volta Place to wait for a telephone call from Chuck Whitmore.

* * *

It was not much of a riot by American standards; probably disturbance was a more accurate word for it. Angry words and shoves were exchanged, nightsticks flew, a few heads were bloodied, a few arrests were made, a few windows were broken by departing demonstrators—that was all. Had the same events occurred almost anywhere else in the world, they would have passed unnoticed. But because they had taken place across the street from the White House, they had political significance. Newspaper accounts would set millions of heads to shaking at breakfast the next day. Television close-ups of one bleeding policeman would seem as ominous as a hundred wounded would. Charles Whitmore had gambled and lost, and no one knew it better than he himself.

"It didn't just happen," he yelled at Ed Murphy. "Somebody stirred it up. It was a setup, and we've got to find out who was behind it."

"It's hard to say," Murphy replied. "The Secret Service and the FBI have checked out the organizers and they're all legitimate. They meant to keep it peaceful. Sometimes things just explode."

"The hell they do," Whitmore shouted. "It didn't just happen. Somebody incited the damn riot, and we've got to find out who. If the Secret Service and the FBI can't get to the bottom of it, you find us somebody who can."

"We'll get to the bottom of it," Ed Murphy promised.

Whitmore poured himself another drink. He was, as he would have put it, unwinding after the tensions of the demonstration. Ed Murphy didn't drink and, as far as anyone knew, never unwound.

"Hell, it wasn't so bad," Whitmore said after a while. "If I had it to do over, I'd still let 'em have the park. What's a few cracked heads? I've been in barroom brawls where more people got hurt than they did over there tonight. We've had it too good, Ed. You don't want to be perfect. If you're perfect, everybody hates you. So we stub our toe now and then. That's okay. It gives the professional criticizers something to do. Now the *Post* and the *Times* and Kraft and Evans and Novak and all those political geniuses will write their little stories about how Big Chuck lost the battle of Lafayette Square. Half of 'em will say I was too wishy-washy and should never have let that red-led rabble into the park. Then the other half will say I was too hard-nosed and should have gone over there and hugged and kissed my unemployed brothers and sisters. Of course, I might have got my head blown off if I'd done that, but then all the geniuses could have kept busy for months writing about what a beautiful corpse I made and what a promising fellow the new President was."

Whitmore leaned back in his chair and laughed aloud. "Ain't it crazy, Ed?" he said. "Ain't this whole thing the damnedest mess you ever saw?"

Ed Murphy grinned and they both relaxed a little. It was a talent Whitmore had, to create tension and then, with a laugh or a joke, to relieve it. Most politicians could only create tension, and their aides had ulcers and drinking problems to show for it, but Whitmore had the gift of laughter, and that was another reason he was surrounded by men who would die for him.

"You want to see the economists?" Murphy asked.

"Oh, God," Whitmore groaned. "Are *they* still here?"

"Yes, sir."

"Send 'em home. I can't listen to that mumbo jumbo tonight."

Ed Murphy picked up the telephone and a few minutes later five of the nation's leading economists, who had been playing gin rummy in the Cabinet Room for several hours, departed unhappily into the night.

By the time Murphy put down the phone, the President's mood had changed again. He was staring glumly out the window into the shadows of the Rose Garden.

"I called her, Ed," he said after a minute. I called her and she wasn't there. Nobody answered."

"Maybe it's just as well."

"No, it's *not* just as well. There are things that have to be settled. Not just this book thing. She and I have got to decide what we're gonna do, one way or the other. Having that hanging over my head, along with everything else, is just too damn much."

"Try her again."

"We can't settle anything over the phone. I've got to *see* her. It's the only way. Hell, we could manage it, Ed. We could drive over there in your car."

"It's too risky," Murphy said. "Claire's upstairs, and there are reporters and cops all over town because of the riot. Somebody would see you and we've got no cover story to explain where you were headed."

"God damn it, I'm tired of people telling me what I can do!" Whitmore roared. "If I want to see her, I'm damn well going to see her!"

But he stayed in his big leather chair, held down like Gulliver by threads of indecision, pondering bitterly the things the most powerful man in the world could and could not do, while Ed Murphy watched and waited in silence.

2

"SHE'S DEAD, all right, Sergeant," the young patrolman in the baggy pants said excitedly. "I seen that right off, as soon as I come in the door."

Kravitz said nothing. He was kneeling beside the dead woman, trying to see everything at once: the bruises on her face, the position of her body, her jewelry, her clothing, the hair or flesh that might be under her fingernails, the thousand and one things you learned to look for.

"Suppose they raped her?" the young patrolman said. "She's a right nice-looking little gal."

Kravitz turned and looked at the young patrolman. He was short—they'd lowered the height requirement

again; soon they'd be recruiting midgets—and homely
and spoke with a West Virginia twang. His nameplate
said "Watson."

"I doubt it, Watson," Kravitz said. "She's fully
dressed, so I doubt it. Why don't you go out back and
talk to the boy? Just try to calm him down. And for
Christ's sake, don't *touch* anything!"

"Yes, sir, Sergeant," the young patrolman said, and
he put his hands deep into the pockets of his baggy
pants and eased himself out the French doors to the
terrace, where the paperboy was sitting motionless in
a deck chair.

Kravitz turned back to the body. For a few more
minutes, before the medical examiner and the fingerprint man and the other detectives arrived, this case
was his alone. He liked that feeling. He felt no particular emotion about the dead woman. He had seen too
many. Kravitz accepted death. To him the dead
woman was only a challenge, a challenge and an opportunity too. He stood up, lit a cigarette, and started
to look around the house.

At first glance it had seemed a more or less typical
Georgetown townhouse, built up and down, with a
tiny "powder room" by the front door and a tiny garden out back, its rooms crowded with books and paintings and expensive furnishings; yet Kravitz sensed
there was something strange, something missing, and
then he realized that the house lacked any lived-in
quality. The furniture was sleek and impersonal; the
paintings were modern and, to Kravitz at least, enigmatic. The portable bar in the corner had a brand
new look, like a bar in a magazine photograph. It held
the predictable bottles of J & B Scotch and Beefeater
gin and, less predictably, a tall unopened bottle of im-
ported plum brandy.

Kravitz studied the books that lined one wall of the
living room. Most were popular novels and books
about politics—the *Making of the President* series,
*The Best and the Brightest, The Selling of the Presi-
dent, All the President's Men.* Kravitz had read most

of the political books. The machinations of Presidents and would-be Presidents fascinated him. Kravitz did not want to be President, but he very much wanted to be chief of detectives, and he was already thinking of how this case would affect the politics of his appointment. It was going to be a big case—he could see the headlines already. And those headlines would help Kravitz become chief of detectives. When he was first on the force, Kravitz had scorned politicians, but in time he had come to understand that politics was not just handshaking and running for office; politics was everything. Even solving a murder could be politics.

Another of the bookshelves contained volumes of film criticism by authors whose names meant nothing to Kravitz—Kael, Simon, Sarris, Agee—and also the screenplays of some movies Kravitz had heard of but hadn't seen: *High Noon, The African Queen, The Blue Angel, A Place in the Sun, Citizen Kane, The Last Picture Show.*

Kravitz wondered about the screenplays. Perhaps the dead woman had been an actress. She'd been pretty enough. He glanced at the body again, wedged between the sofa and the coffee table, wondered where the medical examiner was, and then climbed the steep stairway to the second floor.

The front bedroom was the one she had slept in. The big canopied bed was neatly made, but the dressing table was cluttered with cosmetics and the bedside table held an electric clock, set for seven, a yellow push-button phone, a blank notebook, and a paperback copy of *The Diary of Anaïs Nin.* Kravitz thumbed through the book looking for underlined passages but there weren't any. Next he looked through the chest of drawers, hoping to find identification or letters or a diary, but he found only soft expensive sweaters, bright-colored blouses, neat piles of lingerie, and a box of costume jewelry. It was on the closet floor that Kravitz found what he'd been looking for, a purse stuffed with the usual tangle of tissues, cosmetics, ballpoint pens, and the like, but no billfold or identification. Kravitz cursed and looked at the dresses in the closet. They were size six, about right for the woman downstairs, and came from shops in New York, Washington, and Beverly Hills. He wrote down the names of the shops, then left the bedroom and walked down the narrow hallway to the room at the rear of the second floor, which was some sort of workroom. An antique desk with an electric typewriter atop it faced the windows that overlooked the little back yard. Kravitz glanced out the window and could see the patrolman and the paperboy sitting in the midmorning sunlight. Besides the typewriter, the desktop held a white coffee mug filled with freshly sharpened pencils, a ream of white bond paper, and a dictionary. But there weren't any notes, any manuscript, any indication that actual writing had emerged from this writing room. Kravitz thought of the film scripts downstairs and wondered if the dead woman might have been a screenwriter instead of an actress.

The third floor was no help at all. The two bathrooms were spotless, the two bedrooms were neat, but there were no signs that the rooms had ever been used.

Kravitz heard a car door slam out front. He went downstairs and greeted Crane, the medical examiner, a fat, dour, owl-eyed old man who called homicide cases his "house calls."

Crane grunted a hello and lowered himself onto the floor beside the dead woman. "Who was she?" he asked.

"We don't know yet."

"Strange," Crane said and began moving his stubby fingers over the woman's head.

"I'll be out back," Kravitz said. He and Crane had disliked each other for ten years, ever since a celebrated murder trial had ended in an acquittal because —as Kravitz saw it—the medical examiner had waffled in the crucial part of his testimony.

Kravtiz walked out back where the paperboy was still waiting with the rookie patrolman. The boy was about fifteen, tall and nice-looking. Clean-cut. He had told them his name was Jim Denton and his father was a doctor.

"Is she dead?" he asked when Kravitz sat down in a chair opposite them.

Kravitz nodded and the boy began to cry again. Kravitz sat quietly, enjoying the sun on his face, until the boy stopped. "Jim, you can help us if you'll tell us everything you know about her."

The boy blinked his eyes and nodded. "I'll try. I don't know very much."

"Do you know her name?"

"No, sir."

"Don't you usually know the names of the people on your route?"

"Yes, sir. But the thing is, nobody lives in this house most of the time. But sometimes people stay here, and when I see lights or a car I ask them if they want the *Post*. Usually they do, and I deliver it, and when they leave they're the kind of people who give me a big tip."

"What kind of people are they?"

"I'm not sure. One man might have been in the movies. He gave me ten dollars once to go downtown and get him a copy of *Variety*. Once or twice when I was throwing my route around dawn, there'd be parties still going on here. And I saw cars with Congressional license plates. But most of the time nobody's here at all. I think a maid came once a week—I saw a black woman leaving one afternoon."

Kravitz wondered about the cars with Congressional tags. He wondered if the dead woman might have been a call girl. If so, she was a damned experienced one, to afford the rent on this place.

"Do you remember what day she came? The maid, I mean?"

"No, sir."

"What about this woman, the one who's been staying here?"

"I'd never seen her until about a week ago. I was

out collecting and I saw a light so I knocked and she came to the door."

"Describe her."

"Short, not as tall as I am. Real pretty. Brown hair and big brown eyes. Sort of . . . sort of gentle and graceful in the way she talked and did things. I asked her if she wanted the *Post,* and she said she did. She invited me in and gave me a Coke. She said that a long time ago, when she was in high school, she'd gone with a boy who threw a paper route and she used to slip out of her bedroom window before dawn and go on his route with him and then climb back in the window and her parents never caught on."

"Did she say where? What city?"

"No, sir, I don't think so. Anyway, I threw the paper for a week and then yesterday afternoon I was out collecting and she said she wanted to pay me because she was going to leave the next morning. Today, it would have been. But she said she didn't have any cash and asked if I'd come back this morning—she said she was going out later and she'd cash a check."

"So you came back this morning?"

"Yes, sir, on my way to school. She said it was okay, she'd be up early. I knocked and she didn't answer, so I thought maybe she was around back and I walked down the driveway and looked over the fence. First I saw the French doors open. I called and nobody answered. It didn't make sense that she'd go away and leave the doors open, not around here. So I climbed over the fence and looked in the doors. That's when I saw somebody on the floor. I yelled and climbed back over the fence and ran down the street until I saw this officer writing tickets in the next block, and we came back together."

"You didn't go in?"

"No, sir."

"Did you touch the French doors?"

"I don't think so. I may have."

Kravitz heard car doors slamming in front of the

house and stood up. "I'll want to talk to you some more, Jim."

"I'm already late for school."

"You'd better forget school today. This officer can drive you home. Either I or some other detective will come by this afternoon. Okay?"

"If you say so."

"Good boy."

He shook the tall teenager's hand and watched him leave. He seemed like a fine kid. But he was big enough to have nurtured fantasies about a friendly, beautiful woman on his route, big enough to have made a clumsy pass at her, then to have scuffled with her and knocked her down and fled—and to have had the idea of covering himself by "finding" her the next morning. So he would be checked out. Any record? Window peeping? Fresh talk with women on his route? The boy was a suspect. Everyone was a suspect.

Crane had finished his examination. "For now," he told Kravitz, "I'd say that somebody right-handed hit her with his fist and she fell over backwards and struck her head on the edge of that coffee table. When? Twelve hours ago, give or take an hour. Say between ten o'clock and midnight. Rape? Doubtful. Anything under her nails? Doesn't appear to be, but we'll check it in the lab. Call me tomorrow and we'll have the full report."

"Thanks," Kravitz said, and the old doctor lumbered off toward the black Mercury he'd left parked in front of a fireplug down the block. As he drove off, the fingerprint man and the police photographer arrived. Kravitz stood on the front steps with them, smoking a cigarette and telling them what he wanted done. The neighborhood was still quiet, unruffled, unaware. Soon it would change, when the ambulance arrived, and the reporters and the film crews. Neighbors would gather across the street to gawk and gossip and exchange rumors. And while they did, Kravitz would spend some time studying them from an upstairs window, because the murderer might well be among them, and in any event these were people he'd be questioning soon. But for the moment all was quiet in their smug, rich neighborhood. Kravitz shrugged and went back inside the house.

When the fingerprint man was finished with the phone, Kravitz called a young detective at headquarters who was checking out some things for him.

"We think a woman named Caldwell owns the house, but we can't find her," said the young detective, who'd been put on inside duty because he'd vomited when they found the two nurses stuffed in the trunk of a car.

"Try the Georgetown rental agents," Kravitz said. "See who's paying the taxes. What about the phone company?"

"That's the strange part. The records are missing."

"What the hell do you mean, *missing?*"

"The guy checked and said they weren't where they were supposed to be. He didn't understand it."

"You get the hell over there and make him explain it," Kravitz shouted. "Fast!" He slammed down the phone, sighed, and heard voices out front. He glanced out the window and saw two police reporters he knew arguing with the patrolman who was guarding the front door.

A moment later the patrolman came inside. "Some reporters yelling about deadlines, Sergeant."

"Tell 'em I'll be out in a minute."

Kravitz wanted to stall a few minutes so the other reporters would arrive and he wouldn't have to say the same thing two or three times. Also, he wanted time to think, for what he said to them was important. Mystery Murder in Georgetown—they'd eat that up, so that by the time Kravitz produced the killer the city hall brass would have to make him the next chief of detectives.

It wouldn't have been any sweat at all, except that there'd never been a black chief of detectives and the blacks on the city council were screaming for one and

they had their candidate, a lazy bastard named Cole-
man who would have long ago been fired for incompe-
tence if he'd been white. But Kravitz still thought he
could get the job if he played this case right. There
was a young police reporter for the *Post* who had
spoken of writing a Sunday supplement feature on
Kravitz if he could only find a handle for it. Well, this
case could be the handle for his story and for a lot of
other stories. That was the kind of publicity that impressed people in Washington, the kind of publicity
that made Senators out of Congressmen, Presidents
out of Senators, and could make a chief of detectives
out of Joe Kravitz.

More car doors slammed out front, until finally Joe
Kravitz, student of homicide and politics, snubbed out
his cigarette, rubbed a bit of lint from his sleeve,
straightened his tie, and stepped out confidently to
meet the press.

3

BEN NORTON awoke at nine with a hangover. He'd
come home early the night before but sat up until past
midnight drinking bourbon and trying to make sense
of Phil Ross's story about seeing Donna and Ed
Murphy together. It didn't make much sense, unless
perhaps she'd decided to come back to Washington
to work for the administration. If so, he guessed he'd
hear about it soon enough. He had, however, more
pressing concerns, like reporting back to work at Coggins, Copeland, and Stone. So he climbed out of bed,

made coffee, and called Whit Stone's secretary, a woman every bit as formidable as her boss, a woman who made it a point to destroy some young lawyer's career every few years so the survivors would treat her with respect. Which they did.

"Evelyn? It's Ben Norton, home from the front."

"We expected to hear from you yesterday," said Evelyn, who was quite immune to Norton's boyish charm.

"Jet lag overcame me," he lied. "I slept all day. Now I'm ready to get back to work."

"Whit's expecting you for lunch at twelve thirty," Evelyn said coolly. "Don't be late."

Norton wasn't late, but Whitney Stone was, and as the young lawyer waited in his boss's outer office, flipping sightlessly through an old copy of *U.S. News & World Report,* he felt his sense of unease growing. He didn't like Whit Stone, or trust him, or quite know what he was doing working for him. He respected him, of course, as an eminently successful Washington lawyer, one who gave his corporate clients what they wanted, but there was a coldness about Whit Stone, and about his law firm, that Norton thought he would never get used to. Sometimes he thought he would be more comfortable with one of the older, less overtly political firms, Covington and Burling perhaps, but when he had decided to leave Senator Whitmore's staff a year earlier he'd been in a hurry and Whit Stone had made him the best and fastest job offer, including the assignment in Paris at a time when Norton wanted nothing more than to get as far away from Washington as possible. And, of course, it was a good firm; it had important clients and it paid him a handsome salary. The only trouble was Whitney Stone himself.

There was a story about Whit Stone that for years had been whispered among the firm's younger associates. It had to do with the manner in which Stone, at a relatively early age, had become a partner. The firm had been founded in 1942 by John Coggins, a New Deal lawyer who (legend also had it) had bribed a doctor to declare him 4-F, then left his $6000-a-year Justice Department job to start a private law practice that by the war's end was netting him a quarter of a million dollars a year. By the end of the decade Coggins knew he had to take a partner, and he chose Mason Copeland, a tall, shrewd Midwesterner with lines to the Truman administration. Copeland was not only a good lawyer but an adventurer, a man who savored risk and intrigue, and thus, over the years, when a President's unmarried daughter became pregnant, when a Supreme Court Justice was arrested in a cheap hotel with a teenage girl, when a drunken First Lady smashed a vase over the head of an elderly doctor who was trying to quiet her . . . in these and similar situations it was Mason Copeland who was called upon to wield the persuasion, the flattery, the cash, or the threats needed to put things right.

In the mid-1950s Coggins succumbed to a heart attack and Copeland, now in control of the firm, hired several young lawyers with lines to the Eisenhower administration and planned to elevate the best of them to a partnership. One of the lawyers he took on was a young blueblood named Whitney Stone, whose background included Harvard Law and a stint in the Eisenhower Justice Department. Whit Stone had a wife who was both rich and beautiful, two small children, and the kind of ambition that was sometimes described as rats in the belly.

Mason Copeland respected Stone, liked his wife, and one day in the spring of 1960 sent him to handle some important oil-lease negotiations in Texas. However, the negotiations broke off and Whit Stone arrived home two days earlier than expected, to find Mason Copeland in bed with his wife. The wife, fearing violence, ran naked to the bathroom and locked the door, but she did not understand the legal mind, and while she trembled on the edge of the bathtub her husband and her lover—the latter with a sheet wrapped togalike around his sweaty shoulders—quickly concluded the

negotiations that led to the creation of Coggins, Copeland, and Stone.

The legend had it that when the negotiations were
over the older lawyer looked at his young partner-to-
be and said, "Just one question, Whit. Did you set
me up?"

And, if the legend was to be believed, Whit Stone
flashed a thin-lipped smile and replied, "You'll never
know, Mason. You'll just never know."

"Ben, so good to see you," Whitney Stone said from
the doorway. "Please come in. I didn't mean to keep
you, but the Attorney General called just as you arrived."

Norton tossed aside the *U.S. News,* pulled himself
up from the chair, and shook hands with his boss.
Whitney Stone's hand was small, cool, delicate; to
touch it always made Norton shiver, even when, as
now, Stone was his most charming self.

"Come in, Ben," he was saying. "Some sherry?
Good. Sit down right there."

They sat on opposite ends of a sofa at the far end
of Stone's large office. Stone himself poured their two
glasses of Dry Sack and raised his in a toast.

"To you, Ben," he said. "You did a fine job for us
in Paris."

Norton smiled, sipped his sherry, and responded
with a compliment of his own. "Perhaps you get some
of the credit, Whit. Just when the agreement was coming apart, the Arabs did their turnabout. I thought
you'd punched some buttons on this end."

"Really?" Stone's hooded eyes showed a flicker of
interest. Perhaps, he reflected, Norton was more perceptive than he'd thought. He would remember that.

"Well, the CIA people, or the ones we took to be
CIA, dropped out of sight after the Arabs came
around. We hadn't done anything different on our end,
so I thought there might be a *deus ex machina* on
this end. You seemed a likely candidate."

Stone's smile lingered; he had reached that pinnacle
of power in Washington at which, like certain elected

leaders, he enjoyed being dealt with not only in terms of his self-interest but of his self-image, and the role of *deus ex machina* was one he savored. "I spoke to a few people," he said contentedly. "In the long run, the merger is going to have political as well as economic importance. It will be a factor in Middle East stability. And there are still a few people in this city who are looking that far down the road."

Stone left it vague, left the impression that his murky ties to the CIA had cinched the deal that Norton and a dozen other lawyers had sweated over for almost a year, as quite possibly they had. "But let's not dwell on Paris, Ben. I'd like a full written report from you, but let's think about the future now. You're back, your friend Mr. Whitmore is President now, and you should be entering an exciting time in your career. That's the important thing. Shall we go to lunch now?"

They walked a dozen feet down the hall to the firm's private dining room, one which, had it been open to the public, would have ranked as one of Washington's two or three finest French restaurants. It saved the firm's lawyers time, impressed their clients, and its cost, some $200,000 a year, was of course a tax write-off.

A white-coated Negro brought them wine and turtle soup, and Stone steered the conversation toward the White House. "Tell me, Ben, have you spoken with the President or Mr. Murphy since your return?"

Norton suppressed a smile. "Not yet, Whit."

"It's a courtesy you shouldn't neglect. They'll want to know you're back in Washington."

At that, Norton did allow himself a smile. "I don't think they'll be too concerned about my return, Whit."

"Don't be modest, my boy. They think highly of you. They made that clear to me when you joined the firm. I wouldn't be surprised if they try to steal you back from me. In any event, you'll no doubt be dealing with them on matters of concern to our clients."

That, of course, was the heart of the matter—the reason for this warm reception, and rather than pursue it Norton changed the subject. "How do you think Whitmore's doing, Whit? I got conflicting reports in Paris."

"He's a shrewd man," Stone said with respect in his voice. "Some of his, ah, *populist* inclinations have alarmed certain of our clients, but he's done a remarkable job of consolidating his public support. He's an interesting man."

The waiter took away their soup bowls and served their entrées—shrimp for Norton, rockfish for Stone.

"Well, Ben, you'll be needing some work to do now that you're back."

"The more the better."

"That's the spirit. It happens that we have a new client, Baxter Communications, who has a problem you might be able to help with."

"Harvey Baxter," Norton said, happy to be getting down to business. "Newspapers in Texas. Wants to run for governor."

"Precisely. And also wants to purchase a chain of small-town radio stations, and no one seems to have the vaguest notion how Whitmore's new anti-trust chief would respond."

"Guy Timmons," Norton said. "I read about his appointment."

"Do you know him?"

"We met on the Hill. He did some position papers for Whitmore. He's pretty impressive. He's just about the only professor who ever impressed Ed Murphy."

"Do you feel you could talk to him about Mr. Baxter's proposed acquisition? Informally, of course."

"I think that'd be a last resort. There are other people at Justice I know better who might give me a line."

"Fine," Stone said. "Try to have something by next week. Baxter will be coming to see me."

"What did his papers do in the election?"

"They didn't endorse either candidate."

"Contributions?"

"He and his family contributed about ten thousand to both candidates."

Norton laughed. "That won't help."

"Perhaps his papers could give some editorial support to the President now."

"It couldn't hurt," Norton said.

"I'll speak to him," Stone said. He stirred his coffee and the subject was closed. Just as the luncheon seemed to be over, Stone gave Norton an odd glance. "One other thing, Ben, a rather delicate question perhaps, but there have been some reports . . . Do you recall ever hearing anything about Mr. Whitmore's involvement with a young woman?"

Norton took a last sip of coffee before replying, and he made his lie as quick as possible: "No," he said. "Why?"

Stone pursed his lips in a show of distaste. "I assumed the reports were inaccurate," he said. "You know how people talk. Actually, I thought if we could trace them down, some misunderstanding perhaps, we might be doing the President a favor. It was just a thought." He stood up, and Norton did the same. "Well, Ben, it's a pleasure to have you back with us."

Norton returned the compliment, the two men shook hands rather formally, and the younger man returned to his office. He thought the luncheon had not gone badly, although, like all encounters with Whit Stone, it left him with a faintly sour aftertaste.

The phone rang, and Norton, who temporarily had no secretary, answered it.

"Ben Norton?" a man said.

"That's right."

"Have you seen this afternoon's *Star?*"

"Who is this?"

"You better take a look at the paper, pal," the man said, "because a friend of yours has got herself killed."

"What?"

The man hung up. Norton put the receiver down slowly, annoyed, puzzled. Had crank calls gotten that bad in Washington? He shrugged and picked up a law review article that Whit Stone had urged him to read.

But he couldn't read; something was gnawing at his subconscious. After a moment he walked down the hallway to the receptionist's desk.

"The *Star* come in yet, Josie?" he asked.

"Just did," the young woman said and reached to the floor for one of the two copies that were brought over by messenger each afternoon.

Norton skimmed the front page and found the story at its bottom, with a headline that read, "YOUNG WOMAN FOUND SLAIN IN GEORGETOWN."

He began reading:

District police today are investigating the apparent murder of a young woman whose body was discovered in a townhouse on Volta Place in Georgetown. Detective Sgt. Joseph Kravitz said the woman was still unidentified at midday, and it was not known who owned the expensive townhouse where she was found. Kravitz said the woman had been struck on the face and apparently died of a concussion when her head struck a coffee table. He said she did not appear to have been sexually assaulted. He described the woman as about thirty years old, five-foot-two, 110 pounds, with long brown hair and brown eyes.

Norton read the story twice, with growing apprehension. Then he thought of what Phil Ross had said, about seeing Donna in Georgetown. The description was right.

"Oh my God," he whispered. "Oh my God, no."

The next thing he knew he was running down the street, waving his arms at taxicabs, screaming for someone for God's sake to take him to Georgetown.

4

NEIGHBORS WATCHED from their yards all morning as the police cars came and went, but the tall woman in the pale green pantsuit was the first one to approach Kravitz. She crossed the street and summoned him with a glance; he stepped off the porch and met her in the yard, halfway.

"I'm Mrs. Carter Fleming," she said. "I live over there." She nodded toward an imposing house across the street. "Are you with the police?"

"I'm Sergeant Kravitz of the homicide division."

"Homicide? Does that mean someone is dead?"

"Do you know whose house this is, Mrs. Fleming?"

"Perhaps, Sergeant, you could answer my question first. We in the neighborhood seem to be the last to know anything."

Kravitz tried to place her husband's name. A lawyer? A journalist? A Congressman? He was sure she'd be glad to enlighten him, but that wouldn't be necessary. He knew to mind his manners with Georgetown matrons.

"A woman was found dead here this morning," he said. "She was about thirty, five-two, brown hair, attractive. Do you know who she is?"

"I don't think so."

"Would you be willing to look at the body, for possible identification?"

The woman studied him. She was tall, tanned, and in her late forties, an expensive-looking woman, a woman who Kravitz guessed would be great in bed. Not that it mattered to him. TV repairmen could screw their customers; detectives couldn't.

"I suppose so," she said. "If it might help."

He led her into the house and uncovered the dead woman's body. Mrs. Fleming stared down at it with curiosity and without emotion. Kravitz got the impression that Mrs. Fleming would not mind if more attractive women of thirty could be quietly removed from the scene.

"I don't believe I've ever seen her before," she said finally. "Was she raped?"

"Apparently not."

"That's interesting," the woman said. "I think that if an attractive woman were raped and murdered it would be one thing, but if she were murdered and *not* raped it would be quite another."

"That's quite perceptive," Kravitz said. Actually it wasn't all that perceptive. It was too logical, and crimes of passion weren't often logical. It wasn't logical, for example, that a man murdering his wife would bother to rape her, before or after killing her, but he'd seen it happen a dozen times.

"To get back to my original question, Mrs. Fleming, do you know whose house this is?"

"It *was* Ruth Caldwell's. Could we step outside?"

"Of course."

Out on the porch he lit a cigarette and offered her one. She declined. "Ruth Caldwell was Mrs. Harrison Caldwell," she said. "He was the banker. After he died, Ruth moved to Phoenix to live with her daughter. I don't know if she sold the house or leased it. Sometimes people stayed here and sometimes it seemed to be empty."

"What kind of people?"

"I saw a young actor here on two occasions. I don't remember his name, but he's quite well known."

"Had you noticed anyone here in the past few days?"

"The lights have been on. And I saw a limousine

leaving a few nights ago, coming out of the driveway. The house isn't terribly attractive, but it *does* have off-street parking. I only wish mine did."

"Did you see who was in the limousine?"

"No. I didn't think anything about it. Limousines aren't exactly *unknown* in this neighborhood, Sergeant. Would you excuse me now? I'm beginning to feel faint."

"I'd like to talk to you again. Will you be home this afternoon?"

"I'm not likely to go out with murderers roaming the streets."

Then you'll be inside a long, long time, Kravitz thought, but he bade her a polite goodbye and watched to make sure she entered the house she had said was hers.

Just as she disappeared into her house, a cab screeched to a stop and a big blond-haired man tossed some money to the driver and heaved himself out. He was in his late thirties, Kravitz guessed, was well dressed, was clutching a rolled-up newspaper, and was white as a sheet. Kravitz wondered if it was confession time.

"My name is Ben Norton," the man said. "I'm a lawyer. Is this where the murder was?"

"That's right. I'm Sergeant Kravitz."

"The description in the paper . . . it sounded like someone I know. Has she—the victim—been identified yet?"

"May I see that, please?" Kravitz asked. Norton blinked, looked down at his hand, then gave Kravitz the newspaper. The detective skimmed the story, pleased to see it on the front page. So far, so good. He handed the paper back to Norton.

"No, there hasn't been an identification," he said. "Would you be willing to look at the body?"

The man nodded blankly and followed Kravitz inside.

When Kravitz uncovered the body, the man cried out and fell to his knees. He reached out and touched the woman's face, then gasped at the chill of her skin, at the reality of death. He knelt beside her, pale, tears welling in his eyes, whispering something that might have been her name.

Kravitz watched it all professionally. He had watched such scenes a thousand times. He had seen hysteria, laughter, fainting, shock, anger, fear, heart attacks, and occasionally, the little signs—too much emotion or too little, nervousness, ill-concealed delight—by which killers sometimes gave themselves away. This man Norton's grief seemed real enough. Which meant absolutely nothing.

When Norton stumbled to his feet, the detective covered the body and suggested they go out on the terrace. Once there, the lawyer slumped in a deck chair with his face hidden in his hands. "Just give me a minute," he said.

"Take your time, Mr. Norton," Kravitz said, and he lit a cigarette and waited.

"Her name was Donna Hendricks," Norton said when he could talk again. "She grew up in Cincinnati and came to Washington six or seven years ago. Until recently she'd worked for Senator Whitmore. You can get her full bio from the Senate personnel office. I worked for Whitmore too, and she and I went together for a while. About a year ago we broke up and I went to Paris on business. I understood she'd left Washington and had been living in California."

"You didn't know she was back in Washington?"

"No."

Not until the word was out did Norton realize it was not entirely true. He didn't *know* Donna was in Washington, but he knew that Phil Ross had said he'd seen her with Ed Murphy a few days earlier. Of course, that was hearsay, and Ross might have been mistaken. Still, Norton did not correct his answer, did not mention what Ross had said. Not because he was in a state of near shock, but rather because, even in that state, his political instincts still guided him. He could not bring himself to casually link Ed Murphy, perhaps even the President, to what was probably a routine murder case. He knew too well what the consequences would be—rumors, gossip, headlines, smear campaigns by the opposition, and all of it probably unjustified. Norton would talk to Ed Murphy. He was determined to know more about Murphy's meeting with Donna and what she was doing in town. But he would not send this detective to see him.

"Do you know why Miss Hendricks left Washington?" the detective asked.

Again Norton hesitated. These questions were jarring him like hard left jabs. Why Donna had left Washington was another thing he couldn't tell the police.

"I think she'd just had it with Washington," he said. That was true as far as it went. "She thought it was a man's town and she was tired of fighting it. She wrote me from California that she wanted to be alone for a while, wanted to think about her future, wanted to do some writing."

"Do you still have the letter?"

"I think so," Norton said defensively. He knew damn well he had the letter.

"I'd like to see it."

"Is that necessary?"

"This is a homicide investigation, Mr. Norton. You should understand that. It may be that a prowler killed Miss Hendricks and we'll find his fingerprints and have this cleared up by tomorrow. Or it may not be that simple. We need to know everything we can know about Miss Hendricks, until this makes some sense."

"There's no way this can make sense. No one in his right mind would have killed Donna. She was the kindest, most decent . . ." Norton lowered his head until he got control of himself.

Kravitz watched him impassively. He believed Norton was hiding something. He didn't know what yet, but he knew he would know eventually. "Who were her friends, Mr. Norton?"

Norton frowned with annoyance. "She had lots of friends."

"Give me some names."

"Anyone on the Whitmore staff; they were all her friends. And Gwen Bowers, she was probably Donna's closest friend."

"Gwen Bowers," Kravitz repeated. "She's . . . she's the one I've seen on television, isn't she?"

"Yeah, Gwen's a celebrity now," Norton said. "But she and Donna were old friends. They shared a house for a while."

"Did Miss Hendricks have any enemies?"

"None, none at all."

"Attractive women make enemies. Women resent them. Men get hurt feelings."

"I'm trying to tell you, Donna wasn't like that." Norton sounded exasperated. "People loved her."

"You don't know of any romantic involvements in the past year?"

"No, but I wouldn't."

"Do you know if she had any friends in the movie world?"

"The movie world? She might have."

"Do you know whose house this is?"

"No."

"Ever been here before?"

"No."

"Did you know she was staying here?"

"No," he said again, letting his annoyance show.

Norton hadn't paid any attention to Kravitz at first. He was only a form, a voice, but now he looked and saw the small slate-colored eyes fixed on him, sensed the hostility behind the questions, and he began to dislike this burly, balding man in his cheap suit, smoking his endless cigarettes.

"What were your activities last night, Mr. Norton?"

"It was just yesterday morning that I flew back from Paris. I slept all day, then in the late afternoon I got up and dressed and walked down to Nathan's for a beer—I have a house on Twenty-eighth Street. I ran into Phil Ross, the columnist, and we talked. But I was tired and I went home early, around eight or so."

"You live alone?"

"That's right."

"So you were at home alone from, say, eight o'clock on?"

"That's right."

Kravitz lit another cigarette and got to the question he'd been holding back, the question that was so obvious he thought Norton would have volunteered an answer to it by now.

"Let me see if I've got this straight, Mr. Norton. You haven't seen Miss Hendricks in a year, you think she's living in California, but you read a newspaper story about a young woman dead in Georgetown and you're so sure it's her that you drop everything and take a cab to the scene. Is that correct?"

Norton frowned and twisted uncomfortably in his chair. "No," he said. "There's something else I didn't tell you, this strange thing that happened."

"Yes?"

"Just after lunch today I got a phone call. A man asked for me by name and said I ought to read the paper because a friend of mine had been killed. *Then* I read the paper and saw that the description fit Donna and I came over here."

"The man didn't identify himself?"

"No."

"No idea who it was?"

"None."

"Anything distinctive about the voice? Negroid? A foreign accent? A Southern accent?"

"I took it for a white man. A harsh voice. No particular accent." He thought a moment. "The only distinctive thing was, the man called me 'pal.' Sort of tough-guy style. He said something like 'You better read the paper, pal, because a friend of yours is dead.'"

"Maybe your secretary noticed something," Kravitz pressed.

"No, I took the call myself."

Kravitz studied the other man's face like a scientist peering through a microscope.

"I've tried to make sense of it," Norton continued. "Who knew she was dead? Who would call me and why? I guess you people knew, the police. And people who'd seen the paper. But not that many people knew I was back in town." He stopped, shaking his head in confusion.

"You're forgetting something, Mr. Norton," Kravitz said quietly. "We didn't know who she was. The newspaper story didn't identify her. The only person who knew Donna Hendricks was dead was whoever killed her. Plus anyone the killer might have told of his crime. Which still doesn't explain the call to you."

"Maybe they wanted her identified," Norton said.

"Maybe," Kravitz agreed. "But it would have been simpler for them to call police headquarters or call the newspapers and give her name than to involve you."

To involve you. The words still echoed in Norton's mind when he left the house on Volta Place a few minutes later, after agreeing to give Kravitz a formal statement in a day or two.

It had dawned on Norton rather slowly, in the final minutes of his talk with the detective, that *he* was a suspect in Kravitz's eyes. He began to suspect that the detective didn't believe his story about the telephone call, that he might think Norton had made it up to justify the criminal's supposedly traditional return to the scene. It was ridiculous and yet, Norton knew, it made a certain sense from the detective's point of view: the jilted lover confronts his ex-girl friend, argues with her, kills her. He began to realize what a delicate position he was in. He was not guilty of killing Donna, but he was guilty of knowing things about her he could not tell the police, and that was enough to make his life very complicated. He *was* "involved" in the case, if not in quite the way Kravitz thought he was.

He was involved because he was every second growing more determined to find out who had killed Donna. He stumbled down Volta Place, oblivious to the neighbors staring at him from their porches, oblivious even to the reporter who asked his name and trailed him to the corner. Kravitz might not believe that someone had called him. Kravitz might believe that Norton had killed Donna or that a prowler had killed her. But Norton knew that he hadn't killed her and he knew also that prowlers didn't call lawyers to announce their crimes. Something strange was happening here; Norton didn't know what, but as the reality of Donna's death raced through him like a fever he vowed to find it out. He wanted the truth and he wanted something more than that; like Lear he wanted a revenge so terrible it had no name. The police could look for fingerprints and prowlers and strands of hair, but there were other lines of inquiry for Norton to pursue, like what Donna had been doing in Washington and why she had been riding in a limousine with Ed Murphy and whose house that was on Volta Place.

Abruptly, Norton found himself back at his own house. He went to the telephone and placed two calls. The first was to Gwen Bowers and the second to the White House.

5

As NORTON crossed Gwen's wide lawn, he saw a shooting star blaze across the evening sky; it made him think of Donna.

Gwen was waiting in the doorway, and she had been crying. Norton put his arms around her, surprised at how fragile she was, and thought that he had never known her to cry before. Even on the night Bob Kennedy died, and six or eight of them sat around on the floor of the Capitol Hill apartment she and Donna shared then, Gwen had gotten drunk, cracked bitter jokes, but never shed a tear.

"I'm sorry," she said after a moment. "I tried to get it over with before you came. Come on in. We'll get stinko."

"I want to talk, Gwen. I want to know things."

"We'll talk," she promised and led him down a long hallway. She was wearing pants and a sweater, and her blond hair fell loose around her shoulders.

"This house is incredible," Norton said.

"The wages of sin, my friend. I was offered a quarter of a million for it last week."

It had not been terribly long since Gwen and Donna were young reporters scrambling to make the rent on their Capitol Hill apartment, but Gwen disliked scrambling; there was a hunger about her more often found in Washington's young men than its young women, and she quickly fashioned for herself a spectacular, perhaps unique success story. First she had surprised everyone except herself by marrying a very rich old Congressman. Her friends thought the marriage a joke, and predicted it would last a year. In fact it lasted only four months, at which point the Congressman thoughtfully died of a heart attack. ("It was cold-blooded murder," Gwen had stage-whispered to Norton at a party three weeks after the funeral. "I screwed him to death.")

The Congressman's passing had been followed by some legal unpleasantries with his grown children, but Gwen had emerged from them with the Spring Valley mansion and, perhaps more importantly, with her first taste of celebrity. She liked the taste, and she achieved more celebrity by writing some gossipy aritcles for *Cosmo* about sex in Washington, and that launched her onto the talk-show circuit, that twilight world of people who talk on television because they are celebrities and are celebrities because they talk on television. With it all, Gwen found time to be "linked romantically," as the gossip columnists delicately put it, with a celebrated (and married) young Senator, with one of the more articulate of the astronauts, and with three of four Washington Redskins. Gwen was notorious and she gloried in it. Norton had mixed feelings about her. He thought she was honest and he didn't trust her. He knew she was Donna's friend and he'd often thought she was a bad influence on Donna. But most important, he knew that Gwen was one of the best-informed people in Washington—Gwen collected gossip the way other women collected jewelry—and now he hoped she could tell him things about Donna that no one else was likely to know.

Gwen led him into a huge dark-walled library where a fire was burning. Norton had been there once before when a portrait of the Congressman's mother had been hanging over the mantel. Now it had been replaced by a Larry Rivers painting of a garbage dump.

"Get us some drinks," Gwen said, pointing toward the bar in the corner. "Do you want to see the news?"

"No," he said and poured them both some Scotch, then joined her on the long green sofa.

When he handed Gwen her drink, she clinked her glass against his. "No more tears," she promised. "No orchids for Miss Blandish. No tears for Ms. Hendricks. She was a tough lady, Ben, tougher than you ever knew. Tough and nice. It's easy to be tough and a bitch. But to be tough and nice is just about a goddamn impossibility. Okay, she's dead, but you know something? Donnie lived more in the last five years than most women live in a lifetime. Most women are born dead. They grow up Barbie dolls on the outside and zombies on the inside. Donnie figured out their dirty little game and she beat it. She stood on her own little feet and she said, 'Screw you, world. I'm me and we'll play this one my way.' And she did. Rest in peace, sweetheart, rest in peace and screw 'em all."

She started to cry again, staring straight at him, as

if defying him to deny that she'd loved Donna as much as he had. There had always been an undercurrent of rivalry between them where Donna was concerned. Donna had been like that; people wanted to possess her, and of course that was what she'd always been struggling against.

"I remember the night the two of us came to this damned town," Gwen went on. "Neither one of us had ever been here before. I was a twenty-four-year-old hotshot from the UPI bureau in Cleveland, come to conquer Washington, and I'd talked her into coming along too—did she ever tell you that?—because I knew if I didn't she'd marry some idiot there and spend the rest of her life changing diapers. We had a couple of drinks when the plane took off, and both immediately passed out, but we woke up when the plane came into Washington. I'll never forget how I felt when I looked down and saw the city at night, the cars going across Memorial Bridge, those beautiful damned monuments, the Capitol dome off in the distance. I started to cry. I wanted it all so bad, wanted the whole damn town at my feet. I talked to an actor once who told me he felt the same way the first time he drove up into the Hollywood Hills and looked down on the lights of L.A. I guess everybody's like that when they're young and they think they can have it all. So the plane was landing and I was crying and Donnie didn't understand. She thought I was crying because I was scared, so she squeezed my hand and told me not to worry, that we'd make out all right, somehow. *Jesus,* what a sweet kid she was. Or did I say that?"

Norton knew she meant it, yet for a moment all he could do was hate her, hate her for having brought Donna to this cruel city, hate her for being alive when Donna was dead.

"Well, you got it all, didn't you?" he said softly. "The whole ball of wax, the world at your feet."

"Balls," Gwen snapped. "I'm notorious, is that what you mean? I screw celebrities and blab about it on talk shows. Big deal. Did you know I'm writing my memoirs? Some idiot of a publisher advanced me a hundred thousand."

Gwen ran her fingers through her hair, laughed, and finished her drink. Norton thought she was a little drunk; he hoped so, he might learn more that way.

"Okay," she said. "So much for fun and games. You came to talk. Let's."

"Good," Norton said. "Here's the thing, Gwen. I got back yesterday morning. I thought Donna was in California. Then last night she was in a house on Volta Place and somebody killed her. That's all I know. I want to know whose house it was and what she was doing in town and what's been going on while I was away."

"I can tell you about the house," Gwen said. "Just don't say it came from me. It's Jeff Fields's house. He leased it around the first of the year. Maybe he's bought it by now."

"The actor? What did he need a house in Washington for? And why would Donna be using it?"

"Jeff collects houses. Maybe he thought he'd be spending a lot of time in Washington. He got pretty chummy with Whitmore during the campaign. Or thought he did."

"What do you mean?"

"Well, he raised gobs of money for them; he was Whitmore's line to the show-biz types. But once Whitmore made it to the White House, he didn't want any high-living Hollywood types around that might embarrass him. So now Jeff's not being invited to the state dinners the way he expected."

"What got him involved in the campaign?"

"Well, some people think he's an idealist who wants to help build a better America. Most of us think he was after publicity."

"He'll get plenty of that as soon as they find it was his house. But what was Donna doing there? Was she involved with him?"

Gwen shook her head. "Donna wasn't Jeff's type.

Or vice versa, for that matter. Jeff's into sex the way your friend Whitmore's into politics. Deep. A student of the art. Donna wouldn't have played the games he and his friends play. They got to know each other during the primaries, and he took her to a couple of fund raisers, but it was just for laughs. Still, if he knew she was coming to Washington he'd probably have offered her his house."

"Where do I find Fields?"

"He has an office in Palm Springs—Fields Productions—that always knows where he is. He might even *be* in Palm Springs; he's erected a little pleasure dome there."

"Are you ready for another?" he said.

"Sure. Unless you want some hash."

"Not tonight." He got the drinks, then rejoined her. "Look, Gwen, let's get to the heart of the matter. What was going on between Donna and her friend? I've got to know, and you're the only one who can tell me."

"Why? It's all over now."

Norton wondered how much to tell her. But she had told him about Fields, and he knew that with Gwen you had to give something to get something. "For one thing, someone told me they saw Donna and Ed Murphy together in Georgetown last week. So I don't know what's over."

Gwen looked him over carefully, her eyes cold and sparkling, and he wondered what she really thought of him. Once at a party she'd called him a Southern numskull who wasn't fit to touch Donna's hem, and she'd sounded like she meant it.

"Where were things when you left the country?" Gwen asked. "This all gets pretty complicated."

Norton thought she was stalling, trying to find out how much he knew, but there was nothing to do but answer her. "It all came to a head around Christmas, the one before last," he said. "I wanted us to get married. We'd been living together for five or six months and I thought it was only a question of when. I thought we'd stick with Whitmore through the campaign, then we'd be married and I'd enter private practice and get rich and we'd live happily ever after. But she kept putting me off, saying she wasn't ready to decide. Then she moved back to her own apartment. I didn't know what was happening. I kept asking, 'Why, why, why?' and she couldn't explain it. Then, in early February, when we were about to go up to New Hampshire for the primary, she told me. She was crying and she said maybe she shouldn't tell me, but it wasn't fair not to give me an explanation, so she swore me to seven kinds of secrecy and dropped her little bombshell.

"I almost went out of my mind. I wanted to kill the bastard right then. But of course she calmed me down, told me she had to see this thing through, that I had to understand, that maybe we'd get back together eventually, et cetera. So, I didn't kill anybody, but I didn't hang around either. I left the Hill and when I got the chance I left the country. It was just too much for me to handle; I didn't want to be in the same city with them, or even the same country. Then in July I got a letter from her saying it was all over, that she was going to California to sort things out. I wrote back and asked her to come see me in Paris, or that I'd come to California, but I never got an answer. So I gave up, and that's all I know, except that yesterday morning I came home and last night somebody killed her."

Gwen's eyes never left him as he spoke; she looked, he thought suddenly, like a very dangerous woman.

"I wasn't sure you knew," she said after a moment. "I *thought* that was why you left, but I didn't *know*. Well. She told me about the same time she did you. It wasn't a hell of a merry Christmas for her. She sat right there where you're sitting and told me about him and about you and the whole mess, and then she cried for an hour. She said she'd thought about killing herself. The thing was too much for her, it was tearing her apart. A lot of women could have handled it. A fiancé and a lover, one final fling before the darkness of matrimony descends, it happens all the time. But not Donnie. She was a one-man woman who'd made the mistake of falling in love with two men. After she told me, she came by every week or so, just to talk to somebody, to try to make some sense of it. After you left, I thought it'd be better for her, but then the primaries started and that really screwed things up."

"Why?" he asked bitterly. "It got them on the road together, didn't it? Away from the watchful eyes of Claire."

"Claire was never a problem. I don't think she gave a damn. Other women were just a bargaining chip for her. A lot of Senate wives get like that. They just hang on to see if there's a big white house at the end of the rainbow. Sure, the primaries gave them more time to be together, but it also meant there were a lot of new people around. The logistics of a Senator having an affair are easy—they just stay late at the office or get an apartment on the Hill. But once he starts running for President he's got Secret Service protection, like it or not, and he's got reporters hanging around all the time. Actually, the Secret Service isn't such a problem, because those boys learn fast to be discreet. But you know the reporters are going to assume the worst if a Senator has a pretty, unattached girl on his staff. Donna said once she thought she'd have an affair with a reporter, just to throw them off the track."

"Maybe Jeff Fields performed that function."

"Maybe he did. Anyway, by the time the primaries were over, they were both going out of their minds. Him more than her, I think. The closer he got to the nomination, the less he wanted to run the risk of screwing it up. She came to me in July, just before he left for the convention, and said they'd decided to call if off, and that she was going to quit her job and go out to California."

"Were they calling it off for good, or just for the duration of the campaign?"

"For good, she said. A clean break. She called me

a few times after that and she sounded happy. She never mentioned him."

"What was she doing?"

"She rented a little house near Carmel. She said she was doing some writing. And she had a puppy. His name was Dynamite. One time she called and I asked what she'd been doing, and she said she'd spent the afternoon watching Dynamite chase butterflies."

"What was she doing for money?"

"She had some saved. And she said she expected to get some money for a film treatment."

"A what?"

"Kind of a first draft of a movie, before you do a screenplay. She said she had an idea that some producer was interested in. Or maybe Jeff wanted it. Anyway, she was working on it."

Norton went over and poked the fire; sparks flew, and the heat felt good.

"I could never see it," he said. "Her and Whitmore. I've tried to be objective, to be grown up about it. I know he's attractive, I know all about the power syndrome, but I could never see *her* getting into anything like that."

"You're a baby, Ben. You don't know anything."

"I could see *you* and Whitmore."

"Ha! He and I hated each other the first time we met. We're too much alike."

"Gwen, how many people knew? About them."

"Not many. The two of them. The two of us. Ed Murphy maybe."

"Ed Murphy definitely," Norton said. "Ed knows everything. The question is whether anyone else on the staff knew. Like Nick Galiano."

"That fool?"

"He's such a fool he gets paid thirty-five thousand a year to drink and play golf with his best buddy. Listen, Nick knows plenty. You never know how much Nick knows."

"Well, I don't think many people know. If there'd been gossip, I'd have heard it. So it's *possible* that only the four of us know now—you, me, Whitmore and Murphy. And maybe Nick Galiano."

"Things are going to start happening fast. Tomorrow the stories will identify her and say she used to work for Whitmore. Pretty soon they'll find it was Fields's house. Reporters are going to start digging around."

"Sure, but what do they find? Jeff says he let her use his house. But what else? I don't see anybody uncovering an affair that's been over for months and was kept quiet to begin with."

"There'll be talk," Norton said stubbornly.

"So what? Who's going to print rumors about a dead girl that everybody liked and a President who's famous for his devotion to family, home, and motherhood? My God, Kennedy used to sneak girls into the White House and everybody knew it but nobody printed it. Presidents are allowed to have mistresses, as long as they don't screw them in the Rose Garden in front of the tourists. Or divorce their wives for them."

"Gwen, I talked to the detective on this case and he's a tough, suspicious son of a bitch. He's going to ask both of us a lot of questions, and you're under oath when you answer."

"I don't *care!* Look, some junkie broke in there looking for a stereo he could trade for a fix and she was there and he killed her. It happens every day. If I could help find him I would. But I *won't* tell a detective any ancient history that won't accomplish anything except getting Donna's name dragged through the mud. And you'd better not either."

Norton knew she was right, knew he would have to do the same no matter what the risks. Not for Whitmore's sake—to hell with Whitmore—but for Donna's sake. Once he realized that, he was ready to go. But there was one more thing he had to ask.

"Why did she do it, Gwen? She tried to explain it to me, but it never made any sense."

"Why? Why did she get involved with Big Chuck

when she could have married Dependable Ben? The nice blue-eyed all-American lawyer who'd give her babies and charge accounts and weekends in Acapulco? She didn't do that because that was what she was *supposed* to do. Why didn't you stay down there and practice law in Ringworm, South Carolina, or wherever it is you came from? Because you wanted to test your wings, to see how high you could fly, right? Well, so did she. Why Whitmore? Why *not* Whitmore? Donna always had it too easy. She was beautiful and sweet, so she was spoiled, things came too easy for her. But here was something that wasn't easy. She had to make some hard decisions, had to get hurt, had to grow up. I wanted to help her, but I couldn't, nobody could. She was on her own, and I was proud of her. But that doesn't make any sense to you, does it?"

"No," he said, "it doesn't. And it doesn't make any sense that she'd come back to town and not tell you. Or did she?"

"No," Gwen said. "I didn't know she was here."

He got up, stumbling a little. "I've got to go," he told her.

She looked up at him. "Do you want to stay here?"

He started to laugh but she cut him off. "Not for *that*, you egotistical bastard. Screwing you would be like screwing my half-wit brother. I just don't want you wrapping yourself around a telephone pole."

"I'm all right," he said.

"What are you going to do? About this mess, I mean."

"Keep asking questions until I get some answers."

"Why don't you stay out of it, Ben? Let the police handle it."

"The police and I aren't interested in the same things." He started to leave, then remembered something. "Did you ever know Donna to drink plum brandy? The kind that's colorless, like vodka, and costs twelve dollars a fifth?"

"Why?"

"There was a bottle at the house. She went out and bought it yesterday evening."

"Did the detective tell you that?"

"No, I saw the bottle on the bar at the house. I checked some liquor stores this afternoon and found the kid who sold it to her. He remembered her. Probably the detective will do the same thing."

Gwen got up and came close to him, her face inches from his. "Listen to me," she said. "I'm going to tell you something and I'm telling you so you don't go shooting your mouth off all over town about plum brandy. I don't know how many people know this, but Donna told me once, and maybe I've seen it in print too. Plum brandy happens to be, along with Gant shirts and Bogart movies and the writings of Mark Twain, one of the true and enduring passions of your friend Chuck Whitmore. Think about that one on your way home."

He did, all the way home and most of the night.

6

NORTON HAD not been inside the White House in several years, and he was struck anew by its simple majesty. Not by the power there—power was what you felt when you walked the long naked corridors of the Pentagon—but the beauty, the sheer history of the White House. The worst sons of bitches in the world could inhabit it, as they did from time to time, but the old mansion would only grow more serene, knowing it would outwait them.

Such sentimental thoughts passed through Norton's mind as he entered the West Wing, but he forced them aside as he neared Ed Murphy's office, for he knew better than to visit Ed Murphy in a sentimental mood. Murphy was a son of a bitch too (but *our* son of a bitch, his defenders said), whose sole passion in life was advancing the interests of Charles Whitmore. Even to get to see him was a sign of special favor. Norton had called Mrs. Hall, Murphy's white-haired grandmotherly secretary, and after inquiring about Norton's health and matrimonial status, she'd quickly scheduled an appointment, without even asking what it was about. It had been so easy that Norton was slightly more flattered than suspicious.

Mrs. Hall greeted him like a long-lost son, assured him that her boss would be with him momentarily, but nonetheless ushered him into a small waiting room, where Norton settled back with the new *Time,* prepared to wait the first hour without complaint. Keeping your cool was half the battle. He had, in fact, been waiting only ten minutes when Nick Galiano burst into the room.

"Ben, you old son of a gun, how the hell are you?" Nick bellowed and gave Norton a bear hug that took his breath away.

Norton extricated himself from Nick's embrace and tried to look pleased to see him. He'd always gotten along with Nick—and it was prudent to get along with Nick if you inhabited Whitmore's world—without ever quite liking or trusting him. It was hard to say why, for Nick was the most genial of men. He stayed out of politics and contented himself with being Whitmore's court jester, golfing companion, drinking buddy, and perhaps a constant reminder of Whitmore's rough-and-tumble past.

"How am I?" Norton repeated. "I'm okay, Nick. Or I was, until this Donna thing hit me."

Nick's homely face darkened. "It hit us all, Ben,"

he said. "Hit us like a ton of bricks. I never seen the Boss so shook. He said if he could just get his hands on the guy who did it—" Nick broke off and seemed to pull himself together. "You here to see Ed?"

"That's right."

"Hey, you gonna come back to work for the Boss?"

"No, no, Nick, I want to talk to Ed about Donna. I thought if we compared notes we might come up with something."

Nick stepped close to Norton and spoke in a low, confidential tone. "You know who did it, don't you?"

Norton was startled. "No, I don't."

"Some nigger," Nick said bitterly. "They walk the streets like they owned 'em, looking for houses to rob. And if you happen to be home, it's your tough luck. You know what I'm gonna do?"

"What?"

"I'm gonna watch that house. Just hang around. Because I figure the bastard will come back. They always do. And when he does I'll beat the truth out of him."

Nick's intensity alarmed Norton. He didn't think the answer to the problem was for Nick Galiano to beat up black men on Volta Place. But you never knew how seriously to take Nick.

"Ben, Mr. Murphy will see you now." Mrs. Hall announced from the doorway.

Nick Galiano gave Norton's arm a sudden squeeze. "Let's keep close, pal," Nick said somberly. "Okay?"

"Sure, Nick," Norton said, not at all sure what he was agreeing to, sure only that it was always prudent to be agreeable with Nick. Then he followed Mrs. Hall toward Ed Murphy's office, moving, he reflected, one step closer to the throne.

* * *

Ed Murphy didn't smile when Norton entered his office, but Norton had seen Murphy smile only once in the years he had known him, and that was when a

Senate rival of Whitmore's had broken both legs in a skiing accident.

"Sit down, Ben," Murphy said, and it was, by his standards, an affectionate greeting. "You still working for Whit Stone?"

"That's right," Norton said.

"That guy's as crooked as a corkscrew."

"It's a good firm," Norton protested halfheartedly. "If everything works out—"

"Come to work for us," Murphy interrupted. "I can find you something."

The offer caught Norton off guard; he felt at once the pull of power, the old temptations, the all but irresistible urge to ascend the mountaintop. What was Murphy's "something"? Assistant Attorney General? Special Counsel to the President? His mind raced through the lush green fields of his ambition: do a good job in the first administration, and who could say what reward might await you in the second one? Even a Cabinet post would not be out of the question.

He caught himself, fought back his fantasies, remembered why he was here. "I'm not looking for a job, Ed. I want to talk to you about Donna. This thing doesn't make any sense. I thought you might have some answers."

Murphy sipped his coffee without taking his eyes off Norton. "It's a terrible thing," he said. "The Boss is torn up about it. We all are. I've got a guy checking it out. Maybe you ought to talk to him."

Norton saw the brushoff coming. Murphy would have him out the door in thirty seconds if he didn't dig in.

"Wait a minute, Ed. There are things I want to ask *you*."

"Ask."

"What was she doing in Washington? What was she doing staying in a house owned by Jeff Fields?"

"What she was doing in Washington, I don't

know. As to the other, who says Fields owned the house?"

"I heard from a good source that he either owns it or rents it."

Murphy frowned his agreement. "That's what we heard too. But I don't know what she was doing there. Ask Fields."

"You haven't talked to him?"

"Why should I? He's some pretty-boy actor who hung around during the campaign. I don't worry about who he loans his houses to."

"Ed, had Donna been in contact with you about a job? Was that why she was in town?"

"Nope."

"How long has it been since you've seen her?"

Murphy made a show of concentration. "She left us just before the convention, didn't she? Early July? We had a going-away party for her. That's the last time."

Norton was stunned, not so much by the lie as by the smoothness of it.

"Ed, I talked to somebody who said he saw you and Donna together in Georgetown last week."

"Who?"

"It doesn't matter who."

"He's a liar, whoever he is."

"It was Phil Ross. Why would he lie?"

"He's wrong. He made a mistake."

Norton doubted that. But he had another question he thought he'd better get out fast, while he could. "Ed, how long has it been since *he* saw her?" Instinctively, he jerked his thumb toward the office next door.

"The Boss? The same as me, the going-away party."

"You're saying they broke off the affair and he hasn't seen her since then, is that right?"

"What affair? What the hell are you talking about?"

"Ed, they had an affair, from about Christmas all

through the spring of the primaries. I *know*. You don't have to play games with me."

"You don't know beans, pal. You've got a lively imagination, that's all."

"Ed, I was *going* with her. She *told* me."

"Then *she* had a lively imagination."

Norton sprang to his feet. "Listen, you rotten bastard . . ."

Murphy jumped up too and they glared at each other across his desk. *"You* listen, pal. She threw you over, right? Maybe she thought she needed an excuse, something to let you down easy. Maybe she had a crush on the guy and made it into more than it was. But there was no affair. Christ, the man was running for President. You think he had time to mess around?"

"She told someone else the same thing, Ed."

"Who?"

"It doesn't matter who."

"Okay, she told the story twice. That doesn't make it any more true."

"It won't wash, Ed. You say Phil Ross is wrong. You say Donna made up the affair. Everybody's a liar but you."

Ed Murphy settled back in his chair and lit a cheap cigar. "Sit down, Ben. Relax. We've got no problem. Look, for the sake of argument, let's suppose Donna had a thing with the Boss for a while, and suppose she and I had a talk last week about a job or something. What does it prove? So she's in town, staying at Fields's house, and some bastard breaks in and kills her. Okay, it's terrible, but it happens every day in this city. Lots of other cities too. Look, we've got the cops all over this case. They'll catch the guy and he'll be put away. I promise you that. But what's the sense of you running around chasing down rumors about things that might have happened a long time ago? All you're gonna do is cause problems that nobody needs."

Norton was thinking about the plum brandy.

Donna had made a special trip out to buy it. Gwen said it was a favorite drink of Whitmore's. Couldn't that suggest that Donna was expecting Whitmore to visit her on the night she was killed? Or at least hoping he would? He wanted to ask Murphy where Whitmore had been that night, but he couldn't get the words out. He knew how easily Murphy would tear his theory to ribbons. How many hundreds of people drank the stuff? Maybe she was going to send him the bottle as a present. Or maybe Norton was fantasizing, was out of his mind to think what he was thinking. He didn't know. All he knew was that he couldn't waltz in here and bluff Ed Murphy; he would have to get his facts straight first, then deal with him as an equal.

"We're in this together, Ben," Murphy said. "We both want to see this cleared up. I know you're shook up about this. All I'm asking is that you be careful about riding off in all directions at once. Doesn't that make sense?"

"I guess so, Ed."

"Good man," Murphy said. "Hold on, there's somebody I want you to meet."

He pressed a button on his desk and almost instantly the door opened and a man about Norton's age came in.

"Clay McNair, Ben Norton," Murphy said. "Ben used to work for us. He was a friend of Donna Hendricks. Brief him."

"Sure, Ed," the newcomer said and crossed the room to give Norton a firm handshake and a boyish grin.

Clay McNair was as tall as Norton, but more slender, and he carried himself like an athlete. He wore a pin-striped suit, clip-collar blue shirt, bold regimental tie, black shoes that shone like mirrors, and a college ring with his fraternity's emblem inscribed on its stone in gold. For a moment Norton thought he'd known him somewhere before, but he couldn't think where.

"You want us to go down to my office, Ed?" McNair asked.

"No, stay here," Murphy said. "I've got to go out for a minute. Sit outside, if you want to."

Murphy left the office, and McNair opened the door that led out to a small terrace that faced the South Lawn.

"You ever played on the White House tennis courts?" McNair asked.

"Not yet."

"Call me sometime. Usually they're available. Might as well enjoy the fringe benefits, I figure. Sit down, Ben. Boy, I feel like I know you, so many people have talked about you and said how they wish you were still on board."

Norton decided that McNair was a con man, a smooth one. "How long have you been on board?" he asked.

"Ed hired me right after the Inauguration. He wants me to do some forward planning on the media side of things. And he dumps a lot of special assignments on me." The young man grinned agreeably. "You know how that is."

"What's your background?"

"Corporate management, mainly in merchandising. Our firm worked on the campaign, that's how I met Ed."

"How do you like working for him?"

McNair grinned again. "Well, he can be tough. But how could I turn it down? I mean, having 'The White House' on my résumé isn't going to hurt things any, is it?"

"I guess not," Norton said. He wanted to scorn this amiable fool for using the White House as a rung on the corporate ladder, but of course that was how the game was played. He'd played it himself.

"Well, Ed wants me to brief you," McNair said briskly. "To start with, I'm in touch with the D.C.

police almost hourly. Anything they learn, they're instructed to report to me immediately."

"What have they learned?"

"Not much, yet. They found the liquor store where Donna made a purchase that night. And they found the maid and the yardman, and they're questioning them."

"Have the police found out who owns the house?"

"They're having some problems on that," McNair said with a frown.

Norton looked at him in amazement. Ed Murphy knew who owned the house—he'd just admitted that—so why were the police "having troubles" finding out? He wondered if this eager young man knew everything Murphy knew. He began to sense that this game was being played on several levels.

"What about fingerprints?"

"They didn't find any the first time around. They're going over the house again today."

"Have they checked the airlines to see when she arrived and where she came from?"

McNair wrinkled his brow. "They hadn't mentioned it."

"Maybe you should suggest it."

"Good thinking," McNair said and scribbled something in a little notebook. "That's about it on the investigation, except to say that they're going all-out on this case. It's going to be solved, you can depend on that. Now, do you want me to fill you in on the funeral arrangements?"

"I can get them on my own," Norton said.

McNair looked hurt. "Let me say this, Ben," he said, leaning forward with an earnest expression on his face. "I never knew Donna, but from what people tell me, she must have been one heck of a fine girl."

"She'd have spit in your eye if you called her a girl, pal."

"No offense. I mean a fine *person*. That's why I'm so glad to have this assignment. Ed's asked me to come up with some kind of a memorial to Donna. And just between you and I, I've got a feeling this one came straight from the Boss. What I've been kicking around is a White House intern program in her honor. Like maybe bringing four or five girls—young women—from the Hill to work here each year."

"What kind of jobs?"

"Well, that's still up in the air, so to speak."

"If it's for Donna, they'd better be good jobs. Not girl-Friday stuff."

"Good thought," McNair said. "You're right on target."

Norton was sick of the whole charade. Donna was dead and Ed Murphy had some corporate cutie brainstorming a memorial for her. This bastard didn't care about Donna; he'd have arranged a twenty-one-gun salute for Whitmore's pet canary if Ed Murphy had told him to.

Murphy joined them on the terrace. "You guys finished?"

"Yeah, Ed. Ben's given me some first-rate input."

"You two keep in touch," Murphy said. "Anything Ben wants, you give him."

"Right," McNair said sharply. "Talk to you later, Ben. Don't forget the tennis." With a quick handshake and a friendly wave he was gone.

"That's your new gopher?" Norton asked.

"He's not as dumb as he looks," Murphy said. "What'd you think of him?"

"He reminds me of guys I went to college with," Norton said.

"He gets a lot of good ideas," Murphy said. His phone rang, and the two men walked back into the office.

"I'd better go, Ed."

"Wait a minute. This may be for you." He picked up the receiver, listened a minute, then handed it to Norton. The younger man accepted it reluctantly, suddenly fearful that Murphy had the President on the line to reassure him. To stroke him, as an earlier administration had so nicely put it.

"Hello?"

"Ben. It's Phil Ross."

"Yeah?"

"Ben, listen, I could be wrong about that limousine. It *looked* like Murphy and the Hendricks girl, but I only had a glimpse."

"You were pretty sure the other night."

"Hell, you know how it is. A few drinks and you're sure of everything. But what I'm saying is, I'm *not* sure it was them. Okay?"

"Yeah, sure." Norton mumbled and handed the phone back to Murphy. "You don't waste any time, Ed."

"People make mistakes," Murphy said with a shrug. "We're on the same side, Ben, remember that."

"Okay, Ed. I better go now. Thanks for seeing me."

"No problem, Ben. Anytime. And remember what I said about a job."

"Yeah, sure, Ed," Norton said and stumbled out of Murphy's office in a daze. He was back on Pennsylvania Avenue, back in the world of reality, before he began to think he'd been had.

7

BACK AT his office, Norton had a message to call Sergeant Kravitz. Instead, he placed a long-distance call, and a continent away a woman with a crisp English accent answered: "Fields Productions. Good morning."

"This is Ben Norton in Washington, calling Mr. Fields. He and I met on the Whitmore campaign."

"Oh, of course, Mr. Norton," the woman said, a bit less crisply. "We just had a call from . . ." She stopped, and then her voice became very English again. "Did you say you're with the White House, Mr. Norton?"

"No, I'm a lawyer in private practice," he admitted, cursing himself for not being a better liar.

"Might I ask the nature of your business?"

"Tell Mr. Fields I'm a friend of Donna Hendricks."

"Would you hold, please?"

She let him hold long enough to skim the front page of the *Times,* and when she returned to the phone it sounded as if she'd made a quick trip to the Arctic Circle.

"I'm afraid Mr. Fields is traveling and may be out of touch for some time."

"When do you expect him back in touch?"

"I really can't say," the lady in Palm Springs said, and vanished with a transcontinental click. Norton sighed and dialed Sergeant Kravitz, who asked when he could come to police headquarters to give his statement. Norton said he'd be right there.

In the tiny waiting room outside the homicide division a dozen unhappy-looking black people were slumped morosely in battered folding chairs. Inside, a dozen unhappy-looking white men were scattered about the long crowded room, hunched behind battered old desks, variously drinking coffee, smoking cigars, filling out forms, or talking on telephones. Kravitz met him at the door, offered coffee, then led him to the far end of the office, where three identical doors opened off the hallway.

"These are the interview rooms," Kravitz said and led Norton into the first of the cubicles. It was ten feet square and contained an old metal desk, two chairs, one window with bars over it, a typewriter, a tape recorder, and a pair of handcuffs bolted to the wall.

"You're not going to handcuff me, are you, Sergeant?"

Kravitz was not amused. "Sit down, Mr. Norton. I'll have to ask you to read this."

He handed Norton a small white card which told him some things he already knew about the rights of witnesses in criminal investigations. Norton turned the card over and signed the waiver on the back. Then the questioning began.

An hour later, when Norton emerged from the homicide division, he was more impressed with the detective than he had been. The questioning had been low-key and cordial, but Kravitz had touched all the bases. If Norton hadn't told any outright lies, he had nonetheless told a good deal less than the whole truth, which was just as felonious, if somewhat harder to prove. He hadn't mentioned either Whitmore's affair with Donna or Phil Ross's story of seeing Donna and Ed Murphy together, not because those things weren't relevant—they were, in any normal investigation—but because he thought it the lesser evil to keep quiet for a while than to speak too soon and perhaps hurt, even destroy, the President. Politics, in Norton's experience, usually came down to a choice between greater and lesser evils; the hard part was deciding which was which. In this bewildering affair he didn't know who to trust, so he decided to trust only himself, and to keep on asking questions until he found the truth. And as he walked away from police headquarters, with the Capitol looming to his left and Pennsylvania Avenue, snarled with midday traffic, stretched out before him, he decided where his search would carry him next.

*   *   *

He emerged from the Palm Springs airport in the cool of early evening, just as the orange sun dropped behind the mountains to the west. He took a cab into town, and had just checked into the Canyon Hotel when he spotted her across its canyonlike lobby, a tiny girl with a jet-set tan, a stunning pout, and a pixie haircut; and after a moment he remembered her name.

"Penny! Hey, remember me?"

She looked, slowed, stopped, her eyes wide but blank. Her pout was inching toward her professional welcome-aboard smile when she too remembered and let her real smile explode across her elfin face. "You're . . . Ben! The nice lawyer. We went to the Redskins game together."

She laughed delightedly and bounced upward to kiss his cheek. She had dated a friend of his, a free-lance photographer, and they had been together a couple of times. His friend had always claimed that stewardesses were the only women worth dating, because their unlimited flight privileges made it possible for them to meet him in Paris or Buenos Aires or Istanbul or wherever his work happened to take him.

"How is it up in the friendly skies?" he asked.

"Hostile as all get out," Penny said with a giggle. "I've got this friend who's got this hatpin that's about two feet long, and she swears that the next Corporate Charlie who pats her fanny is going to get it in the eye."

Norton shuddered. "How about a drink?" he asked.

Penny pouted briefly and glanced at her watch. 'Well, I guess I've got time. I'm going to sort of a house party but not much will happen there until midnight or so. So let's."

She grinned and took his arm and he led her across the vast lobby, following signs that promised a bar somewhere in the distance. They reached the bar finally. It was large and dark and elegant, with a bandstand at one end and windows facing a swimming pool at the other. A gorgeous waitress brought them gin and tonics, and Penny leaned toward him, her pixie face aglow with curiosity.

"*I'm* here for a party," she said. "What're *you* here for?"

"Oh, just business," he told her in his most enigmatic Washington-lawyer style. That was one of the fringe benefits of the profession: you were granted your mysteries.

"Have you ever been in Palm Springs before?"

"Never ever."

"How do you like it?"

"I don't know," he admitted. "I don't quite believe it. The sky's too blue. Those mountains don't look real. I feel like I've stepped into the world's biggest movie set."

"It's *not* real," Penny said. "That's why it's so neat. People are so rich they don't bother with anything real."

"Tell me about your house party."

"Well," she said, hesitating a moment, "it's just that I know this fellow who's got money the way other people have got troubles, and he gives absolutely fabulous parties, and *everybody* goes to them, and he's got this incredible house where you can just get anything you want. I mean, if you want to watch a cockfight or drink some ancient wine or see some special movie, all you have to do is ask. The last time I was there, somebody wanted to see *Dumbo,* and the next thing you knew everybody was grooving on this flying elephant."

"Your friend wouldn't be Jeff Fields, would he?"

Her quick frown reminded him what small potatoes a Washington lawyer was alongside a movie star who could stage a cockfight or screen *Dumbo.*

"Yes," Penny said reluctantly, "but I'm sort of not supposed to talk about it. He's kind of, you know, paranoid about his privacy."

"It's all right," Norton told her. "I know Jeff. We met on the Presidential campaign. Back when I worked for President Whitmore."

"No kidding?"

"No kidding. Matter of fact, I'm supposed to see him while I'm here. The President may make him chairman of the Arts Council."

"How neat!" Penny cried. "Does Jeff know yet?"

"Not yet. And don't you tell him. I'm going to call him tomorrow."

Penny's pout worried its way into a frown. "That may not be a real good plan," she said. "I mean, once his party gets going, he may not much feel like talking about politics. Maybe you ought to drive out with me tonight and talk to him before things get too, you know, spaced out."

"No problem getting me in?"

"Well, usually they don't like it if you bring guys, but this is special."

Norton nodded contentedly, thinking that God must have loved lies or He wouldn't have made them so useful. "Do we have time for another drink?" he asked.

"No more for me," she said. "I mean, it might be sort of a long night. But you go ahead. You want to dance?"

Up on the bandstand a combo was tuning up, and suddenly they burst into what Norton would have called a honkytonk version of "Jambalaya."

"Maybe later," he said and waved to the waitress for another drink. "I talk better than I dance. Tell me about Jeff Fields. You know him better than I do."

Penny pouted, then grinned. "Well, the thing you've got to understand is, Jeff's not just another pretty face. He's about the smartest man I ever met. I mean, you don't have three dynamite pictures in a row on luck. And it's not just the pictures. He reads books and hangs out with intellectuals and digs politics and all sorts of things. Of course, he likes to party too. I mean, he built that mansion and he lives like a king. There aren't many guys who can afford to live like that any more. Elvis and Hef and Jeff and not many more. Some of the rock stars could, but they're mostly all wigged out on dope or religion of something. But Jeff's been through all that, and you know what he's into now? Power. Politics and all that jazz. He once told me the only person in the world he looks up to is the President of the United States. Boy, you should have seen Jeff the time he showed Whitmore around his mansion. He was like the king of a little country trying to impress the king of a big country."

Up on the bandstand a young man had begun singing a song that seemed to consist entirely of grunts and groans, plus occasionally a shout of "Do it!" and Penny grinned and jumped to her feet.

"Come on, let's dance."

Norton got up reluctantly. "I'm not much good at this."

She took his hand and led him toward the dance floor. "Did you read that book *Fear of Flying?*" she asked. "I did, because I thought it was about airplanes or something. Wow, was I wrong! Anyway, she says in there that dancing is like sex, it's not how you look, it's how you feel."

Norton, who wasn't feeling too well, but was determined to humor this strange creature, stepped onto the dance floor and began to wiggle his bottom as unobtrusively as possible. The young man on the bandstand kept groaning and shouting "Do it!" and Penny burst into some amazing gyrations, but Norton's mind stayed stubbornly on the mystery that had brought him to Palm Springs. After they had finished the dance and returned to the table, he squeezed her hand and said as casually as possible, "Say, Penny, when was it that Fields showed Whitmore around his place?"

"Huh? Oh, last summer, right after he moved in. There was a problem with the swimming-pool pump and they had to fly a guy in from L.A. to fix it so Whitmore could swim. He took a couple of days off from the campaign to rest up. Didn't you know?"

"I guess I'd forgotten."

"They did sort of keep it secret. That's the great thing about a place like that. You build a wall around it and nobody has to know what goes on inside. I guess the White House is sort of like that too."

"Sort of," Norton said. "Do you think we ought to get going?"

"I guess so," she said. "Listen, Ben, there's just this one thing."

"What's that?"

"Well, we'll *go* to the party together, but when we get there we won't exactly *be* together. It's not that kind of party."

"I understand," Norton said, and she hugged him in appreciation and they were on their way.

8

PENNY GUIDED her rented Mustang down the hill from the Canyon Hotel, past Mawby's, past the Gene Autry Hotel, past date-palm plantations and date-shake shops, out Bob Hope Drive and past the Annenberg estate and into the silver moonlight of the desert. To Norton the desert seemed somehow to stretch into the past—he half expected to see wagon trains and bands of Indians—and then it stopped abruptly in the present, at the dark tangled wall of tropical plants and chain-link fence that guarded Jeff Fields's estate. They drove on until they reached a gatehouse whose flat-faced, vaguely Oriental guardian scowled at Norton, quizzed Penny, but waved them past once she let fall the magic phrase—"a friend of the President"—that opened all doors, even in this unreal desert.

A long driveway twisted between towering palm trees, then stopped at a hulking white-walled Spanish-style mansion. Penny parked the Mustang between a Morgan and a Mercedes, then they walked hand in hand across a lawn as springy as a putting green, up

the steps, through the open door, and into the elaborate confusion of Jeff Fields's party. All the rooms
were filled with people, the women uniformly young
and sleek and lovely, clad in everything from bikinis
to ball gowns, some with little silver spoons hanging
from tiny chains around their necks. Norton recognized one cover girl and one Senator's well-traveled
wife, but the rest were a blur of anonymous beauty.
The men were more a mixed bag. He recognized a couple of rock singers, some young actors, a few giants
from the world of sport, and one cluster of older men
whose cool eyes, permanent tans, and peacock clothing marked them as movie makers. A few men spoke
to Penny, but no one paid any attention to Norton, a
fact that annoyed him; in Washington people at least
found out who you were before they ignored you.

They took goblets of pink-hued punch from a passing waiter, drifted down a hallway toward the back of
the house, heard shouts from the kitchen, and looked
in to see the biggest man Norton had ever laid eyes
on holding a refrigerator off the floor while an ancient
white-coated Chinaman pleaded with him to put it
down.

"Let's get away from him," Penny whispered.

"Who is he?"

"He plays football. He's an absolute animal. He was
balling a friend of mine one time and he flashed in her
face. On purpose."

"Different strokes for different folks," Norton muttered and followed her onto a long flagstone terrace
that overlooked a swimming pool far down the lawn.
The pool glowed an eerie green, and the people near it
moved like phantoms in its pale light, laughing, smoking, drinking, sometimes swimming. A few of them
were naked; otherwise it might have been any poolside
party.

"See that girl by the diving board?" Penny said.

"What about her?"

"Her name's Melinda. She's a super-groupie. She says

she's balled all the Stones and all but one of the Beatles. But she's getting kind of old now."

Norton, stranded between worlds, thought of Gwen, who sometimes claimed to have slept with six Senators, two Supreme Court Justices and one President. He wondered if there was some international scoring system and how Gwen's record might stack up against Melinda's. Did Ringo Starr outclass Ted Kennedy? He watched Melinda for a moment, cavorting beside the diving board with a bearded rock guitarist, and when he turned back to Penny he noticed a slender young man standing in the shadows at the far end of the terrace. The young man was wearing sneakers, a bathing suit and a polo shirt, and holding a can of Coors beer, but there was something in his stance, in his sheer relaxation amid this swarm of frantic people, that told you all this was his.

"There's our host," Norton said to Penny, and just then Jeff Fields crossed the terrace to join them.

"Jeff!" Penny cried. "You remember Ben Norton? From Washington?"

The actor's glance was cool and calculating. "You're the one who called," he said. "Donna's friend."

"Who's Donna?" Penny asked.

"Run and play," Fields told her, never taking his eyes off Norton. "The gentleman and I want to talk."

"Can't I listen? I *brought* him."

"This is business, puss. Why don't you go for a swim?"

He gave Penny a smile that made her glow with delight, and with a shrug to Norton she drifted down toward the pool. It was a trick Norton recognized from the political world, the affectionate dismissal, but Fields was not affectionate when he turned back to his uninvited guest. "How'd you get in here?" he asked.

"I conned the girl. It wasn't her fault."

"No, it was my fault, for giving that crazy chick the run of the place. But you're here now, so let's talk. Come on, we can sit over here."

He led Norton to a picnic table beneath some palm

trees. A waiter appeared and asked what Mr. Fields would like. The actor said to bring them beer. They watched as Penny emerged naked from the cabana beside the pool and jumped into the water with a yelp of pleasure. A moment later the football player who'd been juggling the refrigerator raced screaming down the lawn and threw himself into the pool, sending a tidal wave of water into the air.

"That drunken fool," Fields muttered. "You start with a few friends, Norton, and then you get your friends' friends, and the next thing you've got a zoo." The actor sighed, took a six-pack of Coors from the waiter, and handed one to Norton. "Okay, you came a long way to see me. What's on your mind?"

"You know about Donna, don't you?"

"I saw the newspaper stories. I was sorry about it. Do they know what happened?"

"Not yet. It could have been a prowler."

"It's a dangerous city."

"Fields, what was she doing in your house?"

"What do you mean?"

"Your house in Georgetown. The one she was killed in."

"Who says it's mine?"

"A friend of Donna's told me you'd bought it or leased it or whatever it was."

"Who else knows that?"

"The police will find it out eventually."

"It may take them a while," the actor said. "I bought it in someone else's name."

Norton thought it strange that Fields hadn't already been contacted by the police. Ed Murphy knew that the actor had the house in Georgetown. Either Ed had been slow in passing that information along to the police, or the police had been slow in following up on it.

"Why all the secrecy about a house in Washington?" he asked.

"Why? So I can go there without being bugged by gossip columnists and autograph hounds and would-be screenwriters."

"But what was Donna doing there?"

The actor shrugged. "She called and asked me if she could use the place and I said sure."

"Called from where?"

"Wherever it was she was living. Carmel?"

"Why was she going to Washington?"

"I didn't ask."

"You're not very curious, are you?"

The actor considered him coldly. "Look, Norton, you crashed my party, you're asking a lot of questions I don't have to answer, and now you're getting obnoxious. I should have you thrown out of here."

Norton returned the actor's stare. He had that fine feeling that comes with being angry with someone fifty pounds lighter than oneself. "Go ahead," he said, "but I'll break that pretty nose of yours first."

Fields studied him with the intent look of a man making a perplexing decision, then he shurgged and gave Norton a good-fellow smile. "Look, Ben, there's no use in us having a brawl. You liked Donna? Okay, I liked Donna. You worked for Whitmore? Okay, so did I. We're on the same side. And I'll answer your questions. Just don't push me. Okay?"

"Okay," Norton agreed. "To start, how well did you know Donna?"

"We were friends," Fields said. "You know how people are thrown together during a campaign. I took her out a few times. I liked her. She was bright and she was honest. There was no romance, if that's what you mean. She didn't approve of my life style."

"How much did you know about her and Whitmore?" Norton asked abruptly.

"I didn't know anything about her and Whitmore," the actor said sharply.

"Is it true that she wrote a screenplay for you?" Norton asked.

"She wrote something for me, but I wouldn't call it a screenplay. It was more like a memoir. She thought she had an idea for a Washington movie, so I told her to put something on paper in whatever form she could. As it turned out, she had some interesting ideas."

"What kind of ideas?"

The actor sipped his Coors and stared up at the starlit California sky. Down at poolside the huge football player was tossing Penny into the air like a rag doll, and some other people had started a game of water polo. A young comedian was sitting at a table inside the cabana rolling joints, and a girl beside him was snorting cocaine through a rolled-up dollar bill.

"Her basic story was about a young woman who's in love with a politician who won't divorce his wife," the actor said. "That's conventional enough, but she had some nice detail."

"Like what?"

"Oh, a scene between the young woman and the politician's wife. A nice sketch of the politician's tough-guy assistant. A bedroom scene where she's trying to get his mind off politics. Some funny stuff about the logistics of a politician having an affair."

"This politician didn't happen to be a rugged fifty-year-old Senator who was about to run for President, did he?"

"She was ambiguous about that. She was ambiguous about the whole thing."

"She had good reason to be ambiguous about it," Norton said. "I'd like to see that manuscript. So would a lot of other people."

"That includes me," Fields added.

"What do you mean?"

"My copy was stolen."

"Jesus Christ," Norton whispered. "What happened?"

"I have an office in town where I keep hundreds of scripts. Somebody broke into it. I thought all they took was the petty cash. But when Donna called about her trip to Washington, I mentioned the break-in and she asked me to check on her manuscript. When I told her it was gone, she freaked out."

"Have you told the White House about this?" Norton asked.

"We're not talking much these days."

"Why not?"

"Ask them," the actor said. "All I can say is Whitmore and I were pretty buddy-buddy when I was busting my ass for him, but once he got in the White House he seemed to have forgotten my name. It looks like my old buddy was using me and now he doesn't need me any more."

"Politicians use everybody," Norton said. "You should have known that."

Norton glanced down the hill and saw two men standing in the shadows at the far end of the cabana, talking and passing a joint back and forth. After a moment he saw that the super-groupie named Melinda was kneeling in front of one of the men, the bearded rock guitarist. The guitarist kept talking and smoking, but as the woman's head began to bob violently he lost his cool, grabbed her by the hair, and danced a frantic jig as she completed the act. A few people drifted over from poolside and applauded as the woman stood up, grinned, and swigged a beer.

"Things are picking up," Norton said.

"Fun and games," the actor replied. "Let's go up to the house. You can stay here tonight if you want to. I'd like to talk to you some more."

"About what?"

"About Donna. About Whitmore. I don't know as much as I thought I knew about politics."

The party had moved to poolside and the house was all but deserted now. Fields led Norton into a library that had one wall covered with pictures of himself posing with other people. Norton recognized some of them as actors, actresses, directors. "Here's one of me and our friend," Fields said. The picture showed Fields and Charles Whitmore standing in front of the cabana. Fields was grinning easily at the camera; Whitmore stared suspiciously at it. Norton looked at the picture indifferently. He'd seen a thousand like it

—politicians passed them out like lollipops to children
—but then he looked more closely. There was something wrong with the picture, something he could not at first put his finger on.

"I remember the day that was taken," Fields said, but he stopped when the flat-faced man from the front gate appeared in the doorway.

"Long-distance call, boss," the man announced.

"Take a message."

The man pulled the actor aside, and after a minute's whispering Fields hurried away. The doorkeeper stood with his arms folded and eyes fixed on Norton. Norton turned back to the photograph. He was thinking that Jeff Fields seemed a decent enough fellow; he was intelligent and he'd been helpful. He was still thinking that, and thinking about the picture too, when the actor re-entered the library. Norton turned to him and was startled by the change that had come over him. His face was flushed, his mouth slack, and his hands shook when he lit a cigarette; he looked like a man who had just learned of a death in his family.

But Norton wasn't concerned with the actor's family; he had a question he had to ask. "Jeff, about this photograph—"

"Forget it. The party's over. Jack here will drive you back to your hotel."

"What's the rush?"

"I don't feel good. The party's over."

"Okay, but first tell me who was cropped out of this picture."

"What the hell are you talking about?"

"There was a woman next to Whitmore. You can see part of her blouse, against his arm."

"It was my secretary." His eyes darted from Norton to his bodyguard. "Jack, take Mr. Norton back to his hotel."

"You're lying," Norton said. "I can tell that's Donna's blouse. I gave it to her. When were they here?"

Fields whispered to his helper, then stumbled from the room.

"Let's go, buddy," the other man said. He was built like a weightlifter, and his smug smile dared Norton to defy him. Norton decided not to and walked past him toward the front door.

"We'll take the Imperial," his escort said when they were outside, pointing to a car at the far end of the driveway. Norton started toward the car, wondering what news could so have shaken Jeff Fields. It was no night for bad news. He could hear music and laughter rising up from the party at poolside, and above him the desert sky glittered with a million stars. Then, as they reached the Imperial, the man behind him made a sudden move, and all the stars went out.

9

THE DESERT sunrise was a slow symphony of purple and pink, and Norton had a fine view of it from the ditch he awoke in. Whenever he tried to move, little bombs started exploding in the back of his head, so it seemed more sensible to lie there in the warm sand and watch the new day spread across the sky. When he finally crawled out of his ditch, he found himself not far from the highway. In time a Good Samaritan appeared, in the form of a lettuce farmer in a Chevrolet pick-up, and gave him a ride all the way to his hotel. Norton gave the desk clerk a dirty look instead of an explanation and stumbled up to his room for a hot shower and some hard thinking. The shower was a success; the thinking progressed no further than a decision to bid adieu to fabulous Palm Springs. He thought of seeking out Jeff Fields again, but he feared that he'd only end up back in his ditch, or worse. What he really wanted to do was to get back to Washington. No one had ever knocked him on the head and tossed him in a ditch in Washington. Still, he had one more stop to make in California.

* * *

He found Penny in the airport coffee shop, staring glumly into a cup of Sanka. She didn't even look up when he slipped onto the next stool.

"What happened to the party?" he asked.

"Oh, hi," she said without enthusiasm. "I don't know *what* happened to it. One minute everybody is having a ball, and the next minute Jeff says we've all got to leave. He left too. I asked him where you were, but he said you'd already gone. The whole thing was *weird*. I think the Mafia's after him or something like that."

"Why do you say that?"

"Well, there was this girl who was going to call her boy friend, and she picked up one of the upstairs phones, and she heard somebody saying, 'You son of a bitch, we'll ruin you, you'll never make another movie,' and a lot of wild stuff like that, and Jeff was just sort of gulping, and I figure there's not many people besides the Mafia that'd talk to somebody as important as Jeff like that."

"She didn't hear who the other person was?"

"No, she got scared and hung up. All she wanted to *do* was to call her boy friend."

"Where are you off to now, Penny?"

"Oh, I guess to L.A. Hey, you want to come with me?"

"I've got to get back to Washington. Sorry."

"That's okay. Look. I still want to come see you in

Washington, so we can play tennis and you can teach
me about politics and all."

Norton said that nothing could please him more
than for Penny to visit him in Washington, and that
seemed to cheer her a bit. She was a wilted pixie, but
she flashed her best smile and pecked him on the cheek
before rushing off to catch her plane; and a few minutes later Norton strolled out the gate to catch his
plane, one bound north for Carmel.

* * *

"I bet you thought I was dead, didn't you, fella?"

"Yes, sir, I guess I did," Norton admitted.

"Well, I reckon I *am* dead, by Washington standards," the old man said. "I died twenty-odd years ago
when Joe McCarthy lit out after me and I got whipped
running for re-election. There ain't nothing deader in
Washington than an ex-Senator. I hung around town
for a while, thinking I was still a useful citizen, but
what I was was a turd in the political punchbowl. I
mean to say, it's like being a leper—folks is all mighty
sorry about your affliction, but they'd just as soon you
didn't stay for dinner."

The old man's name was Harry Nolan and four
decades before he'd been called "The Lion of the
Prairie." Norton had read about him in books on the
New Deal. Sometimes the books had pictures of Harry
Nolan with FDR. Now Norton had found him a few
miles outside Carmel in a cottage on a hillside that
overlooked the bright blue waters of the Pacific.

"How'd you find me, boy? She didn't tell a hell of
a lot of people where she was living at."

"She wrote me once. I had the return address."

"You the one that went to Paris?"

"That's right."

The old man peered at him disapprovingly. "That
was a lowlife thing to do, boy. You shoulda stayed
and *fought* for her. Instead you fiddle-faddled around
and let her get away from you. And now she's dead.

Piss-poor, boy, piss-poor. She was a gal worth fighting for. I just wish I'd met her thirty or forty years ago."

"How did you two meet, Senator?"

"Well, she moved in down the way, and she kept to herself for a while, reading or writing or whatever it was she did, but one day that dog of hers got out and run over into my yard, so she come over and we got to talking and we hardly ever stopped talking after that."

"What'd you talk about?"

"Politics, mostly. She was like all you young people, didn't know any history, so I'd try to educate her. She'd get all upset by *scandals* and *corruption*—lordy, it ain't like Nixon *invented* anything. There was worse scandals under Grant and Harding and maybe a couple of others who never got caught. People don't change any. What's changed is television, telling people a lot of things they'd be better off not knowing.

"So, anyway, we'd talk about the New Deal, which is to say I'd talk and she'd listen. That girl was one fine listener. I told her all about how we got TVA and how we put the screws to the Wall Street boys, and all about that old reprobate Jack Garner sitting there being Vice President for eight years and hating every day of it and a-praying morning and night for FDR to wake up dead. Lord, did you ever think what'd happened if FDR had died before he did? You could have had Jack Garner for President. Or Henry Wallace, that blasted fool. Hell, you could've had *me*. Franklin would have made me Vice President in 'forty-four if I'd have had it, which I wouldn't."

"Did Donna have any other friends out here, Senator?"

"You know what she really liked to hear about? She liked to hear about Lucy Rutherfurd and the so-called love affair that she 'n' FDR was having. Hell, like I told her, all they ever did was take rides through Rock Creek Park, like a couple of kids running off and playing hooky. I went with 'em a couple of times, and there ain't nobody else alive who can make that statement. Me 'n' him would talk business and she'd just sit there and listen and maybe pat his arm when we was talking about the war and it was going bad. She hardly ever opened her mouth, and when she did it was just to say, 'Ain't the flowers purty?' or, 'Look how gold the leaves is,' or somesuch nonsense as that. But Donna, she kept after me until I told her. Hell, what did I care about Lucy Rutherfurd? We was trying to win a war and Lucy wasn't helping none. Course, Donna said she *was* helping, just by being there and patting his arm or making him look at the flowers and such. Maybe she was right. I never thought about it before.

"You want a libation, boy? I reckon the sun's over the yardarm somewhere in the world."

"Sure, Senator."

"You get 'em, then. Make yourself useful. The bottle's up there on the counter and I drink mine neat."

Norton poured them two tumblers of Jack Daniel's, then rejoined the old man.

"You in politics, boy?"

"I worked on the Hill for three years."

"Three years? Lord, a man couldn't find the bathroom in three years. I was there twenty years and I was still a babe in the woods when I got cashiered. A politician is a strange breed of cat, boy. These professors, they come in here sometimes and want to talk about *political science* and all. *Science?* What's *science* got to do with anything? Politics ain't no more of a science than eating pussy is. It's an *art,* and either you're born with the talent or you ain't. You want me to tell you about politicans, fella?"

"I wish you would, Senator."

"Well, the main thing you got to understand is they're all the same down deep—it don't matter what party they're with—which is to say they'll all cut your throat if it'll do 'em a dime's worth of good. The only difference between one politician and another is how he'd go about cutting your throat. Take FDR. Say he wanted to cut your throat. You'd be sitting there with him and he'd be just oozing charm at every pore and mixing your martini and showing you his new ship-in-a-bottle, and then maybe you'd blink or look out the window or something, just for a second, but when you did Franklin'd zip across the room, wheelchair 'n' all, and slice you ear to ear, and you'd never know he'd done it, till the next time you turned your head and it rolled off onto the floor.

"Now Harry Truman, he wasn't like most politicians. He might have cut your throat, but it'd have been more his style to punch you in the nose, or more likely to kick you in the gonads. Ike, that baby-faced fool, he'd have prayed over you first. Hubert, he'd have cried about how terrible it was that he had to do it to you, until you'd have been begging him to go on and get it over with. Lyndon, he'd have made a big sloppy speech about how it was all for your own good. Jack Kennedy, he'd have cut loose with some high-falutin' oratory about how it was better to cut throats than to change coats or dig moats or launch boats or somesuch nonsense as that, and while he was giving out with the oratory, Bobby'd have snuck up behind you and put the knife to you. Then there was that reprobate Nixon. You know how he'd cut your throat?"

"How?"

"He *wouldn't*, that's how. He was too gutless. He'd have *delegated* the job to one of those skinhead bandits who guarded the door for him, and they'd have delegated it to some right-wing loon, and *he'd* have screwed up the job. That's one rule of politics, boy, don't delegate nothing, not if you want it done right."

"How about President Whitmore?" Norton asked. "How would he do the job?"

"Whitmore? Oh, that fella's smooth. He could be another FDR, if he don't screw up. I told him that. I told him to forget all about Kennedy and that charisma stuff, and read up on FDR. I told him to talk to folks simple, like the fireside chats. Just go on TV and talk straight, tell folks the truth, and they'd respect it. People ain't dumb. They get distracted easy, but they ain't dumb."

The old man sipped his Jack Daniel's, and Norton asked his question as gently as he could. "When did you tell President Whitmore that, sir?"

"Huh?"

"When? When did you meet him?"

"Oh, hell, I don't know. Three, four, five months ago. Right before he was swore in."

"Just before the Inauguration?"

"That's right. He was in Los Angeles for something, then he snuck up here to see her. He stayed the night and the next morning she brought him over to meet me. She said we was the two greatest men she'd ever met. More's the pity, I reckon. So him and me talked awhile and then they had to take him back to where he was supposed to be. She swore me to all kinds of secrecy, but I don't reckon it matters much now."

"Have you told anybody else about this, Senator?"

"Boy, do you recollect what Jack Garner said about being Vice President?"

"Something about it not being worth a bucket of warm spit?"

"That's right, except what he really said was a bucket of warm piss, but nobody'd print *that*. Well, that's what being old's like. It's got less pleasure in it than a gnat's ass. 'Bout the only good thing about it is that when folks ask you something, and you don't feel like answering, you can just sort of stare off into space and after a while they quit asking. You don't even have to lie, unless you'd rather."

"But somebody did ask?"

"Only that fool yesterday. And I wasn't about to tell *him* nothing. I spotted him for a phony right away."

"Who was he?"

"He said he was some kind of special agent. I took him for a nut. So I just sort of stared off into space and drooled a little, and pretty soon he left."

"Senator, did she tell you why she was going back to Washington?"

"She didn't *tell* me. But anybody with the sense God gave a duck could figure it out."

"How do you mean?"

"I mean, he come out here to see her, three-four months ago, so now it's *her* time to go see *him*. Course, I could be wrong. Could be she was going to check out some books from the Library of Congress or to see the cherry blossoms blossom, or somesuch. But if she was, things has changed since my day. People in love don't never use their heads. Blast it all, I *told* her not to go back there. I told her to stay here where she was happy and let Washington go to blazes. It's a bad place, young fellow. If you stay there long enough, they'll kill you, one way or another, you can depend on that."

10

BACK IN Washington, Norton had work to do.

Not precisely the work he had been trained to do when he studied torts and contracts in his law school days, but a more highly skilled and highly paid type of law he had learned in his years in Washington. He knew why Whitney Stone had hired him and paid him a handsome salary. Stone had pioneered a sophisticated form of recruiting young lawyers. Many firms had for three decades recruited lawyers who had worked for, and presumably had continuing influence with, whatever politician happened at that moment to inhabit the White House. Whitney Stone, ever a gambler, had carried the process further and begun recruiting men with lines to *potential* Presidents. They were cheaper then, and if their patron stumbled on the way to the White House they could always be disposed of. Norton supposed he was one of Whit Stone's better gambles, for Senator Whitmore had only been a dark horse for the Presidency when Stone had snapped him up. And he had been most agreeable about it. He had gone along with Norton's desire to leave Washington for a while, although he obviously thought it rather soft-headed of a young lawyer to leave a potential President, and Norton knew he had done a good job for the firm in Paris. But now his ex-boss was President, and it was time for him to do a good job for the firm in Washington. That was what he had been hired for.

Norton understood the system and had more or less reconciled himself to it. Connections were the name of the game. The trick was to use them properly, to walk the narrow, sometimes almost invisible, line between friendship and influence peddling, and he thought he could do that as well as anyone. His ties to Whitmore might get him inside certain closed doors in Washington; in the long run it would be his own skill and integrity that would keep him there. Or so he hoped.

Thus, the day after his return from California he climbed out of a cab and approached the mighty fortress that houses the U.S. Department of Justice, hoping to discover how certain officials of its anti-trust division would respond if a politically ambitious Texas oilman and newspaper publisher bought fourteen hillbilly radio stations in South Texas. Norton thought he already knew the answer to the question, but he wasn't being paid to guess.

He stepped into the building and found himself face to face with a sleepy-eyed security guard; Norton could remember when there were no guards at the Department of Justice.

"I'm Mr. Norton," he said. "I have an appointment with Allen Gillespie."

The guard looked at him blankly and reached for a pale blue telephone directory.

"He's a special assistant to the Attorney General," Norton said. The guard continued to thumb through the book until he found a number. Then he made a call, announced "Mr. Martin." and after a moment of confusion handed the receiver to Norton.

"Mr. Norton? Mr. Gillespie asked if you would meet him for coffee down in the cafeteria," a secretary said. "He'll be there as soon as he can."

Norton frowned and started toward the dismal little basement cafeteria. He thought this not the best possible start to his mission. Al Gillespie could just as easily have entertained his old friend in the Attorney General's private dining room. But of course they were not really friends. They had been colleagues on Whitmore's staff for a year, rivals in a sense and he doubted that Gillespie had been brokenhearted by his departure. But Al was smart, and he was a political animal. and Norton thought he had a better chance of getting the information he wanted from him than from the former law professor who now headed the antitrust division.

Gillespie joined him in the cafeteria fifteen minutes later. He was a plump self-satisfied young man who was every bit as smart as he looked. They shook hands and Gillespie sat down and began to stir his coffee impatiently. "How've you been, Ben?"

Norton said he'd been fine.

"Which firm was it you went with?"

Norton told him, certain that Gillespie knew exactly which firm he'd gone with.

"You picked a strange time to leave us."

"I'm perverse," Norton said. "When everybody else jumps on the bandwagon, I jump off."

"I heard you might jump back on."

"Where'd you hear that?"

"I heard it. Are you?"

"I doubt it."

Gillespie's glance suggested that he thought his old colleague was demented. That didn't bother Norton. He was wondering how Gillespie knew that Ed Murphy had been dangling jobs before him. Maybe Ed had told Gillespie to check out the available slots at Justice. He began to think this meeting might be more complicated than he'd foreseen. It was still a time of flux in Washington, of professional ups and downs, and perhaps Gillespie was thinking that he and Norton might wind up as colleagues again. Which was fine for him to think.

Norton played out the string. He asked about Gillespie's work and listened intently as Gillespie boasted about the many achievements of the new, revitalized Department of Justice. Norton tried to look impressed by the litany, although it was one he'd heard before from other bright young men in other administrations. Then Gillespie changed the subject abruptly. "Too bad about Donna," he said.

Norton nodded.

"I thought you two were going to get married."

"We didn't."

"What do you think happened?"

"I don't know."

"No theories?"

"I'm not a cop, Al."

"I know you're not a cop. I thought you might be looking into it."

"I don't have any theories."

Gillespie looked skeptical. Norton wondered how much he knew, but that was the last thing you ever found out from someone like Gillespie.

They talked about the Justice Department some more until they had finished their coffee. It was time to go, and neither man had hinted that this was more than a visit between two old friends. Then Gillespie surprised him again. "What've you been working on, Ben?"

Norton took it as no casual remark. Gillespie was

making it easy for him. "Oh, odds and ends." he said. He tossed some coins on the table and they started out of the cafeteria. "One interesting anti-trust thing. A fellow named Baxter, owns some newspapers down in Texas and wants to buy some radio stations, but no one knows which way your fellows would jump."

They walked down the hallway between huge WPA murals of farmers toiling in rocky fields. At the elevator Gillespie turned to him with an absolutely blank expression on his face. "Radio stations?" he said, as if to himself. He made a sour face and then shrugged his shoulders. It was, for Al Gillespie, a most uncharacteristic gesture.

"Good to see you, Ben," he said and punched the elevator button.

"My pleasure, Al."

The elevator rattled its way toward them.

"You representing any tire companies?"

"Nope."

"You're lucky." Then the elevator doors opened and Al Gillespie stepped through them and was gone.

Three minutes later, back in his fifth-floor office next to the Attorney General's office, Al Gillespie made a call to the White House, but Norton didn't know that. All he knew as he walked away from the Justice Department was that he would bet his last dollar that the anti-trust division wouldn't let out a peep if Harvey Baxter bought up all the radio stations in the state of Texas.

The shrug would have been enough, because he knew his man well enough to translate the shrug, and it came out something like "You idiot, do you really think we're going to mess around with radio stations in Texas?" But in case Norton had been too dim-witted to understand the shrug, Gillespie had dropped his line about the tire companies, which made it crystal clear to Norton where the perennially undermanned anti-trust division would be focusing its energies in the months ahead.

Norton knew all he needed to know except the

"why," and he thought about that for a while, because in Washington it was always necessary to look gift horses in the mouth. And he thought he understood the "why" too; it was not all that subtle. He thought that Ed Murphy had talked to Gillespie about this visit. He thought that because of the remark about a job, and also because Gillespie had been pumping him about Donna's death. Norton suspected that Gillespie's million-dollar shrug was just Ed Murphy's way of tossing a few crumbs his way, reminding him how helpful the White House could be to Washington lawyers who didn't make waves. That was fine. He would take their favors and he would keep on doing exactly what he'd set out to do, finding out the truth about Donna. They could underestimate him if they wished. That was their problem.

11

NORTON THOUGHT the finest actresses he had ever seen were Katharine Hepburn, Liv Ullmann, Julie Christie and Frances Hall, and sometimes he believed Mrs. Hall was the best of them all. Of course, Mrs. Hall was unknown to the public at large, and the circumstances of her career had restricted her to one specific, tragic role, but within that role she was beyond comparison. He trembled to think what she might have done as Medea or Lady Macbeth or Mary Tyrone, but she did quite well enough as Ed Murphy's secretary in the anguished portrayal she gave several times each week as she broke the news to some do-gooder or favor seeker that Ed Murphy was not going to see him. In that recurring scene Fran Hall would twist her normally placid face into a mask of pain, tortured tears would well in her soft blue eyes, the twist and flutter of her gentle hands would reflect the sadness in her heart, as she recited the awful facts about Murphy's back-breaking schedule, his failing health, his suicidal devotion to the President's urgent needs, his vast remorse that he would not now or in the foreseeable future be able to work Mr. Favor Seeker into his schedule. She could, as Nick Galiano had once observed, wring tears from a dog turd.

The success of her performances was aided, of course, by the fact that few denizens of the political world were willing to accept the unspeakable possibility that Ed Murphy did not want to see them. It was far easier to take Mrs. Hall's excuses at face value, and to go away believing that on that particular week Murphy could not have worked the Shah of Iran into his schedule.

Ben Norton was no ordinary appointment seeker, however. He knew the game and, as much as he admired Mrs. Hall's talents, he refused to be moved.

"It's pretty important, Mrs. Hall," he said into the telephone. "To Ed too."

"Can I tell him what it *is,* Ben?"

"Just tell him it's a follow-up to our talk the other day."

She would, of course, be annoyed by his refusal to confide in her. No matter.

"Well, I'll do what I can." She sighed. "I'll get back to you."

She didn't get back, so he called again the next day.

"Oh, *Ben,* I was just about to call *you.* Mr. Murphy hasn't had a free *instant.* But I gave him your message, and he suggested you talk to Clay McNair."

"I don't think that would help."

"He's a quite capable young man, Ben," she said, chiding now. "Mr. Murphy relies on him a great deal."

"Mrs. Hall, just tell Ed that I have some new information and I think he'd be well advised to discuss it with me."

"I'll tell him," Mrs. Hall promised, with the faintest of chills in her voice.

Whitney Stone had been most pleased by Norton's success at the Justice Department. When told of it, he had even smiled, a rare occurrence and an unfortunate one, for there was something cobralike about his face, and when cobras smile it destroys the otherwise interesting symmetry of their features. He hadn't questioned the validity of Norton's information, or even pressed him as to its source. He had accepted it and acted upon it.

"I just spoke to Baxter," he told Norton that afternoon. "He was delighted by our report, needless to say, and he's moving at once to acquire the radio stations."

"He really wants those stations, doesn't he?"

"Yes, he's persuaded himself they are the key to his political future. Perhaps they are. Who knows?"

A yellow light flickered on Stone's telephone console. Stone picked up the receiver, listened a moment, then cupped his small freckled hand across the mouthpiece. "Ed Murphy's office calling you, Ben," he announced. "Would you like to take it here?"

"Sure," Norton said and leaned across the desk to take the receiver.

"Ben?" Mrs. Hall said, her voice ringing with good will. "Can you come right over?"

"I'll be there in fifteen minutes," Norton promised. He handed the receiver back to Whitney Stone, who had listened with unconcealed interest.

"Ed wants to see me right away," he explained, hoping Stone wouldn't ask what Murphy wanted to see him about.

"You and Murphy seem on quite cordial terms these days," Stone said.

"We always got along well," Norton said.

Stone walked him to the door of his office, then touched his arm lightly before he opened it. "You know, Ben, if the administration should make you an attractive job offer, something commensurate with your abilities, the firm would of course be most understanding."

Norton didn't doubt that. The only thing better for the firm than having a young lawyer with lines to the administration was having a young lawyer *in* the administration.

"I appreciate it, Whit," he said. "We'll see what happens." He wasn't about to tell Stone that he didn't *want* a job in the administration; as long as the possibility seemed to exist, he had an aura of potential power that was itself a kind of power.

When he entered Mrs. Hall's office she greeted him with a look of unspeakable anguish. "Oh, *Ben*," she cried, "Mr. Murphy was all set to see you, and then the President called him in and it may go on for *hours*." She paused, then brightened. "But let me tell you what Mr. Murphy did."

Just then, as if on cue, Clay McNair entered the room. He was still wearing his college ring and his earnest face, but he'd replaced his pin-striped suit with a sincere-looking Glen plaid.

"He asked Clay to help you any way he can," Mrs. Hall said. McNair strode forward, with boyish smile and outstretched hand, and Norton knew he'd been sandbagged.

"Let's go down to my office to talk, Ben," McNair said.

Norton gave up and followed McNair down the stairs to the White House basement. McNair's office proved to be tiny—from its size and location it might once have been Henry Kissinger's broom closet—barely big enough to hold the two desks jammed into it.

"Space is tight," McNair said defensively. "You know how it is. But the guy who shares this one with me is a kind of consultant who' not here much so it's like having an office to myself. My secretary's down the hall."

"Who is he?" Norton asked.

"Oh, a fellow named Byron Riddle. A funny guy."

Norton shrugged and sat down at Byron Riddle's desk, which was bare except for a small replica of the Iwo Jima flag-raising statue. McNair's desk, by contrast, was covered with neatly arranged stacks of memos, and it also held a photograph of McNair's wife, who looked wanly pretty, and his children, who were blond and toothy. Identical pictures of President Whitmore hung over both desks.

"I thought I might see you at the funeral," McNair began with a mournful look on his face. He was such a clean-cut young man; Norton imagined him passing the collection plate each Sunday at some suburban Presbyterian church.

"I don't like funerals."

"It was nicely done," McNair said. "Very tasteful."

"I don't want to hear about it."

"Well, I thought you'd be interested. There was one rather fascinating sidelight, just between you and I. Sergeant Kravitz had a film crew hidden across the street to have a record of who was there."

"Wonderful."

"Well, Ben, that's heads-up police work, you'll have to admit that."

Norton admitted nothing, and McNair reached into his desk drawer and fished out a pack of Juicy Fruit gum. He offered a stick to Norton, who declined, then unwrapped a stick for himself and began to chew it. The act annoyed Norton, who was already annoyed to be sitting in this broom closet talking to Ed Murphy's flunky. "Are you still in touch with Kravitz?" he asked.

"Of course."

"Then why didn't you tell him that Jeff Fields owned the house in Georgetown?"

"He *what?*"

"You heard me. Why didn't you tell Kravitz that?"

"I didn't *know* that," McNair admitted.

"Then why didn't Ed tell you? *He* knew."

"How do you know he knew?"

"Because I told him, damn it. So why didn't he tell you to tell Kravitz, if you're so full of cooperation for the investigation?"

McNair gave him an all-forgiving smile. "Ben, it must have slipped his mind. Ed's just *incredibly* busy."

"Look, I've worked for Murphy. He never forgets *anything*. Except when he wants to."

"It's different in the White House," McNair said patiently. "It's a quantum jump, Ben. He does forget things now. That's why I'm here, to help him get organized better."

"Ask him about Fields owning the house," Norton said. "And while you're at it, ask him why he called Fields in the middle of the night a few days ago."

He had started to say "*if* he called Fields," but he decided the time had come to bluff.

"Who says he did?"

"I do."

"Okay, I'll pass that on. But is that the urgent matter you wanted to see Ed about?"

Norton hesitated. He disliked dealing with this agreeable fool, yet he assumed he'd get the message through, and that was what mattered. You had to play the game Ed's way.

"No," Norton said. "Tell Ed I want to talk to him about the President's trip to California last January."

McNair looked puzzled. "What trip do you mean?"

"He'll know what I mean."

McNair frowned and scribbled something on a yellow legal pad. Just then the door opened and a man stepped in. He was about forty-five and trimly built, with close-cropped black hair and dark alert eyes that moved quickly from McNair to the stranger at his desk.

"Byron Riddle, meet Ben Norton," McNair said.

Norton stood up and extended his hand, but Riddle ignored him, moving swiftly to the desk and checking all its drawers. Only then did he take Norton's hand, gripping it with such ferocity that Norton had to squeeze back hard to keep from getting hurt. Throughout the handshake, Riddle kept his face close to Norton's, staring at him with such intensity that he had the odd sensation that the man was trying to hypnotize him.

"Ben used to work for the President," McNair said. "On his Senate staff."

"That right?" Riddle said. "What're you doing now?"

Norton didn't answer for a moment. Riddle had a strange way of speaking out of one side of his mouth that so intrigued him he almost missed the question.

"Oh. I'm in private practice."

"Who with?"

"Coggins, Copeland, and Stone."

"Good bunch," Riddle said with a knowing nod. "But you ought to get back on the team, fellow. Big things are happening. This is where the action is."

"What position do you play on the team?" Norton asked.

"A lot of positions. I'm what you call a utility infielder." He grinned at his joke, a rather wolfish grin, and looked at his watch.

"Byron's done some—" McNair began, but Riddle cut him off.

"You men don't want to talk about me," he said. "I've got to get moving. Got a little lady waiting for me, and I don't believe in keeping the fair sex waiting." He winked and vanished out the door.

"That's a real character," McNair said. "They broke the mold when they made Byron Riddle. Maybe you heard about what he did on Inauguration Day."

Norton started to protest—he wasn't all that interested in Byron Riddle—but McNair waved him back to his chair.

"The thing is," McNair said, "Byron had done some work on the campaign. Advance work, crowd security, that type of thing, but he was a long way from rating a job in the White House. Then, on Inauguration Day, when the President's motorcade was on its way down from the Hill, this madman, some long-haired hippie type, sneaked onto the White House grounds with a suitcase he said was full of dynamite. He said he was going to blow up the White House unless he got to speak on national television. He said he had his own Inaugural Address to give. Well, you can imagine the panic. The President's on his way, the whole country is watching, and here's this hippie with a suitcase full of dynamite. For the first few minutes nobody knew what to do. The FBI wanted to shoot him, and the Secret Service wanted to pretend to bargain with him. I mean, *nobody* was in charge. And then Byron Riddle appeared out of nowhere and walked right up to the man and offered him a cigarette and started talking to him, and two minutes later the guy handed over the suitcase to him and surrendered without a peep. It would have been a heck of a big story, except so much else was happening that day, and we pretty well kept it quiet. And as soon as the guy was under arrest Byron just disappeared. That's what you call a passion for anonymity. And believe you me, Ed Murphy appreciated it. So Byron got his job here as a special consultant. He's a funny guy, but he's got guts; you've got to hand him that."

Norton stood up, no longer interested in the exploits of Byron Riddle. "Look, McNair, you just give Ed my message. About California. Tell him if he won't talk to me, I'll have to talk to some other people."

McNair looked most unhappy at that. "I don't like the sound of this, Ben. I don't understand what your problem is, but I think you're barking up the wrong tree. We're all on the same team, aren't we? We all want to help the President."

"Fellow, I don't give a damn about helping the President," Norton said coldly. "I just want to find out who killed a friend of mind. You tell Ed I said that."

McNair looked as if he'd been slapped. He was a young man who sought to please, and Norton inexplicably would not be pleased. But before he could protest, Norton was gone.

* * *

The next day Norton was summoned again to Ed Murphy's office, and he found Murphy in a rage. "What's this about California in January?" he shouted. "What kind of games are you playing? If you've got something to say, say it straight!"

"I will," Norton said. "You told me last week that Whitmore hadn't seen Donna since last summer. But someone else, someone with no ax to grind, told me he went to see her in Carmel in January, just before the Inaugural."

"It's a lie," Murphy shouted. "He didn't see her in January. He hadn't seen her in nearly a year."

"Ed, my information comes from someone who saw him. Who talked to him."

"Who?"

"A friend of hers. Ask Whitmore if you want to know who."

"That old Senator?"

"That's right."

"He's a crank. After the election he started writing and calling, giving the boss a lot of free advice. We tried to humor him, but he got to be a nuisance. So he got his feelings hurt, and he might have made up any story just to get somebody to listen to him. You're a damn fool if you took him seriously."

"That old man's no crank, Ed."

"Maybe you're the crank, then. You're talking crazy. You've got a great future, Ben, but you're gonna blow it if you don't watch out."

"I'm going to find out what happened. You can tell your boss that."

"This is all personal. Your girl friend throws you over, you blame Whitmore. She gets killed, you blame Whitmore. What've you got, some lousy conspiracy theory?"

"Look, Ed, I haven't said a word to anybody about Donna and Whitmore. If I was the jealous lover, I would have, wouldn't I? I don't *want* to cause any problems for Whitmore. All I want is the truth about what happened to Donna. But when you start conning me on little issues, it makes me think you're conning me on bigger issues. If she came to town to see him, or if he went out to see her in January, why don't you just level with me? As long as I think I'm getting the runaround, as long as I think people are hiding something from me, I'm going to keep after it. So why not just tell me the truth?"

Ed Murphy glared at him, but he hesitated before answering, and when he spoke his voice seemed uncertain. "We've told you the truth, Ben."

"Okay, Ed," Norton said and got up. There was nothing more to say. For an instant he thought he had heard regret in Murphy's voice, as if he wanted to tell the truth but couldn't. Perhaps Whitmore was making all the decisions in this matter. That was possible.

But something else was possible too, Norton thought. Perhaps Ed Murphy was right and he was jumping to conclusions. What if Phil Ross *had* been wrong about seeing Donna and Murphy together? What if the old Senator *was* a crank? What if all of it was coincidence? In that case Ed Murphy was right. He was a damn fool, and he could be ruining whatever future he had in this city. Norton was torn by uncertainty. Was he being carried away by his passions? Was he seeing plots where none existed? He knew the kind of people who wandered about town obsessed with this or that conspiracy theory—that the oilmen killed JFK, that Jack Ruby was in the hire of the Mafia, that the Klan had paid for Dr. King's murder—and he had never imagined himself joining their ranks. He was a reasonable man, and part of him feared that he might be behaving like a fool.

Yet Donna was dead. That was a fact. And he

believed Ed Murphy was lying to him. And he didn't think Senator Nolan had been lying about the trip to Carmel. And there was that unexplained phone call that had told him of the murder. He might be wrong, but his best judgment was that the evidence justified his suspicions; he was an angry and stubborn man, and that was enough to keep him going, at least for a little longer.

12

WHEN BYRON Riddle stepped into the office at noon, Clay McNair looked up from his pile of memos and felt a sharp pain deep in his stomach. I am getting an ulcer, he thought. This madhouse is giving me an ulcer. He braced himself for a showdown.

"Byron, where is that security report? Ed's been calling about it."

"Get off my back, buster," Riddle snapped. "I've got some top secret assignments I'm working on."

"Look, Byron—"

"*You* look, Buster. What the hell do you mean letting that Norton character sit at my desk the other day? You think this is Grand Central Station? If I ever catch anybody else using my desk, I'll throw their ass out of here and you too!"

McNair couldn't believe it. "Byron, what *difference* does it make if somebody sits at your desk? I don't care if somebody sits at *my* desk. Let's be reasonable."

"We're not talking about your desk," Riddle said scornfully. "Sometimes I have important documents in my desk."

"Byron," McNair said patiently, "Ben Norton is not exactly an enemy agent, and I was sitting here with him, and anyway your desk drawers are locked, aren't they?"

"Who says he's not an enemy agent? Don't assume anything, Buster. You might have gone to the head for a minute and that's all the time he'd need."

"Byron, the Secret Service said that the locks on these desks are—"

"Screw the Secret Service," Riddle shot back. "A bunch of girls. What do they know? Listen, Buster, the lock's never been made that a real pro can't handle. There are some new electronic devices that . . . Look, you just do what I tell you. If you want to entertain somebody, you take them down to the mess, and lock the door behind you. Understand? If I ever see anybody within ten feet of my desk again, you and me are gonna have problems. Bad problems."

McNair started to protest, but Riddle stormed out of the office, slamming the door behind him. McNair sat motionless at his desk, with the pain in his stomach growing worse. It was such an impossible situation. Clay McNair believed in good organization and good management, and here he was trying to deal with Byron Riddle, who was without doubt the most disorganized, unmanageable person he'd ever met. The idea of the two of them sharing an office seemed to McNair to be an insane, sadistic joke, yet here they were, eyeball to eyeball in their broom closet. McNair wanted to complain to Ed Murphy about their freewheeling consultant, and yet he wasn't sure how Murphy would respond. Riddle was useful sometimes, there was no denying that; he seemed to have sources of information that no one else knew existed. And, worst of all, Clay McNair was afraid of him. When they argued, as they had just now, Riddle would sometimes fix him with that cold, furious stare that seemed to say, I could kill you.

McNair took a stick of Juicy Fruit from his pocket and began to chew it, trying to calm himself. This was not what he had expected when he had been offered a job on the White House staff. He had imagined himself in a fine office near the President's own office, striding down the hallway several times each day to advise the President on affairs of state. Instead, he found himself slaving in a cubbyhole in the White House basement waiting for angry calls from Ed Murphy about this or that fouled-up assignment, and it was a big week if he even *saw* the President. The last time they'd spoken was in a receiving line in the East Room and the President had called him Hank and praised his work on a project he'd had nothing to do with.

McNair's "hotline" rang suddenly—his direct line to Ed Murphy—and he grabbed it with a trembling hand.

"Has Norton been back in touch with you?" Murphy demanded.

"No, Ed."

"Don't talk to him any more. Take a message, report to me, and keep your mouth shut! Understand?"

"Right, Ed."

"And forget what he said about California. The guy has a screw loose. He always was a nut. The best thing we can do is steer clear of him."

"Right Ed," McNair said again, but Murphy had already hung up. Clay McNair lowered the receiver gently. He was a most perplexed young man. He didn't understand why Ed Murphy was so upset about the death of one woman, or why Norton kept asking so many questions about her. But in truth he really didn't want to know. That was one of the rules of good management he'd learned in business school: Keep out of other people's problems. He had problems enough of his own.

* * *

Byron Riddle spent the late afternoon sitting high in the Senate gallery, coolly studying the disorderly spectacle of democracy. The issue of the day was the public-works bill, a proposal of such far-reaching importance to the nation that nearly a third of the Senators were on hand for the debate. Most of the time Riddle focused his attention on Senator Donovan Ripley the aggressive young leader of the pro-public-works forces. Riddle loathed Ripley and everything he stood for yet there was a smug smile on his face as he watched the Senator guide the bill through the parliamentary minefields. Have your fun, Donnie, he thought. Have your fun while you can, because it's not gonna last much longer.

As the debate droned on, Riddle sometimes grew restless, impatient for the larger events of the evening to unfold. Sometimes he would close his eyes and study the various Senators' voices as they spoke. He could identify almost all of them by their voices. That was a little trick he had learned in his work; you never knew when that would come in handy. Once he noticed a certain New England Senator picking his nose. Riddle leaned forward quickly and seemed to straighten his tie. In fact, he was snapping a picture with a tiny camera hidden in his lapel. That was nickel-and-dime stuff, but you never knew when it would be useful. He imagined the nose picking blown up on a campaign poster with the legend "Is this what we picked?" Riddle laughed at that until an elderly lady two rows in front of him turned around and shushed him.

When the Senators finally adjourned, Riddle watched Donovan Ripley march off the floor, surrounded by anxious aides, then Riddle left the gallery and hurried to the nearest pay phone. He dialed a number and a young woman in a small apartment a few blocks away answered quickly.

"Wendy?" he whispered. "It's me."

"Oh, Dr. Green. What's happening?"

"Everything's fine. They just adjourned. He'll go by his office now. He won't be over there until it's dark. Is everything set?"

"Well, *I'm* set," Wendy said.

"Nervous?"

"Maybe just a little."

"Don't worry, kid. You're gonna be great."

"Ha! *He'll* think so."

Riddle grinned into the telephone. "He won't know the half of it. Look, just don't forget about the lights. Tell him that's what turns you on. Tell him you want to see his pretty face. Tell him anything, *but keep those lights on!*"

"Don't worry, Dr. Green. You can count on me."

"Good girl. I gotta go now."

"Look, when do I see you again? What about the rest of the money?"

"I'll call you tomorrow," he promised. "Just keep cool. You're gonna be great."

He walked downstairs, past a huge painting of Washington crossing the Delaware, and was crossing the Rotunda when he saw a familiar figure coming his way, a heavy-set man who was followed by a half dozen high school students.

When the man saw Riddle, he excused himself from the students and hurried over with hand outstretched. "Byron, you old dog, how the hell are you?"

"I'm okay, Senator. How about yourself?"

"Hey, what's this Senator stuff? It's Bill to you, buddy. How's it going? I hear you're doing all right for yourself."

"No complaints."

The man laughed loudly and kept pumping Riddle's hand. "No complaints. Ha. Same old Byron.

You know what your motto ought to be, boy? 'I love a mystery.' Old Byron! What a guy."

Riddle wondered what his companion wanted. He freed his hand and looked at his watch. "How's it with you, Bill?"

The Senator's grin vanished. "Things are tough," he said grimly. "A fellow's elected to do a job and then they won't let you do it. You know I'm dipping into my own pocket to pay for my newsletter? I'm having to give lectures now just to keep afloat. Sometimes I wonder if it's worth it."

"There's a fellow you ought to meet," Riddle said. "Soybean business. New in town. Wants to meet the right kind of people. Maybe could help out."

"Send him around, Byron, send him around. Glad to meet any friend of yours, any time."

"Good," Riddle said and started to move away.

"Listen, Byron, there's maybe something you could do for me." The Senator put his arm around Riddle's shoulders and led him over by the statue of a long-forgotten Vice President. "Some troublemakers back home. One of 'em claims to be a doctor. Opened this storefront clinic. but instead of pills what he's handing out is political advice. I'd like to know who he is and who's behind him."

"Have you talked to our friends?"

"They're no good. They're all scared shitless. It's not like the old days. Look, Byron, I thought if you could go take a look, check it out . . ."

"I'll try, Bill. I'm up to my ears, but I'll try."

"Okay. Byron. Look, I meant to ask you. What do you know about this little lady who got herself killed in Georgetown?"

"Nothing."

"Strange business," the Senator said. "You'd have thought the papers would do more with it."

"You know how they are."

"That's true. Well, great to see you, buddy. You call me now." The Senator winked and started back toward the waiting cluster of high school students.

Riddle hurried outside, down the long flight of steps at the East Front of the Capitol, and over to Constitution Avenue. He smoked two cigarettes before Donovan Ripley emerged from the Old Senate Office Building. Ripley walked rapidly down First Street, past the Supreme Court, and up East Capitol Street. Riddle followed half a block behind him. It was like clockwork. At Fourth Street the Senator turned to the right and walked halfway down the dark block, then darted into an old townhouse that had been converted into apartments. Riddle knew the townhouse well; he was at present renting all three of its apartments. Riddle slipped into his car, which was parked across the street. After a minute he saw Wendy appear at the window and lower the shade. The light stayed on. Riddle lit another Marlboro and began to laugh. It was all so easy, he thought, all so easy when your enemies were as dumb as Donovan Ripley. He sat in the car until Ripley emerged from the apartment two hours later, sometimes laughing and sometimes thinking quite coldly about his future and all that this would mean to him. It was his greatest score, his million-dollar score, and from now on the sky was the limit.

13

JUST AFTER he returned from lunch, Norton received an urgent and unexpected call from his boss's secretary: Mr. Stone wished to see Mr. Norton at once. Three minutes later Norton stepped into Whitney Stone's big dimly lit office and found the older lawyer seated immobile behind his antique desk, with a perplexed look on his narrow face. Stone stared at him for a moment, then waved him into a chair.

"I just had some rather bad news, Ben," he began.

"What's that?"

"As you know, on the basis of your report from the Justice Department, Mr. Baxter moved at once to purchase those radio stations. He signed the papers yesterday morning."

"Yes?"

"Then, this morning, a representative of the anti-trust division told Mr. Baxter that the department has serious questions about the acquisition and is considering injunctive action."

Norton was too stunned to reply; he'd been stabbed in the back and he thought he knew why.

"I'm wondering, Ben," Whitney Stone continued in his gentlest, most dangerous voice, "if you can shed any light on this rather embarrassing turnabout. We of course relied on your reading of the mood in the anti-trust division. Could you have been mistaken? Or misled?"

Norton was too angry to say anything but the truth. "I don't think I was mistaken. I think there's a rather special problem here. Ed Murphy and I are involved in . . . well, call it a difference of opinion, on a personal matter. I think Ed was behind the open-door policy I encountered at Justice. That was Ed's idea of friendly persuasion. But since then we've had another talk and I've continued to disagree with him on the other matter, so he slammed the door on me."

Whitney Stone touched his fingertips together and gazed toward the ceiling, like a man in search of divine guidance. "I appreciate your candor," he said at last. "You see, Ben, I am not entirely unfamiliar with your, ah, difference of opinion with Ed Murphy. It has to do, I believe, with the death of your friend Miss Hendricks."

"That's right."

"I gather that Murphy thinks you're being overinquisitive about the matter, somewhat bothersome from his perspective, and he used this anti-trust issue to set you up, then shoot you down. Is that how you read it?"

"More or less, yes."

"Then perhaps the first question, Ben, is whether you *are* being overly aggressive in this matter."

"I don't think so," Norton said. "Donna was murdered under very peculiar circumstances. No one will say why she was in Washington in that particular house at that particular time. I think Ed Murphy knows and that he's been lying to me."

"Do you suspect that President Whitmore had anything to do with her death, Ben?"

"I have no reason to suspect that," Norton said. That was the literal truth. It was also, as both he and Stone knew, something less than a flat no.

"But you think Whitmore and/or Murphy may have known why she was in Washington or may have been in touch with her?"

"That's right."

"And you are insisting that Murphy satisfy your curiosity on these points?"

"It's more than my curiosity, Whit. I think the truth about her death should be found out, if it posssibly can be."

"The truth about her death, Ben, or about her love life?"

Norton felt his anger rising. "Just a minute, Whit," he began. "I think—"

"Don't take offense," Stone interrupted. "Just let me pursue that line of thought a moment, please. Let us suppose, for the sake of argument, that Miss Hendricks was killed by a burglar. And let us further suppose that the night before she was killed she happened to have spoken with the President or been visited by him or whatever. Are you saying that information would be relevant to her death?"

"It could be. In any normal investigation it *would* be."

"Ah, precisely," Stone said. "But this *isn't* a normal investigation, is it? To the contrary, it's most extraordinary. If you or I had visited Miss Hendricks the night before her death, no one would think twice about it."

"But we're not necessarily talking about the night before her death, Whit. We could be talking about the night *of* her death."

"But you have no proof of that?"

"No. Nothing solid."

"In which case, as I'm sure you're aware, it becomes a most serious suggestion, one you'd not lightly make."

"I know that."

"Of course. So, to continue my line of thought, whatever dealings President Whitmore might have had with the young lady, however innocent, could, if they became known, be used to embarrass, perhaps to cripple, perhaps even to destroy his administration. So we're dealing with a most delicate situation, and perhaps the question is the extent to which your, ah, *inquiries* may be rooted in your, shall I say, emotional attachment to the unfortunate young woman."

Again Norton fought back his anger. "It's not emotional," he insisted. "I just want the truth. Let Whitmore tell the truth like everyone else."

"The truth," Whitney Stone repeated. "You want the truth. I wish you well in your quest, Ben, but I must note that saints and philosophers have been seeking the truth since the beginning of time, and with less than total success. For my own part, I find justice a more practical goal than truth. More men can live with justice than with truth. In the present situation, while the truth might be that Mr. Whitmore is an immoral or imprudent man, I question whether justice requires that he be punished politically for his nonpolitical indiscretions."

He smiled and lit a cigarette without taking his eyes off Norton.

"I don't want to see him hurt politically," the younger man protested.

"Of course not," Stone said. "You only want the 'truth.' But might I suggest, Ben, with no offense intended, that your own dedication to the truth in this matter has been somewhat less than total."

"What do you mean?"

"Well, I gather that you have certain information that you have chosen to pursue on your own, rather than to share with the duly authorized investigative officials. And, while I'd not question your actions, I might note that you may have left yourself in a somewhat compromised position."

Which was a roundabout way of saying Norton might have perjured himself. Which, unfortunately, might be true. Norton wondered how Stone knew so damn much. From the White House? From the U.S. Attorney's office? From the police? But in Washington you never pressed a man for his sources. Not much was sacred in Washington, but good sources were.

"Perhaps I've made mistakes," Norton said. "I've acted in good faith."

"Ah, of course," Stone said with a little puff on his English cigarette. "Understand, Ben, I speak only as a friend who is concerned about your career. Of course, I would be less than candid if I said I was pleased by this Justice Department action."

"I'm sorry about the client," Norton said. "He's getting screwed for something that isn't his fault."

"Well, those things happen," Stone said. "We'll make it up to him somehow. No, Ben, my real concern is you. I don't want to see a promising career damaged. Let's talk about your career for a moment. We really haven't had a good talk since you came back from Paris. Here, let me get you a drink. Scotch?"

Stone stepped to his liquor cabinet and quickly mixed two drinks, an act of hospitality that was, to Norton's knowledge, unprecedented in the firm's history. Norton was a little suspicious of Stone's hospitality, but more than that he was determined to hear the man out. Perhaps he *was* being emotional. Perhaps he *was* throwing away his future.

Stone handed him his drink and sat back down. "Now, Ben, as you look down the road, toward what I'm sure will be a most rewarding career, what are the goals you've set for yourself?"

Norton relaxed, savoring the question. It was nice to look down the road, the farther down the road the better.

"I want to be a good lawyer," he said. "And in the past few years, both here and on the Hill, I've been more and more intrigued by the federal-corporate relationship. It's so much more than just legal. It's political and economic and cultural, and it keeps evolving as the Congress writes new laws and as the corporations keep moving toward a supernational role. The whole thing needs definition. There has to be more communication between the two sides, and we're the middlemen. There's room for, if you'll forgive me, some legal statesmanship, the kind that can serve both parties and the public interest too."

He paused and sipped his drink. He wondered if Whitney Stone, who was not exactly famous for serving the public interest, had any idea what he meant.

"Nicely put," Stone said. "And absolutely correct. Sometimes, Ben, I think I spend half my time trying to explain the corporate mind to politicians, and the other half trying to explain the political mind to my corporate friends. There *is* a need for definition. And for statesmanship. And, one might say, for philosophical considerations. What is *the* proper relationship between the public sector and the private sector? Who is the servant and who the master? Or can it be a meeting of equals? These are intriguing questions."

"Yes," Norton said. "And damned hard questions to focus on when you're struggling with your day-to-day caseload."

"Precisely," Stone said. "And that's what I want to talk to you about. Henry Willoughby will be retiring soon. That isn't known yet, but his health is failing, poor fellow. As you know, he's been our resident philosopher, while I've turned my attentions to more realistic concerns. But I'll be needing a new man to oversee our corporate work. To do some writing. To testify before the appropriate Congressional committees. What I really want is someone who can emerge as a nationally recognized spokesman in the entire field of corporate-government relationships. And of course to work on those cases that most interest him. And I think you're the man for the assignment. If you're interested in it, of course."

"Of course I'm interested, Whit. I hardly know what to say."

"Then don't say anything. Just think about it, and we can discuss the details later. And of course, the importance of the assignment would be properly reflected in our financial arrangement."

"Whit . . . I'm very grateful for this."

"I admire honesty, Ben. I admired the way you told me the truth about your problem with Ed Murphy. And I admire your loyalty to the young woman. All I suggest, as a friend, is that you remember that discretion and caution can be virtues too."

It was all happening too fast. They had moved so quickly from Donna to the dazzling job offer. Was Stone trying to buy him off? Or was he insane even to think that? He debated with himself, and once again his suspicions won out.

"Whit, I can't give any assurances in the other matter. The question of Donna's death."

"None have been requested," Stone said smoothly. "However, perhaps I should alert you to one fact that has come to my attention, on a quite confidential basis. I have, as you may have gathered, certain sources of information on the Hendricks investigation, and I am reliably informed that an arrest is at hand, probably within days. I mention this only to spare you any precipitous action."

"Whose arrest?"

Whitney Stone sighed. "I'm afraid it's a sad end to a

sad affair. The suspect is a demented young man with a history of sex offenses, from window peeping to attempted rape. The young man worked in a Georgetown liquor store and sold her a bottle of brandy the evening of her death. Apparently he followed her home and . . ."

Stone left the sentence unfinished. It was just as well he did. Norton stared at the floor, drained of emotion. So it was all over. She'd been killed by some nut, some window peeper, and they'd caught him and that was that.

"May I freshen your drink, Ben?"

Norton jerked himself back to reality. "No, thanks. If you'll excuse me, I'd better go. All this has been . . . Well, I've just about had it for one day."

"Of course, Ben," Whitney Stone said with his serpentine smile. "We'll talk again tomorrow."

Norton returned to his own office in a daze. He sat there for a while, trying to balance what Stone had said about Donna against what Stone had said about this fine new assignment. His every instinct was to beware Whit Stone bearing gifts. How did he know Stone was telling the truth? Was the kid in the liquor store really about to be arrested or had Stone made that up? Or was he crazy to keep questioning everything and everybody? He cursed himself for his indecision and grabbed his phone. A minute later he had Kravitz on the line.

"Sergeant," he said, "I wonder if I could come by right now to talk to you?"

"Not unless you're about to kill somebody," Kravitz said. "I'm just leaving to see my kid pitch his Little League opener."

"Maybe I could just ask you over the phone," Norton said. "I heard you were about to make an arrest in the Hendricks case."

"We've made no arrest," Kravitz said.

"I understand that. But I was told that the kid in the liquor store has a history of sex offenses and he's under investigation."

"A number of individuals are under investigation," Kravitz said with a hint of irritation in his voice.

"Yes, but can you tell me if the kid in the liquor store is one of them?"

"Look, Norton," the detective growled, "we don't send out advance notices before we arrest somebody. Yes, the boy is under investigation. But that's all I'm going to say."

"Okay, Sergeant. Thanks. I hope your son's team wins."

Norton put down the phone, satisfied at last. Of course Kravitz couldn't tell him what he was going to do. But it was clear enough what would happen next. The mystery had ended, as he might have expected, not with the bang of political intrigue but with the whimper of a deranged young man. Norton shut his eyes and wondered if he'd wanted intrigue wanted Donna's death to have some greater meaning than a prowler's guilt would give it. Then he told himself to put such thoughts behind him. He had behaved honorably. Not wisely perhaps, but honorably and now it was time to look ahead. He had to fight his way out of the cloud of despair that had surrounded him these past weeks. He smiled and thought of the week after he'd finished his bar exams, when he and two friends had gone on a four-day drunk. He didn't want to get drunk now, but he wanted people, laughter, diversion, and he decided to accept an invitation to a party at Gwen Bowers's house that night. She'd called and said she was having some people over to celebrate a friend of hers selling her first short story. It sounded like fun, and Norton thought some fun was exactly what he needed now.

14

HE RANG Gwen's doorbell twice, then he pushed open the door and walked in. He followed the sound of music and laughter down the long hallway to the library, where he found Gwen standing in front of the fireplace telling a story to eight or ten guests:

"So there I am in my new ball gown in the middle of a blizzard and my car won't start and there's not a cab to be had for love nor money and I'm due at the White House in a half hour for the Party of the Year, right? So what do I do? What *could* I do? I put on my boots and slogged down to Mass Ave and stood there in the blizzard with my thumb stuck out till a car stopped, a red Impala to be precise, and I looked at the driver and he looked at me and he was without question the biggest, blackest, meanest-looking mother I have ever laid eyes on. And I seemed to remember reading in the papers about a series of vicious rapes perpetrated by a black man in a red Impala. Now that, children, is what you call a quandary. But I was freezing and there weren't any other cars in sight, so I hopped in and said, 'Look, brother, if you're gonna ravish me, just be quick about it and don't muss my hair, and when you're finished drop me at the White House!'"

The young people scattered around the library laughed politely, the way people in their twenties laugh at jokes by people in their thirties, and someone asked, "When was that, Gwen?"

"Oh, centuries ago," she said. "Back in the last days of Lyndon the Terrible. Actually. he wasn't so terrible once you got to know him. Hey look who's here!"

She greeted Norton with a noisy kiss. "Everybody, this is Ben," she announced. "Ben, these are"—she started pointing to the upturned faces—"Annie. who just had her first story bought by *Cosmo,* and Tim, who's in legalization, and Mitzi who's with the *Post,* and Mike, who writes for *Rolling Stone,* and . . . What's your name, darling?"

"Joe," a bearded boy replied.

"Joe," she repeated. "And Pete, who I think you know, and— Oh, hell, introduce yourselves. Ben's a lawyer and a dear sweet man."

Most of the kids smiled or waved a greeting, except one fellow in the corner who seemed to stick out his tongue. Norton looked again and saw that the boy was busy rolling joints.

"Come on down to the kitchen and we'll get you a drink," Gwen said and pulled him down the hallway. "I talked to that detective," she said. "He's tough, like you said. But all I told him is what I told you I would."

"Gwen, listen, forget about the detective. Forget about everything. It's all over."

"What do you mean?"

"I got word, on a confidential basis, that they're about to make an arrest. It was that kid in the liquor store. He followed her home or something like that. He had a record of sex offenses. He was a nut."

"Did Kravitz tell you?"

"No, somebody else did. I talked to Kravitz. He wouldn't confirm it, because there hasn't been an arrest yet, but he confirmed that the kid's under investigation, and it's pretty clear what's happening. So just don't think about it any more. We've got to put it behind us. It's out of our hands now."

Gwen leaned against the drainboard and shuddered. "Thank God," she said. "I thought that other—the

thing we talked about—was going to drive me crazy."

"So did I, Gwen. Let's just forget it now."

"Okay. But Ben, there's one thing I ought to tell you."

"What?"

"Well, some of those things we talked about—about her and Whitmore—she could have been exaggerating. Or I might have misunderstood her. You never know about things like that. But I guess it doesn't matter now."

Norton didn't understand, but he wasn't sure he wanted to understand, so he busied himself mixing a drink.

"One other thing, Ben. I ran into Phil Ross in the Door Store today and asked him to drop by tonight. I hope it's all right. I mean, wasn't there some problem between you two?"

Norton stared at her, trying to remember if he'd told her about Phil Ross changing his story. "No problem," he said. "Gwen, I've got no problems with anybody. I'm starting over. Let's enjoy ourselves. Come on, let's go meet your friends. Who are they, anyway?"

They started back to the library. "Most them are friends of Annie," Gwen said. "I want you to meet her. She's a sweetheart. A good writer too. Worked for the *Post* for a while but quit to free-lance. She's done articles for *Stone* and the *Washingtonian,* but what she really wants to do is fiction. And she just sold her first short story, so that's why the party."

Back in the library Norton sat down on the sofa beside Annie, who was a tall thin young woman with freckles and long unruly black hair. She was wearing jeans and a flowered blouse open at least two buttons farther down than her mother would have approved. Her breasts were small and jaunty, and as freckled as her face.

"You're Annie," he said.

"That's right."

"I'm Ben Norton."

"I know. Gwen told me. You went with her friend Donna, the one who was killed."

"That's right."

"Tell me about her."

"I don't want to tell you about her."

"Okay, I'm sorry. I just . . . It sounded like a hell of a story."

"She's dead," he said. "The story's over."

"Hey, Annie," another girl called from across the room. "Did you hear about Sophie?"

Sophie was a Congresswoman, age forty-five or so, why was noted both for her outspoken views and her ample girth.

"No, what *about* her?" Annie called back.

"She's pregnant," the other girl, Mitzi, cried. "Oh, God, can you imagine Sophie in *bed* with that tiny little *husband* of hers?"

Everyone roared at that, and the boy who had been rolling joints began a long complicated story, the gist of which was that the Speaker of the House was a shoe fetishist.

"You people don't think much of our elected leaders, do you?" Norton said.

"Should we?" Annie said. "I mean, if you forget what they say and just watch what they *do*, it's ridiculous. I mean, Congress is like the monkey house at the zoo. If they moved the monkeys to Congress and the Congressmen to the zoo, it wouldn't make any difference. Or am I getting too radical for you?"

Norton shrugged. "There are plenty of clowns up there," he said. "But there are some good people too."

"Tell me about Whitmore," she said abruptly. "Is he a good person?"

"I wouldn't accuse him of that," Norton said. "But he might be a great President. Politically, he's the shrewdest man I've ever known about."

"But what's he like as a person?"

"I don't know. I never think of him as a person."

"Women do," she said. "He's awfully attractive."

"He's old enough to be your father."

"I had an affair with a man his age once. A really neat man, all craggy-looking, sort of like Humphrey Bogart."

"Do you have a lot of affairs?"

"I don't know what's a lot. I'm twenty-seven and I've slept with twenty-three men. Is that a lot? How many women have you slept with?"

"I don't know," he said. "I've lost count."

"Seriously, give me a number."

"Oh, hell, too many. Fifty. A hundred. I was into numbers for a few years. It was ridiculous."

"Why aren't you married?" she asked. "You look like the type."

"I am the type, but the ones I wanted to marry didn't want to marry me, and vice versa. I'm too cautious. I look at all my old school friends and they're all divorced, or want to be, or should be. It doesn't make you want to rush headlong into marriage."

"That's the one thing I won't do," Annie said. "Have affairs with married men. I did it a couple of times but no more."

"Why? Does it make you feel guilty?"

"No. But it hurts too much. To make love with someone and then have him get up and leave and go spend the night with someone else. You don't know what that's like."

A joint make its way to them. Norton passed it on to her.

"Don't you smoke?" she asked.

"Sometimes. Not much. I always forget the ends of my sentences."

"Try some," she said. "It'll loosen you up."

He took a hit, annoyed. Women were always telling him he looked stiff, formal, reserved. Hell, he couldn't help how he looked. What'd they want him to do, go barefoot?

"You know what you look like?" she said. "You look like you ought to be wearing a white suit and sitting on the front porch of your plantation with a mint julep in your hand."

"Sort of like Clark Gable," he said.

"Maybe more like Colonel Sanders." She giggled. "But sort of the old Southern aristocracy. Heir to a proud tradition and all that."

"Annie, do you want to know how it was?" he said. "How it was, according to my father, was that in 1820, to celebrate the Queen's birthday they freed all the prisoners in London, on the condition they get out of the country, and all those worthless bastards stole ships and built rafts and swam and otherwise made their way to America, and that's how the Norton clan got here. And the family tree produced a lot of horse thieves and hundreds of Confederate soldiers and one pretty good governor of North Carolina and eventually my father, who lost his farm in 1934 and went to work in a lumber mill for twenty cents an hour and glad to get it. And I'd have been working in the lumber mill too except that, number one, I was pretty bright, and number two, and far more important, I had a talent for knocking hell out of a baseball, which clearly marked me as a man destined for great things."

"How'd you happen to work for Whitmore?" she asked. "I thought he was famous for hiring ruthless sons of bitches."

"Well, he thought he needed one hayseed around to soften his image," Norton said, laughing at his own joke. "No, it was more complicated than that. I came up to work for a North Carolina Senator, as counsel for an anti-trust and monopolies subcommittee. When my Senator died, Whitmore took over as chairman of the subcommittee. After a decent interval, he called me into his office one day. I figured he was going to fire me and put in one of his own people. Instead, we had this very brief conversation. He said, 'You want to keep your job, Norton?' I said I did. He said, 'It's yours. All I ask is loyalty. One thousand percent.' I said that was no problem. We shook hands and that was that. Except that when I got my next paycheck I found out he'd given me a raise."

"You underestimated him," Annie said. "You were doing a good job and he was too smart to fire you."

"You're right," Norton said. "It was the last time I ever underestimated Chuck Whitmore. Eventually he made me his legislative assistant. And here I am."

"I'm glad," she said and touched his hair, and just then they were joined by Pete, the bartender from Nathan's.

"Hey, Mr. Norton, how's it going?"

"No complaints. You know Annie?"

"Sure. Mr. Norton, I don't wanta interrupt, but I have got one hell of a problem. Hey, have a hit."

He grinned and held out a huge joint. Norton took a puff and handed it to Annie. "The thing is," Pete continued, "I borrowed this guy's car last week and I got stopped for running a stop sign and they found six ounces of grass under the seat and they're charging me with possession with intent to distribute. Man, I didn't even know it was there."

"When are you due in court?" Norton asked.

"Two weeks from Monday."

"Drop by my office next week and we'll talk about it."

"Man, that'd be great. But I ain't got much money."

"No sweat, Pete."

"Thanks, Mr. Norton." Pete got up and started to leave.

"Say, Pete," Norton said, "do you remember a couple of weeks ago you said some guy had been in the bar asking questions about me? What'd he look like?"

Pete grimaced and began to tug at his beard. "You know, I don't exactly remember," he said.

"You said he was weird-looking."

"Did I? Did I say that? Well, maybe he was. Or maybe it was some other guy. I might have been stoned. Hey, I'll see you next week, okay?" Pete hurried from the room.

"What was that all about?" Annie asked.

"I'm not sure."

"He's a dealer, you know."

"I know. But the drug laws are stupid and there's no use him going to jail for selling grass."

"Do you do much work like that?"

"I try to. My law firm represents some of the fattest cats in America, so it's good for my soul to help some poor bastard out now and then."

"I like you," she said.

"I like you too. You're honest."

"People ought to be honest," she said. "I mean, you can't help it if you're not pretty or not smart, but anybody can be honest if they want to."

He thought suddenly of Donna, who was the most honest person he'd ever known, so honest, perhaps, that it had killed her, and he wanted to get crazy college-boy drunk, drunk enough to forget about her for a while. But getting drunk wasn't the answer to anything, and instead he squeezed Annie's hand and tried to concentrate on her. She was a nice person, bright and pretty and independent and honest, a little like Donna, but a few years younger and a few years more bewildering to him.

"What's the matter?" she asked.

"Nothing. I may be a little stoned. Tell me about your writing."

"There's not much to tell. I write magazine articles to make money and short stories to . . . well, because it's a challenge."

"What do you want to do?"

"Write a novel. But I'm not ready yet."

"Gwen said you'd left the *Post*. Why'd you do that? I thought everybody was dying to work for the *Post*."

"So was I, until I'd done it for a year. It was like working in a factory. A nice factory, with some nice people, turning out a good product, but still a factory. I mean, some people worked downstairs on the printing presses and some of us worked upstairs at our typewriters. Free-lancing, I make half the money and have twice the fun. Oh, my God, where did *he* come from?"

Norton looked up and saw Phil Ross approaching them. He started to get up, then decided against it.

"Phil. Meet Annie. You're both distinguished writers. Pull up a drink and join us."

Ross shook his head impatiently. "I'm not staying, Ben. Gwen didn't tell me what kind of a party it was. But I'm glad to see *you*. I wanted to tell you that Ed Murphy and I compared notes about that . . . misunderstanding we had." He glanced at Annie.

"It's okay," Norton said.

"Well," Ross said, "on the day in question he *was* riding down Wisconsin Avenue, and with a White House secretary who happens to look a great deal like your friend. So, end of mystery."

"That's great, Phil," Norton said. "Damn fine. Listen, that was a great column you had this morning."

The columnist beamed. "It did make some news," he said. "Well, I've got to run."

"Don't dash off," Norton said. "Stay and meet the younger generation."

Ross frowned. "Frankly, I don't like being places where marijuana is smoked. It *is* illegal, you know."

"That's true," Norton said. "Dirty business."

"Well, so long," the columnist said and hurried out the door.

"That fool," Annie whispered. "He wrote columns supporting Nixon until the day he resigned, and he talks about grass being illegal. What was that about him and Ed Murphy?"

"Nothing. Except that Ross had a column this morning that was a leak from somebody very close to the top, which means that he and Ed Murphy are pretty good buddies these days. Tell me about your girlhood. Did you play baseball?"

"No, I wrote poetry. And about the time your father was losing his farm, mine was starting a grocery store in the Bronx that eventually became eleven grocery stores."

"The Lord giveth and the Lord taketh away," Norton said. "Were you happy?"

"Miserable. I was so damn skinny. Still am."

"The nearer the bone, the sweeter the meat."

"The *what?*"

"An old Southern expression."

"It sounds dirty."

"It is. It means I like the way you're put together."

"I like the way you're put together too."

"I'm mighty pleased to hear that, ma'am. But right this minute, if you'll kindly excuse me, I've got to go pee."

"Will you come back?"

"I'll try."

He floated down the hallway to the bathroom, but its door was locked and someone was groaning inside.

"What's wrong?" Norton asked.

"I'm throwing up," a young man said. Norton thought he recognized the voice of the fellow who'd been rolling joints all night. "I drank some gin. It always does this to me."

Norton wandered out the back door. He crossed the shadowy lawn and relieved himself beneath a huge oak tree, looking up at the stars and feeling in tune with the universe. He stood there for a while listening to the music and laughter from inside, and then he noticed someone come around the corner of the house and crouch in the flowerbeds outside the library window. Norton watched the dark figure for a moment, bemused at first, and then he thought of the window peeper who had killed Donna and he began to run forward.

"Hey, get out of there," he yelled.

The man at the window jumped up and began to race across the lawn. He was wearing a dark suit and seemed slender and wiry. Norton chased him across the lawn, gaining on him at first, and when he was five feet behind the man he dived at him, the way football heroes and movie stars do, floating through the air for a long time, almost flying, but finally landing face

down in the soft dewy grass. Up the street, he heard a
car roar away. Norton had gotten only a glimpse of
the man, but he was sure he'd seen him recently. But
where? In Georgetown? In Palm Springs? At the
White House? He wasn't sure, and it didn't seem to
matter. He thought of a scrap of poetry: "Down in
lovely muck I've lain/Happy till I woke again."
Then he dropped off to sleep. He might have slept a
long time if Annie had not come out and wakened
him.

15

NORTON AWOKE in his own bed, not entirely sure how
he'd gotten there but feeling fine. He threw open his
bedroom window and breathed the sweet spring air.
Then he plopped down on the floor and did fifteen
pushups. It was a time for new starts. He took a long
shower and thought of all the things he would do in
the weeks ahead. He would go on a diet and start
playing tennis twice a week. He would talk to Whit
Stone about his new assignment, he would set aside
evenings for research and writing, and he would check
with the local law schools about lecturing on corporate
law. And Annie. She floated back to him, tall and
tomboy thin, all freckles and unruly hair, and he decided he would call her for dinner. But no more reefer
madness. That was over, all the madness was over
now, and he would think only of the future.

He dressed, had only a cup of black coffee for
breakfast—the new diet had begun—and bounded out

the door to walk to work. It was a fresh, windy morning. Rain had fallen overnight and the sidewalks were still wet, but the clouds were gone and the sky was a dazzling blue. As he passed the Biograph Theater, a pale girl in a granny dress asked him if he'd talked to Jesus lately. Norton's last conversation with Jesus had been some twenty years before, but the girl reminded him of sad-eyed hillbilly girls he'd prayed and played with in his youth and he handed her some bills that were loose in his pocket. "God bless, God bless," she cried as he moved on down M Street, and he smiled at the benediction.

A block before he reached his office, Norton saw Gabriel Pincus coming toward him. He watched Gabe for a minute. Other pedestrians were smiling, whistling, enjoying the lovely morning, but Gabe picked his way down the street like a soldier moving through a minefield, his eyes darting from face to face as if some assassin lay in ambush for him. He was a pudgy, balding, disheveled man of thirty-five who was arguably the best investigative reporter in the world.

When Gabe saw Norton, he fell in beside him without any greeting and whispered, "When'd you get back?" His tone somehow suggested that Norton had been a fugitive from justice.

"About two weeks ago, Gabe. How've you been? I saw where you got the Pulitzer."

"I should have got it last year," Gabe said. "You still working for Whit Stone?"

"Yep."

"I want to talk to you," he said. "I'm onto something big."

"What is it this time, Gabe?"

One of Norton's law partners fell in beside them and nodded a good morning. "Can't talk now," Gabe said. "I'll call you later." Then, with a final glance over his shoulder, he disappeared around the corner.

Norton was not sorry to see Gabe go. Gabe was a great reporter, but he could be a royal pain in the ass. He lived in a world of plots and conspiracies, and be-

cause the real world had in recent years often approx-
imated Gabe's most terrible fantasies he had become
a celebrated journalist. But Norton wanted no more
of fantasies and conspiracies. That was all behind him
now, and he reminded himself to tell his secretary he
would not be in if Mr. Pincus called.

He stepped into the lobby of a sleek modern office
building, took the elevator to the third floor, and
pushed through the big oak door with "Coggins,
Copeland & Stone" inscribed on a plaque of burnished
gold. He winked at Josie, the new receptionist,
marched down the hallway to his office, and began
sorting through his mail. There were letters from clients, one perfumed letter postmarked Paris, some bills
that had finally caught up with him, something from
the Sierra Club, a bulletin from the Duke Alumni
Council, an invitation to a fund-raising reception for
a North Carolina Senator, and finally a letter in a
plain white envelope with his name and address hand-
written in an elaborate old-fashioned scroll. The letter
had a Washington postmark and no return address.
Norton frowned at the small mystery and tore open
the envelope. The note inside was brief.

"Demand to see the autopsy report," it said. "Do
not give up. You are not alone." And it was signed,
"A friend."

Norton read the note over and over. A friend?
What friend? What about the autopsy? What more
could it add. Who had sent this note? He decided it
had to be a joke, a bad joke. One of Gwen's, perhaps.
Or some madman. Or some enemy he'd made somewhere along the line. The police knew how she'd died
and they'd found the killer—what more could the autopsy say? He started to throw the note away and forget about it, but he couldn't. Something told him this
was no joke. He felt the morning's optimism crum-
bling and all his old uncertainty returning as he
reached for the phone to call Sergeant Kravitz.

* * *

Kravitz was discussing the case with Frank Kifner, the young U.S. Attorney, and it wasn't going well.

"If you need men, Joe, we'll get you men," Kifner said. They were in his office, which was large and austere. Kifner himself was small and austere. And, Kravitz thought, a prick. "The men, the back-up work from the Bureau, overtime, priority clearance from me, it's all yours for the asking. No problem. But let's wrap this one up."

"They're either quick or they're slow, Frank. This one's slow. This one takes shoe leather. And luck. Eventually somebody will talk. We're pushing like hell. But it could take time."

Kifner frowned and fiddled with an unlit pipe. He was a precise little man with colorless hair and rimless glasses.

"What about the kid?" Kifner said. "I think there's something there, right before our eyes."

Kravitz suppressed a groan. He'd never seen Kifner like this before. There was pressure on this one, but Kravitz couldn't figure out where from.

"Joey admits seeing her. Period. He left the liquor store at eight and his mother says he got home for dinner at eight thirty and watched television with her till midnight."

"She'd lie for him."

"Sure she would. And she'd convince a jury too. She's a sweet little lady who teaches Sunday school. If Joey did this, we're gonna have to put him there, hard and fast."

"He's a sex criminal."

"He's a kid who blew his brains out on acid and spent some time at St. Elizabeth's and discovered the joy of sex there. You know, in broom closets, under beds, behind the bushes, group therapy they call it. So when he's released he gets deep into window peeping, and the worst thing he ever did was grab a girl in Montrose Park and try to go down on her. But he didn't try too hard because when she got loose and ran away he just laid down on the grass and went to sleep. Which does not make him a violent sex criminal."

"So you don't think Joey did it?"

"The mother could be lying. He could have gone by the house and talked his way in and hit her and accidentally killed her. We don't have any evidence for it, but it's possible. The thing that turns me off is the fingerprints. Or the absence thereof. Somebody wiped off every last fingerprint in that house, and Joey's just not up to that kind of effort. It's all he can do to tie both shoelaces."

"Just keep after Joey," Kifner said. "He could have handled those prints. He could have learned that much on television. What about the others?"

"The paperboy looks like a dead end. We're still looking for the maid's son. We're watching the guy at the service station. The actor's story holds up. He was at a dinner party in Los Angeles that night. And then there's Norton. He called me yesterday. Said he'd heard that Joey was about to be arrested."

Kifner kept fiddling with his pipe. "What do you make of that?"

"I don't know," Kravitz admitted. "Maybe he's got a guilty conscience and hopes we've got the case locked up. I can't figure the guy out. There's that phone call he claims to have gotten the morning we found her, the one that sent him roaring over to Georgetown."

"What's your theory on that one?" Kifner asked.

Kravitz grimaced with frustration. "Either he's lying or he's telling the truth. If he's lying, if there wasn't any phone call, then I figure he killed the girl, then got this crazy idea that it'd make him look innocent if he came over and identified her for us. I don't know. I can imagine the guy clipping his ex-girl friend on the jaw, but it's hard to think he'd be dumb enough to come back to the scene like that."

"What if somebody *did* call him?" the U.S. Attorney asked.

"Then whoever killed her was trying to set him up," Kravitz said. "Which would seem to rule out your garden variety prowler. But if the killer was somebody who knew her, and knew Norton had just arrived back in town . . ."

"He wouldn't have had to know her," Kifner said. "Joey could have talked his way inside the house. Or somebody else. And then talked to the woman for a while. And she mentions that her old boy friend is due back in town. Then she gets killed. Then the killer gets the idea of the call to Norton, to suck him in."

Kravitz cursed under his breath and lit another cigarette. "You know Norton," he said. "What about him? Could he have done it?"

Kifner stared at the ceiling for a while before answering. "Ben's not the violent type," he said at last. "He's big, but he's easygoing. On the other hand, who knows? He comes back from Europe. He's exhausted from his flight. He goes to a bar and has a few drinks and they hit him hard. Then he eyes his ex-girl friend on the street. Remember, we've got him leaving Nathan's at approximately the same time she's leaving the liquor store across the street. So he might well have seen her. She invites him back to the house. Or he follows her back. They argue. He slugs her. It's possible."

The U.S. Attorney looked at his watch and stood up. "Keep pushing, Joe," he said. "This case is important. I know you want to be the next chief of detectives. I'd like to put in a few words for you. But mostly you've got to do it yourself, and this case is the one that can do it."

The detective started for the door, then turned back. "Norton's coming to see me this morning," he said. "Any special ideas?"

"Lean on him," Frank Kifner told him. "Lean on everybody, until somebody cracks."

* * *

Norton arrived at the homicide division at eleven thirty. The place still stank of cigars and stale coffee. They sat down across an empty desk in the back of the room and Norton was about to ask about the autopsy when Kravitz beat him to the punch.

"You haven't been leveling with me, Mr. Norton."

"What do you mean?"

"I talked to Ross, the newspaper columnist. Why didn't you tell me he'd said he'd seen Miss Hendricks with Ed Murphy?"

"Murphy denied it. Ross changed his story. So I assumed he'd made a mistake."

"Mr. Norton, I'd advise you not to assume anything. You know what it means to withhold information."

"You're right. I should have mentioned it."

"What about your little junket to California? Should you have mentioned that? Or did you assume I wouldn't be interested?"

"I don't have to tell you every move I make, Sergeant. I went out on impulse. When I learned about Jeff Fields owning that house, I wanted to question him about it. We talked briefly. He said she asked to use the house and he let her. He claimed not to know why she was coming to Washington. That was about it."

"What about Carmel?"

"I talked to Harry Nolan, an old Senator who lived down the road from Donna. He didn't have a lot to say."

No, not a lot . . . except the small detail that the President-elect had visited Donna in Carmel a few days before he'd been sworn into office. Norton had checked the papers for that week. Officially, Whitmore had gone sailing off the California coast with one of his millionaire friends. But Kravitz was going to have to figure that one out for himself.

"Sergeant, could I ask you a couple of questions?"

"Go ahead."

"Aren't you about to wrap this up? I realize you

can't say anything officially, but my information is that you're about to arrest the kid in the liquor store."

"Mr. Norton, I don't know where you're getting your information, but my advice to you is don't hold your breath until that boy is arrested."

Norton was confused. Either Whit Stone had bad information or Kravitz was lying. "What do you have on the boy, Sergeant?"

"I'm not going to get into the evidence, Mr. Norton. Do you have any other questions?"

Norton hesitated. He'd almost forgotten why he came. The whole damn thing was too confusing. He was sorry he'd let himself get involved again, all because of some crank letter.

"Yes, Sergeant. I wonder if I could see a copy of the autopsy."

"Why?"

"Just curiosity. Do you have a copy?"

"No," Kravitz lied. "But I can tell you the highlights. You know how she died. The impact of her head hitting the coffee table. She hadn't been drinking. There was no rape or other sexual activity indicated. She was in excellent health. There was really only one unusual fact disclosed by the autopsy, Mr. Norton."

Norton saw that he was being set up; he wondered what was coming. "What was that, Sergeant?"

"Miss Hendricks was three months pregnant."

Once, playing baseball, Norton had taken his eyes off the game to wink at a cheerleader and for his trouble he'd been hit between the eyes by a line drive. That was how he felt now. It came out of nowhere, caught him between the eyes, and left him stunned, helpless. Donna, three months pregnant. That meant mid-January and that meant Whitmore and that changed everything. The bastard had gotten her pregnant and she'd come to Washington to see him and . . .

"You look surprised, Mr. Norton."

"Of course I'm surprised."

"Any idea who the man might be?"

"No."

"Mr. Norton, you're holding back something. Why don't you level with me? If you really cared about her, why don't you help me find out who killed her?"

Norton wanted to. He wanted to tell Kravitz everything. That damned Whitmore had gotten her pregnant and then washed his hands of her and if he hadn't killed her himself he knew who had. Or so part of him believed. But another part wasn't convinced and still could not make that accusation against the President. Norton thought of the old Senator, Harry Nolan. If the police talked to him, and he told him about the meeting in January, that would start them moving in the right direction. Norton hoped they would. He didn't give a damn about protecting Whitmore. To hell with Whitmore. He didn't care if Whitmore was run out of town on a rail. He just didn't want the responsibility of having destroyed a President, not unless he was sure.

"Have you talked to Senator Nolan?" he said. "They got to be good friends. He might know who had visited her out there in January, if that's when she got pregnant."

"He's been away," Kravitz said. "We just contacted him last night. A man's going to question him this morning."

"Good," Norton said. "Would you excuse me, Sergeant? I . . . I don't feel very good."

Kravitz dismissed him with a shrug. Norton stumbled out the door, past two weeping black women in the corridor, and down the elevator to the lobby. It was all sinking in, all coming clear at last. That son of a bitch Whitmore, that dirty son of a bitch. Norton vowed to get to the bottom of this. And he wasn't going to count on the police to do it for him. He needed help, but not from the police. He had a better idea. He found a pay phone and called the Washington bureau of the Chicago *World*. Gabe Pincus told him to come right on over.

16

THE WASHINGTON Bureau of the Chicago *World* possessed a quiet elegance more often seen in legal offices than newspaper offices. As a polite young black receptionist led Norton to Gabe Pincus's desk—for you didn't just barge into the *World* bureau—it seemed that the only inelegant thing in the newsroom was Gabe himself. The other desks were neat and their occupants genteelly clad, but Gabe's desk looked like a garbage heap and Gabe looked right at home amid the debris. His tie was unfashionably narrow and his shirt collar was badly frayed. His old tweed coat was torn at the shoulder, his khaki pants were stained with what Norton hoped was red paint, and Gabe's right shoe had come loose from its sole, so that his toes showed through. And lest any passerby overlook his toes, Gabe had propped his feet atop his typewriter as he carried on a loud one-sided telephone conversation:

"Look, Mr. Secretary, why don't you knock off the horse-shit and answer my questions? Don't give me any off-the-record crap. I'm going with this story and you better get on the record fast if you want to save your ass. Okay, then to hell with you!"

Gabe slammed down the phone and winked at Norton. "Let the bastard squirm," he said. "Hey, Sans Souci okay for lunch?"

"Can we get in?"

"The last of the big tippers can get in anywhere.

138

These bastards won't pay me what I'm worth, so I make up the difference on my expense account. After the Harrigan trial I took the whole lousy jury to lunch. It cost the *World* eight hundred dollars, but it was worth it. If those bastards hadn't convicted Harrigan it would have cost us twenty million in libel suits."

The elderly gentleman at the next typewriter, who was clad in a well-worn Brooks Brothers suit and looked rather like a stockbroker, shut his eyes and crossed himself. Gabe ignored him and led Norton out of the newsroom. Near the front door, an elegant white-haired man in a handsomely tailored English suit stepped out of a private office, took one look at Gabe, and jumped back inside. Gabe winked at Norton and pointed to his exposed toes. "The toes drive Mr. Best Dressed up the wall," he said. "Oh, would that jerk like to fire me, but he's just smart enough to know the paper needs me more than it needs him."

At Sans Souci the maître d' greeted Gabe with an enthusiasm usually reserved for visiting heads of state. However, when he offered them a choice table near the center of the dining room, Gabe shook his head and insisted on another table against the wall. As they crossed the room, various political figures looked at Gabe and waved, frowned, avoided his glance or, in the case of one Assistant Attorney General, got up and left.

A young French waiter asked if they'd like drinks.

"A Bloody Mary for me," Norton said.

"Good idea," Gabe said. "Bring us four. Save yourself a trip."

When the waiter had gone, Gabe picked up the bowl of flowers on the table and examined it, then got down on his knees and peered under the table. "Got to watch out for bugs," he explained in a whisper. "I never take the table they offer me, but they might bug all of them. Don't talk when the waiter's around. And don't talk loud enough for anybody at the next table to hear."

Norton glanced furtively at the next table, where

two elderly ladies were chatting innocently. The waiter returned with the four Bloody Marys, and a moment later a small wavy-haired man came over and engaged Gabe in several minutes of small talk.

"That little prick," Gabe said after the man had returned to his own table.

"Who is he?"

"Jerry Vincenti. Don't you know him? He used to be in the White House. Now he's a big-shot lobbyist."

"I'd forgotten him."

"I'll tell you a Jerry Vincenti story. You understand, he's the biggest ass kisser who ever lived, right? Well, the story is, one time his beloved President was having some trouble with a guy in his Cabinet named Harper who he thought was too independent. Not a team player. So the President calls Harper in one afternoon and gives him a long lecture on loyalty. But Harper, who was just a halfwit college professor, kept saying that he didn't understand, that he'd been loyal. So finally the President gets pissed and called in his faithful retainer Jerry Vincenti.

" 'Jerry,' he says, 'did I screw your wife before you married her?'

" 'Yes sir, Mr. President,' Jerry says proudly.

" 'Have I been screwing your wife *since* you married her?'

" 'Yes sir, Mr. President,' Jerry says again, all aglow to be getting this recognition.

"Whereupon our glorious leader turns to Harper and says, '*That,* Mr. Secretary, is what I mean by *loyalty!* ' "

Gabe grinned and wolfed down his first Bloody Mary.

Norton shook his head. "That is a truly incredible story."

"It's God's own truth," Gabe said. "Harper's mistress told it to me. He was so shook up that he quit the Cabinet, whereupon she quit him."

They chatted casually through their second Bloody Marys. For a time, when Gabe was between marriages, he'd dated a friend of Donna's and the four of them had spent a good deal of time together. That was back when Gabe was still on the police beat, before he'd learned that his relentlessness could be applied to higher levels of government with more spectacular results. Now he wore the scalps of Senators and Cabinet officials on his belt the way other *World* reporters wore their Phi Beta Kappa keys. Gabe fascinated Norton. He had the looks of a used car salesman and the morals of a safecracker, and yet it was rumored—although he violently denied it—that he'd studied Greek in college and spent his spare time translating the classics. And it was a fact that he and his second wife had adopted a black child and a Vietnamese orphan.

When their food arrived—veal for Norton, rockfish for Gabe—along with a fine bottle of Montrachet, and the waiter had withdrawn, the reporter leaned forward and lowered his voice. "What's on your mind, pal?"

"Donna."

"I figured. Who do you think did it?"

"I don't know. It could have been a burglar. I hate to jump into conspiracy theories."

"Why not? They're usually true. Why was she in town?"

"I'm not sure. I heard that she saw Ed Murphy."

"That figures. Look, let's get down to the short hairs. She was balling Whitmore, right?"

Norton stared at Gabe in amazement. "How did you know?"

The reporter laughed. "I didn't, you dummy. You just told me. You must be a lousy poker player. So what was going on?"

"They had an affair, about the time of the primaries. They apparently broke it off in July, when she went to California. Or maybe they didn't. I had one report that he went to see her in January."

"Quit pussy-footing around, pal. She was pregnant, wasn't she?"

"Are you bluffing again, Gabe?"

The reporter shook his head. "I got that from a guy in the coroner's office. Look, he knocks her up. She comes to town to see him. She wants money or wants him to divorce his wife or whatever. Or maybe he wants her to get an abortion or wants assurances she won't shoot her mouth off. They have an argument. Big Chuck's on the sauce. He whomps her one, she bangs her head on the table, he gets the hell out of there, and we're back to the old cover-up game again."

Gabe's pudgy face was flushed with excitement. This was his business, to think the unthinkable and then prove it true.

"What you say is possible," Norton said. "I've tried not to think about it. I don't say Whitmore's the most sterling character in the world, but—"

"But what?" Gabe snapped.

"But he's the President, damn it. He's trying to do some good things."

"Baloney!" Gabe Pincus said angrily. "Look, buddy boy, he's a politician and that means he's a thug. They're all thugs, your bunch and the other bunch, and it don't matter which gang's in power. The only difference is that one gang is a little bit more generous with other people's money, and the other gang dresses better. Now, do you want to find out who killed your girl friend or don't you?"

"I want to," Norton said. "And, yes, it could have happened the way you said."

"Sure it could. Or it could have been Ed Murphy who slugged her. Or it could have been some burglar. The first thing I'd like to know is where Whitmore and Murphy were that night."

"It was the night that jobs rally got out of hand," Norton said. "The official record is that Whitmore never left the White House."

"He could have sneaked out," Gabe said. "Just climbed into a limousine on East Executive Avenue and sailed off into the night. Nobody pays any attention to all those limousines. Hitler could be in one and nobody would notice. But I'll check around. *Somebody* would have noticed—one of the guards, a Secret Service guy, somebody."

"Gabe, some strange things have been happening lately."

"Like what?"

"People keep changing their stories. It was Phil Ross who told me he saw Donna and Ed together, then Ed got on the phone to Ross and he said he'd made a mistake."

"Ross is gutless," Gabe snapped. "None of your columnists or hot-shot political reporters are going to touch this with a ten-foot pole. They're the same bunch who were calling Watergate a 'caper' when a few of us crazies were risking our careers to dig out the truth. All you're telling me is that Murphy bought Ross off. Which explains a couple of high-powered leaks he's got recently."

"Some other people too," Norton said. "Pete, the bartender at Nathan's, told me some weird-looking guy was in there checking me out, then he went blank when I followed up on it. And Gwen Bowers told me about the affair, then last night out of nowhere she says she could have been wrong."

Gabe shrugged and signaled the waiter for more wine. "Pete's a doper, which means they can turn him around easy. And Gwen wouldn't be so tough either. Celebrities are even easier to buy off than columnists. You watch, she'll get some big job."

They sat silently for a moment while the waiter took away their plates. The two elderly women were still at the next table. When Gabe saw one of them looking at him, he glared at her until she flushed and turned away.

"Things have happened on my job too," Norton said. "The other day a fellow at Justice did me a favor, but when I kept after Ed Murphy the favor suddenly got undone."

"That was Murphy twisting the knife."

"Probably," Norton agreed. "But the strangest part

was Whit Stone calling me in and instead of being mad he gave me this great new assignment. And it turned out that he knew all about Donna's death. He even told me that the police were about to arrest a kid who waited on Donna in a liquor store. But today I talked to Kravitz, the detective, who said the kid was a suspect but nowhere near being arrested. So I don't know what the hell's going on."

Gabe leaned across the table, his eyes bright with excitement. "I'll tell you what's going on. You're getting the royal runaround. You don't think all this is *coincidence*, do you?"

"I don't know, Gabe."

"You know what's the most interesting thing you've said?"

"What?"

"The stuff about Whit Stone."

"Why?"

"Because your distinguished boss, that luminary of the American bar, is the biggest crook in Washington. Which is saying one hell of a lot."

Norton was taken aback. "Whit's slick, but I don't think he's any slicker than a dozen other big-name lawyers around town. Sure, he's helped kill some good legislation—"

"I'm not talking about legislation. I'm talking about blackmail. Wiretapping. Laundered money. Big piles of money that get from his corporate cronies to his political cronies with you know who as the middleman —and raking his share off the top."

"Okay, Gabe, okay. Suppose he's a crook. What does that have to do with Donna?"

"He tried to cool you out, right?"

"I guess so."

"He knew all about the case, right?"

"He knew a lot."

"Why? What's a murder case to Whitney Stone?"

"I don't know," Norton admitted.

Gabe leaned forward with his hands cupped around his Irish coffee. The thick cream atop the coffee had left a faint white mustache on his upper lip. "Do you know what Whit Stone wants most?"

"What?"

"To be Attorney General."

"You're kidding."

"Kidding hell. That nitwit who's in there now won't last out the year and Stone wants to replace him. He can buy enough votes to get through the Senate. His problem is persuading Whitmore to nominate him and take the heat from the four or five Senators who know what a rat he is. So right now he's looking for favors he can do the White House, and cooling you out might be a pretty big favor right now."

It was almost three and the restaurant was nearly empty. Waiters hovered near the table and Gabe eyed them suspiciously.

"Listen, Norton, this game could get tough," he whispered. "So far, they've just tried to buy you off, but Whit Stone could fire you and Ed Murphy could fix it so no law firm in Washington would let you in the door. Are you in this to stay?"

"All the way, Gabe. That's why I'm here. Between the two of us, we can break this thing."

Gabe chewed on a matchstick for a moment, staring at Norton as if trying to make up his mind about something. "Okay," he said finally, "I'm gonna level with you. And I mean in *confidence*. You may not be afraid of the White House, but if you screw me I'll *really* ruin you."

"You can trust me, Gabe."

"Look, I'll try to find out who zapped Donna, but what really interests me about this is Whit Stone sticking his nose into it. I'm after that bastard, and you can give me some help."

"What kind of help?"

"You understand, this is confidential."

"Gabe, do you want it in blood?"

"Do Washington lawyers have blood?" Gabe shot back. Then he leaned across the table and cupped his hands around his mouth, as if to frustrate unseen lip readers. "Norton," he whispered, "have you ever heard of the Hoover file?"

"The Hoover file? No."

"Do I have to explain?"

"Maybe you'd better."

"Okay. There's been a rumor for a long time that when the old man died he left behind his own personal file. *La crème de la crème.* The works on everybody. You wanta know where Lyndon got his money? You wanta know if Tricky and Bebe played drop the soap? You wanta know what Jackie was doing all those weekends they said she was fox hunting? You wanta know what distinguished Senator seduces the Senate page boys? And that's just the fun and games stuff. There's stuff in that file that could tear this country apart."

"Like what?"

"Like who killed Kennedy."

"Which Kennedy?"

"Take your pick. Listen, if Hoover didn't do it he knew who did. It's all in the file, pal. I know one guy who's got a standing offer of a million bucks cash for it, no questions asked. And that's just where the bidding starts."

Norton stared at Gabe intently. There was a glint in the reporter's eyes that reminded Norton of Bogart's Fred C. Dobbs as he pursued the treasure of Sierra Madre. If Norton had only now met Gabe for the first time, he would have judged him insane. But in fact Gabe was a prize-winning journalist, and arguably was in as close touch with political reality as any man in America.

"Is this for real, Gabe?" he asked. "Or just another crazy Washington rumor?"

"There was only one guy in the world Hoover trusted," Gabe said. "His buddy Zeke McGuire. So a couple of months ago I talked my way into Zeke's hospital room and ran the nurses out and stuck my face right up into his and said, 'Zeke, you know you're about to croak, right? But I'm gonna give you an opportunity few men get. I'm gonna let you write your own obit.' Zeke kinda blinked like he was interested, so I said, 'Zeke, your obit could go two ways. It could talk about forty years of public service, the kind of stuff a fellow'd want on the front page of the *World* when he kicked off. Or, it could talk about how you've been getting two paychecks for the last twenty years and the little one came from the government and the big one from the mob.' Well, old Zeke turns purple and finally he gasps out, *'What do you want?'* and I shot right back, 'The Hoover file.'

"Son of a bitch, you should have seen him. He starts shaking and sweating and I thought he was gonna croak right there. I had him scared, but he was still afraid of the Chief too, scared old J. Edgar was gonna swoop down from the Big File Cabinet in the Sky and cut his pecker off if he gave me that file. So I pushed him. 'Zeke,' I said, 'I've got the goods on you. Checks, letters, memos, and I'll print 'em all unless you get me that file. You'll go down in history as a bigger crook than Grant and Harding and Nixon put together.' So Zeke starts writhing around and drooling and his lips start quivering and finally he gets it out: *'Whit Stone.'* That's all. Two words. Then he lets out a groan and flops back on the pillow and the nurses run in and I split. Two hours later old Zeke was dead. The poor bastard. He wasn't a bad guy when you got to know him."

"So you never printed the checks and letters?" Norton asked.

"Oh, hell, man, I was bluffing. I went in with some rumors and came out with a lead—Whit Stone may have the Hoover file, or at least know where it is. I figure he wants to trade it to Whitmore for the Attorney Generalship."

Norton finished his Irish coffee. They were the only customers left in the restaurant, except for two men in blue suits who were sitting at a table by the door.

"But why would Whit Stone have the Hoover file?" Norton demanded. "If there *is* a Hoover file."

"Because the son of a bitch is evil, that's why. If I made a list of the ten rottenest bastards in Washington, he'd be the only private citizen on the list. The others got sent here by their constituents to rip people off, but Stone does it for *fun,* because he *likes* it. Listen, pal, some of us are trying to save this country, and it's bastards like him we're trying to save it from!"

"Look, Gabe, what's the bottom line? What do you want me to do for you?"

"I want you to get me inside Stone's office," Gabe whispered. "There's a chance he keeps the Hoover file in his office safe."

"Gabe, what you're talking about is sometimes known as burglary."

"Don't give me that stuff!" Gabe snapped. "This is the scum of the earth we're dealing with. They lie, they steal, they make wars nobody wants, and then they go to church on Sunday with little American flags in their lapels. Do you wanta know who killed your girl friend or not? Believe me, whoever's got the Hoover file knows who killed her. It's all part of the same ball of wax. So are you with me or not?"

"I'm with you," Norton said. "What's next?"

"Just hang loose till I call you. Play it cool with Whit Stone and Ed Murphy. Let them think you're playing their game. But keep your eyes open. If there's any more of those 'strange coincidences,' let me know."

Gabe waved the waiter over and got the check. It came to fifty-five dollars. Gabe added a twenty-dollar tip and asked for a receipt.

"There was one thing I forgot to tell you," Norton said.

"What's that?"

"I went to Carmel and talked to this old Senator, Harry Nolan, who's been a friend of Donna's there. He told me Whitmore visited her there just before he was inaugurated."

"At which point he celebrated by knocking her up."

"The point is, I never told the police about that. But Kravitz said they're sending a guy to see him today and if he tells them about Whitmore going there, this thing may start unraveling fast."

Gabe chewed on his lower lip. "I don't think he'll be telling them," he said slowly.

"What do you mean?"

"Hold on a minute," Gabe said and waved for one of the waiters. "Run down to the corner and get me the latest edition of the *Star*," Gabe commanded, and the waiter dashed for the door.

"What's this all about?" Norton asked.

"Just wait," Gabe said. "See those two guys by the door?"

"What about them?"

"They're tailing me. What an assignment. They get to eat at the best restaurants every day at the tax-payers' expense."

The waiter rushed back with the newspaper, and Gabe handed him a dollar and began to thumb through it. "Yeah, here it is," he said finally. "I thought I saw something on the wire this morning but I wanted to make sure."

He handed the paper across to Norton. It was open to the obituary page. Norton first saw a photograph of a familiar face, then the headline beneath it: "Ex-Senator Nolan Killed in Fall. Served in 1933-53."

"Oh my God," Norton whispered.

"I guess you'd call that another 'strange coincidence,'" Gabe Pincus said, then he belched and started out the door.

17

As HOME movies went, it was a masterpiece: First you saw Senator Donovan Ripley enter the grubby little apartment, flash his famous grin at Wendy, then paw her for a minute. She broke free, lowered the shade, and the two of them quickly disrobed, jumped into the big brass bed, and immediately went at it. And at it and at it and at it. Byron Riddle was beginning to wonder when they'd stop.

"You've got to hand it to the bastard," he muttered as Senator Ripley's acrobatics filled the movie screen before him. "He's a real man."

"He's a pounder," Wendy said. "Bam-bam-bam, all night long. No finesse whatsoever."

The Wendy who was watching the film with Riddle was clad in her usual jeans and sweater, but the Wendy up on the screen was wearing only a black mask. The mask had been her own idea. She hoped to conceal her identity and thus be spared any unpleasantries that might arise from this rather unusual film in which she was, as she saw it, co-starring. She had persuaded the Senator that wearing a mask during sex was her ultimate turn-on. And the Senator was easily persuaded. He was a good-natured, rather dim-witted fellow in his early forties who a clever young woman could persuade of almost anything. The people who hoped to make him President knew this, and did their best to keep him away from clever young women.

But they had reckoned without Byron Riddle.

Finding Wendy had been the first, and easiest job. A pro wouldn't do for this mission, for Ripley liked his women young and virginal-looking. So Riddle had wandered about local campuses, one evening dropping into a meeting of a group called the Defenders of American Freedom, and there he had found Wendy, outlining an Impeach Byron White campaign. Afterwards, he took her for coffee, introducing himself as Dr. Horatio Green, a behavioral scientist by profession and a Constitutionalist in politics. Wendy loved to talk politics, and it developed that she loathed Donovan Ripley—"I'd do *anything* to keep him from being President," she had said—and thus was Operation Red Eye born.

The next, and greater, challenge was to penetrate the wall of security around Ripley. The only thing Senator Ripley loved more than serving his fellow man was screwing his fellow man's wife, daughter, sister, or mother. He was, however, not unaware of the possibility of entrapment, blackmail, or scandal, and he chose his partners with extreme care. He staffed his Senate office with young women whose loyalties were beyond question, often the daughters of his political advisers. When Riddle had sent Wendy around for a job interview, she'd barely gotten in the door. But then Riddle had an inspiration. He got Wendy a job in the Senate office *next door* to Ripley's, and counted on Ripley's roving eye to do the rest. It did. Within a week he had winked at Wendy in the hallway, the next week he called her in for a little get-acquainted chat, and it was the next evening that he made his film debut.

Up on the screen both the film and the Senator were nearing a climax. The red-faced Senator and the masked Wendy bounded this way and that, twisting turning, flipping about like sex-crazed acrobats, until finally Ripley let out a whoop of delight and collapsed, limp and sweaty, in Wendy's arms.

"The bastard," Wendy muttered. "I was sore for a week."

"You were great," Riddle told her.

Up on the screen, the Senator glanced at his watch, disengaged himself from the masked woman, quickly dressed, and with a jaunty wave was gone.

"Damn fine," Riddle said. "Quality stuff."

"Will you pay me now?" Wendy asked. "I've got a lab this afternoon."

"Sure, kid," Riddle said. He switched on the lights, pulled out his billfold, and counted out ten crisp hundred-dollar bills. "I'm adding a little bonus," he said. "Just remember, not a word to anybody. Don't compromise the mission."

"Don't worry about me, Dr. Green," Wendy said. "Listen, he wants to meet me here Sunday afternoon after church. Is that okay?"

"Nope," Riddle told her. "The mission's completed now. You quit your job and get back to school."

"Hey, there's a couple of other Senators been giving me the eye."

"Forget it," Riddle snapped.

"Okay," Wendy said. "Look, can you tell me what you're gonna *do* with this thing? I mean, is it gonna turn up at my neighborhood theater or what?"

"Don't get nosy," Riddle said. "You've got your money, now you just button your lip, kid!"

He gave her a look that made her blood run cold. He was such a weird character, Wendy thought. Sort of flaky sometimes, but dashing too, like somebody in a spy movie.

"I won't say anything," she promised. "All I want to do is to stop that degenerate from being President."

"You've done your part, kid."

"Listen, could we get together sometime?" she said shyly. "You know, just to talk about politics and stuff?"

"Sorry, Wendy, I've got to keep a low profile for a while," Riddle said. "So long, kid."

"Goodbye, Dr. Green," she said. "Thanks for everything."

She blinked back a tear and rushed from the apartment.

When she was gone, Riddle yanked off the fuzzy blond wig he was wearing, lit a Marlboro, and sank down on the sofa, deep in thought. Wendy had asked the right question: What *was* he going to do next? He was nearing the most dangerous, most delicate phase of the mission.

Donovan Ripley would never be President now; that much was certain. But the details were tricky and, to Riddle's future, all-important. If all he wanted to do was remove Ripley from politics, he would simply send the Senator a copy of the film with a note saying that if he didn't resign from office by such and such a date other copies of the film would be made public. Ripley would have no choice. He would have to go on television and announce that because of his health or his wife's health or whatever he was resigning from the Senate and leaving politics forever. His only possible alternative would be to find and kill whoever had the film, and Riddle was confident that they couldn't trace him. They might find Wendy, might torture her, but she didn't know his real name or where he lived or even what he looked like, for he'd worn the wig and tinted contact lenses whenever he dealt with her.

Of course, he could make the film public without giving Ripley a chance to resign first. He would have to resign anyway, and it would give Riddle pleasure to see the big oaf disgraced. Riddle had a recurring fantasy about how to make the film public. He had read with fascination about the television studio technicians who had (accidentally, they claimed) shown a porno movie over a cable-television network one night. Riddle's fantasy was to show Senator Ripley's sexploits over national television during halftime of the Super Bowl game. It wouldn't be easy—you'd have to take over the studio——but it would be worth it.

But that was fun and games, and there were more serious considerations at hand. Like money. That film was worth a million dollars. Senator Ripley would surely give that for it, and there were others who would no doubt outbid him. Riddle could get the money and retire to Spain or the Dominican Republic and live like a king, but he aspired to something more than that. He wanted to serve his country. And he wanted to serve his country in one particular job.

Byron Riddle wanted to be Director of Central Intelligence.

It wouldn't be easy. They usually gave the job to bankers and Wall Street lawyers and other big shots, not to the poor stiffs who risked their lives in the trenches. But things were different now; he had the movie that was the biggest bargaining chip in Washington. The question was how to proceed. He could go straight to Ed Murphy, but he wasn't sure how Murphy would respond. That was too risky. He thought he might talk to Whit Stone first; Whit was a smart man, maybe the smartest in town. Perhaps they'd bargain with certain Congressional leaders who could easily arrange the Directorship for the man who'd forced Donovan Ripley out of politics.

However they played the political end of it, there would also have to be a public-relations campaign as well. Riddle would have to surface, to develop the right image for the job he coveted. He had thought it through carefully. There would have to be some lesser job first, perhaps the Deputy Directorship. Then the PR campaign could begin. They could put out a bio telling some of his real exploits and inventing others. He would testify at Congressional hearings, and appear on *Meet the Press*. The *Times* would do a "Man in the News" piece, and an old colleague of Riddle's, now a senior editor at *Time*, could be counted on for a helpful article there. That kind of publicity, plus the right kind of support from the White House and Congress, and the Directorship could be his within a year. Byron Riddle was confident. He had worked hard for years, he had sacrificed much, and now it was all about to be repaid. The time was right. The Agency needed a man with guts and vision, and Byron Riddle was that man.

He got up from the sofa, took the film out of the projection machine, put it into his briefcase, checked his gun, and left the apartment with a smile on his face. Byron Riddle was coming in from the cold.

18

THE PRESIDENT and the comedian were posing for photographers on the first tee at the Thunderbird Country Club outside Palm Springs. The comedian, Pete Gaynor, was wearing a bright red polo shirt and mugging for the photographers and the club members who'd drifted over to watch. The President, Charles Whitmore, was staring over the photographers' heads at the snow-covered mountains in the distance, thinking how fine it would be to play a round of golf without all these people, and most particularly without his wisecracking host, Pete Gaynor.

"I'll tell you this, fellows," Gaynor quipped to the reporters, "I'll play golf with the President but I sure wouldn't run against him. That last guy who did—boy, I hear he's still running!"

The crowd laughed contentedly, reporters and country clubbers alike. Gaynor's off-the-cuff quips weren't all that funny, but he had been making America laugh for forty years, in movies, on radio, on television, and the laughter came instinctively now, as homage to the past.

Nick Galiano was standing off to one side, just out of camera range. Nick was wearing a polo shirt and expensive golf pants too, like all the country clubbers clustered around the first tee, but his face set him apart. Theirs were smooth, rich men's faces; Nick's was forever a Baltimore bartender's face, a workingman's face, and now he was scowling while everyone else was smiling at Pete Gaynor's jokes. After a moment he called to the President, "Hey, Boss, this place is really something. Maybe you ought to paint it white and move in."

The crowd laughed appreciatively, and Gaynor rolled his eyes in mock frustration. "Who is this guy, Mr. President?" he cracked. "He's stealing all my lines."

There was more laughter—the crowd was getting more than it had bargained for—and Nick Galiano winked, lined up an imaginary putt, and came back with another joke: "No kidding, Boss, this Palm Springs is the greatest. Maybe Agnew wasn't so dumb after all."

The reporters and photographers broke up over that line, although the country clubbers didn't find it as amusing. Charles Whitmore, who noticed almost everything, noticed one of the reporters scribbling in his notebook, the bearded reporter, the one from *Rolling Rock* or *Stone Age* or whatever it was called.

"That last remark of Nick's was off the record, fellows," Whitmore said, and the bearded reporter scowled but put his notebook away.

The President had also noticed a certain tightening of Pete Gaynor's mouth at the Agnew remark. He guessed the comedian and the sometime Vice President had been pretty chummy a few years back. To hell with him, Whitmore thought; he wanted this, not me.

But that was not precisely true. It was a decades-old tradition that Presidents and would-be Presidents who visited Palm Springs played golf with Pete Gaynor, for Gaynor was a beloved American institution, America's Clown Prince, and to be photographed with him was part of politics, like putting on an Indian war bonnet or marching in the St. Patrick's Day parade. And it was more than the photographs that would go out over the wire services. Pete Gaynor was a rich man, and he had friends who were even richer. He was a man of influence, like a corporation president or a newspaper publisher, and when he called with his golfing invitations no politician could quite refuse. It was like having lunch with George Meany— you had to grin and bear it.

"Hey, fellows, you know where the President is staying, don't you?" Gaynor called out. "At the Hollenfield estate. Boy, have you seen *that* place? The Hollenfield estate is what God would have done if He'd had the money."

The old joke brought new laughter. Charles Whitmore was getting impatient. He was tired of being used as a straight man.

"Let's get started, Pete," he said. "Nick, you sure you don't want to play?"

"Not me, Boss," Nick Galiano said. "I've got a hangover that won't quit."

"Well, you know what they say, Nick," Pete Gaynor injected. "When a man's got a hangover he needs an aspirin, but when a woman's got a hangover, she needs a brassiere. And there's plenty of 'em needing one these days!"

Whitmore noted that the comedian had been quicker to make a joke than to urge Nick to join their round of golf. But he understood that. Pete Gaynor played golf with Presidents, not with their sidekicks. And Nick *did* look like he had a monster of a hangover. He'd been drinking too much recently. Whitmore made a mental note to find out why, then walked over to tee off.

The President's golf game was strong but erratic. He hooked his first drive over the head of a Secret

Service man who was standing by a palm tree two hundred yards down the fairway.

"Take a Mulligan, Mr. President," Pete Gaynor said. "All visiting royalty gets a Mulligan on the first tee."

Whitmore's second drive was high and straight, and drew a scattering of applause from the bystanders. Whitmore grinned and waved at them, wondering how many of them had voted for him. Twenty percent at best, he estimated.

Gaynor stepped up to his ball, winked at the crowd, did a little dipsy-doodle with his club, then cut loose with a stiff crablike swing that somehow sent his ball soaring thirty yards past the President's.

"Nice shot, Pete," Whitmore said. He meant it. He was thinking that the old bastard was seventy if he was a day.

"I owe it all to clean living," Gaynor said. "Come on, Mr. President, I'll give you a lift."

He led Whitmore to a pale blue golf cart with a fringed canopy atop it and his initials on its side. Nick Galiano spit on the grass and climbed into a cart with Walt Harrigan, the head of the Secret Service detail. Walt was a trim, well-tanned young man with a big nose and shaggy brown hair.

"That guy queer, Walt?" Nick asked as they bounced along the fairway twenty feet behind the President.

"Gaynor? No, he just acts that way. The old goat's up to his ears in girls."

"You met him before?"

"Yeah, I used to go around when he and Agnew played golf, then with him and Ford after that."

"What do you think of him?"

"He's a prick. He cuts off the jokes when the reporters are gone; then he's just another arrogant rich guy. He used to always be asking our guys to help him find his golf balls. Hell, man, we're not here to look for golf balls. The trouble was, back in those days you didn't know if you could argue with guys like that and keep your job. But we straightened him out."

"What'd you do?"

Walt stopped the golf cart and lowered his voice while the President hit his second shot. "Well, let's just say that whenever he asked one of our men to find his ball, that ball *never* got found. Or maybe it got found two feet under water. He caught on. He quit sending us free booze, but it was worth it. These fat cats are all like that. They suck up to the big shots and treat the rest of us like dirt. About the only one I've met I gave a damn for was Jeff Fields, that actor who hung around on the campaign. He was a decent guy."

They parked in the shade of some palm trees to watch the President and Gaynor make their putts. The comedian holed out from twelve feet for his par, and Whitmore two-putted from six feet out for a bogey.

"Hey, let's double the bet," Gaynor cracked and got a ripple of laughter from the reporters and photographers who were following the round. The President frowned and looked sharply at Walt Harrigan.

"I'll be right back," Walt said and jumped out of the cart and walked over to the reporters.

"Sorry, fellows," he said. "No press for the rest of the round."

"What the hell?" said the man from the New York *Times*. "We've always gone the whole round before."

"Sorry," the Secret Service agent said. "I've got my orders."

"From who?" the bearded reporter asked.

"It's security," the agent lied. "Why don't you fellows have a couple of drinks in the clubhouse and pick them up coming in on nine?"

"I could use a drink," one reporter admitted, and after a little more grumbling the gentlemen of the press started back toward the clubhouse.

"Who's the one with the beard?" Nick asked as he and Walt bounced along the golf-cart path toward the second tee.

"We've checked him out," Walt said. "He's harmless."

"There're none of them harmless," Nick said bitterly. "They're vultures. No, they're snipers, that's what they are. They're all buddy-buddy with the Boss when they're with him—drink his booze and laugh at his jokes—but then they sneak off somewhere and they do to you what Oswald did to Kennedy, except they use words instead of bullets."

"Ah, most of 'em aren't so bad," Walt said.

"They're hypocrites too," Nick said. "All so noble and moral and holier than thou. You know where half those bastards are right now? Back at the hotel shacked up with some barmaid or some broad they flew in from L.A."

Walt smiled at that. "Yeah," he said. "They call it the West of the Potomac Rule—no reporter ever talks east of the Potomac about what any reporter does west of the Potomac."

"You guys are keeping an eye on them, aren't you?"

"We know who's where," the agent said. "And with whom." He stopped the cart again and they watched the President and Pete Gaynor make their drives off the second tee. This time the President sliced his shot into the next fairway, and the comedian whacked another straight, solid shot down the middle. Then their little caravan of canopied golf carts went putt-putting off again.

"Somebody told me Jeff Fields is in town," Walt Harrigan said.

"He's in town," Nick said.

"Will he be coming around?"

"No way," Nick said grimly. "Jeff ain't quite respectable. There's too many stories about him and women. Women, men, dogs and billygoats. You can't mess around the way he does and expect to hang out with the President."

"Yeah," Walt said. "And wasn't that strange about that girl being killed in his house?"

"It wasn't so strange," Nick said. "Him and her

were pretty good pals. *Real* good pals, if you want the truth."

The young agent wondered what that meant, but Nick dropped the subject, and it was forgotten as the golf match wound its way up and down the fairways that were like green carpets, past man-made lakes that sparkled like silver in the midmorning sun, past the pastel-walled guest houses that were scattered about the course like Easter eggs on a giant's lawn. After a while Charles Whitmore tuned out Pete Gaynor and began to get his game under control. At the ninth green, as the reporters rejoined them, he chipped in from a sand trap for a birdie. Pete Gaynor threw up his hands in mock dismay and proceeded to three-putt for a double bogey, giving Whitmore the front nine by one stroke. Whitmore watched with interest as the comedian blew an eighteen-inch putt. Had he missed it on purpose? Some people did. It was so damn stupid. Did they think he *cared?*

"How about another nine?" Pete Gaynor asked as they left the green and walked toward the photographers. "Double or nothing."

"Sorry, Pete," Whitmore said. "They've got me working this afternoon."

"Well, I'll see you tonight," the comedian said. "I'm introducing you at the dinner."

"Don't steal the show."

"Ha! I know a scene stealer when I see one."

Whitmore started to leave, but the photographers were calling for more pictures, and Gaynor whipped out their scorecard and made a show of signing it.

"You know, Mr. President," he said softly, "there'll be some fellows at the dinner tonight who hope you'll say something about this welfare mess. These are fellows who're behind you all the way, but they're worried about some of these pie-in-the-sky giveaway schemes that keep coming out of Washington."

The pitch, Whitmore thought; the pitch always comes last.

"I'll keep that in mind, Pete. Thanks for the tip."

"You know me, I'm no politician," Gaynor continued. "But, by golly, it sure seems like there's a lot of people in this country who don't want to work for a living."

"Yeah," Whitmore said. "I run into them sometimes." He turned to the photographers. "That's all, fellows. See you tonight."

He started toward his waiting limousine, but Pete Gaynor fell in beside him.

"Say, Mr. President, maybe after the dinner tonight you'd like to drop by my place for a little relaxation. No politics, just a few drinks and a few laughs. And a couple of sweet young things might drop by too— kids I'm helping get started in show biz. They'd love to meet you. I mean, they'd *love* to meet you."

The white-haired old comedian winked, and Whitmore almost laughed aloud. Did they think he was *that* dumb?

"Well, let's see how things work out, Pete. I've got a pretty rough schedule." He hurried away and stepped into the coolness of his limousine. Ed Murphy was waiting there with a list of phone calls and a pile of memos. As the Lincoln glided away from the Thunderbird Club, Murphy began to open fire with all the new problems of the past two hours and Whitmore shot back his solutions to them. By the time they turned onto Frank Sinatra Drive, the most urgent work was behind them and Whitmore changed the subject.

"Ed, that funnyman back there. I don't want to see any more of him."

"He's introducing you tonight."

"I know that. But no more after tonight. Would you believe this? That character wanted me to come over to his place tonight and meet some girls."

"It's happened before."

"Some of those bastards before didn't have any taste. And not much sense. Listen, I want an insert in my speech tonight. Put some of that stuff in from my Princeton speech about people helping other people, human interdependence. You remember that part?"

"You understand, these are the fat cats tonight."

"I know who they are. I'm thinking maybe they don't know who I am."

"Right."

"Something else. Have you noticed Nick boozing a lot lately?"

"Definitely."

"Keep an eye on him. If he starts making problems on the job, I'll have to do something."

"Right," Ed Murphy said again.

The limousine slowed and turned in at the main gate of the Hollenfield estate, then sped past their absent host's private golf course, past his airstrip, past lakes with swans gliding atop them, past outdoor and indoor tennis courts, and past an Olympic-size pool beside which six off-duty Secret Service men were playing an endless poker game. Finally they rounded a curve and the Hollenfield mansion rose up in the distance, a pink-walled palace shimmering against the bright blue desert sky.

"Did I tell you he's got this place for sale?" Whitmore said. "Eight million bucks."

"It's not big enough?"

"Not private enough. See that building over there?"

Far in the distance the upper floors of a new luxury condominium could be glimpsed above the trees "He says the people in the penthouse might see him playing golf, if they used binoculars," Whitmore explained. "He says it's an invasion of privacy."

"The poor suffering bastard," Ed Murphy said. He began to gather up his papers as the limousine neared the mansion. "You know," he said, "a couple of the reporters were saying that maybe it's not a good idea for you to use this place. They were saying—"

"I know what they were saying," Whitmore replied. "To hell with them. They'd be here if they could be. Let's go first class while we can."

The Lincoln stopped in front of the mansion and a marine captain jerked open the door for the President. But Whitmore turned back to Ed Murphy.

"Did I ever tell you what Huey Long used to say about the way he dressed? They used to jump on him about dressing like a millionaire. He said he wanted every mother in Louisiana to look at Huey Long and think her boy could grow up and dress like that some day."

Ed Murphy grinned one of his rare grins. Whitmore started to climb out of the car, then turned back again. "Did you talk to our actor friend?"

"I talked to him."

"Is he okay?"

"He's okay. Not happy, but okay."

"Good," the President said and moved gracefully out of his limousine and up the steps of his borrowed mansion.

19

THE HOUR was late, the office was quiet as a tomb, and Ben Norton was trying without success to concentrate on an article in the *American Law Review*. He kept seeing Gabe Pincus's face leering at him between the lines, and whenever he glanced at his watch he saw Gabe there too, grinning at him like a malevolent Mickey Mouse. He tossed the law journal aside and stared glumly at the wall, wondering why he had let Gabe talk him into this. It was madness. Worse, it was *criminal*. But it was also necessary, Gabe had argued, and he had prevailed.

Norton heard George Evans, the only other lawyer still left in the office, coughing in his cubicle next door. Norton got up and looked out his window. He watched some people emerge from the French restaurant below him, then he looked down the street and thought he saw a figure lurking in the shadows of a record store's doorway. Gabe? Or Norton's imagination? He shook his head, then turned at the sound of a rapping on his door.

"Come on in, George," he said, and a slight, nervous man in his early thirties stepped uncertainly in.

"Don't let me interrupt you," he said.

"You're not, George. I'm about to knock off for the night."

"Me too," George Evans admitted. "What's got you burning the midnight oil?"

Evans obviously wanted to talk, and Norton wanted to postpone the madness ahead, so he motioned for his colleague to sit down.

"Just catching up on my reading," he said. "So damn much is happening."

Evans nodded sadly. "I've heard you're getting a new assignment, Ben. Riding herd on corporate policy, is that it? Sounds like a coup."

Norton guessed Whit Stone was letting the word spread. That was interesting. He hadn't said anything more to Norton about the assignment. Norton wondered what *that* meant.

"Whit and I have discussed it," he said. "But I don't know how it will work out."

Evans managed his hangdog smile. "That's how Whit operates, isn't it? You never know where you stand. Sometimes I wonder if it's worth it."

Rather than reply, Norton busied himself pouring two iceless Scotch and waters. George Evans was a decent fellow, and a competent lawyer, who was in the process of having his heart broken—and his career mangled—by Whitney Stone. Or, in a larger sense, by the unwritten, all-powerful system by which the nation's biggest law firms decide who is to succeed and who is not.

The system was simple enough. The most prestigious firms hired three or four young lawyers for each one they expected eventually to take into partnership. After five or six years on trial, it was up or out. The chosen few became partners, with life tenure and an ever-increasing share of the firm's profits. The rejects were expected to leave, not exactly in disgrace, but knowing they would thereafter be second-class citizens of their chosen profession. Men were blackballed by the senior partners—for it was much like the college fraternity system—for varied reasons. Some were incompetent. Others wore the wrong ties, espoused the wrong causes, or had married the wrong wives.

Most of the men who were passed over moved on to smaller law firms. Some left the profession or turned to booze. Now and then you heard of one who'd killed himself. Sometimes they hung on in limbo for a year or two, hoping for a miracle. That was what George Evans was doing, and Whitney Stone was letting him twist slowly in the wind. Norton didn't know why Evans didn't face reality. Perhaps it was because he had an ambitious wife pushing him on.

"I just don't know if it's worth it," Evans repeated, rubbing at his stubble of beard. "Sometimes I think I'd rather teach. The money isn't everything. Don't you ever feel like that?"

Norton was reminded of the all-night bull sessions about Life and Truth and the Future that had gone on endlessly in his college days. Life is just college continued, he thought, blackballs and bull sessions and big men on campus, until finally you graduate into death.

"Sure, I feel that way sometimes, George," he said. "To part of me teaching would be great. No sweat, no pressure, and the joys of pedantry. But practicing law appeals to part of me too." He couldn't say to George Evans what he wanted to say about the challenge and the competition of the big leagues, about the thirst to make it, to prove himself, that had been so deeply and permanently ingrained in him and in almost all the men of his generation. His generation didn't drop out of the system; they dug in and did their damnedest to beat the system.

"If Whit just wasn't so damned *secretive*," Evans said. "You never know what's in his mind. I've never known anyone like him. Sometimes I want to punch him in the nose."

He smiled wanly and glanced at the ceiling. "Just kidding, Whit," he said. It was a standing joke among the younger lawyers that Stone bugged their offices.

"Well, it sounds like your future is all set," Evans continued. "You haven't heard anything on the grapevine about us other poor slobs, have you?"

That was a bit much. Part of Norton pitied Evans and another part scorned his helplessness. "There isn't much of a grapevine around here," he said. He finished his drink and stood up. "You ready to call it a night?"

"I guess so," Evans said. They got their things together and walked the long corridor to the law firm's front door.

Norton shut the door, started toward the elevator, then stopped. "Would you double-check the door, George?" he said. "I'm not sure it locked."

Evans went back and rattled the doorknob. "It's locked," he said.

"Good," Norton said, and they took the elevator down to the lobby, where Norton said a loud "good night" to the drowsy guard and wrote his name and the time more legibly than usual on the sign-out sheet. It was midnight.

"Can I give you a lift anywhere?" Evans asked.

"I think I'll walk," Norton said. They waved good-bye, and Norton started down the street, past the French restaurant and around the corner by the record store.

"Ben, over here," a voice called from the darkness.

Norton moved into the doorway and found Gabe Pincus.

"Is it all clear?" Gabe whispered.

"That guy and I were the last to leave," Norton said.

"Who was he?"

"Just a lawyer."

"What about the cleaning women?"

"They've finished, the office is empty and the lights are out," Norton said. "Gabe, I'm not sure about this."

"Quit your bellyaching," the reporter snapped. "Where are the keys?"

Norton reached reluctantly into his pocket, just as a man and woman rounded the corner. Gabe pulled him back against the wall. The couple walked on by, talking excitedly about the new Bergman movie.

"The keys, the keys," Gabe whispered impatiently.

Norton handed them over. "The big one opens the door from the parking lot," he said. "You can take the stairs up without going through the lobby. The other one opens the front door to the office. After that you're on your own. Stone's office is the last one, all the way down the corridor."

"I know where it is," Gabe said. "You just get the hell away from here and make yourself conspicuous somewhere."

"For Christ's sake, be careful," Norton said and hurried off to find a cab.

Gabe stayed in the shadows for a few minutes watching the dark windows of Coggins, Copeland, and Stone. He was better dressed than usual, in a dark suit and vest, and was carrying a leather briefcase, looking as much as possible like a lawyer who had been working late. But his dark shoes had rubber soles and his briefcase contained burglar's tools, not legal briefs. He didn't like this any better than Norton did. He'd cut a lot of corners in his police-beat days, but in recent years he'd relied on more subtle means than burglary to achieve his journalistic ends. He had too much to lose now. But there wasn't much he wouldn't do for a shot at the Hoover file.

Gabe took a deep breath, squared his shoulders, stepped out of the shadows, and marched confidently down the street. Minutes later he was standing in the darkness of Coggins, Copeland, and Stone's reception room. He switched on his flashlight, shone it down the long corridor that led toward Whitney Stone's office, and began to creep in that direction. When the corridor jutted to the left, he peered around the corner cautiously—and jumped back when he saw a light beneath an office door. Gabe froze, silently cursing Ben Norton. Lawyers were all worthless, he thought; the ones who weren't crooked were dumb. Was someone in the office? Or had Norton been wrong about all the lights being off? Gave could hear his heart pounding. His choice was to leave or to wait. If he heard any sound from the office, or if anyone emerged from it, he was sure he could beat them to the front door. So he waited. The only sounds he heard were those from the street, the roar of buses, the slamming of car doors, an occasional peal of laughter. Gabe tuned them out and focused on the sliver of light beneath the door. As he waited, his thoughts were on the Hoover file, which might be fifty feet down that hallway, which might be in his hands in half an hour. *The Hoover file!* Gabe trembled at the thought of it. The whole blinding, overpowering truth about thirty years of American politics, a tale of greed and lust and deceit and hyprocrisy and corruption on a scale unmatched in the history of the world. The truth that even the most dedicated journalist could only see in bits and pieces. The truth that only God knew (if, indeed, God existed, which Gabe doubted) and that in any event God was not sharing with journalists.

Oddly, perhaps, Gabe wasn't sure what he'd do with the file if he found it. He didn't want to sell it, and he doubted that his paper would print much of it. It was for his soul's sake that he wanted it. He wanted to look truth in the face. He wanted to look at other men and see past their well-crafted public facades into the darkness of their souls. Gabe had spent a decade being lied to, used, tricked, condescended to, and scorned by politicians, and he had come to think of himself as one of the few honest men in Washington. That was his vanity, not the prizes he had won but the temptations he had resisted. The Hoover file, if it could be found, would at once confirm all his prejudices and justify all his vanities.

When thirty minutes passed with no sound or movement within the lighted room, Gabe decided that the cleaning woman must have left the light on and that fool Norton not noticed. He slipped silently around the corner, paused before the lighted office, heard nothing, and moved on toward Whitney Stone's door. A passkey opened it, and Gabe shut the door behind him and shone his light about the silent office. It was a big rectangular room, with the desk at one end and a sofa and chairs at the other. He noticed a door near the sofa—Norton hadn't mentioned that —and hurried across to try it. The door opened into a small room with a file cabinet and a bed, and it contained another door that led to a bathroom.

Satisfied, Gabe returned to Stone's desk. He unlocked the top drawer and found a bottle of aspirin, a vial of amyl nitrite capsules, a Bible, several legal briefs and a small blue address book. He put the address book in his pocket and searched the other drawers, finding nothing of interest until the bottom one, where his light fell upon a large manila envelope. He eased the envelope from the drawer, opened it, and found a typewritten manuscript inside. His hands shook as he searched for the title page, hoping to find Hoover's name, but the words he found were:

A FRIEND IN POWER

A Novel By
DONNA HENDRICKS

Gabe cursed bitterly but slipped the document into his briefcase, then began his search for the safe. He found it on the wall behind one of the prints of red-coated English gentlemen riding to hounds, and he soon found that it was, as he'd feared, beyond his safe-cracking capabilities. He'd been instructed in the art by an ex-con of his acquaintance, but his fingers lacked the master's touch. When he twisted the dial, his fingertips were not sensitive to the telltale clink of the tumblers within. He shrugged, put his gloves back on, and replaced the hunting scene; in truth, he doubted that Stone would be so foolish as to leave the Hoover file in so vulnerable a spot. He crossed the dark office again and stepped inside the small room with the file cabinet. Just as he pushed the door to, he heard a sound.

He cut off his light and peered out through an inch of open door. As he watched, the office door swung open and a light shot across the room toward the empty desk.

"I've got you covered," a man barked. "Come out with your hands up."

Gabe saw in profile a wiry dark-haired man with a revolver in one hand and a flashlight in the other. Gabe shut the door to a crack and watched as the man moved to the desk, tried its drawers, and then turned in a slow, uncertain circle, his gun before him, peering around the silent office. When his gaze reached the door behind which Gabe was hiding, he began to inch forward. Gabe slammed the door, locked it, and pushed the file cabinet in front of it. Then he stepped into the bathroom and locked its door too. He figured he had three choices. To do battle with an armed man, to surrender and hope he had enough on Whit Stone to negotiate his way out of jail, or to escape.

"Come out in five seconds or I'm coming in," the man shouted. Somehow, the melodramatic cry gave Gabe hope—the man sounded like a fool. He began struggling with the bathroom window. Then he heard a muffled explosion. The son of a bitch was shooting the lock off. Gabe threw open the window and looked out. The sidewalk was twenty feet or more below him, too far to jump, but there was a narrow ledge running around the building.

He heard the man push open the outer door and knock over the file cabinet. Gabe heaved himself out the window and began inching his way along the ledge, but he'd gone only a dozen feet when his pursuer emerged from the bathroom window and pointed his gun at Gabe's wildly pounding heart.

"Come on back, buddy, or I'll blow your brains out."

"Okay, pal, you've got me," Gabe said. "Keep cool."

"You bet I've got you," the man whispered triumphantly.

Gabe looked down. A dozen feet below him the big blue-and-white striped canopy of Chez Pierre stretched out over the sidewalk. Well, Gabe thought, when the going gets tough, the tough get going, and he plunged into space.

The canvas groaned, ripped, and deposited Gabe none too gently on the sidewalk. Still clinging to his briefcase, he got to his feet, pleased with himself—it was like his old police-beat days—then looked up and was astounded to see his pursuer inching along the ledge and then leaping into the air toward the torn canopy.

Good Lord, Gabe thought, that character is *crazy*. And then he turned and ran for his life.

His pursuer plunged through the canopy and hit the sidewalk hard, howling with pain as his ankle seemed to crack. But when a taxi driver slowed down and asked what the hell was going on, the man waved a gun at him and began trotting painfully down the street after Gabe Pincus.

Gabe rounded a corner, running for all he was worth, then spotted a police car at the next intersection. He feared the police almost as much as the madman behind him, so he turned for refuge to the only building open on the block, a theater called the Gaiety which, its marquee announced, was presenting a double bill of *The Joys of Boys* and *Hole Lot of Fun*. Any port in a storm, Gabe thought, and tossed some bills at the ticket taker and darted inside.

The theater was dark, smoke-filled, and packed with men of all ages. Up on the screen some naked boys of sixteen or so were dancing the Charleston. Gabe looked for a fire exit, couldn't find one, and dropped into an empty seat near the front of the theater. Twisting his head around, he saw his pursuer limping down the aisle, shining his flashlight along the rows of theatergoers. Gabe sank deeper into his seat, glanced once at the naked lads on the screen, and was startled to feel a hand settle gently onto his thigh.

Jesus H. Christ, Gabe thought, and jabbed the man beside him hard with his elbow.

"You needn't be *rough*," the man said indignantly, removing his hand.

Gabe looked around again and saw his pursuer advancing relentlessly down the aisle, shining his flashlight down each row, and in the process revealing some remarkable scenes: men stripped to the waist, men in wigs and dresses, men with their heads in other men's laps. When his pursuer was three rows from him, Gabe dropped to the floor and began to crawl through a tangle of men's legs toward the back of the theater. Soon, curious hands began to pinch and prod him. He tried to ignore them, but when one hairy-legged tormentor goosed him beyond all decency, Gabe twisted his ankle until he heard it crack. Gabe crawled on, trying to avoid the warm puddles that dotted the floor like land mines on a battlefield, as all around him men stood and shrieked at the two intruders, the one crawling underfoot, the other shining his light into their dark pleasures. When the circle of light was three feet from him, Gabe struggled to his feet and found himself face to face with his pursuer.

"Don't make a move, buddy," the man barked out of the side of his mouth. Gabe knocked him into a row of hysterical moviegoers and raced out of the theater, only to find two square-jawed D.C policemen blocking the sidewalk.

"What's your hurry, mister?" one of the cops asked.

"It's a lousy show," Gabe mumbled.

"Hey, don't I know you?" the other cop said. "Ain't you some reporter?"

"Yeah," Gabe said. "I'm Evans Novak."

"Sure," the cop said, beaming. "I read your column every day. What're *you* doing in *this* dump?" His face suddenly darkened. "Hey, you're not—"

"Hell, no!" Gabe said manfully. "I'm out to expose the bastards. Security risks. Half the State Department's in there. Hey, you better get inside. Some madman's on the loose."

"We'll get him," the cop promised. "You just keep writing them columns, Mr. Novak."

The two policemen charged into the Gaiety Theater, and Gabriel Pincus ducked down a nearby alley, weary but victorious, clutching his briefcase to his heart.

20

NORTON AWOKE at dawn feeling like a man on his way to the gallows. He switched on his bedside radio and twisted the dial madly, searching for the bad news. Unable to find it, he sat by the front door until the boy delivered his *Post*, then tore through its many pages in search of the story that would be headlined: "Famed Reporter Held in Law Firm Break-in; Accomplice Sought."

But there was nothing. Norton threw down the paper, unable to summon even his usual morning's smile for Doonesbury. He started to call Gabe's house, but decided that Gabe's phone was surely bugged, even if his own was not. He pictured a defiant Gabe at police headquarters, being grilled, threatened, beaten, but refusing to name his accomplice. Then, in a burst of realism, he pictured Gabe making a deal with the police and putting all the blame on Norton.

Finally he decided to face the music. He dressed and walked to work, trying in vain to savor the gorgeous May morning, telling himself it might be his last morning of freedom for a long time. He was half surprised to find no police cars outside his office building, only some workmen unloading their truck in front of Chez Pierre. He pushed open the door of Coggins, Copeland, and Stone despairingly, expecting to face a platoon of detectives, but in fact facing only Josie, the receptionist.

"Boy do you look zonked," Josie said. "What'd *you* do last night?"

Norton stammered, unable to frame a reply, and finally Josie giggled and said, "Well, anyway, you just had a phone call."

"Who was it?" he asked anxiously.

"He wouldn't say. He said he'd call back."

Norton clutched at the slender straw of hope. It must have been Gabe. He was still at large. Perhaps he'd gotten away with it. Norton breathed deeply and stumbled down the hallway toward his office. Halfway there he encountered George Evans.

"Say, Ben," Evans began, "did Whit ask you about what happened last night?"

"Last night?" he repeated innocently.

"Somebody tried to break into his office. He saw on the sign-out sheet that you and I were the last to leave, and he thought we might have noticed something. Hasn't he talked to you?"

"Not yet," Norton said. "He probably figures you

know everything I know. How was he? I mean, was he upset?"

"Not at all," Evans said. "It was strange. It was the most pleasant he's been to me in years."

Beware the pleasant cobra, Norton thought, and dragged himself back to his little office, which, he mused, was about the size of a jail cell. Mercifully, his thoughts were interrupted by the phone.

"It's your mystery caller again," Josie said, her voice aglow with curiosity. "All he'll say is that he's a friend of yours and it's important. Do you want to talk to him?"

"Why not?" Norton sighed.

Josie clicked off—or would she be listening?—and Norton waited to hear Gabe's harsh conspirator's voice; instead the voice he heard was familiar, gentle, and distraught.

"Ben, I can't say who it is over the phone. I've got to talk with you."

"Well, why don't you just drop by the office, my friend?" Norton said. "We have visiting hours from noon till two."

"I can't come there. I have my reasons. Let's meet somewhere. It's urgent."

Norton would have hung up, but he was tantalized by the voice. He knew this man. He had talked to him recently. But he could not for the life of him remember where.

"You don't think my *phone's* tapped, do you?" he said, stalling, amusing himself with his gallows humor.

"It could be."

"That's right, it could be. But if you want to get into paranoia my friend, you've got to dive in all the way. If they're tapping my phone, they'll follow us to our meeting place too. The bastards are everywhere."

"Won't you be serious?" the man said. "This is urgent. I'll be in Lafayette Square at noon. Will you meet me?"

Norton's shoulders rocked with silent laughter.

"Sure," he said. "Why not? Who'd ever look for us in Lafayette Square?"

"Good," the man said.

"If you don't know me," Norton went on, "I'll be the guy with two men in dark suits following ten feet behind him." But his mysterious caller had hung up.

* * *

Lafayette Square at noon on a bright day in May. Fearless squirrels sharing bureaucrats' lunches. Black secretaries eating tunafish sandwiches on concrete chessboards. Andy Jackson astride his horse in perpetual triumph, with pigeons taking aim at him from above and tourists with Japanese cameras taking aim at him from below. The White House, serenely indifferent, glistening across Pennsylvania Avenue. Norton found an empty bench and skimmed the first edition of the *Star* for news of Gabe's incarceration. Then a slender young man, tanned, tieless, wearing an expensive sport coat and wraparound dark glasses, dropped down beside him. The dark glasses concealed his identity for a final instant. His face had not been so lined with care the last time they'd met.

"Well, Jeff, long time no see," Norton said. He thought he was cracking, freaking out, that Lafayette Square and the people there and the White House across the way were all part of a gigantic movie set and he was the only man alive who hadn't read the script.

"Look." Jeff Fields began impatiently, "I've got a lot to say and not much time to say it."

"Why don't you begin by telling me why your goon banged me on the head the last time we met?"

"He wasn't supposed to," the actor said. "It was a mistake. I'm sorry. Okay?"

"Sure," Norton said. "All is forgiven. What brings you to the citadel of democracy?"

"Wait a minute," the actor whispered, and nodded toward the park bench across from them. A grizzled old man in a shapeless suit and a soup-stained tie had flopped down and begun reading a paperback copy of *Tales of Power*.

"Let's move," Fields said.

"You picked the park, fellow," Norton protested, but the actor was already on his feet. Norton sighed and followed him down the gravel path past the statue of Andy Jackson until they found another empty bench. A furtive young black wearing a Sly Stone T-shirt was sitting on the grass nearby. After one glance at the two white men *he* got up and left.

"There are only the hunters and the hunted, Fields," Norton said. "Even the squirrels are wired for sound. It helps to mumble."

"Look, Ben, I've done a lot of thinking since I saw you in Palm Springs. You were playing straight with me but I didn't play straight with you. Now I'm going to level with you. I'm going to tell you some things you may not like, but they're true. All I ask is that you hold them in confidence."

"No promises," Norton said. "No promises to people who have their house guests tossed in ditches."

"I knew Donna better than I told you I did," the actor said. He seemed so intent on his own lines that he had tuned out Norton's side of the dialogue. "The thing is, I have this reputation about women. Most of it's true. Most of the women I meet don't know anything but sex, don't think anything but sex, don't *want* anything but sex. But Donna was different. I met her on the campaign—that was my first mistake, trying to play *that* game. It was fun for a while, but I was out of my league. Whitmore was just using me. I finally figured that out. I was like a pet monkey they used to draw crowds. And I picked up a lot of checks. But I hung around. And then I met Donna, and she was the only decent person in that whole damned traveling circus. I liked to talk politics, and she was the only woman I'd ever met who knew as much about politics as I did. Hell, she knew more. I flipped over the chick. After the campaign, after she moved to Carmel, I went up to see her a couple of times. She was lonely and we had some good times and I finally got her to come see me in Palm Springs. Listen, what I'm trying to tell you is, I asked her to *marry* me. And she turned me down flat. Thanks but no thanks. I couldn't believe it. I mean, you don't *know* what some chicks have done to try to marry me. My lawyers say if I don't have a vasectomy I'll be fighting paternity suits till I'm eighty."

"Use the knife, end the strife," Norton mused.

"Man, will you quit making *jokes*? I'm trying to tell you, I dug the chick as much as you did."

"Then why don't you quit calling her a chick? And why don't you get to the bottom line of this heart-rending tale?"

"The bottom line is—and maybe you won't like this, but I'm leveling with you—if she was pregnant, like I heard, then it was me. I spent the second week in January with her. She came to my place. That must have been when it happened. She'd been having some problems with the Pill—you can ask her doctor—and she went off of it and she much have miscalculated."

Fields stopped, his wiry body tense, his finely chiseled mouth taut, his famous brown eyes blinking behind his wraparound dark glasses. Norton was thinking that an actor can't properly ply his trade behind dark glasses, that too much emotion springs from the eyes.

"Why are you wearing the shades, Jeff? To protect you from your fans or to protect you from Big Brother?"

"Is that all you've got to say?"

"What do you want me to say?"

"Don't you want to hear the rest?"

"What rest is there?"

"Look, I know how you must feel, but I didn't know she was pregnant. After that week in January I had to go to Spain for three months. I called her when I got back. That was when she asked if she could use my place in Washington. I told you before that she didn't say why she was coming back here. That was another lie. She told me she wanted to see some friends and do some research for her book. And she mentioned you. She said she'd heard you were due back from Paris and maybe she'd surprise you. Look, I knew there'd been some . . . *attraction* between her and Whitmore for a while and I asked her if that was part of it. She said that had nothing to do with it, that it was all dead and buried."

There were little beads of sweat glistening on the actor's forehead and, Norton thought, a few little beads of truth glistening in what he said.

"How did you find out?"

"Find out what?"

"That she was pregnant."

"My lawyer found out. Don't ask me how. I pay him a fortune to find out things."

A mop-topped youth in overalls ambled by holding aloft a cluster of brightly colored balloons.

"How much?" Norton called to him.

"One dollar, brother," the young man said.

"That's a rip-off, brother," Norton replied.

"Man, everything's going up. Rubber's eighty bucks a ton now."

"Do *they* go up?"

"Huh?"

"The balloons. Do they rise above this world of care? You know, *fly.*"

"Oh, sure, man. Like, up, up, and away."

Norton handed him a tarnished Kennedy half dollar and two quarters and picked a bright blue ballon. He admired it for a moment, jerking its string, letting it bounce before his eyes, then he let go of the string and watched the balloon rise above the trees. In seconds the wind caught it and sent it soaring above the White House.

"What was *that* for?" Jeff Fields asked wearily.

"I'm testing the White House DEW line," Norton said. "You watch, in a minute ten Phantom jets will streak across the sky and blast that little balloon to kingdom come. Say, why didn't you come to my office?"

"What?"

"Why didn't you come to my office to tell me all this? Why the park? Are you a squirrel freak?"

"I don't like lawyers' offices," the actor said. "I spend too much time in them already. They turn me off."

That, Norton thought, was the most sensible thing the actor had said all day.

Fields pulled a monogrammed handkerchief from his pocket, took off his sunglasses and wiped his brow. There were circles under his eyes and lines in his face that hadn't been there the last time they'd met. "Ben, this last month hasn't been easy on me. But now I've told you the truth and I feel better about a lot of things. You can check it out, you can forget it, you can slug me if you want to, but that's the *truth!*"

Norton yawned.

After a long phase the actor said, "Damn it, will you *say* something?"

"What can I say? It's a hell of a story. I just don't happen to believe it."

"You don't *believe* it?" Jeff seemed truly crestfallen.

"Nothing personal."

"Man, I give you my word—"

"Look, Jeff, maybe, just maybe, I'd have believed you if I'd put a gun to your head and sweated the story out of you. But I'm getting leery of Greeks bearing gifts."

"Ben, I *truly* do not understand you. I've come a long way to tell you the truth and—"

"Okay, okay, don't run it again. This is where I came in. So long, Jeff." He stood up, stretched, and started off, but the actor fell in beside him.

"Think about it, Ben. You've got reason to be suspicious, but think about it. I don't want any hard feelings between us."

"No hard feelings," Norton said. "You're my favorite actor. Except for W. C. Fields. He any relation?"

"Ben, there's something else I've got to say. Will you *wait* a minute?"

Norton turned to face the actor, and behind him he saw the statue of some oft-forgotten Polish patriot. That's what America needs, he thought, more Polish patriots. Where are you, Kosciusko, now that we need you?

"I've got this production company," the actor said. "We've got five pictures stacked up. Budgets anywhere from two million to ten. I'm making so damn much money that I'm thinking about starting a foundation to do some good with it. My only problem is that my lawyers are driving me bananas. They're all corporate types—greedy, right-wing, unimaginative—"

"Good men," Norton said.

"Listen, I need somebody young and smart and straight, somebody to watch over the whole thing, somebody I can trust who'll give me good advice—"

"And the money's fantastic and I'm just the man for the job, right? Oh, Jeff, Jeff, as gift-bearing Greeks go, you are the new Aristotle Onassis."

The actor sagged, as if someone had kicked him in the stomach. Norton realized how much he was enjoying this, what a sadist he'd become. So many people had been screwing him over that it was sheer unadulterated bliss to screw someone else over, even this poor fool.

"Let me tell you something, Jeff. You have made a miscalculation. Or whoever sent you here to do this snow job on me has made a miscalculation. You said I was young and smart and straight. Not so. Maybe I am relatively young and relatively smart, as lawyers go, but I am not straight. True, I used to be. But I have of late been undergoing a transformation. Like Clark Kent ducking into the phone booth and coming out Superman. The full moon is rising, my friend, and Dr. Jekyll has turned to Mr. Hyde. Beneath this mild exterior there lurks a bloodthirsty beast who would cut your handsome throat for a dime. I've been screwed over for the last time, pal. You tell that to whoever sent you here. You tell them that hell hath no fury like an honest man screwed over once too often. You tell them the worm has by God turned and there's gonna be blood on the moon. Now get out of my way before I break your worthless neck."

He marched away from the actor and crossed Jackson Place against the light. A car screeched to a stop and its driver shouted furious obscenities at Norton, but Nortion didn't even notice. He was drunk with his own new-found fury, and for the first time in a long time he felt fine.

21

NORTON'S NEWLY kindled passions were all but extinguished by the time he reached home that evening. Caught in a sudden downpour, unable to find a cab, he was drenched as he splashed the final five blocks to his house. Then, safe on his doorstep, he noticed a light within. He guessed it was either Gabe or the police. Neither prospect cheered him. He pushed open the door and found Gabe stretched out on his sofa alternately nibbling at a hangnail and guzzling Norton's Cutty Sark. He was dressed in a filthy three-piece suit and had a purple bruise on his forehead.

"How'd you get in?" Norton asked, peeling off his soggy coat and tossing it into the bedroom.

"You better get some decent locks on your doors," Gabe said, "or else some crook's gonna back a truck up here and clean you out."

Norton flopped down in a chair and began taking

off his shoes. "Okay, Gabe, what happened last night?"

"Turn on your radio," the reporter whispered. "This place may be bugged."

Norton switched on the radio, dialed WGMS, and a Mozart concerto filled the room. Then he pulled his chair up close to Gabe.

"What happened last night, you incompetent son of a bitch, is that you almost got me killed," Gabe said. "There was a guy with a gun in there."

"My God! Who was he?"

"He didn't introduce himself. I thought maybe you'd know."

"What'd he look like?"

"Five-eight or -nine. A hundred and fifty pounds. Black hair cut short and parted on the right. Forty-five or so. Squinty eyes and kind of a sneer on his face."

Norton shook his head. "That could be a lot of people."

"There was an office with a light on. He must have been in it."

"Gabe, all the lights were off when I left. Which office was it?"

"After you turn the corner, on the left, past the men's room."

"That one's vacant. You can hear the toilet flush in there. The last guy hired always gets it."

"This guy had kind of a sharp, twangy voice. He talked like old gangster movies. 'I got you covered,' stuff like that."

Distant bells chimed in Norton's memory, but all he could think was that his feet were cold and he ought to take some aspirin. "I don't know, Gabe," he said. "It sounds familiar but I can't make the connection." He bent over and began taking off his clammy socks. "So was the whole thing a bust, Gabe? You risked your neck for nothing?"

"I didn't say that!" Gabe snapped. "This ain't exactly nothing." He reached into his briefcase and handed Norton a manuscript. Norton looked at the title page, gasped, and turned quickly to the next page, which was headed Chapter One and which began: "Linda Henderson arrived in Washington one windy day in the spring of 1968, which was perhaps not the best time for anyone to arrive in Washington."

Norton put the manuscript down. "This is Donna's novel," he said. "The one Jeff Fields said was stolen from his office. How the hell did it get into Whit Stone's office?"

Gabe shrugged. "Maybe somebody working for Stone stole it. Or maybe somebody else stole it and sold it to Stone. That'd be a good thing to find out."

"I'll find out!" Norton declared. "I'll go to Stone first thing in the morning and we'll have this out."

Gabe threw up his hands. "You big oaf, will you just once use your head? You ask him where he got the manuscript and he says somebody mailed it to him anonymously. Then he asks how you happen to know about it. What do you say? That a pal of yours stole it?"

Norton sighed. "Okay, Gabe. I'm new at this. Listen, something strange happened today. Jeff Fields came to see me, right out of the blue."

"What'd he want?"

"He wanted to tell me that *he'd* been to see Donna in January and *he'd* gotten her pregnant. And that she told him she'd come to Washington to see friends, but not to see Whitmore. And to top it off he offered me a job."

"So what'd you say?"

"I told him I didn't believe a word of it."

"You idiot!" Gabe cried. "Didn't I tell you to go along with them?"

"I'm sorry, Gabe. I have this habit of telling the truth."

"You call Fields and apologize. Tell him you want to talk some more."

"He'd never believe me now."

"People believe what they want to believe. Tell him

you want to talk about that job. The way you're going, you'll need a job."

"I ought to resign," Norton said. "I can't keep working for Stone. I could resign and maybe beat the truth out of him."

"You hang on there, fellow, and keep playing dumb." The phone rang. Norton jumped up, then stopped and looked at Gabe.

"Answer it," the reporter said. "It might be good news."

Norton doubted that, but he grabbed the phone on the third ring.

"Hello?"

"Ben? It's Penny."

"Who?"

"Penny. You know, we went to the party in Palm Springs."

It seemed long ago. He remembered a tiny girl with a pixie face. "Sure, Penny," he said. "How've you been?"

"Ben, I'm in trouble."

"What's the matter?"

"I can't talk now. I've got to see you."

"You can come by tonight if you want to."

"I'm in Chicago now. But I'll be in Washington tomorrow night. Can I see you then?"

"Sure, come on by my house. I'll be home by seven. Do you know my address?"

"I'll get it," Penny said and hung up.

Norton put down the phone and saw Gabe staring at him. "What was it?" he asked.

"A girl I met in Palm Springs. A stewardess. She got me into Jeff Fields's place. She says she's in trouble."

"She's not the only one," Gabe said. "Look, there was something else I found last night. Stone's address book. There are some damned interesting names and numbers in there."

"Like what?"

Gabe pulled the blue address book from his coat

pocket. "Some of them I recognize, but some of them are just initials. Like this. 'G. 546-3646.' "

"That's Gwen Bowers's number. You know her."

"Yeah, but I don't know why Stone has her number in his book."

"I'll try to find out."

"Try using a little finesse when you do. Here's another one. 'R. 456-7236.' "

"The 456 is the White House prefix. The R. I don't know about."

"I called it today. A secretary said, 'Mr. McNair's office.' "

"That's Clay McNair. He works for Ed Murphy. I met him a couple of weeks ago."

"Describe him."

"About my age. A corporate type. Tall, good-looking. Pin-striped suits and cufflinks. The young executive. I met him when I started asking questions about Donna. Ed had him keeping tabs on the police investigation."

"Maybe he was reporting to Whit Stone on the side."

"I doubt it. McNair doesn't strike me as somebody Ed would trust with anything heavy. He's the All-American boy. He wears his college ring and chews Juicy Fruit."

Norton frowned, sneezed, then sat up straight. "Hey, wait a minute! McNair has this little cubbyhole in the White House basement. He shares it with a guy named Byron Riddle. A strange character. McNair says he's some kind of a consultant, one who does special assignments. The time I went to see McNair I sat at Riddle's desk and he hit the ceiling when he came in and found me there. A weird guy."

Gabe's face came alive. "What does he look like?" he demanded.

"Average height. Slender. Dark hair. In his forties."

"That's gotta be the one." Gabe sighed.

"What one?"

"The one last night. The guy with the gun. Does he

talk crazy, like in gangster movies? Out of the side of his mouth?"

"Yes! Maybe it *is* the same guy."

"I'll run a little check on Mr. Byron Riddle," Gabe said.

Norton started pacing around the living room. "Listen, I just remembered something. Last week I went to a party at Gwen Bowers's house. It was a wild night and I got loaded and at the end I went outside and there was some guy lurking in the bushes. I chased him but he got away. It could have been Riddle."

"It probably was," Gabe said. "I've got to get a look at this guy. You've got to point him out to me."

"How?"

"If we watch the White House long enough, we're bound to see him coming or going."

"*If* he's coming and going. McNair said he travels a lot."

"Like to Palm Springs to steal a manuscript? Like to Carmel to push an old Senator off a cliff? It sounds like this guy Riddle has been doing a lot of traveling."

Norton slumped down in his chair, staring glumly at his cold bare feet. "It's just too much, Gabe," he muttered. "Do you really think a guy on the White House payroll—the *Whitmore* White House—could be a burglar? A murderer?"

Gabe laughed and ran his fingers through his hair, sending a shower of dandruff cascading down onto his shoulders. "Buddy boy, that's what this is all about. Where have you been?"

"Okay, okay, it's possible. Anything's possible. But if that's so, I think it's time we took what we know to the proper authorities."

"*What* proper authorities? Chuck Whitmore? Ed Murphy? That nitwit Attorney General? Or maybe Whit Stone if he gets to be the next Attorney General?"

"No, not them. But there's an investigation of Donna's murder in progress, and her manuscript being in Stone's desk involves him somehow. We could take what we know to the U.S. Attorney's office and let them take it from there."

"Point one: There's no way you put that manuscript in Whit Stone's desk without putting me in the slammer. Point two: Do you happen to know who the new U.S. Attorney for the District of Columbia is?"

"Sure. Frank Kifner. Except I doubt that Frank's personally involved in Donna's case. One of his assistants would be handling it."

"Wrong again. He's taken personal charge of the investigation. And the way I hear it, he's busting ass to get an indictment. Except he's got the minor problem of not having a case against anybody."

"What about the kid? The one with mental problems?"

"No evidence. Which may or may not mean they won't indict him. They frame him, he pleads insanity, and he gets sent to an institution, which is where he belongs anyway. Everybody's happy."

"I don't think Frank's that kind of a guy."

"You know him?" Gabe asked.

"I knew him on the Hill, four or five years ago. He's younger than I am."

"That's right. He's the youngest U.S. Attorney in the country. And he'd like to be the youngest federal judge, or maybe the youngest Assistant Attorney General if Whit Stone gets the top job. That was another thing. Stone's address book had Kifner's unlisted number with an F. beside it."

"It's not unusual that a top Washington lawyer would have the U.S. Attorney's phone number."

"No, except that all the names in the book were spelled out except G. for Gwen and R. for Riddle and F. for Frank Kifner. He's in select company."

"I know Frank well enough to go have a confidential talk with him. Nothing about you or the manuscript. Just a little talk about some of the strange things that have been happening."

"Kifner would steal your socks. All you'd do is give away everything we know, and then all the rest of the doors would start slamming in our faces."

"I think Kifner's honest. I *know* he's smart. Too smart to play games with a murder investigation."

"My God, no wonder the South lost the war," Gabe moaned. "Can't you get it through your thick head that nobody but you gives one happy damn who killed Donna Hendricks? Whitmore wants to protect himself. Murphy wants to protect Whitmore. Kifner wants to score brownie points with the White House so he gets another promotion. Hell, the detective on the case is bucking for *chief* of detectives. And so it goes. Everybody's looking out for Number One."

"What about you, Gabe?" Norton said bitterly. "Do you care what happened to Donna? Or just about finding that Holy Grail you call the Hoover file?"

Gabe grinned at the question *"Now* you're catching on," he said. "Sure, I'm helping you because you can help me. That's how the world works. But you can't help anybody if you don't start using your head. Look, you call Jeff Fields and say you want to talk to him again. Talk to Gwen Bowers and pump her about Stone. And find some excuse to see McNair again. If he shares an office with Riddle he must know something about him."

Gabe got up and shook some dandruff from his coat. "I got to go," he said. "Look, are you still with me? The game's getting serious. That wasn't a popgun that character pointed at me last night."

Norton started taking off his soggy necktie. His shirt felt plastered to his back. "I'm with you, Gabe. I just wish I knew what was going on."

"I'll tell you what's going on," Gabe said. "We're about to bust this thing. Look at that!"

He extended his hands toward Norton, who gazed at them and saw nothing unusual, except that Gabe's fingernails were dirty.

"Look," Gabe said and pointed to one of his wrists. "See them? Spots!"

Norton looked closely and saw two or three faint pink blotches on Gabe's wrist.

"It never fails," Gabe said. "When I get close to breaking a story, the spots start. Then, when I'm *really* close, I break out in a rash. It's a sixth sense I've got."

Norton was speechless.

"So don't worry, buddy," Gabe said. "We're gonna get the bastards. We're gonna nail them to the wall." Gabe winked, gave Norton a friendly punch on the arm, and slipped out the door.

Norton sighed, locked the door, turned off the radio, and went to the bathroom to take some vitamin C. He caught colds easily and he felt one coming on.

22

HE OPENED the door and she threw herself into his arms.

"Careful, I've got a cold," he said.

"I don't *care,*" Penny said and kissed him, and she began to cry into his cashmere sweater.

"Come on in," Norton said. "Have you eaten? I could scramble some eggs."

"No, thanks," Penny said glumly. "I'm not really hungry."

"How about a hot toddy? I'm living on hot toddies and Contac this week."

"Maybe just a Coke or something," Penny said. "I'm already in such trouble that I don't want to drink booze or smoke grass or jaywalk or anything." She tried to smile, but her face cracked and she began to cry again.

He got her a Coke and joined her on the sofa. "Okay, Penny, tell me what the trouble is."

"I don't even *know* what the trouble is," she cried. "I met this guy on the plane and the next thing I know the cops are asking me questions and talking about the grand jury and how I could go to jail, and I'm about to lose my *mind!*"

It all tumbled out at once, like the debris from Fibber McGee's closet, and it frightened Norton.

"Slow down, Penny. Start at the beginning."

She fumbled in her purse for a Virginia Slim. Her hands shook as she lit it. "I *think* it started on the plane," she said. "The L.A. to Washington run. I was working the first-class cabin and I got to talking with this very peculiar guy. He came on strong about what a bigshot he was and all these adventures he'd had. Finally I told him I thought he was putting me on, and he got all snippy and showed me a White House pass with his picture on it, so I guessed he was for real."

"Did he tell you his name?"

"He *said* his name was Wendell Baxter, but when he showed me his White House pass he kept his hand over the part with his name. And his cufflinks had an R on them. So you figure it out."

Norton wasn't even surprised. He was starting to think Gabe was right: the whole world was one vast conspiracy.

"Penny, was he about forty-five and slender, with dark hair cut short and kind of a wild look in his eyes?"

"How'd you know?" Her eyes were big as saucers.

"It's a long story. Tell me more about what he said."

"Well, he talked like he'd been some kind of international spy. He talked about guns a lot. He said he had a gun that could shoot around corners, but I guess that was a joke. He talked about these private clubs where he gambled in London and he said he knew the Shah of Iran personally and he dropped the names of a lot of movie types. I guess that's how we got to talking about Jeff."

"Jeff Fields?"

"That's right. Like a dummy I said I'd been to some of Jeff's parties, and he picked up on that. Started asking me questions about Jeff and his parties until I changed the subject and then he went back to his snow job."

"Did he say what he was doing with a White House pass?"

"He said something about special assignments. He made it sound like *he* was doing *them* a favor. I mean, he wasn't all that infatuated with President Whitmore. He got to talking about politics and how what the country needs is new leadership and 'Constitutionalist principles,' whatever that means. It was wild to hear him talk. I mean, none of it made any sense at all—but I couldn't take my eyes off the man. He was positively hypnotic."

She sipped at her Coke. "So anyway, when we landed at Dulles he asked me to dinner, and I didn't have anything better to do, so I said okay and we went to dinner at some Arab place, and the long and short of it is I got bombed out of my mind and he took me to some apartment, this grubby place on Captiol Hill, and instead of him trying to hustle me, which at least is what I expected, he starts asking me questions about Jeff and whether people use drugs at his parties. And I guess I told him everything I knew, just to shut him up. So sometime in the middle of the night he calls a cab and takes me to the friend's house where I was staying."

"Penny, could you find that apartment again?"

"I don't think so. You know how Capitol Hill all sort of looks alike. I guess I'd know the place if I got inside it."

"I want us to take a walk around the Hill tomorrow to see if we can find that place. Okay?"

"Sure, Ben."

"So what happened next?"

"Nothing, for about a week. Then one morning I'm at work, about to leave on a flight, and these two guys ask to see me and flop out these silver badges and say they're narcotics agents and I may be in trouble and they want to ask me some questions. And I say, 'Gee, fellows, I don't know. I've got this plane to catch.' And they say maybe I want to check it with my boss first—real polite, like they were doing me a favor, but it sent me up the wall to think about my boss knowing there were two narcotics agents there to question me."

"They knew it would."

"I guess so. Anyway, I asked them what it was they wanted to talk about, and they started asking me about drugs, and did I use drugs and did I know other people who did. It was ridiculous. I said, 'Look, fellows, let's face it, everybody smokes grass, everybody sniffs the happy powder.' Honestly, Ben, half the stewardesses I know smoke a joint or snort some coke before flights, just so they can keep on smiling at those fanny-pinching fools we have to take care of. But these two guys just kept on asking their questions and pretty soon they zero in on Jeff Fields and who uses drugs at his parties and where do they come from and all, until finally I told them I didn't want to talk any more."

Penny paused and finished her Coke. Norton sneezed and blew his nose.

"You better have a toddy," she said. "Maybe I could stand one too."

"Good idea," he said. He went into the kitchen, heated the water, poured each of them two jiggers of Early Times into a coffee cup, filled the cups with boiling water, and added some honey and a couple of nutmegs.

Penny tried her drink and grinned. "That's *good*," she said. "If I'd just stuck to bourbon, I wouldn't be in this mess I'm in. Or maybe I would, with my luck."

"Penny, did these men ever tell you that you didn't have to answer their questions? That you could call a lawyer? That anything you said could be used against you?"

"Well, not exactly. I mean, maybe one of them said something about how I didn't *have* to talk to them, and the other one broke in and said of course it'd be better for me if I did, since I was already in so much trouble. I was all confused. One of them started talking about how awful prison was for a girl like me, and I guess I started crying a little, and the other one gets all friendly about how all they want is the truth and the truth never hurt anybody."

Norton groaned. "Penny, if a cop ever asks you what *time* it is, you tell him to talk to your lawyer. Please."

"I knew I should have called you," she said. "But I flew to L.A. and had a few days out there and it was like the two cops hadn't ever happened. I thought it'd all go away. But when I got back to Washington, those same two guys were waiting for me and this time they said the U.S. Attorney wanted to see me. I just about dropped my teeth. I thought about calling you then, but they'd already talked to my supervisor and he said I'd better cooperate or I'd be out of a job. And, you know, jobs aren't exactly growing on trees these days, and a lot of girls are having a hard time, so I figured the best thing I could do was to go see the U.S. Attorney. So I did."

"Frank Kifner?"

"You know him?"

"Yeah," Norton said. "What'd he say?"

"Well, he started out all warm and friendly, saying how wise I was to cooperate and how there were just a few little points to clear up, and then we're back to playing Twenty Questions again. And most of the questions were about Jeff and cocaine. Like he asked me if I used coke. 'Only to brush my teeth with,' I said, but he didn't think that was funny. So he asks if people snort coke at Jeff's parties. I said sure. Did Jeff do it? Sure. But they kept trying to get me to say that it was Jeff's coke and that maybe he sold it to people, and I told them I didn't know, and that's when they started talking about the grand jury. I guess I started crying again, so finally they told me I could leave but they might be in touch. And then a few days later they called and said Kifner wanted to see me again. And that's when I called you. That man—I couldn't face him again. Ben, he's got the coldest eyes I ever saw."

"God, I wish you'd called me sooner."

"I'm sorry," she said. "I'm so darn dumb."

"No, you're just an average person who any half-way competent cop, much less a lawyer like Kifner, can tie up in knots."

"How much trouble am I in?"

"I don't know. My guess is that they're not interested in you. I think they wanted to build a case against Jeff Fields, to pressure him into doing a little favor for them, so they leaned on you and probably on some other people to get evidence against him. It's called 'dealing up.' They use the little guys to get the big guys."

"I don't understand," Penny said. "What did they want from Jeff?"

"I don't know," Norton said, although he was almost certain they had used the cocaine investigation to pressure Fields into telling him the story about getting Donna pregnant.

"But why do they want to see me again?"

"I don't know. Maybe they're just going through the motions, trying to make this look like a legitimate investigation instead of a cheap political squeeze play."

Penny blinked in confusion. "You make it sound like *blackmail!*" she said. "Like the government uses the laws to push people around, just like crooks use guns. Can they *do* that?"

"They do it every day," he told her. "And the drug laws make it easy as pie for them. Just remember, Penny, every time you smoke a joint, much less use cocaine, you're putting yourself at their mercy. And they don't have a hell of a lot of it."

She shuddered and put her face in her hands.

"It's getting late," he said. "Where are you staying?"

She looked up at him and tried to smile. "Nowhere, really. I mean, I could stay here, if you've got room and all."

He shook his head. "I don't think that'd work, Penny."

"We wouldn't have to *do* anything," she said.

Norton was starting to feel uncomfortable. "The thing is, Penny, that since the last time I saw you, I've . . . well . . ."

"You've got a girl," she said.

"Yeah, more or less. It's all happened sort of quick, but . . ."

Penny grinned. "But she wouldn't exactly approve of me moving in with you."

"I think that's a fair statement," Norton said. "Look, maybe you could stay with her. She's got a little house over in Foggy Bottom, not far from the Kennedy Center, and she's got a spare bedroom. The thing is, I'm going to talk to Kifner about you, and I don't want you talking to *anyone* before I do."

"What's her name?" Penny asked.

"Annie," he told her.

"Annie," Penny repeated glumly. "I'll bet she's smart, not a dope like me." She put her face against the back of the sofa and started to cry.

Norton touched her shoulder. "Listen Penny, you're wrong. You and Annie are a lot alike. You're both honest. You're both good people. You'll get along fine. We'll all three be friends. We'll all three try to help each other. Okay?"

She turned and blinked at him, then hugged him tight. He held her for a moment, then he went to the phone and called Annie. She listened to his explanation and then said that if he didn't get Penny to her place within ten minutes she'd break his neck.

23

CLAY MCNAIR was pondering a memo in which the White House chef pleaded for a 30 percent budget increase and hinted of rebellion among the kitchen help if he didn't get it, when Byron Riddle burst into the office, slammed the door behind him, and turned on the little Sony TV set on the shelf beside his desk.

McNair looked up angrily. "Byron, if you don't mind, I'm trying to work," he said.

Riddle ignored the complaint. His eyes were fixed on the television screen, where a fat woman was hopping up and down beside a new Dodge Charger.

"Byron, I'm *working!*"

"Take a break, pal," Riddle said out of the side of his mouth. "Don't you know what's about to happen?"

McNair sighed and put aside the chef's memo. "No, Byron, what *is* about to happen?"

"Donnie Ripley's called himself a news conference," Riddle said, with an air of smugness that mystified McNair.

"A news conference? What for? It's too early for him to announce for President."

"Ha!" Riddle said, grinning fiendishly. "Let's us just wait and see."

McNair shook his head in frustration. The political pundits were forever speculating whether Senator Ripley would challenge President Whitmore for their party's nomination three years hence, but the question did not interest McNair at all. He expected to have returned to the relative sanity of corporate life by then. Furthermore, he didn't *care* who was President. He had decided that politicians were like toothpaste, products you advertised as uniquely different but that were in truth all the same. You merchandised your candidate to get him elected, and once he was elected you did his work for him. McNair was coming to see a certain fatal Catch-22 to the political process: the more talent a man had for getting himself elected to office, the less talent he would have for performing his duties of office.

"Come on, damn it, come on," Byron Riddle said impatiently. The television station was airing a seemingly endless series of commericials before the Senator's news conference. At the moment a perky-looking older woman was advising a befuddled-looking younger woman of the virtues of a certain washday detergent. "If we had the right kind of government in this country," Riddle snapped, "people wouldn't have to watch garbage like that."

"Byron, we've got to have advertising," McNair protested. "It keeps the wheels turning."

"Listen, pal, what this country needs is to put some steel in people's spines, not to sell soap," Byron Riddle snapped.

He groaned and began searching through his pockets for a cigarette. Finding none, he hurriedly unlocked his desk drawer and extracted a fresh pack of Marlboros. Just as he lit one, a can of dog food was replaced by the Capitol dome, then by the perplexed face of a well-known political commentator, who was saying, ". . . unexpected news conference has caught Washington by surprise. Veteran Washington watchers believe it is far too early for Senator Ripley to announce Presidential plans, yet that possibility remains . . . possible. And now we're ready to switch to . . ."

And there he was, Donovan Ripley, his imposing and rather weary face dominating the screen, the flag furled behind him, his wife and children seated beside him. His wife was a gorgeous creature with strangely dazed eyes, like a debutante who has stumbled into a mine disaster.

"My fellow Americans," said Donovan Ripley, the hope of millions, every inch a President-to-be, "I am here this morning to announce a difficult decision, one I have reached after much prayer and much discussion with my beloved wife and the many friends who have encouraged my career of public service . . ."

Clay McNair frowned and Byron Riddle let out a whoop of joy.

". . . and every public man must constantly weigh his duty to his country alongside his duty to those he holds most dear . . ."

Byron Riddle was pounding his desk and rocking with silent laughter.

". . . the painful but necessary decision that, out of devotion to my beloved wife and children, I shall not now or at any time in the future be a candidate for President of the United States . . ."

Riddle jumped to his feet and began dancing around the room like a man gone mad. On the television screen there was similar chaos. The urbane political commentator was gasping like a fish out of water: ". . . political bombshell . . . totally unexpected . . . deep devotion to his family . . . completely alters the future of national politics . . ."

"He did it," Riddle shouted. "He's out!"

McNair, annoyed, got up and turned off the TV. "Byron, let's settle down. It's not that big a deal, is it?"

"Not that big a deal?" Riddle repeated and started laughing again until tears filled his eyes. "I'd say it's about as big a deal as I've ever had a hand in."

"Had a hand in, Byron? How is that?" McNair thought his companion had taken leave of his senses.

"Just a figure of speech," Riddle said and pulled himself together. "I've got to go now. This changes everything. I've got to talk to Ed Murphy. See you later, McNair."

"Byron, what about those reports . . . ?" McNair began, but the other man raced from the office, slamming the door behind him.

Clay McNair sighed and returned to his desk. This madness had gone on long enough. He didn't know what valuable services Riddle was performing for Ed Murphy or others in the White House, but all he was doing was disrupting McNair's own work schedule. He would have to talk to Murphy. At the very least, Riddle had to move to another office. Enough was enough.

McNair was reaching for the chef's complaint again when something quite unexpected caught his eye. Riddle had left his desk drawer open. McNair was stunned. Riddle had always guarded those drawers like a tiger. He felt a sudden almost irresistible urge to see what was inside the drawer.

No, he told himself, that would be beneath his dignity; that was not the kind of thing an executive did.

And yet, he thought, perhaps he would find something compromising, something that would strengthen his case with Ed Murphy, and he would do almost anything that would get Byron Riddle out of his office and out of his life.

He crossed the office swiftly and pulled open the drawer. There was a carton of Marlboros inside. And a map of California. And two manila envelopes. McNair picked up the first one. It was sealed, and someone had written "D. H. Tape" across the front of it. McNair could feel the round spool of tape inside. D. H. Tape? Who or what was D. H.? Department of Housing? David Halberstam? McNair frowned, replaced the first envelope, and picked up the second one. This one was bulky and unsealed, and when McNair peered into it he was startled to find it was full of money.

Most of the bills were hundreds, with a few fifties scattered about. At a glance, McNair guessed there was at least ten thousand dollars in the envelope.

As McNair gazed at the money, his heart began to pound and he was thinking very fast. He thought of the financial sacrifice he was making to work in the government. He thought of the expense, more than five thousand dollars a year, of keeping his daughters in private schools. He thought of his wife's complaints that he was working too hard, that they hadn't taken a vacation in two years, and he thought how fine it would be it he could take his family to Acapulco or perhaps Caneel Bay for a week or two. If he could afford it. He reached into the envelope. Just two thousand he thought. Twenty bills. Riddle would never notice. And what a fine vacation he and his family could have.

Suddenly the door opened and Byron Riddle stepped into the office. McNair gasped and dropped the envelope.

"You shouldn't have done that, McNair," Riddle whispered.

"You left the drawer open," McNair said smoothly. "I was closing it for you. You ought to be more careful, Byron."

McNair flashed his boyish grin, but it faded quickly in the face of Riddle's murderous stare. McNair shrugged and started back to his own desk. "Look, Byron," he said. "I think it's time you and I had a little talk. I'm getting tired—"

Riddle's fist shot out and sank into the pit of McNair's stomach. McNair doubled up with pain and thought he was going to be sick. Riddle grabbed his Countess Mara tie, shoved him up against the wall, and slapped him hard across the face. McNair struggled to defend himself but Riddle judo-chopped him in the neck and his arms suddenly went limp.

"Byron, for God's sake," he cried.

Riddle slapped him again. "How'd you get in that drawer?" he demanded.

"You left it *open*."

Riddle punched him in the stomach again and Mc-

Nair sank to his knees. He's going to kill me, he thought. This madman is going to murder me right here in the White House basement.

"Byron," he pleaded, "if we have a problem, let's discuss it like——"

Riddle banged his head against the wall so hard that McNair thought he would pass out. "You want some money, punk?" Riddle whispered savagely. "You like the money? Okay, we'll give you some money."

He reached into the envelope, pulled out a hundred-dollar bill, and stuck it in McNair's face. "Eat it, punk!"

"What?"

"I said eat it!"

Riddle slapped him again and stuffed the bill into his mouth. "Chew it up. Swallow it."

McNair started to protest, but when Riddle raised his hand, as if to slap him again, McNair began to chew the bill. It tasted dirty, and he thought he was going to vomit. He started to cry.

"Swallow it before I kill you," Riddle said.

McNair swallowed, gagged, then got the bill down. He sagged forward on all fours, staring sightlessly at the floor.

"What'd you see in that drawer?" Riddle snapped.

"Nothing, Byron. I swear. Please——"

Riddle kicked him in the ribs. "You're a liar. What'd you see?"

"The cigarettes. A map. Some money."

"What else?"

"An envelope."

"What'd it say on it?"

"I don't know."

Riddle kicked him again. *"What'd it say?"*

"I swear to God I don't know."

Riddle knelt down, whispering into his ear. "If you ever say anything to anybody about what was in that drawer, I'll kill you. Do you read me?"

"Yes, Byron."

"I won't kill you fast. I'll kill you slow. And your wife and kids too. You think I'm kidding?"

"No, Byron," McNair whispered. "Can I get up now?"

"Stay where you are."

"Byron, we can't go on like this, sharing an office—"

"That's the first smart thing you've said," Riddle told him. "So you better tell Murphy you want to move out. Okay?"

"Okay. Byron. Anything you say."

"That's more like it. You can get up now."

McNair struggled to his feet.

Riddle leaned against his desk and lit a Marlboro. "I don't like getting rough with you," he said. "That's not my style. But you got to understand I'm doing some confidential assignments for the big boys and there can't be any leaks. So you just keep your mouth shut and we won't have any more problems. Right?"

"Right," McNair said. His side throbbed where Riddle had kicked him. He thought he might have a broken rib. "And Byron . . . I'm sorry I looked in your drawer. That was bad procedure."

"Spoken like a man," Riddle said and suddenly extended his hand. Dazed, McNair shook hands with his tormentor.

"There's no reason for us to have problems," Riddle said. "You're a team player, McNair, and there's a place for your kind. But Byron Riddle's a lone wolf, out there on his own, doing the tough jobs that nobody else wants to do. And from now on the best thing you can do is stay out of my way."

"I agree," McNair said.

"Good! Now, turn around and face the wall."

"What?"

"You heard me. Turn around. *Fast!*"

McNair turned around, fast, and heard the sounds of Riddle opening his desk drawers and removing their contents and putting them into his briefcase. "So long, McNair," he said after a minute. "Remember what I said. Keep your lip buttoned and you'll be okay."

The door closed. McNair turned around slowly, saw that Riddle was gone, and quickly locked the door. As if any lock could protect him from Byron Riddle. He slumped down at his desk, throbbing with pain, trying to decide what to do. He would have to tell Ed Murphy. He couldn't go on working with a maniac who'd threatened to kill him.

And yet . . . what if all Riddle said was true? What if he was working on confidential projects for Ed Murphy or even for the President? What if he told them McNair had somehow compromised their secrecy? What if, instead of getting Riddle fired, he got himself fired? If that happened, all his plans would go up in smoke. No corporation would give him the kind of job he wanted. Maybe it was better to keep quiet, to move to another office and keep away from Byron Riddle, even if it meant leaving the White House for the limbo of the Executive Office Building next door. That might be best just to mind his own business. And yet he couldn't help wondering. Why was Riddle so upset? What was so important about those two envelopes?

D. H. Tape.

Donna Hendricks Tape.

It hit him all at once and left him limp with fear. What did Riddle have to do with the dead woman? What kind of tape? What secrets could be on that tape that would inspire a threat of murder? McNair was starting to think thoughts he did not want to think. All he wanted was to do his job, to please his bosses, to get ahead in the world. But now, somehow, he was dealing with a madman who had threatened to kill him and his family. McNair put his face in his hands. His ribs ached where Riddle had kicked him and he had a queasy feeling in the pit of his stomach. He wondered what germs might have been on that bill. Perhaps he should see a doctor. But how would he explain having swallowed a hundred-dollar bill? Mc-Nair's telephone began to ring, but he ignored it. He didn't want to talk to anyone. He wished he was far away from Washington, D.C. He almost wished he was dead.

24

THEY ARGUED on the way to the airport.

"You can't trust Gabe Pincus," she said.

"I *don't* trust him," he told her. "But I need him."

"He'll screw you," Annie said. "All he cares about is his scoops. His name in lights. You can't control him."

"He's useful. Half of what I know about this mess came from Gabe."

"And how much do you know? So much that now you're flying off to California on a wild-goose chase?"

"Annie, it's all I know to do," he said wearily. "There's got to be a weak link somewhere. McNair won't talk to me. Riddle has vanished. So I'm going to try Jeff Fields again."

"You could go public," she said. "Call a news conference. Lay out everything you know. Then let *them* explain it, instead of beating your head against a wall like this."

He turned off the Beltway onto the Dulles Access Road and shook his head stubbornly. "I'm not *ready* to do that yet. It could destroy Whitmore and I won't do that until I'm sure he was involved in Donna's death."

"Sure? How sure can you *be?*" she cried. "You know he got her pregnant. You know somebody killed Senator Nolan. You know they pressured Fields into claiming *he* got her pregnant. What do you want, a confession?"

A taxi whizzed past them at eighty miles an hour. "Some poor bastard late for his plane," Norton said. "Look, I tried to explain last night, all those things could be coincidence. The case against Whitmore is still circumstantial. There's a line between what I *suspect* and what I *know*. If I were a juror, I couldn't say that I was convinced beyond a reasonable doubt that Whitmore was involved."

"Oh, *God,*" she cried. "*Lawyers.*"

When he stopped the car in front of the airport he took her hand. "I'll call you tonight," he said.

"Get some rest out there," she said. "Lie by the pool for a while and soak up some sun."

"I'll try to," he said. "Look, I'm really sorry about last night."

She scooted across the seat and kissed him. "I loved last night," she said. "Just get some rest. I'm going to eat you up when you get back."

He kissed her quickly and hurried into the terminal.

When his plane lifted off the runway a half hour later, Norton thought he'd never been so glad to leave a place as he was to leave Washington now. Even if it meant leaving Annie. For the past week or so he had felt the walls closing in on him. He had begun noticing people on the street whose faces had only been blurs to him before. Now he imagined them watching him, following him, conspiring against him. He assumed all phones were tapped, all mail was opened, all conversations were overheard.

The last straw had come the night before, when he and Annie had gone to bed together for the first time. And that was all they had done, gone to bed, for something maddening had happened to him. Impotence, it seemed, was one of the final symptoms of paranoia. In bed, with her arms around him, her thin body warm against his, he heard sounds outside the door, saw shadows at the windows, imagined spies, hidden cameras, secret microphones. It was too much. She tried to help, but it only got worse. Finally he gave up and, hoping to make her understand, told her what was troubling him. Of course, even as he whispered to her about Donna's death, part of him feared that she was somehow part of the conspiracy, but he had to trust someone.

Once he began talking, she sat up in the bed, switched on the light, and cross-examined him for an hour. She thought he was being too cautious, too trusting. She had no doubt of Whitmore's complicity. But of course she was ten crucial years younger than he was. He had come of age trusting his government, and she had not. Finally, when all her questions were answered, she'd switched off the light and put her arms around him and held him close. He fell asleep half in love with her.

"Would you like a cocktail, sir?"

He opened his eyes. The stewardess was blue-eyed and pert. He thought of Penny and wondered if this stewardess might also be stoned.

"Two Bloody Marys, please," he told her. He had a plan: to drink two Bloody Marys and sleep all the way to California.

* * *

The flat-faced man was still guarding Jeff Field's gate, but this time he caused no problems. "The boss is expecting you," he said a bit sullenly. "Down by the pool."

Norton parked his rented Ford in front of the mansion, beside a sparkling canary yellow Jaguar, and walked around the house and down the long lawn that sloped toward the pool. It was not like before, when partygoers had cavorted in and around the pool. Now there was only Jeff Fields, lying on a chaise beside the pool, and a big white rubber raft bobbing gently on its surface.

"Hello, Norton," the actor said without getting up.

"Hello, Jeff. I appreciate the hospitality."

"I owed you some, after last time. Just don't give me any more nonsense about coming out here to talk about a job. How about a beer?"

"Great."

"I'll get them," Fields said. "There's a refrigerator in the cabana."

He went into the cabana and returned a minute later with two icy Coors. "You're a Southerner, aren't you, Norton?" he asked.

"Sure. North Carolina."

"Do you say refrigerator or icebox?"

"I grew up saying icebox. We had one. Literally, a box you put ice in. Sometimes I still catch myself saying it. Why do you ask?"

"I made a picture once that was set in Mississippi in the thirties. I had a hell of a time convincing the director I should say icebox."

"I saw that picture. You played the bootlegger. You were good too. I used to get so damn tired of seeing pictures about the South starring people with Brooklyn accents. The kind of people who think 'you all' is singular."

Fields smiled. "It's plural, isn't it? 'You all shore been right nice tuh me.' I'll have to remember that."

"Look, Jeff, I was pretty rude to you that time in Lafayette Square. The problem was, I didn't believe what you were telling me. To get right to it, do you want me to tell you what I think's happening here?"

"Sure. Fire away."

"To begin with, I don't for a minute believe you got Donna pregnant. I think Whitmore did and they pressured you to come to me with your song and dance. The only thing I couldn't figure out is how they could make you do something so dumb."

"Why dumb?"

"Why? In the first place, it's always dumb to involve

yourself in a murder case if you don't have to. Besides that, if you told your story under oath, and it could come to that, you'd be running the risk of perjury. Whenever you lie for somebody else, Jeff, there's always the chance they'll decide to tell the truth and leave you way out on a limb."

The actor shrugged and began rubbing suntan lotion on his chest.

"I couldn't figure how they'd got to you," Norton continued. "Then the other night a stewardess named Penny came to see me. Remember her?"

"Yeah."

"Well, the U.S. Attorney's office put the screws to her until she told them everything she knew about drug use at your parties. And I figure they did the same with other people too, until they got enough evidence for some kind of a cocaine charge. Was that it? Is that how they turned you around?"

"Let me tell you something, Norton. Just hypothetically. The government wouldn't have to convict someone like me to ruin them. They might not even have to indict me. They could probably ruin me just by leaking certain evidence to the papers. 'Actor Accused in Cocaine Plot.' 'Wild Orgies at Actor's Estate.' Stuff like that. A cocaine charge today would do to my career what a marijuana charge did to Bob Mitchum thirty years ago."

"So you think they've got you cold?"

"Don't you?"

"No. I think you're making a hell of a mistake."

"Look, Norton, if you ever repeat what I'm about to tell you, I'll deny it. But you're not far off the mark. They did ask their little favor and I said no, and the next thing I knew they had an army of narcotics agents talking to my friends. So I talked to my lawyer and his advice was four words: Do what they say. And I did. And that was the end of the cocaine investigation. So maybe I wasn't so dumb after all."

"Hey, boss." It was the fat-faced man calling from the terrace. "I'm going to town. You want anything?"

"Get more beer," Fields yelled back. The man waved and disappeared.

"Just you and him now, Jeff?" Norton asked. "No gorgeous babes? No music? No parties?"

"The party's over," Fields said. "Now, you tell me where you think my lawyer's wrong."

"He's wrong because he's letting you get into trouble you don't have to get into. He's underestimating your position. Sure, you're vulnerable, but so is Whitmore. He can hurt you, but you can hurt him too, and he's got even more to lose."

"It's a no-win situation."

"What you're doing is a no-win situation. Look, I think you know something about Donna's affair with Whitmore, and why she went to Washington to see him, and maybe about how she died. And if you know even half of that, there's no reason for you to let them push you around. *They're* the ones in trouble, not you. *You* didn't kill anybody. Why let them drag you into a cover-up?"

"Damn it, because they can ruin me."

"Other people could get ruined too. Do you know who Frank Kifner is?"

"Yeah."

"He's talked to you about the drug investigation?"

"One of his assistants did."

"Okay. I'm going to see Kifner when I get back to Washington and I'm going to tell him that I know that he's been putting the screws to Penny for no good reason except political pressure from the White House. And that he's been doing the same thing to you. They can't *do* that, Jeff. They can't just walk over people with impunity. They can't use the judicial process to blackmail people. Frank Kifner's a smart, ambitious man, and he's going to listen to me. He's got to look out for his own interests, and what I want to do is convince him that it's in his interest to get the truth about Donna's death. And you're one of the people I'm going to urge him to talk to. And I hope you'll get smart and tell him the truth."

Fields got slowly to his feet, as if weighed down by indecision. "How about another beer?" he asked.

"Sure."

Fields returned with two more Coors and handed Norton one. "Look, let me ask you a couple of questions."

"Go ahead."

"Why are you telling me all this? That you think Whitmore got her pregnant and knows who killed her? That you're going to see Kifner about it? Aren't you afraid I'll call Whitmore or Ed Murphy or whoever's behind all this and tell them what you've said?"

"I've talked to Murphy. He knows what I think. Right now we're playing poker. They're betting I can't prove I'm right and I'm betting I can. And you're in the middle."

Fields got up and moved his chaise farther away from the cabana. It was midafternoon and the palm trees were beginning to cast long shadows across the lawn. Norton stayed in the shade.

"Ben, don't you ever feel that you're tilting at windmills? That whoever it is you're up against controls the police and the FBI and the U.S. Attorney's office, and there's no way you can crack through that wall? Aren't you gambling—and asking me to gamble—on one hell of a long shot?"

"Sure I've felt like that," he said. "I've been in Washington long enough to know just how screwed up and corrupt the political system can be. But the thing is, Jeff, deep down inside I believe in our system. I think of it as being like an old mule. It's lazy and stubborn and selfish and stupid—but the damned thing can *work!* If you just kick it in the ass enough, you can *make* it work. That's all I'm trying to do, just trying to kick ass until I get that old mule moving in the right direction."

"What if the mule kicks back, Ben?"

"Let it kick. I'm just as stubborn as it is."

"I'm not joking. I think there are people who want to shut you up and if they can't discourage you one way they'll do it another way. If I were you, I'd be careful where I went and who I turned my back on. I had a friend once, a director, who crossed the Mafia. A small thing, a gambling debt, eight or ten thousand dollars. The cops found him stuffed in a garbage can behind the Brown Derby with eighty-three icepick holes in him."

"We're not dealing with the Mafia, Jeff."

"No? What about that old Senator? Do you think he fell off that cliff accidentally?"

"I don't know," Norton admitted. "I'd like to think he did."

Fields laughed bitterly. "Then don't call me dumb, pal. You may be dumber than I am. If that's possible."

"Maybe so," Norton said. "We'll find out eventually. What I want to know right now is whether or not you're going to cooperate with me. I want to know who at the White House told you to tell me that story. And why Donna went to Washington. And what you know about her death. All of it. What do you say?"

Fields crumpled his beer can in half and flung it into the air. It landed in the grass and lay sparkling in the sun. "Damn it, I don't know what to do," he said.

"Just tell the truth, Jeff. You can't go wrong telling the truth."

The actor almost smiled. "You know something funny? I believe in Whitmore. I think if anybody can straighten out this screwed-up country, he's the one. The last thing I want to do is cause him problems."

"I feel the same way," Norton said. "But we didn't cause his problems. He caused his own. You've got to think about your own interests. Whitmore's got plenty of people looking out for his."

Fields got up and began to pace beside the pool. "God *damn* it," he said. "I didn't ask for any of this. It's not my problem. If it just wasn't for that damn *tape.*"

Norton froze. "What tape, Jeff?" he said softly.

The actor stopped pacing and seemed to come out of his trance. "What? Oh, nothing. Forget it."

"Jeff, *what tape?* What are you talking about?"

Fields sat on the end of the chaise with his head in his hands. "I can't talk now," he muttered. "I've got to think. I've got to talk to my lawyer. I don't *know* what to do!"

"There isn't much time," Norton said. "I go back to Washington tomorrow. I need to know which way you're going to jump."

"Come by at nine in the morning," Fields said. "I'll make up my mind by then."

Norton stood up, then made one last try. "The tape, Jeff. Just tell me what you meant by that."

"In the morning," the actor repeated, and Norton gave up.

He started up the hill, then stopped beside the mansion and gazed back down at the pool. Fields had gone in for a swim. After a lap or two, he had climbed onto the white raft that had been bobbing in the water, and now he was lying on his back, eyes shut, drifting about the pool like a man perfectly at peace. It was a pleasing sight: the lean tanned young man floating on the white raft atop the turquoise water, with the cabana and the palm trees and the mountains and the endless desert sky for his backdrop. Norton thought the vista would have made a nice ending for a movie, if movies had nice endings any more.

Fields opened his eyes, saw Norton, and lifted one hand in farewell.

"Paddling your own canoe, Jeff?" Norton called down the hill.

"Maybe," the actor called back. "Or maybe I'm just up Shit Creek without a paddle."

Or maybe both, Norton thought, and he waved and walked around the house to his car.

25

BACK AT his hotel, Norton ducked into the bar, ordered a gin and tonic, and asked the bartender if he would turn on the evening news. Norton was of course a news addict; any night he missed Walter Cronkite he began to shake and sweat like a junkie without his fix. The bartender gave him an odd stare, but switched on the huge color television set above the bar. No one else in the dark little barroom seemed remotely interested in the news, and Norton noticed a few people seeming to frown at him.

The news that evening was mostly from Washington and was all bad. Prices up, employment down, food scarce, experts baffled. Another Congressman had been indicted for tax evasion, and the Senate was immobilized by a filibuster. The State Department warned of new violence in the Middle East, the Pentagon wanted more money, and the Treasury hinted at another tax increase. As more and more bad news flowed out of the television set, Norton began to feel uncomfortable, began to see the news from a new, disturbing non-Washington perspective. In Washington he accepted the nation's political woes as part of everyday life, like the smog in Los Angeles. Moreover, he and most of the people he knew made their livings off the nation's political agonies, one way or another. But here in this posh little bar in this desert paradise, Washington's ill tidings seemed cruelly out of place.

He saw people up and down the bar beginning to grumble and shoot angry glances his way, and he thought suddenly, startlingly, How they must hate us! Hemingway called Paris a moveable feast, but Washington was a moveable disaster, each night sending its message of gloom and doom across a helpless and uncomprehending land.

"Say, mister, you still watching that?" the bartender asked. "Some folks want to see the golf tournament."

"Good idea," Norton said, and Walter Cronkite was abruptly replaced by the comforting sight of Johnny Miller sinking a thirty-foot putt. A collective sigh filled the barroom, and even Norton felt relieved.

* * *

The next morning Jeff Fields emerged from his mansion just as Norton parked his rented Ford beside the actor's Jaguar. Norton walked over and met the actor at the foot of the steps. Fields was wearing sneakers, white linen pants, and a lime green sport shirt, and he looked nervous and distracted.

"Morning, Jeff."

The actor looked at him and laughed. "Ben, you look like hell."

"I didn't sleep well," Norton admitted. "I lay there until dawn trying to make sense of this mess. You don't look so great either."

The actor plunged his hands in his pants pockets and stared glumly at the driveway, kicking absently at a chunk of gravel.

"Something strange just happened," he said. "Just when I'd made up my mind what to do, this very strange thing happened."

"What?"

"Look, I'm going to level with you, as far as I can. You made sense yesterday. Last night, after you left, I called my lawyer and we talked a long time. Then I called somebody in Washington—I'm not going to say who—and we talked too. And finally I decided you were right, that I ought to tell the U.S. Attorney the truth about this mess and let the chips fall where they may."

"Great," Norton said.

"Then, just now, ten minutes ago, this thing happened," Fields said. "I got a phone call from the commander of the army base just outside of town. He said I had to get over there immediately, that I had a call from the White House."

"What the hell," Norton protested. "What do they want? And why can't they call you here?"

"The implication was that it was the President calling and he wanted the call on a secure phone—which the phone at the army base is and my phone isn't."

"So you're going?"

"What else can I do?"

"Jeff, even if it is the President, nothing he can say can change anything."

"Maybe not. But I have to talk to him, just as a courtesy."

"I guess you do," Norton said. "But don't let them snow you. Your position is very simple: you're going to tell the truth. Don't listen to any of this jazz about how Western civilization will collapse if Chuck Whitmore gets involved in a scandal. That's *their* problem."

"I guess so," the actor said uncertainly.

"Another thing," Norton said. "I guess I'm a little slow this morning, but why is this call coming at this particular time?"

"The only thing I can figure is that after I talked last night to my lawyer—he's in Los Angeles—and to my contact in Washington, one of them called the White House and told them what I was about to do. That's the hell of it, Ben. They hold all the cards. No matter what you do, they're one step ahead of you."

"Don't think that way," Norton said. "Don't let the bastards get you down."

"Look, I might as well get this call over with. It's about a twenty-minute drive to the base. Do you want to come with me?"

Norton threw up his hands. "I don't know. I guess so."

"I don't guess there'll be any trouble getting you in," Fields said. "It's some sort of a communication center. Top secret stuff. Come on, we'll take the Jag."

They started across the driveway to the yellow Jaguar, then Norton stopped. "Jeff, I missed breakfast, and if it's all the same with you I'll stay here and have some coffee."

"Suit yourself," the actor said. "Everything you need's in the kitchen. Try a Bloody Mary too."

"Just coffee and eggs," Norton said. "That's what I need."

"Okay, see you in an hour or so. Keep your chin up."

The actor grinned, skipped across the driveway, and slipped gracefully into the Jaguar. The engine started the first time and purred gently as Fields buckled his seat belt. Then he waved a jaunty goodbye and the car shot forward along the driveway. Norton, watching from the steps, smiled at the picture before him: the actor's perfect profile, the bold lines of the Jaguar, the freshly watered lawn sparkling in the morning sun, an instant of almost perfect beauty, and then he was falling backward as the picture exploded into a pillar of flame. Windows broke across the front of the mansion. A cloud of smoke drifted up over the lawn. Beneath it, what had been the yellow Jaguar was a knot of charred, twisted metal with fingers of flame leaping up from it. The man in the gatehouse shouted something and began running toward the ruined car. Norton picked himself up and started forward, then stopped when he noticed something small and pinkish white in the driveway. He bent down and saw it was a thumb. He stumbled toward the house and vomited into a flowerbed. Then he made himself go inside and call the police.

* * *

The Palm Springs detectives weren't finished with Norton until midafternoon. He told them he'd come to see Fields about a job. He also told them about the mysterious call from the army base, and by the time he left the police station the detectives had established at least one fact: there had been no call from the White House to the army base and no call from the army base to Fields.

Norton was still shaken when he reached the Palm Springs airport that evening, but certain facts were starting to fall into place. The bomb had been put in the car overnight; Fields's bodyguard told the police that the Jaguar had been driven the previous afternoon. That meant that somehow the killer had found out overnight that Fields intended to tell the truth about Donna's death. How? Maybe he'd called the wrong people for advice. And who was his mysterious Washington contact? Or maybe his phone had been tapped. However they'd found out, someone had slipped in and planted that bomb. And then there'd been the phony phone call at nine in the morning, timed to come just as Norton arrived, calculated to be the one message that would make Fields drop everything and hop into his Jaguar.

Norton was shaken, dazed, as he boarded his plane. Donna's death might have been unintended. Senator Nolan's could have been an accident. But Fields's death was carefully planned, cold-blooded murder. And something else: the more he thought about it, the more he was convinced that the murderer had intended for him to be blown to bits along with the unlucky actor.

26

NORTON CLIMBED out of the cab and splashed through the puddles that dotted the vast expanse of concrete in front of the federal courthouse. As water soaked his shoes and rain drenched his head and shoulders, he cursed himself for not wearing a raincoat that morning, but in truth he almost never paid attention to the weather in Washington. It had been different back home in North Carolina. There, the coming of rain meant picnics and hayrides canceled, baseball games postponed, football games played in the mud; and he had watched the sky many nights to see what havoc the elements might play on his young life. But Washington was different. He thought of Washington as a city without weather. Washington had moods instead of weather—the political commentators were its true weathermen. The mood of Washington tonight is calm. The mood of Washington tonight is tense. The mood of Washington tonight is pessimistic. Moods drifted over his adopted city instead of thunderstorms or heat waves. Politicial weather, with the barometer always falling.

Safely inside the courthouse, he asked the guard where Frank Kifner's office was. It was not the easiest of questions to answer, for Kifner shed offices the way a snake sheds skins, and each new office was always bigger and more imposing than the last. He had been a Supreme Court clerk, a Senator's legislative aide, a star of the Watergate Special Prosecutor's team, an assistant U.S. Attorney, and now the U.S. Attorney for the District of Columbia. And that was not the end of the line, not at all, for Kifner had ambitions to match his abilities. The private practice of law still lay ahead of him, and perhaps politics after that. It was an interesting progression. This year he would make his name by putting men into prison so that next year he could make his fortune by keeping other men out of prison. Then someday he might go on the bench, where he could do both, or into politics, where he could set the rules of the game.

Norton found the proper office, announced himself to an efficient black secretary, and moments later was ushered into Kifner's large, rather austere office. Kifner greeted him with a limp handshake and a cold stare. He was a small man with thinning hair and rimless glasses who gave off an aura of absolute precision.

"I'm glad you called, Ben," he began. "We've been trying to reach you."

"I was in California for a couple of days."

"I know. We've had reports from the Palm Springs police."

"Do you want to talk about that?"

"Let's settle your business first. You're representing Miss Carr?"

"That's right. And I'm as confused as Penny is. Is she the subject of an investigation? If so, what's its status? I want transcripts of your interviews with her. And I'd like to know why you never advised her of her rights. You people played it fast and loose with this girl, Frank."

Kifner was unruffled. His fingers tapped the top of his desk impatiently and his eyes stayed fixed on Norton, seeming never to blink. "She was advised of her rights," he said. "The status of the investigation is that it's closed, so far as she's concerned. If you want the transcripts, tell my secretary."

You bastard, you're like a computer, Norton thought, click-click-click, making punch cards out of people's lives.

"The investigation is closed?" Norton said. "Closed because Jeff Fields got himself blown up?"

"Closed."

"Not as far as I'm concerned," Norton said. "You people put the screws to my client for no good reason, except whatever political games you're playing."

Kifner stared back at him with a detachment that was very close to contempt. Somehow the expression reminded Norton of Whitney Stone. "Your client is an admitted drug user—"

"Come on, Frank! There are millions of—"

"Who admits attending parties where large amounts of cocaine were in view. Our investigation involved some major West Coast drug dealers."

"So you zero in on Jeff Fields, whose last picture made eight million dollars. He's dealing?"

"He was one link in the chain of evidence."

Norton chewed at his lower lip and wondered if Kifner really believed the things he was saying. "Don't you know what's going on, Frank?" he asked.

Kifner glanced impatiently at his watch, like a man who was living his life five minutes behind schedule instead of five years ahead of schedule. "Why don't you enlighten me?" he said.

"To begin with, Donna Hendricks was three months pregnant when she died. I assume you know that. And old Senator Nolan told me that Whitmore visited her in Carmel in January, three months before her death. I think they'd been having an affair and he got her pregnant and she'd come to Washington to talk to him when she was killed. And I think he or maybe Ed Murphy knows something about who killed her. All I can get from Ed is a runaround. Jeff Fields came to me a few weeks ago and said *he'd* been having an affair with Donna and had gotten her pregnant. This didn't make much sense, then I talked to Penny and found out about this drug investigation and realized it was all intended to put pressure on Fields to make him tell me he'd gotten Donna pregnant. He admitted as much to me the night before he was killed. So what

I'm suggesting, Frank, is that you'd better start worrying less about airline stewardesses who use cocaine and more about whether Fields and Senator Nolan were killed because they knew too much about Donna's death."

"All three deaths are under investigation," Kifner said calmly.

"Yeah? Who's in charge? You or Ed Murphy?"

Kifner's eyes narrowed but his expression never changed. "Remarks like that won't help you any, Ben."

"Help *me*? Frank, haven't you listened to what I've said? Don't you realize what's going on?"

"Our investigation is progressing," Kifner said. "I'm not obliged to give you all the details." Kifner looked at his watch again.

Norton was starting to feel desperate. "Frank, do you know who Byron Riddle is?"

"I know who he is, yes."

"Have you questioned him?"

"I'm not going to comment on that."

"Well, you damn well better question him, because that guy keeps turning up everywhere. He set Penny up on that drug rap—don't bother to deny it. I caught him spying on me one night. Someone who fit his description visited Senator Nolan not long before he was killed. And I'll bet my last dollar he was in Palm Springs when Fields got blown up."

"Do you have any proof of that?"

"No, damn it. You're the one in a position to get proof. There are all these loose ends and it's your job to tie them together."

"Do you have any more advice for me, Ben?"

"Yeah, I do. Get on top of this thing before it blows up in your face. Maybe the White House has been conning you, but now you've been warned. Question Ed Murphy, and Riddle, and maybe McNair and Galiano too. Get them on record, under oath. Maybe somebody will break. Maybe there's an innocent answer for all this. Maybe the President is in the dark—

he may well be—and you ought to take it straight to him. It's your move, Frank. Everything I've told you I'll repeat under oath, but the ball's in your court now."

Kifner's fingertips drummed against the top of his desk. There was no other sound in the office.

"I think I know how to do my job, Ben," he said finally. "Although it would certainly be easier if I had your remarkable powers of persuasion. People always seem to tell you the truth. Senator Nolan tells you about this mysterious assignation that no one else knows about. Jeff Fields tells you about mysterious pressures from the White House. Then they both conveniently die, and only you are left knowing the truth. Everyone else in the world seems to be crooked, Ben, except you."

Norton stood up. "Okay, Frank, I won't waste any more of your time. I thought you were trying to do an honest job."

"Sit down, Ben."

"I don't want to sit down. But let me leave you with one parting thought. I know about the tape. Fields told me about it the night before he died."

Kifner's fingers stopped drumming on the desk and he sat perfectly still for a moment, like a poker player trying to decide whether to call a bluff. "Did he tell you where it is?" he said at last.

But Norton could not push the bluff any further. You couldn't bluff a man who had the power to subpoena evidence. "No," he admitted. "No, I don't know where it is. Yet."

"Sit down, Ben."

"I've said all I have to say. I could give you details, but you obviously don't want my details."

"Sit *down*. You may be finished, but I'm not."

Norton lowered himself back into his chair.

"Whether you choose to believe it or not, Ben, we have an investigation of Miss Hendricks's death in progress. Sergeant Kravitz, the detective in charge of the investigation, is just as anxious to see the case solved as you are. Perhaps more so. Kravitz has had a breakthrough in the investigation. And since you've been so generous with your information, I think I should share our new information with you." There was a cutting edge in Kifner's voice that made Norton uneasy.

"We have a witness," Kifner continued, "who claims to have seen someone leaving the house on Volta Place around midnight on the night Miss Hendricks was murdered."

"Who is your witness?" Norton asked.

"I'm not going to identify the witness," Kifner said. "But I am going to tell you who he claims to have seen leaving the house that night."

"Okay, who was it?"

"You, Ben."

27

GABE WAS stretched out full-length on Norton's sofa with a tumbler of Scotch balanced on his belly. As he talked, he was alternately running his hand through his dandruff-filled hair and scratching dead skin from his mottled forearms.

"We're getting close," he said fervently. "My rash is starting."

"Getting close?" Norton said glumly. "Gabe, I got close to being blown to bits the other morning. It was pure dumb luck that I wasn't in that car. I'm not sure it's safe for me to go out on the street any more."

"Nobody's gonna kill you in Washington," Gabe

said, flicking his stubby fingers so that scraps of dead skin fluttered to the floor. "It's just out in the field that they pull stunts like that. Some guy bucking for a promotion, trying to impress the home office. Just think, if you'd got blown up some up-and-coming spook would have made GS-12. Back here in Washington the boys are more sophisticated. They don't plant bombs, they plant ideas—that's the way to really work a guy over."

"You're right about that," Norton said. "My old pal Frank Kifner planted some ideas with me the other morning that have just about driven me up the wall."

"Like what?"

"Well, he might have a perjury count against me, which I knew already. And then he claimed to have a witness who saw me coming out of the house on the night Donna was killed."

Gabe laughed so explosively that his drink spilled onto his pants leg. He cursed and grabbed the glass, managing in the process to knock his ashtray onto the floor. By the time he rearranged himself his smile had vanished and he stared at Norton with narrowed eyes. "Did you?" he said sharply.

"Did I what?"

"Did you come out of the house that night, you dummy?"

Norton groaned with disbelief. "No, I didn't come out of the house that night. I didn't kill her, if that's what you're thinking."

The reporter shrugged and pulled at his wet pants leg. "Stranger things have happened," he muttered.

"The thing is," Norton continued, "that Kifner wouldn't tell me who his witness is. If there really is one. I mean, he could be bluffing."

"He's not bluffing," Gabe said. He lit a Lucky and tossed the match in the general direction of the ashtray he'd spilled onto the floor.

"How do you know he's not bluffing?"

"Because I know who his witness is."

"*Who,* for Christ's sake?"

"Joey Smallwood."

"The crazy kid in the liquor store?"

"That's him. He's a professional window peeper, always prowling around Georgetown at night, and they've got him claiming he was across the street and saw you coming out."

"Some witness," Norton said bitterly. "You'd think they'd do better than that."

"They don't have to," Gabe said. "Sure, Joey's too nutty for his testimony to hold up in court, but they can ruin you just with the scandal. Or maybe they do bring a prejury charge and maybe they make it stick. You get disbarred, maybe do a year or two in the slammer, and by that time nobody's gonna listen to what you say about Donna Hendricks. The boys are putting the squeeze on you, pal."

Norton got up and poured them both another drink. Gabe stretched out on the sofa again, blowing smoke rings toward the ceiling and scratching his arms. His left wrist had begun to bleed and he licked the blood away occasionally.

"I've got a theory about this case," Gabe said after a while. "I haven't got all the details pinned down yet, but it's coming."

"Let's hear it."

To start with, you have to assume Whitmore or Murphy or somebody else in their inner circle zapped Donna. Otherwise, all this cover-up doesn't make any sense. So, what they need is a fall guy, and it looks like you've been elected."

"Why me?"

"Why not you? It makes sense—the jilted lover and all that. That's what that phone call to you telling you Donna was dead was all about. To make you do exactly what you did—dash to the scene and get the cops interested in you."

"Who do you think called me?"

"My guess would be Riddle. He's up to his ears in this thing. But—and here's where things get complicated—then Joey comes along. The nutty kid who waited on her in the liquor store and maybe followed her home or something. Joey, not having a law degree, or even much sense, figures to be an even better fall guy than you, so I figure they change strategies in midstream. Frame Joey."

"Then why have they now got Joey saying I did it?"

"Because, one, he's got an All-American Mom who swears he was home that night, and, two, you're such a pain in the ass they figure they'll shut you up."

"Okay, Gabe, but if they're trying to frame me for the murder, why did they try to blow me up the other day? Or doesn't your theory extend that far?"

"It gets a little fuzzy there," Gabe admitted. "Somebody might have figured that it'd be easier to frame you if you were dead. *In absentia,* so to speak."

Gabe took a swallow of his drink and then chewed at a hangnail for a minute. "Or," he said finally, "it could be that there's one bunch trying to frame you and another bunch trying to kill you. You never want to underestimate the fuck-up factor when you're dealing with the government."

They sat in silence for a moment, Gabe chewing on his hangnail, Norton pondering his uncertain future. "One thing I'm wondering," he said after a moment, "is whether Joey really saw *somebody* coming out of the house and honestly thought it was me."

"Use your head," Gabe said scornfully. "All that kid saw was the light. Either he puts you at the scene or they put him at the scene. Even a loony can figure that out, if they lean on him long enough."

Norton wondered how Gabe knew who the witness was, but he knew better than to inquire about his sources. He had an idea it was Sergeant Kravitz. The week before, Gabe had written a long feature article about Kravitz that portrayed him as the very model of a resourceful homicide investigator, and Norton knew that Gabe, like most political reporters, rarely flattered anyone in public life without a *quid pro quo*.

"You know, it's damned interesting that Kifner told me about this witness at all. Under the rules of evidence, you don't have to tell a defendant about a witness against him until his trial starts. So it's like Frank was doing me a favor."

"I don't trust the bastard," Gabe said.

"I don't either, but I trust his sense of self-interest. I told him enough about Donna and Whitmore to shake him up, I hope. He's got to be thinking about what happens to him if this thing breaks the wrong way."

"That's something else," the reporter said. "This thing could break fast. Any day now. Because ever since Fields got himself blown up, some reporters have started putting two and two together. I figure in a week or so somebody might write a story asking if Donna's death and Fields's death and Senator Nolan's death weren't connected. And they might toss you in as the link connecting all three of them. They might even have the bit about Joey seeing you leave the scene. Except they're not going to break it, I am. I'll hold off as long as I can, but I'm not gonna get beat on this."

Norton sighed wearily. "Damn it, Gabe, I don't understand how the media works. After Jeff Fields got killed, I figured every reporter in the country would link his death up with Donna's and the whole thing would start to unravel. Instead, I pick up this morning's paper and there's this idiot story about the *Mafia* killing Fields. 'Sources close to the case . . . unpaid gambling debt . . . mob-style execution . . . blah-blah-blah.' I couldn't believe it."

"Why not?" Gabe said. "That's all the Mafia is, a whipping boy for the FBI and the CIA to use when they get theirselves in a jam."

"It's *what?*"

"Look, Billy Blue-eyes, the Mafia ain't nothing but a figment of J. Edgar Hoover's imagination. Him and his PR-boys took a couple of hundred pot-bellied low-life Eye-talian hoods and pimps and bootleggers and blew them up into the International Crime Syndicate, which they then informed a trembling nation was second only to International Godless Communism as a threat to Home, Flag and Mother. Hell, the FBI's got more PR-men than agents, and they spend half their time building up the Mafia Menace in books and movies and TV shows, so they can soften up Congress to give them more money so the FBI honchos can ride around in Lincolns and fly around in Lear jets."

"Gabe," Norton protested, "are you saying there *isn't* a Mafia?"

"I'm saying that the Mafia, as an institution, is about as big a menace to public safety as the Boy Scouts, and is one hell of a lot less of a menace than the people who make cigarettes or the people who make those big dangerous goddam Detroit automobiles or the American Medical Association. Hell, those damn doctors kill a hundred times as many people every year as the Mafia does, and they deal in two hundred times as much dope, and they charge more for it too. The lousy bastards."

Norton looked at Gabe with interest; there was something more than the usual cynicism in his voice.

"You don't like doctors, Gabe?"

Gabe turned on Norton the coldest stare he had ever seen. "A doctor killed my mother and charged my old man thirty thousand bucks for it," he said. "And then my old man killed himself trying to pay the bastard off. Yeah, you might say I don't like doctors. Among other pillars of our society. But that's not your worry."

Gabe killed his drink and after a moment Norton did the same. "Okay, Gabe," he said, "the Justice Department or the U.S. Attorney's office or somebody is putting out this story about the Mafia killing Fields. So what does that prove?"

"For one thing, it proves once more the truth of Pincus's Law."

"Which is?"

"Which is, and I quote, 'The more vigorously a politician denies a given assertion, the more likely that assertion is to be true.' As for example, 'We seek no wider war' or 'I shall never resign' or 'I am not a crook' and et cetera. In the case at hand, if you go poking around the White House, the line they're putting out is that Whitmore never heard of Jeff Fields, or maybe, just *maybe,* he might have shook his hand once or twice on the campaign. And since that's a dirty and demonstrable lie, they got the U.S. Attorney's office to trot out the Mafia story, in hopes that a crime-crazed media will swallow it, which most of the idiots will. But the bottom line, my friend, is that they're scared shitless of somebody making the linkup between Fields and Whitmore and Donna."

"But who is 'they'?" Norton asked, with something close to agony in his voice. "Is it Whitmore? Murphy? Kifner? Riddle? Who the hell is running this damn show?"

Gabe shrugged and spit a sliver of hangnail onto the floor. "That, in case you hadn't noticed yet, is what we're trying to find out. We don't know yet. But, like I said, it's best to assume the worst. I wouldn't want you being disillusioned later on."

Norton slumped forward and stared at his shoes for a while. They needed shining. Then he remembered something.

"Gabe, listen. Jeff Fields told me something I forgot to tell you about. That last afternoon, when he wanted to talk to me but was afraid to, he kept saying something about a tape."

"He said *what?*"

"What he said was something like 'This isn't my problem . . . If it just wasn't for that damn tape.' He wouldn't explain, but he was worried as hell."

"Holy shit," Gabe cried. "Then it's true."

"What's true?"

"One of my sources had heard about the tape, but he didn't know what to make of it."

"What to make of *what?*"

"See, when the cops searched the house on Volta Place, they found this fancy voice-activated taping system. Anything you said in that house was taped. Or could be."

"What for?"

"Who knows? Maybe Fields liked to pick up dialogue for his movies that way. Maybe he was just dirty-minded and liked to know what his friends aid in bed. Maybe he planned to set up politicians with girls there and play some blackmail games. Maybe all of the above. I don't know. The point is that the cops found the taping system but no tapes. Fields claimed he'd never used the system—never put any tape in it —but he could have been lying. From what you say, it sounds like he was. Which means the whole damn murder may be on tape and the tape is still floating around somewhere."

He paused to lick some blood from his wrist. Norton stared at him in disbelief. "Gabe, if there was a tape, and the killer found it, the first thing he'd have done would be to destroy it. That's as plain as the nose on your face."

"Then why was Fields worried about it?" Gabe shot back.

"I don't know," Norton admitted. "It doesn't make sense."

"It makes sense if it wasn't the killer who found the tape," Gabe said. "If somebody else found it, and if Whitmore was somehow involved, then that tape would be worth a nice little bundle. That makes plenty of sense."

"How do you mean?"

"I mean money. I mean whenever anything strange happens in this city and you can't figure out why, don't look for sex or revenge or glory or jealousy or anything like that to be the reason. Just keep your eye on the money, because that's why people do things in this place. And that tape would be worth a pretty penny, my friend. Next to the Hoover file, that'd be just about the hottest item on the market."

"Wait a minute, Gabe, wait a minute. How would

somebody else—someone other than the killer—have got his hands on the tape?"

"Look, there was eight or ten hours between the time she was killed and when the paperboy found her. A lot of people could have gone clomping through there in that much time. I don't know who. But the point is we know what we're looking for. A tape."

Norton sat slumped forward with his chin cradled in his hands. "What do you think we should do next?" he asked.

"I'll call Fields's lawyer and the Palm Springs police and see if I can shake anything out of them. You talk to McNair again. See if you can find out where Riddle is. The son of a bitch has disappeared."

"He'll turn up," Norton said. "I'll bet anything he was the one who planted that bomb in Fields's car."

"He might have," Gabe said. "I found out some stuff about Riddle. You wanta hear the story?"

"Sure. You want another drink first?"

"Don't mind if I do," Gabe said and lit a Lucky while Norton refilled their glasses. "The thing is," he began, "that the guy we call Byron Riddle has reached a point where nobody knows exactly who he is. Probably *he* doesn't know any more.

"But, I think that the guy who now calls himself Riddle used to be called Bob Caldwell. A guy by that name who looks like Riddle was in the Yale class of 'fifty-four. Back then it was real fashionable for young Yalies to join the CIA. It was kinda like joining the Peace Corps after Kennedy came in. Actually, as I got the story, this guy Caldwell didn't join right away. He spent a couple of years trying to write the Great American Novel, and when that didn't pan out he gave up and joined the Agency. After that things get sketchy. I *think* he was involved in the Bay of Pigs. And he *may* have been in jail in Cuba for a while. Anyway, he turned up in Washington in the mid-sixties. His specialty was communications. Radios, wiretaps, bugging. He had a cover job, working in some phony PR agency. And when he wasn't tapping phones, he was back at writing novels. Except now he's into spy thrillers. I read a couple of them. They weren't bad. Lotsa sex. But the plot was always the same—the heroic agent out in the field being double-crossed by the cowardly paper shufflers back in Washington. The Bay of Pigs syndrome.

"Anyway, as I get the story, Riddle began to go off the deep end a few years back. I don't know why. Maybe he was frustrated. Maybe he was just crazy. But the word got around the Agency that he'd do more that tap phones for you."

"What do you mean?" Norton asked.

"I mean he'd zap the guy using the phone, if that seemed to serve the cause of freedom. He was on some hit squad they had. So there you are. An ex-Yalie who hates Commies and bureaucrats and lives in a fantasy world and doesn't mind bumping somebody off now and then."

"It's just fantastic, Gabe."

"It's not fantastic," the reporter shot back. "The trouble is, you only know the upper crust in this town. They're bad enough, but lift up the rocks sometime and take a look at all those consultants and lobbyists and political hustlers and private-eye types crawling around down there. By their standards Riddle was a pretty high-type guy. He'd been to college and liked to talk about F. Scott Fitzgerald—he just happened to kill people sometimes."

"Okay, Gabe, but how does a guy like that make the jump to the White House?"

"The way I get the story, Riddle hooked up with your distinguished employer, Whit Stone. Don't ask me how, but Riddle started doing odd jobs for Stone —who, if you didn't know it, has plenty of lines to the Old Boy network that's always run the Agency. Anyway, Stone uses Riddle to tap phones, deliver money, stuff like that. And eventually Riddle gets himself a new cover. Opens an office as a private investigator. Gets respectable."

"Okay, but what about the White House?"

"I'm getting there. Whitmore got nominated last summer, right? Before that, Stone and his oil-industry pals had been backing another horse, but they jumped on the Whitmore bandwagon fast. Stone brings in money, lawyers who want to volunteer their services, et cetera. And one of the et ceteras was Byron Riddle. He signed on to help with crowds, advance work, security, all that stuff, and naturally he did a hell of a job. But that still didn't mean he was going to amount to anything after Whitmore got elected, even with Whit Stone pushing for him. He might have got stuck over at the Treasury or something like that, but that's when—"

"That's when Riddle pulled his hero act on Inauguration Day," Norton said.

"Right. You remember it? The crazed assassin slips onto the White House grounds with a suitcase full of TNT, and fearless Byron Riddle ambles over and disarms him. Thereby winning himself a job in the White House. Very, very neat."

"Well, the guy *does* have guts," Norton said.

"Like hell he does," Gabe said. "The whole thing was a setup."

"What?"

"Sure. I checked up on the so-called crazed assassin yesterday. He spent a month at St. Elizabeth's, until everything quieted down, then he disappeared. I'm telling you, Whit Stone and the CIA really wanted their boy Riddle inside the White House. And they got him there. And it looks like it paid off for them, at least it did if Riddle got them the goods on Chuck Whitmore."

"You mean you think . . . ?"

"I think that Riddle's either got something on Whitmore, something about him and Donna, or he's trying his damnedest to get it. And that means it's dirty pool we're playing, Buster. Riddle may think he's fighting the fires of Bolshevism, but Whit Stone and his crowd know what *they're* after. Money. They'd like to bleed this country white. Look what they did with Nixon.

Contributed five or ten million to his campaign, then when the time was ripe the bastards doubled the price of oil, and practically everything else, which was worth God knows how many billions to them. Jesus, can you imagine what they'd do if they had something big on a President? Like a *murder rap?* Listen, they'd have us paying five dollars for a gallon of gas. And that ain't all. The CIA would want its pound of flesh. Like there were some mighty sad spooks when Big Chuck closed down the assassination bureau. Christ, there's fellows over there who don't know how to do nothing but bump off radicals. You think they wouldn't blackmail Whitmore to get back in business? And there's Riddle himself. I heard he's got this fantasy of being Director of Central Intelligence."

"Jesus Christ," Norton whispered.

"Pretty, ain't it?" Gabe said. "Just like they taught you in your civics class. Democracy in action."

28

FRANK KIFNER called the next morning and said he wanted Norton to testify before the grand jury the next week. He was quite precise and business-like; he wasn't obliged to give any particulars and he didn't. After their talk Norton sat at his desk for a while brooding over a number of things, among them what he should do about his employer, Whitney Stone. The situation had become impossible. Norton was about to call Stone when Stone, as was his habit, one-upped him. His secretary called and in the most frigid of voices announced that Mr. Stone wished to see Mr. Norton immediately.

This time when Norton entered his boss's office, there were no smiles, handshakes, or offers of Scotch, only Whit Stone coiled behind his desk with his hooded eyes glowing like coals in the dimly lit office.

"You have a problem with the grand jury, I understand," he began.

"An appointment. Not a problem."

"I would call it a problem," Stone said. "Or perhaps your problem is Washington, Ben. Perhaps you need to get away for a while. Perhaps you need time for reflection."

"Maybe so," Norton said. "But not until I finish what I've started."

"The question, Ben, is whether you can continue your, ah, *investigation* in association with this firm."

"I agree."

Stone's eyes showed a glimmer of surprise. "Perhaps a leave of absence . . ." he began.

"No, not a leave of absence. I think the situation calls for a clean break. In other words, I quit."

Stone leaned back in his chair. Norton guessed he was overjoyed to be rid of him so easily. "Well, Ben, if that's your decision, and I'm sure you know what's best for you, I think some severance agreement could be worked out."

"I don't want any more of your money, Stone. Not a dime. All I want is to take this opportunity to say that you may be the sorriest, crookedest son of a bitch it's ever been my misfortune to encounter."

Stone shot up out of his chair. "Get out of here," he snapped. "Get out before I have you thrown out."

Thus ended Norton's association with the firm of Coggins, Copeland, and Stone. Five minutes later he had cleaned out his desk and was in a phone booth on M Street calling Annie.

"Guess what?" he began.

"You're hopelessly in love with me."

"Worse than that. I'm unemployed. Whit Stone and I just reached the parting of ways."

"Wonderful."

"What's more, the grand jury wants to see me."

"You've had a busy morning."

"Fridays are always bad," he said. "But last night was good. Or did I tell you that?"

"Tell me again."

"Last night was beautiful. You were incredible."

"You were pretty good yourself. Would you be interested in a return engagement this evening?"

"I don't think so, Annie. I've got a lead I've got to follow up. But how about lunch tomorrow? I've got an errand on the Mall in the afternoon."

"Hey, is tomorrow the kite-flying day?"

"Maybe so. There's some kind of folklore festival going on. And maybe we could stop by the Hirshhorn."

"Sounds great."

"I'll call you later."

"Okay. Bye."

She had a sudden breathless way of saying that final "bye" that always left him reeling. In fact, a lot about her left him reeling. They'd gone to bed a second time, and this time there'd been no problem. If there'd been spies hiding under the bed, he hadn't known or cared. He wondered if it was insane for him to be falling in love in the midst of all this madness. Maybe not. Maybe it was one of the few sane things that anyone was doing in Washington these days.

* * *

At six that evening Norton parked his car in front of a comfortable brick house on a quiet tree-lined street in one of the Maryland suburbs. He double-checked the address, crossed the well-kept lawn, and knocked on the door.

When Jane McNair opened the door and greeted

him with a shy, quizzical smile, he knew her at once, for he had known women like her all his life. He knew she had progressed from dutiful daughter to teacher's pet to sorority president to blushing debutante to virgin bride to loyal wife, devoted mother, and Junior Leaguer. She looked nice, decent, innocent; and from the first he liked her and felt sorry for her.

"Mrs. McNair, I'm Ben Norton. Is your husband home?"

She looked confused. "Have you tried his office?"

"They said he'd left," Norton lied. "And in any event, it's a personal matter, one I'd just as soon not discuss at his office."

"I'm sorry," she said, "but what was your name?"

"Ben Norton."

"Yes, I think Clay has mentioned you."

"We've talked several times. I'm a lawyer."

"You were a friend of the woman who was killed, weren't you?"

"That's right."

"Is that what you want to talk to him about?"

He made a show of hestitation. "Not exactly," he said. "You see, Mrs. McNair, I think your husband may be in some trouble. But I don't want to bother you with it."

He took a step back, as if to leave, and she pushed open the screen door.

"Please come in, Mr. Norton. Perhaps we should talk. Clay should be home any moment. He promised to be home early tonight." She smiled. "It's our anniversary, and we're going out to dinner."

He followed her into a living room that looked anything but lived-in. She motioned Norton to the sofa and sat down across from him in a straight-backed chair, face somber, back straight, knees together, ankles crossed, the very model of a proper young matron.

"Now, Mr. Norton . . ." she began.

"Ben."

"Ben. Please call me Jane. And please tell me what kind of trouble you think my husband is in."

"I'm not sure it's right—"

"Not sure it's right to worry the helpless little wife? Ben, let me tell *you* something. I think my husband has been in trouble ever since he set foot in this city. I think it's destroying him. I don't mean the ulcers. They can treat ulcers. But they can't treat what all the pressure and all the cynicism and all the self-seeking do to a person's mind and heart and soul. I know my husband. He's not a great man or even a brilliant man, but he's a decent man. Or wants to be. He works hard to provide for his family. The trouble is, he measures success in terms of money. But I see his job . . . this city . . . *politics* . . . turning him into a machine. A very efficient, effective machine, I'm sure, but the job gets all his time and energy and what's left over is only a shell of the man I married. So don't be afraid to tell me anything, Ben. Nothing you could say could disturb me more than I'm already disturbed."

Norton liked her more, and for a moment hated himself for the game he was playing with her. It was always like this in the Washington wars; it was the noncombatants who suffered the most.

"Of course, Clay would say I'm naïve," she continued. "He would say I don't understand the political world. Clay and I come from quite different backgrounds, really. He's more accustomed to the rough and tumble of the world. I'm afraid I led rather a sheltered life before I married him. So I see Washington as a jungle, while he sees it as exciting and challenging. I don't know who's right."

"Perhaps you're both right. Jungles can be exciting and challenging."

"If you're a savage," she said bitterly. "Or a politician."

"It's a destructive place," Norton said. "Destructive of most men and almost all marriages."

"But why does it have to be like that?"

"Why? Perhaps because ours is a competitive society. We compete in the playground, in school, in sports, in sex, in business, in politics, in just about everything, and there happen to be a few places, like Washington or Wall Street or Hollywood, where the stakes are highest so the competition is the most ferocious. Let's say your husband was making twenty-five thousand a year when he went to work at the White House. If he plays his cards right, he'll leave there for a job making two or three times that. But to do that he's got to give it everything he's got, because if he won't there are a hundred others who will."

The front door burst open and two young girls appeared, talking and laughing excitedly. When they saw Norton they fell silent and looked at their mother expectantly.

"Girls, this is Mr. Norton," she said formally. "These are my daughters, Emily and Anne."

Each child stepped forward in turn, extended her hand, and said "I'm very pleased to meet you" in a polite singsong.

"Go have some milk now," their mother said, "while Mr. Norton and I finish our talk."

"They're lovely children," Norton said.

"Lovely children who are having terrible problems because they don't understand why they don't have a father any more. But I'm boring you with my problems, Ben. Tell me what trouble it is you think my husband's in."

"I'm not entirely sure," Norton said. "He may not have done anything wrong at all. But he may be in the middle of something he doesn't understand. It all relates to Donna Hendricks's death. I think there are people in the White House who know more about it than they've told the authorities. I think one of them may be a man named Byron Riddle who shares an office with your husband."

Jane McNair shut her eyes for a moment. "Yes," she said, "I might have known he'd be part of the trouble."

"You know Riddle?"

"We met once, which was quite enough. He was extremely rude to me, for no apparent reason. But that's nothing compared to the difficulties Clay has had with him. Clay came home about two weeks ago more shaken than I've ever seen him and it all had something to do with that man."

"How shaken?"

"How? His face was white as a sheet. His hands were trembling. He could hardly talk. He was even sick at his stomach. All he would tell me was that he'd had an argument with Byron Riddle. The very next day he arranged to change offices."

"Didn't he ever tell you the specifics of their argument? Or anything about what Riddle was involved in?"

Jane McNair frowned in concentration, and two small vertical lines marred her quite lovely brow.

"No," she said at last. "Only that Riddle was some kind of investigator. And that he was a lone wolf but valuable sometimes. He kept calling Riddle a 'madman' and saying he wasn't going to have anything more to do with him. He kept saying, 'I'm just going to mind my own business.' "

She seemed close to tears. Norton wondered if he should leave. She looked at him and seemed to read his mind.

"I'm being a terrible hostess. Let me fix us a drink. Clay really should be here any moment."

"Well," Norton began, thinking that a drink sounded good, and then the front door opened again and Clay McNair stepped in.

"Hi honey," he began, then he saw Norton and his expression passed in distinct stages from weariness to surprise to geniality. But he still looked tired beneath his boyish smile as he crossed the room with his hand outstretched.

"Well, Ben, to what do we owe this honor?"

Norton stood up to shake hands. "I wanted to talk

to you. Your wife was kind enough to invite me in to wait."

"We were just about to have a drink," Jane Mc-Nair said. "What would you like, Clay? I'll get them."

"No, honey, that's my job," McNair said. "What's your pleasure, Ben?"

"A Scotch and water would be great."

"Honey?"

"A martini, please."

"Coming up," McNair said cheerfully, and as he started out of the room his daughters raced in to greet him. He picked each girl up and kissed her, and they followed him happily into the kitchen.

"He tries," Jane McNair said sadly. "He really does try." They sat in silence, listening to the girls' laughter and the clink of ice into glasses in the kitchen, then McNair reappeared with the drinks and the girls went quietly upstairs. McNair sat down on the opposite end of the sofa.

"Well, Ben, I'm afraid Jane and I have to go out soon for a little celebration, so perhaps we'd better have our talk right away. Honey, if you'll excuse us . . ."

"No, Clay, I think I should stay. Ben and I have already talked some, and this seems to concern me too."

McNair frowned and took a sip of his drink, which was several shades lighter than the one he'd mixed Norton. "Well, what is this mysterious business?"

"Clay, you know that I'm trying to find out about Donna's death, and I'm convinced there are people in the White House, including Ed Murphy, perhaps including the President, who know more than they've admitted. And I have reason to believe that this man Byron Riddle is deeply involved in whatever's going on. I've found out some things about his background that prove he's a dangrous man. All I'm asking you to do, for your own safety, is to tell me whatever you know about him."

McNair gripped his drink tightly and shook his

head. "I can't tell you anything. I shared an office with him for a while, but I don't know anything about his work."

"What was the argument you had? Why did you change offices? Why did you tell Jane 'I'm just going to mind my own business'?"

McNair looked angrily at his wife. "Honey, what have you been telling him?"

"Only the truth, Clay. That's what you should do. Whatever's happened, just tell the truth. You have no reason to protect that man."

"She's right, Clay. Why protect Riddle? Would he do it for you? What's that guy up to?"

McNair stood up. "I think the question right now is what you're up to. You had no right to barge in here and take advantage of her—that's what you did, don't deny it. I want you to leave now. If you have questions, talk to Ed Murphy. I don't mean to be rude, but that's all I have to say to you."

Norton got up slowly. "You're making a mistake, Clay. This thing is going to break wide open and—"

"It's none of my affair."

"Clay . . ." his wife began.

"Keep out of this, Jane. You don't know anything about it. Good night, Norton."

Norton shrugged and started for the door. "Good night, Jane," he said. "Thanks for the hospitality."

The last thing Norton saw was Jane McNair staring helplessly at her angry husband. McNair shut the door behind him, and he walked to his car. Some little girls playing hopscotch next door looked at him and smiled. He drove away wondering if McNair might change his mind after he'd had time to think it over.

But inside the house, Clay McNair was far from changing his mind. "Jane, you had no business letting that fellow barge in here and pump you about my affairs."

"Clay, it sounded to me like he's trying to *help* you."

"Help me? He's the one who's in trouble. The grand jury has called him to testify next week. I'll bet he didn't tell you *that*. Don't you see? He's just looking for a way to protect himself."

"Clay what *do* you know about Riddle?"

"Nothing."

"You told me yourself he was crazy. Now you act like you're afraid of him. What *is* it?"

McNair paced about the room in frustration. "What is it? Do you really want to know? Okay, I'll tell you what it is. Byron Riddle threatened to *kill* me. That's why I changed offices. And that's why I'm staying out of whatever it is that's going on. I don't know anything and I don't *want* to know anything." He sat down on the sofa with his head in his hands.

She crossed the room and sat down beside him, reaching out to touch his hand. "*Kill* you, Clay? Surely he was joking."

McNair jumped to his feet. "He *wasn't* joking! Can't you understand? He beat me up. He pointed a gun at me. He *would* kill me, that's what I'm trying to tell you."

"But why?"

"I can't tell you."

"You must."

"Darn it, I *can't!* It's . . . it's politics. I can't explain it. I'll just have to live with it."

"Live with it? With a man threatening to kill you? Clay, either you tell me what this is all about, or I'll . . . I'll take the girls and go somewhere where people are sane and there's no talk of killing people."

McNair groaned and slumped back down on the sofa. His world seemed to be falling apart. Why wouldn't people just leave him alone, just let him do his work?

"Jane, I happened to look into Riddle's desk once and there was a tape recording inside it that had something to do with Donna Hendricks. He caught me and that's when he threatened to kill me if I told anyone. And he would. And that's why I've got to stay out of this."

Jane McNair eased herself down in a Queen Anne chair that had been one of their wedding presents fourteen years before. "Clay, you must tell this to . . . to someone. To Norton or the police or someone."

"I can't," he moaned. "I can't." He sat there dejectedly, staring at the beige carpet, unable to make any sense of what was happening to him. Now, more than ever, he thought the world was mad.

29

THEY TOOK a cab to the Hill and had lunch in one of the Senate restaurants; the bean soup there was one of Norton's few enduring passions. After lunch they walked across to the Capitol and descended the long flight of marble steps that led to the Mall. It was the start of the Memorial Day weekend, and stretched out before them on its long grassy expanse they could see hundreds of tourists moving between the museums, out-of-state cars circling about in an endless search for nonexistent parking places and, far down by the Washington Monument, a bright swarm of kites dotting the sky.

They stopped at Fifth Street. "What'll it be?" Norton asked. "The Hirshhorn or the National Gallery? My God, this'd be a great city to visit."

"How's our time?" Annie asked.

"Not too good. I want to get down to this folk festival in a half hour or so."

"Let's just wander through the Sculpture Garden then. I don't want to be rushed."

She took his hand and they started to the left, toward the Hirshhorn.

"Have you ever done the Hirshhorn high?" Annie asked.

"Not yet."

"We had a picnic on the Mall once and smoked some grass and then I went and spent an hour standing in front of one of the Jackson Pollocks. I'd never gotten into him before—I'd just seen all these little squiggles of color—but this time the picture actually came alive. The colors were moving and all that energy was pouring out of it and grabbing me . . . I felt like I was being *ravished*."

"Cheap thrills," Norton said grumpily, and they entered the Sculpture Garden and moved slowly a-mong its nudes, fallen warriors, giant mobiles, stone saints and sinners, past the Picasso baby carriage, around Rodin's majestic "Burghers of Calais," finally stopping in the shadow of the great brooding Balzac.

"It's too much," she said. "If there's a heaven, it'll be like this."

"Maybe God will turn out to be like Joe Hirshhorn," Norton mused. "A lovable little stock manipulator who collects statues. Let's go get some ice cream."

They crossed the museum's crowded plaza, tossed pennies in the fountain, circled the doughnut-shaped building, bought two Good Humor bars from a surly Puerto Rican, then returned to the Mall. Norton led them to a grove of trees near Twelfth Street where two dozen teenagers had set up an outdoor bazaar. Their wares were displayed on card tables and Indian blankets: pottery, paintings, leather goods, shawls, jewelry. The makers of these wares stood quietly be-hind them, strangely passive salesmen with blissful smiles and innocent eyes.

"They're retarded," Norton explained. "It's some sort of special program. Joey Smallwood is supposed to be here, but I don't see him."

They walked slowly down the line of tables. Annie bought a dozen ceramic cups and an Indian necklace. One boy told Norton that Joey Smallwood was expected later.

"What now?" Annie asked.

"Let's leave and come back."

"Where to?"

"I've never been in there," he said, pointing to a big building that stood between the Mall and Constitution Avenue."

"Neither have I. What is it?"

"The Museum of History and Technology."

"What's that mean?"

"I don't know. Let's go see."

The museum proved to be an amazing treasure house of everything, from the world's biggest American flag to model ships, antique cars, and a huge statue of George Washington clad as Jove. Upstairs, they explored a room devoted to a history of the media. They stepped into a tiny movie theater that showed newsreels of FDR's "nothing to fear but fear itself" speech and of grinning young Americans sailing off to fight the Second World War. They passed on to a circle of old television sets which showed Joe McCarthy denouncing communists in government, Ike playing golf, JFK's Inaugural Address, LBJ promising a Great Society, and grinning young Americans sailing off to fight the war in Vietnam. Norton grabbed Annie's arm and pulled her toward the door.

"What's the matter?" she asked.

"Nothing," he said. "Except that my whole life is back there and I don't want to look at it."

He led her back to the bazaar in the grove of trees. "That's Joey," he whispered. "The one in the baseball cap."

"He looks so sad."

"Let's go talk to him."

Joey Smallwood was selling brightly colored crude paintings of horses, houses, and children at play. He beamed as Annie examined them.

"I love your colors," she said. "Have you been painting long?"

Joey seemed confused by the question. "Sort of," he said. "They say it's good for me."

"I'd like to buy this one," she said, pointing to a picture of two children playing in a wheatfield. "How much is it?"

"You can have it if you like it," Joey said.

"No," Annie protested. "Here, take this." She handed him a ten-dollar bill. He put it in his pocket without looking at it.

Norton stepped forward and faced the boy. "Joey, do you know me?"

Joey took a step back and began to tremble.

"Do you know me?" Norton repeated. "Have you ever seen me before?"

"Maybe."

"Where?"

"I don't know. Somewhere. Are you a policeman?"

"No, Joey, I'm not a policeman. But you've been telling the police some things about me that aren't true."

Joey turned and began to run across the Mall. They watched him dart between tourists until he disappeared over by the old Smithsonian Building.

"Did you have to scare him?" she asked.

"I wanted to see what he'd say. It might have helped."

"It was cruel."

"Look, they're using him to frame me on a murder rap."

"Well, let's get out of here now. What about his pictures?"

Norton stacked Joey's pictures and asked the girl at the next table to watch them.

As they turned to go, a short husky man with a crewcut stepped into their path. "Hello, Ben."

"Hello, Nick."

"I want to talk to you."

"Talk."

"Alone."

Annie looked from Nick Galiano's face to Norton's and shrugged elaborately. "I get the hint," she said. "I'll meet you in the Sculpture Garden."

"I won't be long," he said. "Here, I'll carry that."

He took the bulky sack containing the coffee cups and Joey's picture and watched as she walked, long-legged and graceful, across the Mall. Then he turned back to Galiano. "Okay, Nick, what's on your mind?"

"I hate to see you making such a fool of yourself," Nick said. "I hear you're out of a job now."

"Don't worry about it."

"I'm not losing sleep. But there's no sense in it. The Boss feels bad about it."

"Did he send you to see me?"

"The thing is, if you'd stop making waves, if you'd just use your head, there wouldn't be any problem. Hell, Ben, you could come back to work for us. Just like the old days."

"The old days are dead and buried, Nick."

"You're gonna be dead and buried, pal, when that grand jury gets through with you."

"I don't think so. I think it's some other people who ought to be worrying."

"You're making trouble," Galiano muttered. "And you're asking for trouble."

They walked along in silence for a while. They were nearing the National Gallery and for a moment Norton watched the endless line of tourists swarming up and down its steps. He wished he was with them, instead of here on the sidewalk arguing with a court jester who wasn't funny any more.

"Have you said all you've got to say, Nick? If you have, just tell your friend that I'm still digging."

Galiano stopped walking and the two men turned to face each other. "You've got it all wrong," Galiano said. "The Boss ain't worried about this thing. He hardly knows what's going on. You're the one who keeps blowing this thing up."

Norton was fed up. "Nick, I'm sick of hearing

about 'the Boss.' He may be your boss. He may be your meal ticket. He may be the President—I know that. But the laws apply to him too, just like the rest of us."

Galiano leaned forward until his face was close to Norton's. "You piss me off, Ben," he whispered. "You really piss me off."

For a minute Norton thought Nick was going to hit him. He tensed, ready for the blow, ready to punch back, but instead Nick abruptly turned away and began walking rapidly toward the Capitol.

Norton watched him for a moment, then started across the Mall to the Hirshhorn, where he found Annie sitting on a bench in the Sculpture Garden staring at Rodin's Balzac. He took her hand and they started back up the Mall toward the Washington Monument. The kite-flying contest was still going on, with the kites dipping and soaring against a pillar of clouds tinted pink by the late afternoon sun.

"It's such a damned beautiful city," he said. "It would be so great if . . ." He stopped, searching for the right words. "If only people weren't crazy."

Annie laughed. "You're wrong," she said. "If people weren't crazy, this city wouldn't even be here."

He squeezed her hand and watched the soaring kites and tried his best to forget about Nick Galiano.

* * *

A few blocks away Charles Whitmore was standing in front of his bedroom mirror and fumbling with his black tie. He cursed, jerked it loose, and was starting to tie it a third time when there was a soft knock at the door.

"Charles?"

"Come on in."

Claire Whitmore stepped into the room and smiled at her husband's plight.

"Let me do that," she said. He sighed and lifted

his chin while she deftly knotted his tie for him. "We could get you a valet, you know," she said.

"I tried that first one," he said. "I didn't mind him laying out my shirts and stuff like that, but the guy would hang around, all poised for action, and whenever I started to put my pants on, he'd run over and try to hold 'em for me. Jesus Christ, can you imagine such a thing? One man holding another man's *pants* for him? Course, he was English. Jeeves? Cleeves? I think probably that's what's wrong with England—too many politicians over there got valets holding their pants for 'em."

"I suppose that might be part of it," his wife said. "Everything set downstairs?"

"Everything's fine," she said. "The Rose Garden looks lovely and the weather is going to be perfect."

Whitmore slipped on his tuxedo jacket and admired himself in the mirror. "You ever met the king before?" he asked.

"Not really."

"He's not a bad guy. A little stiff at first, but you get a few drinks down him and he loosens up. The last time I saw him I told him the one about 'Tuesday is your day in the barrel' and he just about split his gut."

"It should be an interesting party," Claire Whitmore said. "No thanks to your Mr. Murphy."

"What does that mean?"

"It means that when we decided to have the dinner outdoors, which meant we could invite a few more people, I sent Elizabeth to clear the new guests with Ed Murphy and he was rude and recalcitrant. Really, Charles, I realize that Ed's boorishness can be useful to you sometimes, but when he's rude to my social secretary it's the same as being rude to me."

"I'll speak to him," Whitmore said. "He's had a lot on his mind lately."

"I'm sure he has," she said.

"You want some sherry?" he asked.

"If we have time, please."

"We have time," he said and poured them each a glass of sherry. They sat down in chairs that faced out over the South Lawn.

"Isn't that pretty?" she said. "The kites in the sunset, with the Monument behind them."

"Yeah," he said absently. He was wondering why she'd come to see him. Small talk was not part of their relationship.

"Any other complaints?" he said. "Besides Ed Murphy, I mean. Or constructive criticism? Or compliments?"

She smiled and tried to look surprised. "Well, I thought your speech last night was excellent."

"Thanks."

"And I think your entire handling of the school-construction bill has been brilliant."

"I hear you've been pretty brilliant yourself," he said. "Ed told me about your session with the—what do you call them, female Congresspeople? Anyway, he said you knocked 'em dead."

"They're human, Charles. They're middle-aged women, most of them, who like to be listened to and perhaps flattered a bit. If you'd turn your famous charm on them I'm sure you'd have them eating out of your hand."

"Just what I need," he said and laughed, and they sat in silence for a moment, watching the kites bobbing against the sunset.

"Charles," she said finally.

"Yeah?"

"There *is* something."

"What?"

"I don't *know* what. This *thing*. Donna Hendricks's death. Then the old Senator who had been her friend."

"Coincidence."

"People are talking, Charles."

"I can't help that."

"A reporter for the *Post,* one I've been friendly with, told me in confidence that they've got a team of reporters working on the story."

"Let 'em work. If they can figure out what happened they're better detectives than the D.C. police have got."

"Charles, I don't think you can shrug it off. I have made a few inquiries—"

"You've *what?*"

"Very discreet inquiries. Do you think I'm going to depend on you and the newspapers for what I know? In any event, without pretending to understand all this, it seems to me that some very disturbing things have been happening, and that people in your employ are somehow involved. In which case, I think you should set your house in order."

He got up and began to pace about the room. "What's past is past, Claire. You always had it wrong about Donna."

"I'm not talking about *Donna,*" she cried, "Do you think I'm jealous of a dead woman? I'm talking about several *deaths*. I'm talking about this man Riddle and his patron Whitney Stone—and you know what I think of *him*—and the runaround that Ben Norton's been getting."

"Hold on," he shouted. "Riddle's out. Gone for good. Stone's out too, as long as I'm President. And Norton . . . well, he's a good fellow but he was in love with Donna and now he sees plots and conspiracies everywhere he looks. He'll calm down."

"I'm not so sure he'll calm down," she said. "And I'm not sure it matters if Riddle has been fired or you've dropped Whitney Stone. Things have happened, Charles. I have this sense that things are about to explode, unless you do something."

"Just let me worry about it, will you?"

"But are you? Or are you just hoping it will go away?"

He sat down on the edge of his bed, and just then a buzzer went off. He reached over and pressed a button on a small box on the table beside the bed. "Yeah?" he said wearily.

"Sir, the king and queen are waiting," a man's voice said.

"We'll be there in a minute."

"Yes, sir. Another thing, sir."

"Yeah?"

"Mr. Galiano would like to see you."

Claire Whitmore spoke before her husband could reply. "I don't want him anywhere near tonight's dinner," she whispered.

Whitmore nodded without looking at her and said to his unseen assistant, "Tell Nick I'll see him after this shindig tonight. Around eleven or so."

"Yes, sir."

Whitmore punched the button again and finished his sherry.

"Where were we?" his wife said.

"I don't know where we were," he said. "But let me tell you where I am. Some bad things happened. Worse than bad, dumb. But they've stopped happening. The only question now is whether some people get embarrassed or not."

"I don't like it," she said.

"I don't like it either," he said. "But that's how it is."

They got up and stood looking at each other.

"You look nice," he said. "That a new dress?"

"I got it in New York last week."

"You always look nice," he said.

"Thank you, Charles," she said and kissed him on the cheek, and she straightened his tie unnecessarily. He grinned and opened the door for her. The marine captain waiting outside snapped to attention.

"Charles?" she whispered.

"Huh?"

"What's the queen's name?"

"Olga? Irma? I forget. Ask the protocol fellow. He gets paid to remember queens' names. Me, I save myself for the big problems."

She laughed and took his hand, and they walked gracefully down the hallway to the room where their royal guests were waiting. She was thinking that he was right, that there was no use her worrying about it, because he was going to do what he was going to do, the way he always had. But sometimes she worried, sometimes she wondered how much longer his luck could hold.

30

HE TWISTED, moaned, burrowed beneath the pillow, resisted the awakening as long as possible, but finally the persistent call of the telephone jerked him awake and he fumbled for the receiver and mumbled a hello.

"Ben?" a woman said. "I hope I didn't wake you. It's Jane McNair."

He groaned a good morning to the lady.

"The reason I'm calling is . . . well, Clay and I have gone over and over it, and now he agrees with me that he should tell you what he knows about Byron Riddle and . . . and all the rest of it."

Norton pulled himself upright and looked at the clock. "When?" he said. "I could be there in an hour."

"I'll let you talk to Clay," she said.

"Norton?"

"When do you want to talk?"

"We're just leaving for church," McNair said. "After that we're driving out to Virginia. I'm playing in a tennis tournament. My match should be over by five. Why don't you meet me there? You could drive me home and we'll talk on the way."

"Clay, that's seven hours from now. Couldn't you cancel your match?"

"I'm in the finals," McNair said. "People are counting on me."

"Okay, okay," Norton said impatiently.

"I want you to understand one thing," McNair continued. "What I tell you has to be in confidence. You can do with it whatever you like, but I don't want to be involved. Is that agreed?"

"Sure," Norton said, lying again. "Just give me directions to the tennis club."

Norton drank some coffee and spent a few minutes thumbing through the Sunday *Post*. There wasn't much news except that people were killing themselves on the highways in record numbers. Then he came across a small item headed "Attorney's Home Robbed, Burned." It said that persons unknown had broken into the Potomac estate of attorney Whitney Stone, ransacked the house, blown open a wall safe, and set fire to the house before departing. Police said the burglary appeared to be the work of professionals. Norton wondered if those professionals might have been in the employ of his friend Gabe Pincus. Had Gabe finally gotten his hands on the Hoover file? Or would it elude him forever? Norton started to call Gabe but decided against it. He didn't trust the telephones, and for that matter he didn't trust Gabe. Instead, he turned on his television set and watched a few minutes of *Face the Nation*. The President's chief economic adviser was being interviewed, but he seemed to be speaking some language other than English. After a while Norton thought of something else to do.

* * *

Gwen was smiling when she opened the door, but her smile vanished the moment she saw him. "Hello, Ben," she said coldly. "This is a surprise."

"I called your new office to congratulate you," he said. "What do they call you now? Special Assistant for the Arts? That's very impressive, Gwen. But you ought to return your calls."

"I've been busy," she said. "Was there something you wanted?"

"Would you like to invite me in?"

"I'm expecting someone. What do you want?"

"Maybe I just wanted to congratulate you. I saw your picture in *Time*. You're getting up there. Next thing you'll be on their cover. Girl of the Year."

"What do you *want?*"

"I want you to refresh my memory. Just after Donna died we talked about her affair with Whitmore. Then a couple of weeks later, at your party here, you talked like maybe there hadn't been any affair. I've got to tell my story to the grand jury this week, Gwen, and I may need some backing up. So what's your story going to be?"

"Don't get me involved, Ben."

"Involved? Just tell the truth."

"The *truth?*" She made the word sound ugly. "You make everything so simple."

"Everything is simple," he said. "What's your story?"

Gwen's green eyes were bright and cold and furious. "She talked about him a lot. She had a thing about him. I don't know if it was true. She might have made it all up."

Norton couldn't believe it. "She was your best friend, Gwen."

"Don't give me your holier-than-thou crap!"

"And you'd sell her out for a job you don't need. For your picture in *Time*."

"Go to hell, you thick-headed, self-righteous Boy Scout son of a bitch!"

"How do you sleep, Gwen?"

She slapped him hard and slammed the door in his face. He rubbed his cheek and started back to his car. It was time to drive to the tennis match.

The tennis club was near Middleburg, an hour's drive west of Washington. Norton drove slowly, savoring the rich Virginia countryside. He followed a twisting dirt road past horse farms, over old wooden bridges, beneath towering oak trees, until he came to a sign that said "Northern Virginia Tennis Club. Private." He bounced along the private road for a quarter mile to the rambling old clubhouse. He parked in a field crowded with foreign-made sedans and American station wagons, many with their tailgates down and picnic lunches spread out on them. Off to his right, children shouted and splashed in a spring-fed pool. Norton walked across the field to the left, where fifty or sixty people were sitting on blankets and lawn chairs beside a clay tennis court.

Out on the court Clay McNair was battling a heavy-set bearded opponent, but for a moment Norton ignored the match and studied the spectators. They seemed to be of all ages, from a cluster of teenagers to a row of young marrieds to several dozen well-tanned, well-preserved middle-aged couples, and even one regal *grande dame* who looked as if she'd been watching this tournament for many decades. Many of the younger people swigged beer from the can, and many of the older ones sipped martinis poured from shining thermos bottles. One woman in a flowered dress and carrying a big straw bag stood alone at the far end of the court, but everyone else seemed clustered with family or friends. Jane McNair and her two daughters were sitting on a blanket beside the court cheering her husband on. Norton, who was a decent tennis player, turned back to the match, and soon he was watching it with admiration.

McNair and his bearded opponent were both first-class players, although their styles could not have been more different. McNair's was a classic game. Slender and elegant in his tennis whites, he served, volleyed, and lobbed with free-flowing grace and with never a wasted motion, and his court manners were perfection itself. His opponent, clad in red shorts and a striped shirt, was a scrambler, grunting and groaning as he raced about the court, falling down, getting up, hitting ferocious shots, seemingly outclassed but staying in the match on sheer guts and determination. The crowd applauded both men, but McNair was clearly the favorite. His opponent had a habit of muttering at unfavorable line calls, a habit that met with obvious disapproval among the onlookers.

They were in the third and final set when Norton arrived. Both men held service to 6-6, then McNair unleashed a barrage of blistering baseline shots that broke his opponent's serve and put him ahead 7-6. Then, as shadows began to fall across the court, McNair served three straight aces to reach match point. His opponent grumbled to the umpire that the light was bad. McNair eased up on his final serve, and when his opponent returned it and charged the net he sent a gentle lob inches above his reach. The lob landed a foot in bounds, the crowd roared, and the bearded opponent slammed down his racket, then grudgingly started to the net for a handshake.

Jane McNair and her daughters hurried onto the court to hug McNair, other well-wishers surrounded him, and an elderly gentleman in a blue blazer stepped forward with a trophy in his hands. The old gentleman made a short speech, McNair beamed, someone took pictures, and there was a final burst of applause before people began to fold up their lawn chairs and blankets and drift back toward the clubhouse. Norton watched as McNair walked off the court with the trophy cradled in one arm and his other arm around his wife's shoulders. It was strange, Norton thought, that such a sorry bastard could be such a fine tennis player. Maybe he wasn't such a sorry bastard in his private life. Who could say?

Suddenly McNair's knees buckled and he pitched forward onto the grass. His wife screamed and dropped down beside him. The old gentleman in the blue blazer began calling for a doctor, and people began running in all directions, some toward McNair, some away. Norton stepped forward until he saw the red circle spreading across McNair's tennis shirt, then he turned and began scanning the crowd. He saw the woman with the flowered dress and the straw bag running around the edge of the clubhouse. There was something wrong with the way she ran. Norton watched her disappear behind the clubhouse, then started racing across the field after her. When Norton reached the clubhouse, a blue Mercedes roared past him. Byron Riddle had jerked the wig off by then and had slipped a jacket over the flowered dress. Norton raced to his own car, only to have his path blocked by the bearded tennis player.

"Where do you think you're going?" the man demanded.

"The guy who shot him's getting away. Get out of the way."

"You're staying here, mister," the bearded tennis player said and grabbed Norton's arm. Norton knocked him down, jumped into his Mustang, and roared down the dirt road after the Mercedes. The Mercedes was out of sight, but there was no place for Riddle to turn off until the road had twisted three or four miles to Route 50.

He kept his Mustang floorboarded and after a mile, as he banged across an old wooden bridge, he saw the Mercedes ahead of him, caught behind a horse trailer, unable to pass on the narrow road. Norton pulled up close behind, almost bumper to bumper, looking for a chance to force Riddle off the road. Suddenly Riddle twisted around and stuck his head out the window. Something shattered Norton's windshield. Norton slammed on his brakes and dropped back fifty feet, weaving from side to side and trying to keep an eye on Riddle through the cobwebbed glass before him. He saw the horse trailer swerve to the side of the road and the Mercedes pull around it. Then suddenly something green appeared around a curve in the road, there was a mighty crash, and the Mercedes tumbled off the road and down a steep hill to come to rest beside a tiny creek.

Norton braked to a stop and jumped out of his car.

The driver of the green pickup truck, a red-faced old man in overalls, staggered out onto the road with blood gushing from his nose. Chickens, abruptly freed from the back of the pickup truck, flapped and squawked about the road. Norton ignored the man in overalls and ran down the embankment to the crumpled Mercedes.

Byron Riddle was pinned in the front seat. The flowered dress was soaked in blood and the man inside it was deathly still. Norton reached in, searched Riddle's pockets, then grabbed a manila envelope that had fallen between his feet. He tore the envelope open and stuffed the spool of tape into his pocket just as the driver of the pickup stumbled down the hill and looked inside the wreckage.

"Jesus Christ," the old man said. "Sumbitch is queer."

"I'll go for a doctor," Norton said.

"All these weirdos move out here from Washington," the old man grumbled. "Queers, hippies, liberals. You reckon the sumbitch has got insurance?"

"Check his pockets," Norton said, and he scrambled up the embankment, climbed into his Mustang, and drove very, very carefully back to Washington. He got home about eight, locked his door, and played the tape. He played it twice, then he called the White House. He asked to speak to the President and, more quickly than he had expected, he got him.

31

OVER THE years, Norton had attended receptions in the East Room of the White House and meetings in the West Wing offices of various Presidential aides, but he had never been inside the Oval Office itself. In his mind it had remained mythic, inaccessible, an Olympus that few mortals scaled, and thus he was a little shocked the next morning to discover how easy it was to enter the President's office—if you were wanted there. When he gave his name at the gatehouse outside the West Wing, a guard checked his identification, waved him past and grabbed a phone. A moment later Joe Saradino stepped out of the West Wing to meet him. Saradino been a Pentagon lobbyist back in the Senate days, and one of Whitmore's golfing buddies, and now he was one of his military aides. Joe was a lanky horse-faced Floridian, charming, easygoing, and shrewd. He'd recently been promoted to brigadier general, but he was wearing civilian clothes—a garish sport coat and two-tone shoes. He pumped Norton's hand and led him inside the West Wing.

"Ben, what the hell's going on?" Saradino asked as they marched past dark-suited security guards who seemed hardly to notice them.

"What do you mean?"

"I've never seen the Chief so uptight. What's the story?"

"I can't talk about it, Joe."

Saradino shot him a quick suspicious glance, then

stopped in the green-carpeted hallway outside the Oval Office and checked his watch. It was two minutes until ten.

"Well, I'll tell you this, Ben," he said. "If you got any way to ease that man's mind, I wish you'd do it. He's got more troubles now than he can say grace over. That whole Middle East thing may blow again, any day, any hour. That man is really between a rock and a hard place. I tell you, it's agony to watch sometimes, the things that are tearing at him. That fancy office of his is more a torture chamber than anything else. So don't you go causing any more problems, old buddy." He glanced at his watch again and as the second hand moved straight up, at precisely ten, he knocked once and opened the door to the President's office and Norton stepped inside.

He indulged himself in one quick glance around the beautifully appointed room. His eyes took in the Peale portrait of Washington above the mantel, the busts of Lincoln and Kennedy, the President's big desk with the Plexiglas-covered globe beside it, the tall windows looking onto the Rose Garden, and then he focused all his attention on the two men who were rising to greet him. Ed Murphy was rumpled, watchful, grim. Frank Kifner was crisp, cordial, precise.

"The President will be down in a minute," Murphy said.

"Fine."

"Let's sit down," Murphy continued. "We can talk until he gets here. He said you have something new in the Hendricks case."

"That's right," Norton said and eased himself down onto one of the sofas opposite the two other men.

"Maybe you should have talked to me or to Frank first."

"It has to be directly with him," Norton said. "He agreed to that."

Murphy frowned. "I hope you know what you're doing," he said.

Norton hoped so too, but he said nothing. The door

opened and the three men tensed, ready to rise at the President's entrance, but the man who stepped into the room was a red-coated Navy steward bringing coffee. Norton and Kifner declined; Murphy took a cup and his hands shook embarrassingly as he drank it.

"You spoiled my weekend at the beach, Ben," Kifner said. "That's an indictable offense, you know."

Norton managed a smile. He didn't think the joke very funny, but it was better to make small talk than to sit there listening to Ed Murphy's coffee cup rattle.

"A lot of people's weekends have been spoiled, I guess," he said. "Has anybody heard about McNair?"

"I talked to the doctors this morning," Murphy said. "He'll be all right. They say he'd be dead if the bullet had entered an inch lower."

"Incidentally, Ben," Frank Kifner said, "there's a warrant out for your arrest in Virginia. Something about leaving the scene of a crime."

Norton wasn't sure if that was a joke or not, but before he could ask, the door opened again and this time the President strode into the room. Nick Galiano followed a few feet behind him. The three seated men rose to their feet, and the President, after nodding to Murphy and Kifner, came straight over to shake hands with Norton.

"Ben, it's been a long time," Charles Whitmore said. His voice was rich and resonant, his face well-tanned and confident, and as they stood for a moment with their faces a foot apart, Norton felt himself succumbing to the aura of certitude and power that was part Charles Whitmore himself and part the office that he held. Norton wanted to believe this man, to trust him, to help him. He felt himself weakening, as if some gas had been piped into the room that made men lose their resolve.

He let go of the President's hand and took a step back. "It was good of you to see me," he said, deliberately leaving off the almost obligatory "sir." He kept telling himself, He is a man like other men.

"Well, from what you said on the phone I didn't

have a whole lot of choice," Whitmore said. "Let's sit down, gentlemen, and see what Ben's got to tell us."

The President took his place behind his desk and reached into the top drawer for a box of cigars. Nick Galiano drifted across to a chair by the fireplace. The three other men took chairs that faced the President's desk.

"Anybody want to join me?" Whitmore asked and held up a Montecristo cigar. The other men shook their heads and Whitmore laughed. "I recognized Cuba so I could smoke these damn things," he said and lit the cigar. After his first satisfied puff he leaned forward and stared at Norton.

"You may not know it, Ben, but I've been in the dark about Donna's death as much as anybody. I told Ed to ride herd on the police, but all I heard back was that they had some suspects but nothing firm. Now, out of the blue, you call and say you know who killed her." He shook his head and took another puff of the cigar. "I guess after what happened yesterday that this man Riddle had a lot to do with it. Jesus, I only met the character once, and now it's starting to look like he was some kind of a plant."

"I take the blame for Riddle," Ed Murphy said. "I knocked some heads together last night and began to find out some things nobody bothered to tell us the first time around. Like his CIA record and his tie-in with Whit Stone. We'll probably never know everything that guy was up to. But we know he shot McNair yesterday and my guess is that he killed Donna. I've got a feeling that's what Ben has found out. And I want to say that I for one owe Ben an apology. He warned me about Riddle and he was right. That guy was a rotten apple and we're damn lucky we're finally rid of him. That's about what it comes to, doesn't it, Ben?"

Norton stared at Ed Murphy with grudging respect. He was so smooth, so reasonable. Blame everything on Byron Riddle, pass out cigars and congratulations, shake hands all around, and exit smiling. Except that wasn't how it was going to be.

"Riddle didn't kill Donna," Norton said.

"How do you know?" Frank Kifner asked. "What evidence do you have?"

"I think I ought to start at the beginning," Norton said. "Is that all right, Mr. President?"

"Go ahead," Whitmore said, hunched forward over his desk, still fondling his Cuban cigar.

"Okay. To begin with, I found out that Jeff Fields had installed a voice-activated tape-recording system in his house on Volta Place."

"You found out how?" Ed Murphy demanded.

"From Gabe Pincus, who I think learned it from the police."

"That's correct," Frank Kifner said. "Our men found the system but no tapes. Fields denied that tapes had ever been installed."

"Yes," Norton said, "but the night before he was killed he told me there was a tape somewhere. He didn't say where, but by then I was convinced that Byron Riddle was at the center of whatever was going on, and that's why I kept after McNair, hoping he could tell me something about Riddle. Yesterday morning McNair agreed to talk to me, after that tennis tournament, but Riddle shot him first."

"How did Riddle know that McNair was going to talk to you?" the President asked.

"I'm not sure," Norton admitted. "But Riddle was a wiretapping expert, so you can draw your own conclusions. He seemed to know what a lot of people were doing and saying. I'd bet that if you find out where Riddle lived you might find a lot of tapes and transcripts and God knows what."

"Get on that fast, Ed," the President commanded. "Ben, what's your fix on this character Riddle? What was he after?"

"I don't know," Norton said. "Adventure? A big job? I think the guy was half crazy. It's my information that he was tied in with Whit Stone—that Stone pushed you to hire him and hoped he could come up with something that could be used for some kind of blackmail. I'd like to know what *Stone* was up to."

"That guy plays a lot of games," the President said. "He had this fantasy that I'd make him Attorney General, and I kidded him along and maybe he thought it'd happen. Meanwhile, he's the lawyer for some of the big boys in the oil industry, and those guys play the game rough. If Stone had gotten anything on me, they'd have been around to make their little deal. So what about that tape, Ben? Let's get back to that."

"A point of information," Frank Kifner said. "When I talked to McNair at the hospital this morning, he said he once saw a spool of tape in Riddle's drawer that was labeled 'D. H. Tape' and Riddle threatened to kill him if he talked about it. That's what McNair was going to tell Ben yesterday."

"That makes sense," Norton said. "Because after Riddle wrecked his car, I found the tape. That's why I got out of there so fast. I wasn't handing that tape over to the Virginia state troopers or anybody else. I took it home and played it, and after that I called the President and asked for this meeting."

He might have added that once he finished that call he took the tape and went to a hotel and spent the night there under an assumed name. Even now part of him feared that at any moment someone would push a button and he would fall through the floor and never be heard from again.

"And you've got the tape with you?" the President said.

"Yes, sir," Norton said, instinctively patting his coat pocket. "I'll play it whenever you're ready."

"I'm ready," the President said. "There's a tape deck in that cabinet over there."

Norton got up and crossed to the cabinet.

"Tapes don't prove nothing," Nick Galiano said, speaking for the first time. "You can fake 'em, splice 'em, do anything you want with 'em."

"An expert can tell," Kifner replied.

"Damn experts are what's wrong with this country," Nick grumbled.

Norton opened the cabinet and was examining the finest recording equipment he'd ever seen.

"I don't leave it on all the time, if that's what you're wondering," Whitmore said. "You know how to work it? Or you want me to get somebody?"

"I think I can manage," Norton said. He took the tape from his pocket and began to thread it on the spool.

"I wonder if this is the right thing to do," Ed Murphy said. "If this is new evidence, maybe it ought to go straight to the U.S. Attorney's office. We don't want to screw anything up, just to satisfy our curiosity."

"Frank?" the President said, glancing at the young U.S. Attorney.

"I see no objection to our playing the tape," Kifner said. "I represent the Justice Department. And you are, after all, the President."

"So they tell me," Whitmore muttered. "Okay, Ben, let 'er rip."

Norton stared at the President, amazed at how relaxed he seemed. Didn't he know what he was about to hear? Didn't he care? Or was he acting, trying to feign innocence? Either way, he was one cool son of a bitch.

Norton pressed the "play" button. There was a hum, then the sound of a telephone ringing, then a woman's voice saying hello. Norton punched the "forward" button and there was a loud whirring sound as the tape spun ahead.

"That was Donna answering the phone," Norton said. "But I don't think the conversation is particularly relevant."

He wondered if the President understood whose conversation it was. He let the tape spin for a few seconds, then he punched "play" again; the whir became a quiet hum again. Frank Kifner coughed and the President's chair squeaked. Abruptly, the Oval Office was filled with the sound of someone knocking on a door. That sound and the sounds and voices that followed were perfectly clear; Norton was reminded of the old-time radio dramas he had listened to as a boy, stretched out on his living-room floor.

"Who is it?" Donna asked.

"Me. Open the door." It was a man's voice, gruff and impatient. Norton wondered if the others recognized it. He sat staring at the spinning tape, for some reason not wanting to watch the faces of the other men in the room.

"Who? Oh, all right."

There followed the sounds of a chain lock rattling, a bolt clunking, a door opening.

"Oh, it's *you*. What do you want?"

"To talk, that's all."

"We don't have anything to talk about."

"I think we do. Look, are you going to invite me in or not?"

"Oh, all right, come in."

The door closed, and footsteps echoed down the hallway of the house on Volta Place.

"You can sit there," she said. "What do you want to talk about?"

Norton stole a glance around the room. The other men were motionless, expressionless. Yet he felt the tension rising. Surely they understood by now.

"That book of yours," the man said. "The letters. Don't you realize—"

"My God, is *that* why you've come here?" she said impatiently.

"Look, you're just causing problems nobody needs!"

"Oh, go to hell, will you?" Donna shouted. "Get out of here!"

They heard the sound of the man's angry curse, the scraping of a chair against the floor, footsteps—then, like an echo, they heard a curse, a chair moving, and footsteps there in the Oval Office.

"Turn that damn thing off!" Nick Galiano shouted

and dived toward the tape machine, knocking Norton aside.

Nick turned the machine off, Norton grabbed him, and Nick suddenly had his thumbs in Norton's Adam's apple when a shout filled the room: "Nick. Stop it. Right now!"

It was the President, and when Galiano heard him he dropped his hands instantly and stood beside the cabinet white-faced, his hands trembling.

"You don't have to play your damned tape," Nick said bitterly. "I'll tell you what happened next. I asked her for that manuscript of hers. We had an argument. She slapped me and I hit her back. She fell down and banged her head on the coffee table. That's all. It was an accident. I didn't mean to hurt her. I was just trying to help you, Boss."

He sank back down in his chair and buried his face in his hands. The President's face was twisted into a scowl. Ed Murphy lit a cigarette with trembling hands. Finally Frank Kifner broke the silence.

"Then what happened, Nick? Who did you tell? Who took the tape?"

Nick Galiano raised his head slowly and looked directly at the President as he spoke, as if there were no one else in the room.

"I could see right away she was dead. There was nothing I could do for her. I panicked. I went home. Then I started thinking about fingerprints. I didn't know what the hell to do. I didn't care about me— I still don't, Boss, I swear to God—but I knew they'd use it to get at you. I wanted to go back there to wipe off the fingerprints, but I just couldn't make myself do it. There had to be somebody else. Then I thought about Riddle. He was the guy who was supposed to be the cloak-and-dagger expert. So I called him. I told him I'd gone over there and found this woman dead and I didn't know who'd done it but I knew that somebody important had been over there the night before and it could cause a big stink. I told him if he'd fix things right I'd take care of him. All he said was 'No sweat, Nick, Byron Riddle can handle it.' So I waited, and after a couple of days it looked like he had handled it. Then I heard about the tape being gone and I knew he'd screwed me. I went to see him and we had a hell of a fight but he claimed he didn't know nothing about the tape. Then the guy disappeared. That's all I know."

Nick got up and stood before the President's desk like a prisoner in the dock. He looked old, tired, deflated. "I was just trying to help you, Boss. You said she had that book and she was gonna screw you with it, so I thought I'd get it away from her. I didn't even get the damn thing—I guess Riddle did. I thought I could keep it quiet. But I screwed it up, like I've screwed everything up in my stupid life. But I take all the blame. It was me and Riddle. I'll sign a confession, make a statement, plead guilty, whatever you say."

Whitmore got up slowly, walked around his desk, and put his arm around Nick's shoulders. "You really did screw this one up, didn't you, Nick?" Whitmore shook his head sadly. "You're just gonna have to hang tough, pal. I can't help you now. I'm still your friend, but I can't help you."

Nick tried to smile. "That's all that matters, Boss. Now I got to get out of here. I've said all I can say. From now on, you just tell me what to do."

Frank Kifner cleared his throat before he spoke. "Mr. President, I think I should take a statement from Mr. Galiano as soon as possible. And of course he should have counsel present if he wishes."

"I don't want a lawyer," Nick said. "I'll go wait in my office. I'll be there when you're ready."

Nick dragged himself out of the office, his hands in his pockets, his eyes downcast, all the life gone out of him.

There was silence for a moment, then Frank Kifner spoke. "Mr. President, there are some points that need to be wrapped up as soon as possible," he began.

"What's left to wrap up?" Ed Murphy asked sharply. "Nick and Riddle did whatever was done. Nick admits it and Riddle's dead."

"Hold on a minute," the President said. "I've got to go talk to Nick. If that man thought it would help me to put a bullet through his head, he'd do it. I've got to calm him down. And I want to make sure he gets himself a lawyer. I'll be back in fifteen minutes and we'll finish this."

The three other men stood up as Whitmore marched out of the office, then sat back down. Norton was thinking about a pardon and wondering if it was proper for the President to be talking to Nick. But what could you do?

"What a morning *this* has been," Ed Murphy said wearily. "This is terrible about Nick, but at least the damn thing is over. Say, does either of you guys want a drink?"

Norton and Kifner shook their heads.

"Ben, I'll say it again," Murphy continued, "you've done a hell of a job on this. You were right and I was wrong. You're a stubborn son of a bitch, but I admire you for it. The Boss does too. And believe me, when all this settles down, that offer of a job is still good."

Norton didn't know what to say, and he was relieved when the door opened and Joe Saradino, the dapper military aide, came in. "I have a message for you, Ben," he said and handed Norton a slip of paper.

"He's busy now," Ed Murphy growled. "It'll have to wait."

Norton took the note, read it, and stood up. "No, it can't wait," he said. "I'll be back in ten minutes."

"What the hell?" Murphy protested, but Norton was already out the door.

He went only a few feet down the hall to the Cabinet Room. She was waiting for him inside, sitting alone at the big conference table, looking out at the

Rose Garden. She stood as he entered and held out her hand to him.

"Mrs. Whitmore . . ." he began.

"We haven't much time, Ben," Claire Whitmore said. "Can you tell me what's happening in there?"

"Nick killed Donna accidentally. He admits it. Riddle, the man who was killed yesterday, helped him conceal it."

Claire Whitmore stared at him in disbelief, then nodded for him to sit down beside her. "What happens now, Ben?"

"I don't know."

"But it's not going to be as simple as some people hope, is it?"

"No, it's not," he told her.

"May I make a request of you?"

Norton stared at the shining mahogany table; he felt worse than he'd felt all morning. "I don't even know if we should talk at all," he said. "This is hard enough for me already. You know I'd do anything I could for you personally, but—"

"I won't ask anything for myself. Or for Charles, either. Ben, I want to see justice done as much as you do. Do you remember the note you received about the autopsy?"

He was stunned. "Did you . . . ?"

"I had a friend making inquiries for me. Don't you think I wanted to know if my husband was involved in that poor woman's death? But there was so little I could do without attracting attention, so when I found out about her pregnancy I thought the most useful thing I could do was to pass the information to you. So you see, I'm not trying to cover up anything."

"I never thought you were. What did you want to tell me, Mrs. Whitmore?"

She twisted a handkerchief in her lap. "Now that I've got you here, it's hard to put into words. I don't know all the facts in this case. Perhaps no one ever will. But some very momentous things are going to happen soon, and you as much as anyone are going to determine what they are. I guess what I'm trying to say, Ben, is that whatever you do, you try to remember the pressures that Charles has been working under since he took this office. You can't imagine what it's like. No one can. It's like Hamlet said, one man taking arms against a sea of troubles. It's an impossible job, Ben. So he has to rely on other people and perhaps he didn't always pick the right people. He's like every other President. When it comes to it, and you have to choose between a brilliant man and a loyal man, you choose the loyal man. And somehow their very loyalty is always what makes them go wrong.

"Charles has made mistakes; no one knows that better than I. But for all his faults, I think he's always tried to do what's best for the country. Do you remember what Mark Antony said of Caesar? 'When the poor hath cried, Caesar hath wept.' Charles has wept too, Ben, and paced the floor all night and cursed and prayed and gotten roaring drunk—all those things, and more—because of the pressures of this office and the impossibility of getting done all the things he wants done.

"I see all these things, and my heart goes out to him, not for the husband I lost a long time ago, but for the man I admire and believe in and, ultimately, I forgive. So all I'm asking you, Ben, when you make whatever decisions you have to make, is to try to understand how hard it's been for him, and try to remember how much good there is in the man."

There was a knock at the door. "I've got to go," he said. "I'm sorry. I wish I could tell you how I feel. I agree with so much that you say. I . . . well, I'll remember what you said. Thank you."

He got up and left her there, staring out at the Rose Garden.

The President was back, seated at his desk. No one asked where Norton had been. Perhaps they knew. He had the feeling that everyone knew everything, except himself.

"Frank and I have been talking this over," Ed

Murphy said to the President. "He thinks Nick should go before the grand jury right away. He can tell them what he did and what Riddle did and the whole thing can be wrapped up as quick as possible. We figure you should make the announcement, Mr. President. Call the reporters in, tell them what you've found out, tell them what Nick says, admit our mistakes, give Ben here credit for all he's done, and then we can put this mess behind us. That's damn important, because there's rumors spreading all over town, and unless we squelch this thing fast we'll have a crisis on our hands."

The President looked from Murphy to the U.S. Attorney. "Is that how you see it, Frank?"

The young prosecutor looked grave. "Sir, obviously I need to hear Mr. Galiano's full story. But on the basis of my present knowledge, I would say that once he has told his story to the grand jury the matter might well be terminated in the manner that Mr. Murphy suggests. Of course, on the basis of his confession, Mr. Galiano will probably be indicted in Miss Hendricks's death and might well go to prison."

The President nodded slowly and turned to Norton. "What do you say, Ben? Do you think we can wrap this up like Ed says?"

Norton looked back at Whitmore without really seeing him. He was thinking of many things. Of what Claire Whitmore had said. Of his own weariness, his own anxiety to see this ordeal ended. But he thought of the tape too, the part that Nick had stopped him from playing, the part where Nick yelled, "You lousy bitch!" and there followed quickly a slap, a thud of fist against face, her cry, the crack of her head against the table, then Nick shouting, "Wake up! Wake up!" and finally a long, terrible silence.

He shut his eyes, opened them, and saw the President waiting for an answer to his question.

Norton looked at the other men in the room and tried to see them as they were: Charles Whitmore, the most talented, most total politician he had ever known, a man of considerable courage and of infinite guile; Ed Murphy, a professional son of a bitch, a man whose occasional rough charm could never conceal his perpetual, perhaps necessary, ruthlessness; Frank Kifner, the young man in a hurry, playing out of his league here, perhaps, but driven by ambition toward whatever accommodation might best serve his bosses' interests and his own future. Norton thought he understood these men better than he understood himself. He knew what they were; the question was what he was. He thought of Sam Rayburn's famous advice to the young Congressman, a line he had heard repeated so many times on Capitol Hill that he thought it should be engraved in stone there: "If you want to get along, go along."

And they always made it so easy to go along.

"Mr. President," he said, "I think we're moving too fast. I think we're ignoring a lot of questions that haven't been answered yet."

"Like what, Ben?" the President asked.

"We know from the tape that Nick killed Donna and left the house," Norton said. "We know that someone——Riddle, according to Nick—returned to the house later and wiped away all the fingerprints and also took the spool of tape. It probably was Riddle, since he's the one who eventually had possession of the tape. But one question is who sent Riddle to the house?"

"Question? What the hell do you mean question?" Ed Murphy demanded. "Nick *told us* he called Riddle for help!"

"I know what Nick told us," Norton said. "I'm saying I'm not sure I believe him. I'm not convinced that Nick, in a desperate situation like that, with a murder charge hanging over him and God knows what consequences for the President, would turn for help to someone like Riddle, whom he barely knew. I think he would have turned to someone he trusted absolutely."

"What are you driving at?" Whitmore asked.

"Mr. President, being as objective as I can, I would suspect that Nick would have gone for help either to Ed Murphy or to you."

Ed Murphy jumped to his feet with an angry shout. "You sorry son of a—"

"Shut up and sit down," the President snapped, and Murphy did. "All right, Ben, I follow you. You think Nick would have called me or Ed, and one of us would have made the decision to send Riddle over there. That makes some sense. But I can say flatly that Nick *didn't* call me that night, or any other night, about what happened to Donna."

"He didn't call me either," Ed Murphy yelled. "And I resent the hell out of the suggestion that he did. Put up or shut up, Norton. Show me any proof against me and I'll resign. Otherwise you ought to get the hell out of here."

"I don't have any proof," Norton said. "I'm just raising questions. And there are plenty of others that need answering."

"Like what?" Whitmore asked.

"A lot of things, Mr. President," Norton said. "A lot of things that individually might be coincidence, but that taken together suggest an attempt to conceal what Nick did. There was the mysterious call to me the morning they found Donna's body. There was the newspaperman who told me he saw Ed and Donna together, then changed his story after Ed talked to him. There was Gwen Bowers's getting a big government job after she changed her story about Donna's relationship with you. There was Senator Nolan's telling me you'd visited Donna in Carmel, and then getting killed. There was this drug charge the Justice Department manufactured against Jeff Fields, which pressured him into coming to me and claiming he'd gotten Donna pregnant—and then him being killed when he was about to tell the truth. There was the Justice Department playing some games with me, and Whit Stone playing some games with me, the point of the games being to shut me up."

"Hold on, hold on," Ed Murphy said. "Half of that stuff is speculation and the rest of it is Riddle. Didn't you hear what Nick said? He and Riddle were in this together."

"I wouldn't be surprised if Riddle called me the morning they found Donna, to try to get me involved as a suspect," Norton said. "And I wouldn't be surprised if Riddle killed both Nolan and Fields. But the question is whether he was acting on his own or whether someone was directing him. And some of the things I mentioned—getting Gwen a job or using the Justice Department to pressure Fields—were things Riddle couldn't have managed on his own. What I'm saying is that all the evidence suggests a high-level coordinated cover-up, intended to hide both the fact that Nick killed Donna and the fact that the President had been involved with Donna."

"You can't prove a word of that!" Murphy shouted. "All you want to do is dig up dirt and ruin this man. All because your girl friend threw you over."

"All I want," Norton said, "is a routine investigation of Donna's death, following up all the leads. Right now, it looks like Nick is trying to take the blame for people higher up and it looks like the U.S. Attorney's office is keeping its head buried in the sand."

"I resent that suggestion," Frank Kifner said.

"Then treat this like any other murder case," Norton said.

" 'Like any other murder case,' " Murphy repeated bitterly. "Why won't you be honest? You're after revenge. You know damn well that once the reporters find out about him and Donna it's going to bring down this administration."

"I don't know if that will happen," Norton said. "If so, it can't be helped."

"You cold-blooded son of a bitch," Murphy whispered. "You—"

"Cool down, Ed," the President said. "Maybe you and Frank ought to wait down in your office while Ben and I talk some more."

The two men stood up. Murphy glared at Norton for a moment, then followed Kifner out of the office. The President got up, stood looking out the window for a moment, then turned to Norton with a bemused look on his face. "This is supposed to be a holiday, Ben. Some holiday. You want a drink or a cigar or anything?"

"No, thanks."

Whitmore sat back down. "You've done a hell of a job on this thing," he said. "You always were a hard worker. And stubborn as a mule. Donna used to talk about you. She said you were the most dependable man she'd ever met. I wish to hell you'd married her."

"I was planning to, before you stepped in," Norton said, and no sooner were the words out than he was shocked at his own bitterness. Did he hate Whitmore that much? Was Murphy right, was he out for revenge?

Whitmore saw the opening and stepped into it quickly. "I know how you feel, Ben, and I can't say that I blame you. But you might try to put yourself in my shoes for a minute. I won't apologize for getting involved with Donna. Hell, I can't even explain it, it just happened. But it happened to both of us and it was real. We tried to break it off, two or three times, but it wouldn't stay broken. So I saw her in January —you know about that. And two months later I find out she's pregnant. She wasn't even going to tell me. I called her one day and I could tell something was wrong and finally she came out with it. I just about went out of my mind. I finally got her to agree to come to Washington to talk to me about it. She was just going to have the baby and not say anything to anybody."

Norton looked down at the floor; he didn't want to hear this but he had no choice.

"That wasn't good enough for me," Whitmore continued. "I was afraid she'd get married and some other guy would end up raising my kid. But I didn't know what to do. That last couple of weeks before she came here I almost went crazy. Sometimes I thought

I'd divorce Claire and marry Donna and tell the country it could like it or lump it. Sometimes I thought I'd quit after one term and then marry Donna. Except I didn't know if she'd agree to that. That's what her trip here was all about. So she comes. And Ed sees her about some of the details. And then the night I'm supposed to see her, there's a demonstration across the street and things get all fouled up. Plus, I get upset about this book she's supposed to be writing, and that gets Nick upset, and you know the rest."

"Yes, I know the rest."

"All I'm saying is, however you feel about me and Donna, don't let that decide what you do about other things."

"I don't think it is," Norton said. "Donna's dead and Nick killed her. She's not the issue. The issue is that after her death some people tried to cover up the crime."

"Okay," Whitmore said, "let's get down to that. You think Nick called Ed after he killed her and Ed called Riddle, and that ever since then Ed's been trying to cover things up. Right?"

"I think that's very possible. It's also possible that other people were involved."

"Like who?"

"Like Whit Stone. Like . . ."

Whitmore grinned. "Come on, Ben, out with it."

"Like you."

Whitmore held his grin for a moment, seeming to savor it, then let it fade away. "Anything's possible, Ben," he said, "but I wasn't involved. I told you that. As for Whit Stone, my guess would be that he was playing his own game. Of course, it could be that this character Riddle was playing a double game, working for both Murphy and Stone. I don't know. But the main thing is that even if Ed was involved it's gonna be damned hard to prove, as long as he and Nick both say he wasn't involved. And if you can't prove it, the whole thing is gonna be damned messy for all parties concerned. Am I right?"

"I imagine you are," Norton said.

"Then let me ask you this. What if Ed resigned? Walked out of here today and never came back. And then we buried this mess right there. Nick pleads to manslaughter, Ed leaves, and there's no use to carry it any farther."

Norton shook his head. "It's no good, Mr. President. If Ed ran a cover-up, he's committed a crime. If he didn't do it, he ought to keep his job. There's no in-between."

"There's usually a way to work things out."

"In politics, yes. But not in law."

"The law means a lot to you, doesn't it?"

"It's all we've got," Norton said. "Either we've got law or we're back in the jungle."

"We've got some top-level slots open over at Justice," Whitmore said. "We could use you over there."

Norton looked into Whitmore's somber face and realized they were barely speaking the same language. The realization depressed him and made him speak a little more bluntly than he would have. "I'm not interested in a job at the Justice Department," he said.

Whitmore concentrated on his cigar for a moment, relit it, puffed on it approvingly, and then turned his attention less approvingly back to Norton. "So you're not interested," he said scornfully. "Well, Mr. High-and-Mighty, let me ask you this. Are you interested in my health-insurance bill? Are you interested in my school program? You were pretty interested in them back when you were working for me, I seem to recall."

"I still am."

"Yeah? Well, you're gonna see them go right down the tube once you get me mixed up in a scandal. Look, Ben, I've been pretty far out front, and I've been bringing the country along with me, but it this thing breaks, the other side will use it to discredit me and everything I stand for. Don't you see? You're playing right into their hands. At the very least, my program gets gutted. And that might not be all. Congress has been feeling its oats the last couple of years, and they just might decide to take it all the way. I mean impeachment."

Whitmore paused to let it sink in. Norton twisted uncomfortably in his chair.

"You know who the Vice President is and what he stands for," Whitmore said. "I took him because I needed him to get elected, but if I go out and he comes in he's gonna turn things around one hundred and eighty degrees."

Norton lifted his hands helplessly. "Mr. President, all those things might happen if Donna's murder is investigated. I don't know. But there's nothing I can do about it."

"Nothing you can do about it!" the President said angrily. "For openers, you can come down off your high horse. You can't just open up this can of worms and then walk away from it. You've got to take responsibility for your actions."

"So do you. That's the point."

Whitmore got up and began to pace about the office. "Ben, once this thing gets started, some people are gonna question your motives. You better figure on getting called some names."

"That's all right."

"And from what Kifner tells me, you may have a problem yourself for not telling the police everything you knew."

Norton almost laughed. "Believe it or not, I was trying to protect you. I didn't want to tell them about you and Donna unless I had to. But I'll take my chances on that one."

"It's not just you and me and Congress," Whitmore said. "See that globe there? Listen, we've got troubles in places you never heard of. And don't think the other side wouldn't try to take advantage of it if they see me getting cut up at home. And if they push, I push back, and that's how wars get started. Think about it. What you're doing could screw this country up for a long time."

"If you're above the law, then it's screwed up permanently," Norton said.

"Is that your last word?"

"More or less."

"And you're so sure of yourself that you'll risk tearing this country apart, just to have your way?"

"I'm not all that sure of myself," Norton said. "I'm scared to death I may be doing the wrong thing. But I've thought hard about it, and I've made my decision, and I think it's the only decision I can live with."

"What if I won't play your game?" Whitmore asked suddenly. "What if I tell Kifner the grand jury investigation shouldn't go beyond Nick, and the Attorney General backs me up?"

"Then I'll call Gabe Pincus and tell him everything I know, including this conversation. Either way, the story goes public. But it's better if you put it out."

The President sighed and his body seemed to sag a little. "It'll take some time," he said.

"I won't say anything for twenty-four hours," Norton said. "Not until noon tomorrow. You can arrange a news conference by then."

"Do you want to be there?"

"Not particularly," Norton said. "I'll watch on TV."

"What happens to you, Ben?" the President asked. "After all this is over, I mean."

"I don't know," Norton said. "I think maybe I'll go back home to North Carolina and practice law."

Whitmore stared at him in amazement, then abruptly he stood up. The decision was made; the meeting was over. "Okay, I guess that's it. You're tough, Ben. I wish you were on my side."

"I am, Mr. President. Honest to God, I am."

The two men shook hands and a moment later Norton left the White House for what he thought would be the last time. As he passed through the gates and started along Pennsylvania Avenue, part of him wanted to turn back, like Lot's wife, for one last look, but part of him was afraid to, so he just kept on walking.

32

THE CALL came about ten minutes before eleven. Norton didn't want to take it—he'd quit giving interviews —but the reporter was a fellow he'd known in Washington and whose work he respected, so he thought he'd better talk to him.

"Ben? How is everything down there?"

"Everything's great, Bill."

"You busy?"

"Sort of. What can I do for you?"

"Well, with the trial coming up next week, I was thinking of doing a piece on you. The star witness returns to Washington, and all that. It's been almost a year now since you opted out. People are curious about you."

"Bill, I can't say a word for the record. Any publicity at this point might somehow affect the trial, and I can't risk that."

"Let's just talk for background then. No attribution. Just tell me what the hell you're *doing* down there."

"I'm a small-town lawyer, that's all. I have an office on the second floor of an old building that faces the Vance County Courthouse. Right now, looking out my window, I can see the courthouse square with the dogwoods in bloom and the statue of Johnny Reb in the middle of the square and beneath it a bunch of old codgers who sit there and whittle and chew tobacco and tell lies all day. This afternoon I'll be over at the courthouse trying a personal injury case. After that I'll meet with a tobacco farmer who wants to change his will. And so it goes."

"And you're *happy* doing that?"

"Happy as a hog in clover."

"You never get the itch to come back to Washington?"

"Bill, do you remember what Huck Finn said at the end of the book? He said, 'I can't stand to think about it. I been there before.' Well, that's how I feel about Washington. I been there before."

"How about Annie? Is she adjusting to the rustic life?"

"She loves it. She's working on a novel. And she gardens and rides a lot. We play bridge with friends. On Sundays, if the weather's decent, we go fishing out at the lake. It's a simple life—and it's no story."

"I think it's a hell of a story," the reporter said. "A guy in your position just dropping out like that. My God, with all that publicity you could have had any job you wanted."

"I'm telling you, I got the job I wanted."

"Look, Ben, I'll see you during the trial, and then maybe after it's over I could come down there and visit you. I think there's a Sunday piece in it."

"After the trial would be a lot better for me," Norton said. He looked out the window and saw Judge Harper emerge from the courthouse and start walking briskly across the square.

"Bill, I've got to get off the phone. I've got an appointment with someone I can't keep waiting."

"Anything interesting?"

"I don't exactly know. This man, Judge Harper, is the local political power. Has been as long as I can remember. Sort of a benign dictator. I *think* he's coming because he wants me to fill a vacancy on the Vance County Democratic Committee. Which I don't much want to do, because I'm not sure I'm a Democrat any more. I think I may be some kind of anarchist. Anyway, he's coming up the stairs now and I've got to go."

"I'll see you at the trial," the reporter said. "So long."

Norton put down the phone, sighed, and went to open the door for Judge Harper. "Hello, Judge."

"Good morning, Ben. You're looking well."

"So are you."

It was true. The judge was a tall, raw-boned, white-haired man who hadn't gained a pound in the thirty odd years that Norton had known him.

"And how is your lovely wife?"

"She's fine, Judge. She sends her regards."

They sat down and Norton waited in silence while the judge lit his pipe. Norton liked the old man. It could be argued that he was a racist and a reactionary, among other things, but he had a certain integrity about him and he was without malice. His son, who had been killed in Vietnam in 1965, had been Norton's best friend in high school.

"Well, Ben," the judge said, once he had his pipe fired up, "I guess you're going up to Washington next week for the trial."

"That's right."

"How long do you expect that to take?"

"They say the trial could last two months. I hope I can leave sooner than that."

"But you are the chief prosecution witness, are you not?"

"I suppose so. It's a complicated case."

"How do you see it turning out? Or is that a fair question?"

"It's a fair question," Norton said. "I just don't know the answer to it. I think the trial could go either way. You've got the three alleged conspirators, Ed Murphy, Nick Galiano and Whitney Stone. And the prosecution has me and Frank Kifner and a couple of other witnesses making an essentially circumstantial case. Conspiracies are never easy to prove. In this case, you've got Nick Galiano—who's already pleaded guilty to manslaughter and hasn't got a hell of a lot to lose—saying he and Riddle did it all. And you've got Ed Murphy and Whit Stone denying everything. So in the end it'll come down to who the jury chooses to believe."

"Mightn't the thieves fall out?" the judge asked.

"It's always possible. I figure that Whit Stone is the joker in the deck. I think Galiano and Murphy are willing to go to jail to protect Whitmore—always hoping for a pardon, of course—but if Whit Stone ever decides he's in danger of prison he'll make a deal with the prosecution so fast it'll make your head swim."

"The President must be watching this trial with interest," Judge Harper said.

"An acquittal would be damned helpful to him. He's actually weathered the storm pretty well, all things considered. The papers went pretty easy on his involvement with Donna. And the way Mrs. Whitmore stood by him helped him a lot. And there's never been any evidence that he knew about the cover-up. Maybe he did, but nobody's proved it. All he's been found guilty of so far is having a love affair and trusting some of his friends too far. The impeachment campaign never got off the ground. And if Ed Murphy gets acquitted, a lot of people will take that to mean that Whitmore didn't know what was going on."

"But he has been hurt politically," the judge said.

"Oh, no doubt about that. Maybe two years from now he'll decide not to run again. But if those are two years of peace and prosperity, he might be in pretty good shape."

"You seem remarkably free of rancor, Ben."

"All I wanted was to see an honest investigation of Donna's death, and I got that. I happen to think that Whitmore knew more than he admits knowing about the cover-up, but if you can't prove it you can't prove it. I told my story to the grand jury and the Congressional committee and I'll tell it at this trial and after that I'm out of it. I'm just a country lawyer now."

The judge smiled. "You're a bit more than that, my boy, after all that national publicity you received."

Norton shrugged. "People forget."

"Only if you let them," the judge said. "Actually, Ben, there was a local political matter I'd hoped to discuss with you today."

Norton nodded and waited. He had decided not to argue; if the judge insisted, he'd serve on the county committee. It was only one night a month, and the meetings were funnier than anything on television.

"I'm afraid I must begin with bad news," Judge Harper said. "John Flagg is a very sick man. I spoke with him yesterday. There's no possibility whatever of his running for re-election this year."

"I'm sorry to hear it," Norton said. "He's been a good Congressman."

"He has indeed," the judge said. "But now, those of us with an interest in party affairs must look for a candidate to replace him."

Norton laughed. "Judge, the last time I looked, there were three or four young lawyers standing over there on the courthouse steps who I suspect are available. And some of them wouldn't be bad."

"We want more than not bad, Ben. We want a young man who can go up to Washington and serve with distinction and build some seniority and perhaps move up to the Senate when the opportunity presents itself. I think I know who our man is. The only problem will be convincing him, because he's a little pig-headed sometimes."

"I'm sure you'll convince him," Norton said. "Who's the lucky fellow?"

"You."

"*What?*" Norton almost fell out of his chair.

"You don't have to give me an answer now, Ben."

"It's just such a shock, Judge. I'm not a candidate for dog catcher, much less Congress. And I'm not that well known. I've only been back less than a year."

"Oh, poppycock. You're one of the best-known men in this part of the state. A great many people remember you from your high school days, and they've certainly been reminded of your existence by all this recent publicity. I haven't the slightest doubt that you can be nominated and elected. The only question is whether you're going to be pig-headed."

"Maybe I am, Judge. I've enjoyed being home. The pace is slower than Washington, but it's a good life. I guess I'm a little sour on Washington."

"And understandably so," the old man said. "But we're talking about you returning as a member of Congress. As your own man. And there's no telling where the path might lead. You're destiny's child, Ben."

Norton shook his head uncertainly. "I'll talk to Annie," he said. "I'll give you an answer tomorrow."

A half hour later Norton left his office and walked around the courthouse square. He passed the Vance County Farmer's and Merchant's National Bank, which held the mortgage on his new home; passed the White Palace Cafe, where he ate the $1.25 special with the town's other lawyers on the days he didn't go home to lunch; passed Doc Hayes's drugstore, one of the few remaining places in the world where you could still buy a real malted milk; passed the boarded-up Rialto Theater, where he'd spent the Saturday afternoons of his boyhood watching Roy Rogers, John Wayne, and Abbott and Costello. Then he turned up Oak Street and began walking past big graceful Victorian houses with long porches and huge old trees to shade them from the sun. In his youth the town's leaders—the doctor, the banker, the three lawyers, Judge Harper—had lived on Oak Street, and Norton had mowed their lawns in the summers for spending money.

Annie was sitting at the kitchen table glaring at her typewriter. He bent down and kissed her. "How goes the Great American Novel?" he asked.

"Slowly," she said. "I spent the morning putting in

a comma and I'll spend the afternoon taking it out."

He laughed. "That's a good line."

"I know. It's Oscar Wilde's. What's new with you?"

"Oh, not much. The high school wants me to speak at their commencement."

"Are you?"

"I guess so. I turned the others down, but it is my own alma mater. Is there anything for lunch?"

"There's leftover chicken. And I could make a salad."

"Great," he said. She went out to pick some fresh lettuce and spinach while he got out the chicken, set the table, and poured them each a glass of milk.

"The bugs are into the lettuce again," she announced when she came in.

"Speaking of bugs," Norton said, "Gabe Pincus called me this morning. From Singapore."

"Collect?"

"He tried. Anyway, he's hot on the trail of the Hoover file, and he wanted to check with me on a theory that a former law partner of Whit Stone's might have stolen it. I told him I thought his theory was ridiculous, so now he thinks I'm part of the conspiracy. He may turn up here next month."

"I won't let him in the house."

"He'll say you're anti-Semitic. Say, do you want that last drumstick?"

"Be my guest."

"Thanks." He grabbed the drumstick, took a bite, then put it down. "Listen, Annie, something serious came up this morning. Judge Harper paid me a visit. He said Congressman Flagg is sick and won't run again. And the bottom line is that he wants me to run. He thinks I can win."

She dropped her fork and stared at him. "What did you tell him?"

"That I'd think about it and talk to you."

"What are you thinking about it?"

"I don't really know yet. I'm still stunned."

"But tempted?"

"Sure, who wouldn't be? It's just that—"

"That what?"

"That I thought we'd made our decision. To get out of the rat race. To live sensible lives. And it hasn't worked out so bad. Maybe things are a little slow here, but we've had fun, haven't we?"

"Sure we have."

"I think I've almost got politics out of my system. The other night I was out on the porch reading that biography of Jefferson and I kept reading right through the news. Just didn't give a damn what Walter Cronkite had to say. Didn't even think about him. It was a breakthrough."

"I've got my novel half finished," she said. "If you got into politics I'd never finish it."

"And it'd be so great for our kids to grow up in a small town like this. Washington in no place for kids."

"It's no place for anybody."

"I'd have to be crazy to run for Congress," he said. "I know what it does to people. It'd ruin our marriage. It'd make monsters of our children. It'd be sheer, utter madness. There's no question about it."

"Not a bit."

Norton laughed and finished his milk. "It's funny, actually. I mean, all over America men my age are lying and scheming and selling their souls for a chance like this, and I don't want it."

"You're smarter than they are."

"I'm lucky," he said. "I've got a great wife and I make a good living in a nice quiet law-abiding community, and I'm out of the rat race, and I'd be insane to give up this life for politics."

"So your mind is made up?"

"Absolutely. I'll tell the judge tomorrow."

They sat in silence for a minute. He was staring out the window toward the distant hills. She was looking at him. "You know what I say?" she said finally.

"What?"

"I say bullshit."

"Huh?"

"Ben Norton, you know you want to run for Congress. You've probably wanted to since you were six years old."

"I *said* I was tempted. But Washington is—"

"Washington is dirty and dangerous and expensive and corrupt and hypocritical," she said.

"That's right."

"It's also where the action is."

He winced and looked out the window again.

"And it's where we ought to be," she said. "Because we're Washington people."

"Damn it all."

"It's an addiction. Worse than gambling. Worse than nicotine. It gets in the blood. You haven't kicked it just because you skip Walter Cronkite one night. Ben, you're going crazy here. I see it every night when you come home glassy-eyed and mumbling about whose cow got into whose pasture. And I'm going crazy too. I know that Bill Dawson is your oldest and dearest friend, but if I have to play bridge with him and that dippy wife of his once more I'll leave you. People in Washington may be crooked and hypocritical but they're not often dull."

"I *know* he's dull. But I've known that guy for thirty years. He'd give me the shirt off his back."

"And his doubleknit suit too? Oh, Ben, don't you know that you can't go home again? Didn't you read Thomas Wolfe? Or if you do go home it isn't really home any more, it's just some grubby little backwater town and pretty soon you remember why it was you left in the first place."

He nodded sadly. "You know what happened last week?" he said. "I wasn't going to tell you. Mrs. Cowan, the schoolteacher, came in and said she didn't understand the interest rate she was paying on her new car. And to make a long story short, I found out that the bank and the car dealer have got a deal where they gyp people about two hundred dollars on the interest when they finance a car, and then they split the difference. Of course, if you complain, they say it was all a big mistake."

"What are you going to do about it?"

"I talked to Billingsly, the bank president, and of course he said it was a misunderstanding and he was very indignant that I would suggest that *he* could be part of any impropriety. But the point is, Annie, that Billingsly, our bank president, our elder of the church, our neighbor on Oak Street, is as big a crook as Whit Stone. Or would like to be."

"And if you're going to spend your life fighting crooks like that, you may as well fight them in Washington as in the boondocks."

"That's right," he said. "I wanted to come home and give it a chance. I wanted to put down roots."

"Who needs roots? You're not a turnip. Be a rolling stone, baby, and gather no moss. You'll probably be President someday."

"Annie, please don't say that. Not even as a joke."

"Who's joking? I'll nag you into the White House."

"Listen, Annie, seriously, if I make it to Congress, I don't want to start thinking about the Senate and the White House and all that. I just want to work hard and get good committee assignments and do a good job for my district. Congress would be a tremendous challenge. It's not just this simple black-white liberal-conservative stuff any more. The issues are tough and complicated as hell. What about the energy crisis? What about the economy? Somebody's got to come up with some answers."

"Ben," she said, "I'll work for you, I'll stuff ballot boxes for you, I'll launder money for you, but I'm damned if I'll listen to your speeches."

He began to pace about the kitchen. "I'm sorry," he said. "But thinking about it gets me all worked up."

She got up and put away the dishes while he continued to pace. "I've got an idea," she told him.

"What?"

"Unless you have any pressing legal duties, we

could go up to bed and see if we could calm you down."

"That's a hell of an idea," he said.

"I've got a million of them," she said and took his hand and led him upstairs.

Keep Up With The BESTSELLERS!